SH

MW01235642

It's a Hard, Hard, Hard, Hard World

An Erotic Novel by

John Butler

STARbooks Press

Herndon, Virginia

Published in the United States by STARbooks Press, PO Box 711612, Herndon, VA 20171. Printed in the United States.

Many thanks to graphic artist John Nail for the cover design. Mr. Nail may be reached at: tojonail@bellsouth.net.

Herndon, VA

STARbooks Publications by John Butler:

Novels

"model/escort"

WanderLUST: Ships that Pass in the Night

Boys Hard at Work – and Playing with Fire

This Gay Utopia

Teacher Is the Best Experience

Heels Over Head in Love

WanderLUST

Ships that Pass in the Night

Boys Will Be Toys

Showboy

John Butler Editions

Seduced 2 (Co-editor)

Wild and Willing (Co-editor)

Living Vicariously – The Best of John Patrick (Editor)

Short stories in the following anthologies:

Any Boy Can

Seduced 2

Fever!

Taboo!

Fantasies Made Flesh

Wild and Willing

Virgins No More

Dedication

And yet another one for Derek, the most exciting man I have ever encountered-- all man, but marvelously versatile and gentle as well. Our regular meetings are the stuff of books like this one, but his sexual performance routinely outstrips in reality the fancied accomplishments of my most thrilling fictional characters. However, the performance of "Chad Meredith," whose lovemaking is briefly chronicled in the following pages is an accurate exemplar of Derek.

Contents

1.

Life Upon the Wicked Stage

They loved looking at his dick. They seemed to be either fascinated by it, or maybe just envious. He knew that most of them wanted to do a hell of a lot more than just look at it, too. But he couldn't blame them; he was aware that it was something special. Whether in the locker room or shower at school, at the nude beach, or here on the stage of the *Top 'n Bottom Theatre*, he enjoyed showing it off as much as they loved looking at it.

He had always felt a tingle of pride when he knew another boy was drinking in the sight of his impressive prick, and that tingle usually made the sight grow even a bit more impressive. When a number of admirers were in evidence, as at the nude beach or in a large shower room, he could rarely restrain that growth, and he frequently had to either hide the prodigious hard-on or find somewhere to share it with another boy. On stage now, he knew there were a dozen hungry men out there, willing his cock to grow, and he was unable to keep it from obeying their desires. Almost from the moment he had shed his tiny Speedo and freed his bare cock, it had sprung up and grown to its very fat, astonishing length of ten-plus inches without his even touching it.

Standing there in the spotlight, he thought of the audience as a gathering of cobras, hypnotized by a young, hard cock rather than by a snake charmer's reed. Like a cobra, it swayed from side to side when he moved, and bobbed up and down. Every pair of eyes in the audience seemed to be transfixed by the lumbering shaft of throbbing flesh, and he felt sure their mouths were salivating as they imagined closing their lips around its challenging bulk. He knew that if he were out there watching a young man parade such an impressive endowment around the stage, he would be greedy to do so, and his asshole would be twitching with anticipation as he imagined settling down over it, reveling in the wonderfully satisfying thrill of a huge cock filling him, its bulk suffusing his entire body with heat as it drove eagerly in and out in rapturous hunger. Until a few days ago, the only cocks he had taken up his ass that were as big as his own were made of latex or hard rubber, and he longed to be filled regularly by a comparable one that was warm, engorged flesh, bursting with a huge load of hot cum. He had often wished he could fuck himself, ramming and slamming his monster dick in and out wildly until it erupted inside him. He knew it would be what most of his fuckbuddies claimed it was: the thrill of a lifetime.

He loved looking at it, himself. At home, as he stood in front of his closet-door mirror, contemplating his own cock, thinking about all those exciting dicks he saw regularly in P.E. class and some of the monster equipment his favorite porn actors showed in the videos he loved to watch, his prick invariably filled out and grew to proportions that would make many of those porn studs burn with jealousy. Then he would stroke it, and get it so hard it stood straight out from his young body, springing from the luxurious thatch of pubic hair at his crotch, so dark in contrast to the golden-blond hair on his head. He loved to see his dick jutting out so gloriously, throbbing for attention, looking both sublimely beautiful and, at the same time, monstrous and threatening. He'd studied so many other pricks he knew his was beautiful in comparison—as smooth and perfectly formed as those of porn stars like Jeff Stryker or Tom Steele. Very few of the porn idols he admired had cocks as long or as fat as his, and almost none had the stunning combination of length and girth that made his look so dangerous, especially so, given his relatively slight frame.

Many of the boys he took into his bed, perhaps the majority of them, asked how long his cock was. He kept a 12-inch ruler next to his bed so he could show them, not just tell them. He usually claimed he had an eleven-inch dick, and by pressing the end of the ruler very hard against the flesh under his pubic hair as it rested on top of his shaft, the tip did, indeed reach the eleven-inch mark on the ruler. No boy had ever been looking at the other end of the ruler at the time, so the ruse went undetected. When he measured it for his own information, he did not push the base of the ruler into his flesh, and the end of his cockhead just exceeded the ten-inch mark by a small margin.

A number of boys he fucked, especially the younger ones, were convinced the blond stud had a prick over twelve inches long—the fabled 'foot long' dick so many well-hung men claim to sport. To sell this fable to his more naïve admirers, he produced a joke ruler he had commissioned a friend to construct, one he called his "pecker checker," or his "peter meter." By reducing the photographic image of a foot-long ruler by about fifteen percent, and printing it on a strip of wood, he had a one-foot ruler that was actually only ten inches long, and it measured his cock at well over the fabled twelve inches.

His enjoyment at the sight of his glorious cock in the mirror was multiplied exponentially when he had another naked boy lying with him, or standing or kneeling next to him, sharing his admiration for it. To see that boy trembling with anticipation as he reached out to take hold of the fat, throbbing shaft, or to watch as his stunning cock disappeared into the boy's wide-stretched mouth or between the cheeks of his hungry ass gave him great pleasure. Perhaps the greatest pleasure, though, was when he pulled the head of his cock out of a worshipping mouth or asshole to watch it spraying the initial spurts of his customarily large orgasm over a smiling face or twitching buttocks before he savagely rammed it back inside to finish blowing his massive load, thus sealing the satisfaction both he and his partner gained from the masterly fuck he was administering.

Casey Lowe, this big-dicked stud, was not one to allow his sex partner to go unfulfilled, however. He loved getting fucked almost as much as his eager bottoms thrilled to the feel of his monster cock plumbing their depths, and he adored sucking dick and swallowing the hot cum his efforts produced—especially in sixty-nine, when his partner was servicing his own cock the same way. He liked to suck some of his own cum out of the mouth of a boy who had just taken a load there, or swipe his hand over the back of a boy he had coated with the early shots of his first orgasm, to provide enough of his own cum to lubricate his partner's cock or his own asshole. He would position himself over his partner's supine body, and with a joyous cry, impale himself on the lucky boy's dick, inspiring him to provide Casey with the kind of fuck Casey had just given him. But in truth, few of the boys he made love with were able to fuck at the level of intensity and excitement Casey could—and almost always did—provide.

His regular sex partners knew, and his initiates immediately learned, that if they wanted it, Casey was almost always ready to administer a follow-up fuck after he had taken his partner's load—a fuck as intense, and usually considerably more protracted (thus even more satisfying) than the first. He had yet to screw a boy who declined his offer to give him an immediate *encore* fuck. He, himself, had never turned down the offer of a second load from those few of his fuckbuddies who were capable of giving it to him, and he had successfully exhorted several to give him another fuck who didn't realize they could.

Considering the large number of boys and men who had gloried in Casey's masterful and mature lovemaking, it is surprising to note that he was barely eighteen years old.

He had been born in Atlanta, Georgia, but his parents moved to San Francisco when he was five years old, and he had lived there ever since. His beauty was not limited to his sexual equipment. He had a slight body, about 5'9" tall, but it was nicely muscled, with strong arms, broad shoulders and a very narrow waist. His tits were unusually well rounded for such a trim body, with prominent, large nipples. His eyebrows and the hair under his arms and around his cock were unusually dark for his coloring, but except for the blond fuzz on his balls, his body was otherwise completely smooth. His ass was full, but in proportion to his body, with prominent buttocks and a deep cleft between them, concealing the tight pink sphincter he loved to offer for his partners' enjoyment. As an infant and small child, he had been head-turningly beautiful, and maturity had not lessened his attractiveness in the least. In addition to his glorious head of golden hair, he had an angelic face that completely belied the *fuckmaster* within, with wide-set green eyes, a generous, full-lipped mouth that smiled to reveal dazzingly white, even teeth, classic high cheekbones and a strong, jutting jaw. It would be hard to conceive a more perfectly formed or more attractive young man of his ethnicity and body type.

He was a senior at San Francisco's Junipero Serra High School, where virtually all the girls were more-or-less in love with him, as were virtually all the gay boys—and there seemed to be an extraordinary number of the latter in the student body.

In all likelihood, there was no higher percentage of gay boys at Serra High than one would find at most high schools around the country, there were just a greater number of them who admitted they were gay and chose to do something about it. San Francisco has an unusually high percentage of gay men, but it does not follow that there will be a greater number of gay students in the public schools because of that. After all, the city's large gay population mostly moved there from other areas to be citizens of a gay-friendly community, and, of course, to be able to enjoy a reasonably free sexual and social life style—not to raise children. Moreover, the relatively gay-friendly atmosphere in which San Francisco's students are raised probably keeps far fewer gay boys in the closet. They are basically born that way, after all, not converted to their sexual orientation, whatever many bigots and evangelists would have people believe.

At least a dozen of the male teachers, and most of the female teachers at the school were equally smitten with Casey's looks. The basketball coach had learned about Casey's exceptional talents and endowment from one of his players, with whom he was having an affair, one who was also a frequent sex partner of Casey's. The coach kept a picture of the blond Adonis pinned up near his bed at home, and he frequently fantasized about him while he masturbated. His player-lover usually fucked with the coach in his office after school, but when he made love with the coach in his bedroom he often stared at the same picture, remembering the last time he had been with Casey and looking forward to the next.

Few of those admirers who had not had sex with Casey suspected what splendid sexual equipment, phenomenal technique and endurance he possessed. Those who knew through experience sought him out eagerly and unceasingly for repeat performances. He never bestowed his favors on a female, however; they simply did not inspire any arousal in him—and most seemed to sense he was not interested. Although quite a number of the gay boys at Serra High were open about their sexuality, Casey played his cards close to his chest. His regulars tended to avoid letting others know what a treasure they had found, reasoning that the more who knew how splendidly satisfying their idol was, the less time he might have for them.

The stunning quality of his cock tended to detract from the fact that he also had such an adorable ass and exciting chest. Many a boy who had just reveled in the taste or feel of Casey's ravening prick was momentarily diverted as he ate out Casey's sweet rounded ass, or fucked it while he played with the blond's equally well-defined, hard tits.

Aside from those boys he had sucked off, or who had fucked him or spent a rapturous hour or two sharing his deliriously passionate kisses—and there were an amazing number of them, considering Casey's age, probably thirty or more—his sexuality was a mystery, a subject for conjecture and dreaming. There were ten or more boys who had sucked him off or taken his incomparable weapon up the ass, who were not absolutely sure he was gay, since he had not reciprocated.

Occasionally, Casey liked to feel the sense of power and superiority that his failure to reciprocate suggested.

He was so attractive and smolderingly sexy that a fairly surprising number of straight boys at Serra High also fantasized about going to bed with him, especially those few who had somehow come to see his magnificent cock in its full glory. There were a dozen or so of those straight boys who had pursued their fantasies, and serviced Casey's glorious prick. One or two of those had for some reason later felt ashamed or guilty, but all had enjoyed the experience fully at the time and had been especially astonished at how exciting and stimulating they had found Casey's feverish kisses. After joyously eating several loads of Casey's cum or taking his ten inches up the ass a few times, a handful of them had begun to question their sexuality or abandon heterosexual pursuits entirely.

Not one boy who had ever had sex with Casey, whether gay or straight or undecided, failed to make it clear to the blond Adonis that he wanted to repeat the experience—although a couple of them were dilatory about doing so. Those latter two were straight boys who had seemed to act guilty around Casey after having been fucked by him, and were obviously pretending to themselves it hadn't happened. Neither had seemed to change his attitude after a couple of weeks, and in both cases Casey cornered each alone in a locker room or bathroom, with his dick out, hard and huge, saying "You mean to tell me you really don't want some more of this?" After a moment's hesitation, each had tentatively reached out to put a hand around the tantalizing fat shaft and begun to stroke it as they admitted they did. As a sort of mild punishment, Casey had made each one kneel and suck his cock for a few minutes after admitting he wanted it again. But he wasn't mean; he simply enjoyed dominating any sexual encounters, even if he was the one sucking dick or getting fucked. He raised each of the two reticent boys to his feet and kissed him deeply, really fucking his mouth with his tongue, promising he'd also take every drop of cum the boy could give him down his throat or up his ass. And he made good on his promise to both of those recalcitrant boys—so well that one of them eventually mended his heterosexual ways and became a regular in Casey's stable.

Except for a handful who had proven to be unsatisfying sex partners for some reason, Casey cheerfully honored requests for repeat sex—and as frequently as he could manage. All but a few of his regular fuckbuddies were students at Serra High; those few were students at other, near-by high schools. For three years he had not fucked anyone who was not a high-school student.

It might seem that Casey spent most of his free time pursuing, or engaging in, sex—and that would be quite close to the truth, especially by the time he reached his senior year. His sole extra-curricular activity at Serra High was fucking, but that was not something that would be listed under his name in the yearbook. Clearly, Casey was obsessed with sex to some degree, but as one would never criticize a fine athlete for spending all the time he could in pursuit of honing his athletic skills, so the young sexual athlete should rather be admired for constantly improving his unique, virtuoso sexual talent. It was fortunate that he attended classes without fail, and had a quick mind and an excellent memory, or he would have been in serious academic trouble.

Perhaps the most astonishing thing about Casey's adventures was that except for Dave Cotter, he had fucked every single boy he had sex with—and even by the time he was sixteen his cock had been nothing short of gargantuan. Most of the boys he fucked had never had a dick up the ass the first time Casey made love to them, and Casey's cock was as far from 'training size" as most of them would ever suck or ride. Probably the greatest single factor in convincing those who were initially hesitant or fearful about getting fucked for the first time was Casey's winning beauty; no one wanted to disappoint such an Adonis. But he also virtually exuded an irresistible sexiness, and he cajoled and sweet-talked so convincingly that before a boy knew it, he would be on his back with three of Casey's well-lubed fingers all the way up his ass, and hearing "I've gotta have it, please," whispered into his ear during those moments when his mouth wasn't being fucked by Casey's insistent, writhing tongue. By the time Casey had gently insinuated his cock all the way up his ass, the boy was in heaven, with his joy far overcoming any initial pain as he took the prodigious thrusts and cum eruptions Casey proceeded to bestow on him. No boy had ever failed to suck Casey's cock, either, in spite of the challenge of such a fat shaft. Many failed to take it all the way in their throats, especially the first few times they worked at it, but they all wanted to, and did their best. Whether sucking Casey or getting fucked by him, they all wanted to please such a beautiful, marvelously endowed boy, such a persuasive lover.

Casey's parents had separated when he was twelve years old. His mother had found a stash of 'physique' magazines—basically soft gay porn, in spite of the alleged target market of bodybuilders—hidden in her husband Bill's closet, and laid a trap for him, hoping to learn if he was gay. *God knows he hasn't had much interest in fucking me for the last five years*, she thought. She supposedly left for a week-long visit with her sister, but came home early to find Bill kneeling naked on all fours at the edge of their bed, his toes hanging off the side, with two sailors, both naked from the waist down. One sailor knelt on the bed in front of Bill, holding his head and fucking his mouth, and the other stood at the side of the bed, holding Bill's waist while he fucked his ass. "Faggots!" she growled in a harsh voice, turned on her heel and walked out of the bedroom—and, effectively, out of Bill's life. Bill was rattled, of course, but when the sailors fucking him insisted he at least let them finish what they were doing, he agreed—after all, these two were good, among the best he had serviced in months.

In leaving her husband, Casey's mother effectively abandoned her son as well, unfeeling although that might have appeared; she suspected the twelve-year old Casey was a fledgling cocksucker. She had no use for gay men—faggots as she thought of them, and as she invariably referred to them—but living in a gay-friendly city like San Francisco, she kept her feelings pretty much to herself. She was disgusted to think that the man who had shared her bed for so long was in reality a faggot who lay down and let other men fuck him. She had no way of knowing that just before she walked in on the scene of Bill getting fucked by two sailors at once, he had not only fucked both of them, and blown a load in each, he had promised he would fuck each of them and give each another load as soon as they finished fucking him. The sailors knew Bill would be as good as his word since he had given the same assurance to them in a hotel on Market Street only the day before, and had delivered the promised two-loads-apiece in exceptionally satisfying style. He had, in fact, performed something like this same kind of service for those same sailors quite a few times before, even on one occasion when they brought along a third sailor to share in the fun.

Although he was not yet quite a teen-ager when his mother exited his life, Casey was already productively masturbating to pictures of men and boys and fantasizing about some of his more attractive acquaintances. He was barely twelve when he produced his first orgasm, while he was playing with himself and looking out of his bedroom window, wishing he was being held in the strong arms of the sexy high-school boy who was cutting the grass in his front yard. He was well aware of what he found sexy, but he failed to draw obvious conclusions about what his dad might be finding equally enjoyable from hints his mother dropped when she later told him she was leaving them. She had observed her son watching other boys and men, and concluded that the apple doesn't fall far from the tree, as they said. *A fruit tree, of course,* she thought, ironically. Casey had lived with his father ever since.

To her credit, Casey's mother was not acrimonious. She loved her son, but she knew Bill adored the boy, and his deep affection was returned. Casey would be better off with his father. Moreover, she would be free to openly pursue the passionate, clandestine affair she had been having for well over two years with a man only about ten years older than her son—one who gave her what she hadn't been getting at home for a long time.

If Bill Lowe suspected what a sexually active and mature son he was raising, he gave no indication, although he was well aware that his son was gorgeous and was hung like the proverbial mule. Bill's philosophy of parenting was *laissez faire*, and Casey mostly enjoyed relatively free reign to exercise his talents and appetites. His father well knew the ways of gay boys: God knows he had fucked enough of them during his time in the Navy and beyond. Knowing that Casey seemed to evince no interest in girls, he had a pretty good idea of what went on in his son's bedroom when he was not home—and often when he was actually in residence—but he gave no indication, and did not interfere. Casey, on the other hand, did not think his father was gay, even as he grew in sexual knowledge and experience, or that the same thing he was doing in his bedroom was often going on in his dad's room. Naturally he wondered if his father might be gay. After all, since his mother left—for reasons never explained adequately—he had not dated any other women, nor had he shown any interest in women at all. Had Casey snooped around his father's bedroom, he would have found ample evidence to prove his father was as interested in cock as he was, but as his dad respected his own privacy, so did Casey respect his dad's. Since he had never seen it hard, Casey never knew that his dad had a monster cock the equal of his own ass-reamer.

The road from high-school stud to the stage of the *Top 'n Bottom Theatre* — the T 'n B, as its habitués called it — was a surprisingly short one.

Most of Casey's classmates had fake California driver's licenses, attesting to ages that made the purchase of alcohol and tobacco appear to be legal. Casey had never been especially interested in drinking or smoking; his father's smoking and occasional drunken binges did nothing to attract his son to the use of either alcohol or tobacco. And since he had already attained legal age to pursue fucking, his principal form of indulgence, he had never been especially eager to obtain false identification. However, there were several locations in the city he was curious about, all of which he assumed would require him to be twenty-one before he could enter. These included a pair of 'baths' and three gay strip theatres. He didn't know it, but he only needed to be eighteen years old to patronize them.

His sexual activities were frequent and satisfying enough that one would assume he need look no further afield. However, practically all of his sex partners were around his same age, and very few of them were sufficiently experienced or adventuresome that they brought real excitement to Casey's bed — or to whatever place they went to have sex. The kind of sexual excitement and mature technique he saw in many gay porn videos intrigued him. He longed to share himself with the mega-hung and dirty talking Jeff Stryker; to relish the fat, perfect prick of Tom Steele; the magnificent chest, succulent tits and dark, dangerous-looking monster cock of Brad Stone; the golden facial beauty and stunning physique of Steve Fox, ravenously hungry to get fucked, in spite of his extreme masculinity; the commanding sexual aura of Michael Christopher or Tim Kramer; the perfect combination of face, body and cock embodied by Erik Houston; or the stunning sexual athleticism of the endlessly fascinating Matt Ramsey, who was as enthusiastic and hungry a bottom as he was a top, and whose orgasms were as explosive as they were copious. Casey was glad he was living in 1983, when access to sexually explicit gay films of such beauties was available to him. He knew that only a dozen-or-so years earlier, hard-core gay porn had been all but unavailable. He was also frustrated, however: some of his porn idols occasionally appeared at the strip theatres in San Francisco, but he was too young to enter — or so he thought. It seemed cruel that he could, for instance, only look at those magnificent tits of Brad Stone or Steve Fox on film, when he could have a chance to see them in person, and perhaps fondle them or even suck on them, if he were old enough to gain admission to their live shows.

One of Casey's most favored fuckbuddies at Serra High was his classmate Joey Stone. Joey was not, unfortunately, a relative of Brad Stone of the epic chest, whose real name probably wasn't Stone, anyway. Not only was Joey cute, he had the most rounded, most adorable, most perfectly fuckable ass Casey had ever seen — and Casey frequently proved its fuckability to Joey, usually once a week or so. (It should be noted that Joey felt the same way about Casey's ass.) Casey liked best to fuck Joey from behind — doggie style, or bending Joey's body over a table — so he could glory in the endlessly fascinating sight of the firm, golden orbs of his sweet ass shivering with hunger and excitement while he watched his own fat shaft sliding in and out between them. Joey actually preferred lying on his back, with his legs thrown high in the air or resting on Casey's shoulders, while the young fuckmaster plowed him, or riding Casey's cock while Casey lay on his back, because he was then able to study his idol's stunning facial beauty and its generous crown of golden hair as his friend made love to him; moreover, those positions allowed Casey to lean over and share fiercely passionate kisses with Joey while he fucked him, something Joey adored almost as much as getting fucked by his lover of the moment. Joey actually felt, or wanted to feel, that Casey really was his lover He knew, however, that Casey regarded him as a good friend, a favored fuckbuddy and a great piece of ass, but nothing more meaningful than that — and Joey wisely settled for what he could get from his godlike friend.

Joey had a very authentic-looking fake California Driver's License and an equally impressive fake U.S. Navy ID Card, both of which gave him a birth date in 1962, making him apparently eligible to do anything he wanted. Joey — who, like Casey, was barely eighteen — had managed to get the documents from a sailor who had connections he was happy to exercise in return for a pair of very hot nights in bed with Joey. Joey was not averse to telling Casey how he had managed to score the IDs from the sailor, since at the time he had just spent quite a bit of time enjoying the wonder of his classmate's fucking and cocksucking talents.

"Casey, he'd get you stuff to prove you're the King of Spain if you fed him that cock of yours," Joey laughed.

A meeting was arranged. Hank, the sailor, brought a camera and part of a Navy uniform for the boy to wear in the Navy ID photo. He got the pictures and information he needed for Casey's documents, along with an extremely enjoyable fuck. A week later, Hank delivered the completed cards to receive two equally satisfying fucks from the boy in payment—and a surprise, as well. Joey had told Casey how much he enjoyed getting fucked by Hank, so between the two fucks Casey gave Hank on the day he brought the ID, the young blond stud sucked the sailor's cock until he was near coming, then lay on his back and threw his legs in the air as he invited him to shove his cock up his ass, telling him to "fuck me for all you're worth." The sailor did exactly that—and he was 'worth' a lot! Casey later told Joey the fucks the sailor had given him were undoubtedly the best he had ever been given.

Casey had not been exaggerating. Hank was burly and extremely masculine, not very good looking, but fairly well hung, muscular, and, at thirty-five years, quite the oldest man Casey had ever had sex with. He was also the roughest fucker Casey had ever encountered, who threw the boy's legs over his shoulders, grinned as he said, "Jesus Christ, kid, you're fuckin' gorgeous," and pounded his ass mercilessly until he had blown two consecutive loads without stopping, all the time deliriously sharing passionate kisses. The second fuck Casey gave Hank was inspired by the one he had just been given, as rough and relentless as the sailor's had been, also yielding two consecutive orgasms—the first time Casey could remember having got his load three times in one unbroken sex session.

If Hank proved to be the most thrilling, satisfying top Casey had until then bottomed for, he also demonstrated abilities as a bottom that served as a lesson and a standard for the young blond fuckmaster's future performance in that role.

Very few of Casey's conquests were able to deep-throat his dick—even stretching their lips enough to admit the massive shaft was a considerable challenge for many of them. So far, only one had taken all ten fat inches down his throat the first time he tried, and that was, surprisingly, a supposedly straight star halfback of the Serra High football team. The football player, coincidentally, had a very challenging cock of his own, which Casey had gagged on repeatedly before finally being able to swallow completely. The halfback had snickered, "They all do that" when Casey gagged, which, combined with the football star's superb cocksucking ability, seemed to give the lie to the boy's alleged heterosexuality. The only other boys who regularly buried their lips in Casey's pubic hair when they sucked him had only achieved the ability to do so after diligent and extremely enjoyable practice. But the sailor, Hank, had gobbled Casey's cock down to the root with one swoop, licking feverishly at the same time as he exerted fierce suction on the gargantuan shaft, providing greater ecstasy then Casey had up to then derived from a blowjob. Casey knew he, himself, had never brought that kind of intense dedication to the task of sucking a dick, whether it had been one he could easily deep-throat, or one he had to struggle to take completely. As Hank serviced him so fully and so excitingly, Casey determined he was going to do a better job of sucking dick in the future, to give the kind of pleasure Hank was giving him. It crossed his mind, and later proved to be true, that he might then enjoy sucking cock even more than he always had.

When Casey first poised his cock-head at Hank's asshole and was preparing to plunge it inside the sailor who knelt on all fours, obviously hungry for a fuck if his moans and groans of encouragement meant anything, Hank drove his ass backwards fiercely, and completely impaled himself on Casey's monster dick in an instant, uttering a shout of complete joy as he did so. That in itself was unusually thrilling for Casey, but it was what followed that made him reconsider his own technique for taking a dick up the ass.

Hank rode Casey's cock like he was a bucking bronco, gasping and moaning with lust as his ass writhed in circles and drove back and forth on the shaft that was filling it so completely—at times grinding and pumping more fiercely and rapidly than the boy would have thought possible. The muscles of Hank's chute squeezed and pulled on Casey's fat dick, seeming to provide the same kind of intense suction the sailor had applied to it with his mouth. Hank almost seemed to be sucking Casey's cock again, but with his ass, and even more intensely than before. Many years later, Casey would watch the Czech porn star Ion Davidov celebrate getting his ass plowed by the glorious Lukas Ridgeston in exactly the same way, in the film *Lucky Lukas*, and would recall Hank's performance of two decades earlier with vivid fondness. As Casey screamed, "I'm coming" the first time be blew a load inside Hank, the older man's ass did, in fact, seem to be sucking every drop of cum from Casey's cock. When he erupted inside Hank's ravenous ass and collapsed over the sailor's back, Casey knew he had just delivered his greatest fuck ever, and that a considerable portion of the credit for its special quality was due to Hank's superb technique as a bottom.

As he had resolved to become a better cocksucker when Hank was blowing him earlier, Casey now swore he would become a better bottom, to use his ass in active worship of a cock that was fucking it, that he would not just lie there or kneel there and enjoy getting fucked, as he basically had in the past. Seeing the ecstasy Hank evidenced when he was servicing him, Casey knew he could get even more thrill from taking a cock up the ass than he had in the past, and he could apparently achieve that by assuming a more active, more dedicated part in the process when he bottomed.

When Hank fucked Casey a week later, he had no reason to suspect that the fiercely joyous way the boy sucked his cock and took him up the ass was at least partly attributable to his own example.

And Casey was immediately an even more exciting top as a result of his first encounter with the older sailor. In the week that intervened, while Casey waited for his new ID cards, he had sex with three other boys, 'regulars,' who responded happily to the new brand of fierce exhortations Casey grunted at them while he rammed his fat prick in and out of their mouths and asses: "Suck deeper, eat every inch of that fat dick, really suck it! Ride that dick faster and harder—suck the cum out of my big cock with your hot fuckin' ass!" And in return, Casey sucked and rode their cocks with a fierceness and mastery they had not before experienced, with the big-dicked blond personally demonstrating what he now expected from them when they fed him their dicks.

Joey and Casey compared their new ID cards—and they appeared to be authentic. In addition to being a twenty-one-year-old licensed California automobile driver, Casey was now "William Casey Lowe, Yeoman Third Class, United State Navy," and the sailor uniform Hank had brought for him to wear in the photograph looked great on him. Hank had thought Casey looked so cute as a sailor, he insisted he wear the uniform while they fucked—then, and on his return a week later. Joey agreed with Hank's assessment, and from then on, the uniform—which Hank had laughingly donated, as he said, in the cause of young love—always came out for one of them to wear when they had sex in Casey's room.

Armed with his new bogus identification, Casey scouted out the baths and strip theatres, something that had not before seemed worth devoting any time to, since he thought he could not gain admission. They seemed to promise even more excitement now, since after Hank, he had reason to suspect that really mature men might have more to offer than he had hitherto suspected. The porn gods he worshipped were all at least older than he, and several of them considerably more mature; they now seemed even more desirable than they had before — and even then he had desired them very, very strongly.

The first strip theatre he stopped by was on a clean, well-lighted street, only about a block from Union Square. The exterior and lobby were clean and well appointed, and the 'dancers' pictured in the lobby display were fairly attractive, but none of them particularly appealed to Casey. He observed that there was a hefty admission fee, good for walk-ins all day and evening, with a show every half-hour, featuring one of the dancers — supposedly regular employees — or the visiting porn "star." The visiting star was one Casey had never heard of, and who didn't strike him as irresistible. The ticket-taker allowed him to peek quickly into the theatre's auditorium without having to purchase a ticket. A lanky young man was dancing on the small stage, completely naked, boasting an erection that bobbed and swayed as he gyrated his hips to the music. His heart didn't seem to be in his work, even though his hard-on definitely was. Just as Casey began to watch, the dancer stepped down from the stage and stopped in front of one of the patrons, holding his cock out as he presented it not six inches from the man's lips, clearly tantalizing him. There were probably a dozen men scattered around, in a space that would probably seat a hundred or more, and in the dim light-spill from the stage, Casey could see that at least a couple of the men had their cocks out and were stroking them while they watched. Before he could see if the dancer was going to get his cock sucked, the ticket-taker pulled him away, saying he would need a ticket to see more — adding that Casey had better be able to prove he was eighteen before he could buy one. *Eighteen!* He hadn't needed to get the fake ID cards, after all. But had he not, he wouldn't have learned the lessons Hank had brought to their lovemaking. He thought he would return to the theatre when, and if, one of his favorite porn stars was appearing there.

The second theatre was in the Tenderloin district, in a run-down building on a ratty street. Everything about the marquee and lobby looked seedy and dirty. The performers shown on a board outside were not attractive, and no established porn star was promised. Casey didn't bother to look further, but went on to look at the two 'baths' he had located, since they were nearby.

He had heard enough about the baths to know what to expect if he visited: sizeable numbers of men wandering around nearly naked, or even completely so, cruising each other to arrange for uninhibited sex in the private rooms—in pairs, or larger gatherings. According to what his sources told him, most of the men would be considerably older, and many not at all attractive, but there was liable to be a sprinkling of younger, attractive men as well. It would not be unlikely that groups would gather to watch the more attractive and better-hung patrons having sex. It sounded like fun to Casey, but only if he found a sufficient number of the other patrons attractive. Since fucking with Hank, he thought it likely he would find at last some of the older men more attractive than he would have before.

The first bath he stopped by was also in an old, dirty building, and from what Casey could see in the lobby and the advertising cards, he wanted no part of it. The second one, on Polk Street, looked infinitely more promising. It appeared to be clean, and photographs of the pool and social areas showed an inviting atmosphere, with a mixture of older men and some hot young ones. Of course the pictures were probably either posed, or very selectively chosen, but Casey thought he would give it a try. Again, he learned that eighteen was the minimum age—not twenty-one, as he had supposed.

The final strip theatre he found was the *Top 'n Bottom*, located on Folsom Street, near Fourth. If it wasn't quite as slick-looking as the one near Union Square, it didn't miss it by much, and the arrangement for shows was virtually identical to that of the first theatre he had visited. More importantly, the house dancers' photographs showed them to be much sexier, in Casey's opinion. Of overriding interest, however, was the fact that the visiting star was Race Rivera, not only a well-known porn stud, but one that Casey had frequently focused on while he masturbated. He eagerly anticipated sitting in the auditorium while Race teased him in person by wagging his famous big dick or wriggling his gorgeous ass up-close and personal.

In two weeks, the theatre advertised an appearance by Michael Christopher, the goofily cute, very popular star of many porn movies. Michael looked a little coarse, and—frankly—not terribly bright, but he was sexy, sexy, sexy! And his body was massive, his vast tits were nothing short of glorious, and he wielded an amazingly fat, uniquely crooked cock of staggering dimensions—no doubt even bigger than Casey's. Michael was a top, of course—with that body and dick, how could he have been anything else? But he sucked dick like the professional that he was, and, amazingly, would occasionally bend over or throw his legs toward the sky while he took a big dick up his generous, rounded ass as well. Casey had seen him get fucked by Tim Kramer in a video, and the utter joy Michael seemed to be feeling while taking Tim's dick was almost palpable—just as any sane man would feel if he had a chance to get fucked by Tim Kramer. Casey thought Michael Christopher—and Tim Kramer, for that matter—were easily on his top-ten list of men he wanted to have sex with.

Casey resolved to return to the *Top 'n Bottom* the next day, a Saturday, to ogle and drool over Race Rivera, and he swore he would be among the first in the theatre the day Michael Christopher opened, even if he had to cut school to do so.

The baths and theatres were expensive, however, and Casey's finances were limited. His dad gave him a fairly generous allowance, but not enough to permit him to indulge this new expense. He had no idea how he was going to fund his new activities, but he could afford the first day's admission, and he would worry about financing the trip to see Michael Christopher when the time came.

Some of his high-school fuckbuddies made money by hanging around Polk Street, propped up against certain buildings and wearing pants that revealed what they had to offer to the men who paid handsomely to give them blowjobs. Joey Stone was one of those, and he had encouraged Casey to offer his stunning meat that way to make some extra money. "With your looks and your cock, you could make a fortune," Joey said. "But you won't enjoy it. Most of the guys who wanna blow you are shifty-eyed, sad old men. You'll only wanna leave your eyes open or even think about what's happening with about one in fifty." That didn't appeal to Casey, but still, he might consider putting on some faded, very tight Levi's he owned, which practically showed the veins in his dick if he didn't wear underwear under them, and offering his gargantuan prick for a few blowjobs. Given the size of what he had to offer, he felt sure he could make all the money he needed, in fairly short order. As it happened, he didn't need to display himself along the 'meat racks' on Polk Street to finance his new interests.

2.

A Destiny with Race

Race Rivera was a tall Latino from Los Angeles whose dark good looks and monster cock, combined with a nicely muscled body and an adorable 'bubble butt,' presented the kind of physical appearance that qualifies one for pornographic films. Race was further qualified for porn stardom by his sexual endurance, massive, explosive orgasms and his furious, unrestrained lust in lovemaking. He was generally thought of as a top, and did serve in that role in every one of his films, but he was often shown bottoming as well, and his sexual fierceness was as impressive when he was sucking dick, eating ass, or getting fucked as when he was plowing a rapturous bottom. His actual name was Tony (actually, Antonio) Lopez, but anyone who knew him called him by his family nickname, 'Gundo,' which was a familiarized form of the Spanish word segundo ('second'), recognizing the fact that his father's name was also Tony Lopez—so he was Tony Junior, or Tony the Second. Gundo had a sunny disposition and a generous good nature. He was, in fact, a very nice person. He was also, true to his reputed Latino heritage, a very hot-natured lover, tireless and voracious in sex. And 'sex' for Gundo strictly meant 'sex with guys,' as it had for his father, Tony Lopez the first—with a single exception.

Gundo's father had impregnated his mother through a single encounter, the only sex he ever had with a woman. She was Patty, the live-in lover of Don Mojica, a gorgeous Latino-Cherokee boy Tony worked with, and who Tony desperately wanted to have sex with, but had pleaded for in vain up to that point. Patty knew Tony was hot for her husband—and she, in turn, was hot for the dazzlingly handsome Tony. One night when Tony came to visit, Don had been suddenly called away on a family emergency, and she told Tony her cunt was full of Don's cum, since he had fucked her twice not an hour earlier. Tony didn't know what to say, but when she grinned crookedly and told him she wanted him to stick his dick in Don's hot cum and add to it, he took her up on the offer, fucking her savagely, thinking all the while of the ghost of Don's cock inside her cunt and Don's slippery, hot cum bathing his own prick while he fucked her. He deposited a great deal more cum in her before he stopped fucking—and soon she discovered she was pregnant.

Don, as it happened, was sterile, but Patty was unaware of it. When she became pregnant, Don knew it was someone else's baby she was carrying. When he learned it was Tony's, he was furious, but relented when Tony explained the circumstances surrounding the impregnation. Don threw Patty out, and rather than have the abortion Patty wanted, Tony's mother took care of her until the baby boy was born, then provided her with resources to settle somewhere else and leave the baby—as they had agreed she would do. Tony raised Gundo, with the help of his mother, and he was a beautiful baby, the spit and image of his father. A happy corollary to the situation was that Don finally gave Tony what he had wanted so badly, and discovered that sex with the big-dicked Latino was much better than what he had been enjoying with Patty: Tony's ass was much tighter than Patty's pussy; Tony could not only suck cock much better than she could, but his kisses were much more passionate and satisfying; and Tony gave himself completely to Don when they had sex, in a way that Patty never had. It was not long before Don was giving himself to Tony in the same way—tentatively at first, but soon joyously meeting the lip-stretching, ass-reaming challenge of Tony's colossal dick. Sucking cock and taking it up the ass were things he had never been able to experience with a woman, nor had he imagined he would enjoy them, but he found them to be so pleasurable that when he also considered the advantages he found in topping Tony, he largely gave up on women.

Many of Tony's friends were in the burgeoning porn film and video business, and his son grew into it, first hanging around the sets on porn shoots as a kid and surreptitiously sucking off the stars between takes, Sometimes he acted as a 'fluffer,' in the parlance of the business, one who sucks dicks on a porn set to get them hard for a take, and sometimes just for the sheer pleasure he gave and received. Many of the actors were so taken with the cute Latino kid with the big dick that Gundo was soon taking as many dicks up his butt as he was taking in his mouth, and fucking just as many guys around the set as were fucking him. He finally moved in front of the cameras as an experienced prodigy, filming his first on-camera fuck on his eighteenth birthday.

The star of Gundo's first film, *Rick Gives It Up*, was a well-established, extremely popular stud, who was exclusively a top on camera—but only on camera. His debut as a bottom had been widely anticipated by his many thousand of fans. The ecstatic fuck Gundo threw into him during the shoot was completely masterful, and clearly sent the star of the film into seventh heaven—as Gundo's fucks had done several times earlier, but off-camera, "in the wings." *Rick Gives It Up* was a smash hit, and Gundo was an instant star in his own right.

His popularity as a porn actor made him a good 'draw' when he appeared at strip clubs and theatres around the country; his reliability and good disposition made him popular with the managers of those venues. Moreover, he had the knack for providing a first-rate experience for most of the men who paid him for sex—whether impromptu sexual encounters during a club or theatre appearance, or on a pre-arranged 'escort' date. He closed his eyes and fantasized about sex with gorgeous young men, especially gorgeous young blond men with big dicks, while kissing or sucking and fucking with less attractive men—sometime very, very far less attractive ones. He had done three week-long appearances at the *Top 'n Bottom* before that spring of 1983 when Casey Lowe appeared in the audience for a morning show. Casey Lowe: exactly the kind of young man Gundo fantasized about when he needed extra inspiration.

After the announcement that Casey learned would precede almost every half-hour 'show' at the theatre—saying that patrons were forbidden to touch the buttocks or genitalia of the performers, a prohibition that was frequently ignored—the first house dancer was introduced. Unlike most of the 'dancers,' who, Casey later learned, simply paraded the stage instead of dancing, this one actually moved rather well to the soft-rock music that accompanied his striptease. He was probably in his twenties, nice-looking, although nothing special, and a bit on the thin side. He wore a tiny Speedo bathing suit and boots as he danced, then stripped off the Speedo to reveal a tiny g-string, which he wore when he went out into the audience and gyrated in front of each patron, shaking his well-filled pouch in each face, and turning around to wriggle his ass seductively. And his ass was actually bare, since there was only a tiny string behind him to hold the pouch in place in front. Since there were only about ten men in the auditorium, he had ample time to spend a few moments with each, and Casey noted that each man put a dollar bill in the dancer's g-string before he moved on to the next patron.

The dancer spent more time with Casey than with any of the others in the audience; he could clearly see that Casey was extremely attractive, and probably decades younger than the average patron. He hesitated before moving on, apparently expecting Casey to put a bill in his dollar-stuffed pouch, but gave up after an awkward moment. Then he returned to the stage and removed his g-string. He stood here gyrating to the music while his dick fattened and stiffened as he stroked it, until it stood straight out from his body. He manipulated his hard cock as he returned to the audience and again teased each man there. Casey observed that several of the men reached out and stroked the hard cock bobbing only a few inches from their lips, and several reached up between the dancer's legs to play with his busy ass. He could only see into the laps of three of the other patrons, but Casey noted that two of the three had their own cocks out of their pants, and were masturbating as they enjoyed the house dancer's visit. Their dollar tips were put into the dancer's boots now. After allowing the tip of his cock to brush Casey's lips, the boy leaned over and whispered in his ear, "You want it?" He reached down and groped Casey, immediately discovering the fat, hard shaft straining against his left pants leg, and then almost gasped as he stroked it, "Jesus, I hope you do. I sure would like to get this." He straightened up and slapped his dick—now apparently even harder and longer—against Casey's cheek. He smiled down and said, "A hundred bucks, kid. See ya out front," and moved on to the next patron. He hadn't apparently figured out that if Casey had failed to put a dollar in his g-string, he wasn't likely to give him a hundred times that much for a personal crack at his dick.

A hundred bucks! Christ, Casey thought, if he expects to get a hundred bucks for a blowjob, or whatever he's offering, a guy wouldn't be able to get anything from Race Rivera more than a close-up look without having to mortgage his car!

Since he knew he had no money to pay for sex with any of the dancers at the T 'n B—and didn't have any desire to, except maybe with Race Rivera—Casey didn't agonize about the apparent cost of doing business at a strip theatre. Besides, if the first dancer was representative, Casey was already having great sex with much cuter and hotter guys for free. He knew a dozen or two boys from Serra High, and a half-dozen from other high schools, who were at least as attractive as this guy, who wouldn't charge him anything except the chance to suck him off or take his monster up the ass. And if he wanted some guy to do a sexy striptease for him, he knew most of his regulars would happily do a private performance of whatever he wanted if it was followed by his special brand of lovemaking.

The second show featured another house dancer, who looked and 'danced' pretty much the same as the first. When he came around wearing glaring white Jockey shorts, and thrust the well-filled crotch in Casey's face, Casey whispered, "I'm sorry, I don't have any money to put in your underwear." The dancer smiled down at Casey's angelic face, and cupped his chin as he murmured, "Honey, anything I got you can have free." He turned around and pulled down his shorts in back, completely baring his ass. He looked back at Casey over his shoulder as he added, "Any time you want it, baby," then turned back around and stroked the tube of flesh that was filling out the left side of his shorts until it grew noticeably. He pressed his cloth-covered hard-on against Casey's lips, then leaned down and kissed him, whispering, "I'll be back, handsome," before he restored the back of his shorts and moved on.

The dancer stripped off his shorts when he returned to the stage, and gyrated to the music for a few minutes, his prick jumping up and down when he humped, and growing noticeably as he did so, until it was hard—and pretty impressive. He had a cute, round ass, which he was clearly proud of, judging by the way he stroked it and wriggled it as he displayed it—presented it, really—for the audience to admire. When he returned to Casey's seat a bit later, with his impressive prick still fully hard and lumbering in front of him, he put it up against the base of Casey's neck and pressed the boy's chin down on it, creating a chute into which he fucked for a while, as Casey reached up between his legs and fondled his pretty ass.

He turned around and sat in Casey's lap, reaching down between his own legs to grope Casey's prick—which was straining against his pants leg. The dancer gasped and stood to face Casey as his hands went down the front of Casey's pants to squeeze his enormous shaft. He whispered into Casey's ear, "Son of a bitch, would I love to ride this dick! I can do some wonderful things to this big ol' thing of yours, baby. Come backstage if you want me to show you." He held his prick and rubbed it all over Casey's face, especially rubbing the cock-head against Casey's lips. And then he moved on, shortly moving back up on the stage and masturbating furiously until he stepped down to the edge of the stage apron and held his throbbing prick still while he fucked his fist until he shot an impressive load of cum out into the audience—and shot it an impressive distance. Holding his dripping prick, he pointed out into the audience, directly at Casey, and blew a kiss before he exited to an appreciative round of applause.

Finally, it was time for the star to appear, and the announcer repeated the caveat about groping the performers before trumpeting, as all the lights suddenly went out, "And now the T 'n B brings you the hottest stud in fuck films, the long-dong Latino lover, Race Rivera!"

The spotlight picked up Race's head at the side of the stage. Some fairly sustained applause greeted him—much more enthusiastic than any Casey had heard so far. The spotlight opened up to show Race's bare chest as he grinned and waved. The light followed him while he moved downstage and center, where it broadened further, and all the stage lights came up to full. Aside from floppy paratrooper boots, Race was wearing only skin-tight, glossy black tights that clearly showed his impressive legs and ass as he turned around to display himself. The bulge at the crotch of the tights looked impossibly full, but Casey knew from having seen Race's films what an impressive set of cock and balls was squeezed into it; he wondered it didn't look even bigger. Apparently all the men in the audience were aware of the treasures the black tights concealed, for they whistled and clapped loudly as Race grinned and stroked the bulge, humping it against his hand.

Casey was bowled over by the physical presence of this man he had watched fuck and get fucked so many times, but whom he had never seen in person. He looked every bit as good in real life as he did in his videos. Casey and his fuckbuddies often had porn videos playing while they made love, and they sometimes liked to match their real actions to the passionate sex play their porn gods were enacting in the videos. Race Rivera was a favorite inspiration to them, and here he was in the beautiful and ultra-sexy flesh, not thirty feet away from where Casey sat while he massaged the long, hard tube of flesh that snaked down his left pants leg, wanting the Latin Adonis far more than he ever had when he had been only an image on a television screen.

Race moved well to the hard-rock music that was playing, bumping and grinding frantically, but always in rhythm with the beat. He leered at the audience as he cupped his bulging crotch and pinched his tits. He turned around and bent over so they could watch him stroking his ass, and then he stood, as with a sudden yank he pulled his breakaway black tights completely off, from his front, leaving his ass covered only by the straps of a white jockstrap. He turned around and grinned, clad now in only his jockstrap and boots. He humped his ass wildly to the music, causing the jockstrap to bounce up and down, and then he began to swivel his hips so that the jock swayed from side to side. Soon it was clear that the contents of his jockstrap was growing. After he reached inside and played with his dick for a few minutes—always in time with the music—the pouch lengthened and jutted out, with his cock clearly straining for release from the tiny garment.

Race stroked his fabric-sheathed hard-on suggestively, and began to tug it down. He lowered it to the point where his pubic hair was completely exposed, and the base of his hard cock could be seen. Then he put a hand to his mouth and mimed a modest "Oh!," as if he had just remembered he couldn't show the audience his dick. So he turned his back as he pulled the jock strap down and dropped it at his feet. He stepped out of it, and spread his legs wide as he bent over, almost touching his toes. He reached behind to spread the cheeks of his ass, and moved from side to side as he did so, in order that everyone could get a good look at the pink rosebud hiding there. He released his buttcheeks and looked back over his shoulder so the audience could clearly see him exaggeratedly moistening the second finger of his right hand. Then with his left hand he pulled one cheek aside, and he brought his right hand up from between his legs so he could position his moistened finger at his asshole. Someone called out 'Do it!,' followed by a few whistles, and he honored the request. He slowly pushed his finger into his asshole and began to drive it all the way in and out slowly and seductively. The audience applauded and Race grinned at them over his shoulder while he continued to finger-fuck himself, sometimes quite violently.

Removing the finger from his ass, Race stood up and turned around, with his hands cupping and concealing his prick. He moved his arms so that it looked like he was going to bare his cock, but he mimed another surprised "Oh!" as he turned around again, bent over to pick up his jockstrap—exaggeratedly wriggling his ass as he did so—and drew it back up, after which he turned to reveal his cock barely concealed inside the inadequate cloth pouch, not completely hard, but pressing mightily against the flimsy constraint. He stepped down from the stage and began his first tour of the audience.

The man several seats down from Casey had his cock out, and had been masturbating as he watched Race's performance. Casey's own cock was painfully hard, and he had been massaging it through his pants leg. He thought, *What the hell, probably most of the guys here are beating off. Why not pull it out and join the fun?* He had intentionally avoided wearing tight pants; figuring he might be jacking off at some point, and he didn't want to struggle to extricate his cock, as he had to do when he had an erection while wearing Levi's. Hard as it was, his prick was still too big to pull out without lowering the waistband of his pants, so he undid his belt and opened the flaps of his fly. He had intentionally not worn underwear, and his throbbing cock was now free so he could stroke it properly.

Race did not spend as much time with individual audience members as the house dancers had. Of course his 'show' had gone on longer than the others', and since there were almost twice as many audience members to visit, those visits had to be relatively brief. When he finally positioned himself in front of Casey, he looked at him and said, "My god, kid, what dream did you step out of?" He caressed Casey's chin and said, "You're the cutest thing I've ever seen in this place." With his other hand he reached down, saying, let's see what you got down here that you wanna give me." His hand closed over Casey's naked, throbbing shaft and he gasped, "Holy shit, kid, fantastic dick! I hope you do wanna give this to me. He pressed his bulging crotch against Casey's face and added, "I sure as hell would like to give this to you, if you want it. Look good to you?"

Casey gulped, and was barely able to stammer, "It looks wonderful. You can't imagine how much I want it. But, I don't have any money, and . . . "

He was cut off when Race put a hand over his mouth. "Kid, with a dick and a face like yours, you don't need any money to make it well worth my while. How about it? You wanna fuck my ass? You gonna let me fuck you?"

With his heart racing so he could hardly speak, Casey managed a very fervent "Yes!" Race grinned, and said, "Keep that beautiful thing out—I'll be back in a few minutes," and moved on to visit the other patrons. Then he stepped back on the stage and very seductively peeled off his jockstrap, exposing his huge bare cock in all its glory. He stroked it in time to the music, getting it fully erect so that it stood out parallel to the floor. Then he stepped back down to re-visit the patrons

He gave each a close-up view of his dick and luscious ass, and allowed any of them who wanted, to caress his cock for a minute, or plant a kiss on it. Several of them also planted a kiss on his ass—and even deep down between the cheeks. As he left the man nearest to Casey, he veered off and returned to the stage, where, with exaggerated gestures, he allowed everyone to see him apply lubricant generously to his asshole and finger-fuck himself again. Then he was down in the audience and with Casey. He leaned over and whispered, "You really want it, stud?" Casey barely whispered his affirmative reply before Race's lips closed over his, and the porn god was kissing him as passionately as he had always done in Casey's fantasies, virtually fucking his mouth with a wonderfully greedy tongue.

Race turned around, facing away from the big-dicked blond Adonis. He reached down and stroked Casey's cock as he applied to it a coating of the lubricant he had been concealing in his hand. Then he positioned the head of Casey's cock at his asshole, and gradually sank down into Casey's lap, taking every inch of Casey's fat ten inches inside him. He bobbed up and down and took Casey's hands in his, placing one on his cock, and guiding the other to his tits. Race's cock was stupendous, incomparable—the biggest one Casey thought he had ever held, even bigger than his own. Casey was so thrilled to be stroking Race's throbbing meat in his hand, and to feel his idol riding his cock, he almost forgot to play with Race's tits. He fucked violently upward to counter the downward plunges of Race's ass. Race groaned with joy, apparently as insensible as Casey was to the dozens of men watching them, all of them keenly aware of what was going on. The way Race's body was riding up and down, with his head thrown back and his mouth open in obvious ecstasy, there was no question about the fact that Race was riding the young blond's cock.

After about five minutes, Race reached back and pulled on Casey's sides, turning his head back to growl, "Stand up." Still fucking Race, Casey stood, and as he did so, his pants slipped down to puddle around his shoes. Race leaned over the seat in front of him, and Casey seized his waist while he picked up the pace of his fuck, slamming his prick ferociously and unmercifully into the eager porn stud's ass, with strokes as long as only one as gloriously hung as Casey could achieve. If he thought at all about the fact that twenty or thirty men were watching his bare ass humping while he hammered Race's hungry butt, he was too completely seized with fuck-frenzy to care.

Casey was so excited that after a few minutes he knew he was going to shoot a load very soon. "Race, "I'm gonna come if I don't stop right away."

"Give it to me, baby, fill me with your hot load!" Race cried

Both Race and Casey were so completely engrossed in their lovemaking that they were unaware that the volume of the sound system had been gradually ratcheted downward as they got more and more passionate, until there was complete silence in the theatre long before Casey stood and started fucking Race while he was bent over the seat in front of them. Since the fuck had started, Casey's grunts and cries of joy, and Race's gasps and groans of appreciation had been clearly audible to all, and as Casey's orgasm neared, Race's feverish exhortations were clearly heard: "Give me that fuckin' big cock, baby! Fuck my hungry ass, kid! Fill me with your big load, lover—I want your cum!"

Casey seized Race's waist in a vise grip and his ass froze in muscular spasm as he drove his prick as far inside Race's twitching chute as it would go, and held it there, grunting bestially just before he began to explode spurt after spurt of what he knew was going to be the biggest load he'd ever given anyone. He screamed, "I'm coming, I'm coming! Take my big load!" followed by a muffled scream of joy as he erupted, "Oh god, Race! Aaaaaaahhh!"

The celebrants were also unaware that the spotlight had been focused on them for some time, and most of the patrons were either standing and craning their necks to get a better look at the two god-like studs locked together in a delirium of lust, or had moved closer to get a better view; all but a few had their cocks out and were masturbating as they watched, and a couple of the more eager ones already had cum dripping from them.

As Race's ass continued to work Casey's now somewhat less engorged cock, the boy reached around and began to jack off Race's cock again, now using both hands—something only possible when you're stroking the kind of major meat the Latino stud had to offer. Race stood up and moved Casey's hands back to his tits, turning his head to say, over his shoulder, "I'd love for you to beat me off, but I can't blow my load right now, baby—got work to do." As he said this, they both realized that they were in the spotlight, and audible to all around them. Speaking in a very low voice, Race said, "What a fuckin' stud you are, baby. I almost shot my load while you were plowing me, but I wanna save it to shoot up your pretty ass, You really gonna give me a crack at it?"

"Any time you want it," Casey whispered.

'Can you come to my seven o'clock show? I'll have at least three hours after that, and we could go to my hotel room if you want. Sound good?"

'Sounds great! I'll be here." His cock began to stir again inside Race's ass as he considered the possibilities.

"Okay. And sit in the front row—I'll have a surprise to give you. But I can tell I'd better get on with this show or you're gonna start fucking me again. Save it for later, okay?" He turned, allowing Casey's still almost fully hard dick to slip out of his ass. He pushed Casey down into the seat, positioned his cock-head at the boy's lips, and pushed. Casey opened his mouth wide to admit the challenging shaft as Race seized his head in both hands and began to thrust his prick into Casey's throat. Casey quickly relaxed his throat and brought all his cocksucking expertise to bear as he managed to admit every inch Race fed him. He sucked happily and profoundly, not caring that every eye in the auditorium was on him, and his slurping and Race's murmurs of satisfaction were still clearly audible. After far too few minutes, Race pulled his cock out of Casey's mouth and whispered in his ear, "Jesus, baby, you suck cock as good as you fuck." He kissed Casey again, but a very long, gentle, sweet kiss—the kiss of a satisfied lover. Casey thought it was even sexier than Race's passionate tongue-fuck had been—if that were possible. The audience broke into sustained applause as they kissed, and returned to their seats when Race slipped away to visit the few other patrons he had not visited when naked. As Casey watched, he observed that each of those patrons had their fingers up Race's cum-slick ass while he tantalized them with his dick.

Then Race returned to the stage. He picked up his discarded tights and jockstrap and draped them over his cock—protruding upward, and sufficiently hard that it held them like a coat hook. The audience was applauding loudly. He bowed, and then extended a hand toward Casey as he reached behind to hold his ass with the other and pantomimed an ecstatic "Ooooh …Wow!" He flashed an engaging grin and swaggered off the stage, still playing with his luscious ass, which rolled seductively, with his tights and jockstrap still draped over his cock and swaying as he walked.

Casey was so exhausted and euphoric he did not remember to put his cock back in his pants until he realized the house lights had come back up and several men were coming by to get a close-up glimpse of the cock that had just fucked Race Rivera. A few even made comments, expressing their enjoyment at having watched him fuck Race, conveying their envy of Race for taking him up the ass or of him for having fucked the Latino stud. Several indicated their willingness to take his cock themselves, any way he would be willing to give it to them. Casey smiled, and was polite to them, but made no reply to those who were soliciting sex with him. He knew he should be embarrassed for having just sucked Race's cock and having fucked him in front of dozens of witnesses, but oddly enough, all he felt was pride and excitement. He knew he didn't want to watch any more of the house dancers—at least not that day. He'd seen the best, he'd fucked the best, he'd sucked the best, and he was going to go to bed with the best in several hours.

He began to leave the theatre, and as he passed through the lobby on the way out, he encountered the second house dancer, who stopped him to say, "You're one lucky bastard, you know that? And I'll bet Gundo's gonna meet you later, right?"

"Gundo?"

"Race. That's his real name. I'll bet you're gonna get a royal fucking from that fabulous dick of his. When, tonight?"

Casey grinned, proudly, "That's right."

The dancer rolled his eyes. "Believe me, I know from personal experience exactly what you're gonna feel when Gundo fills your butt and starts slammin' it. I'll be thinkin' about it, and wishin' it was me he was fucking again." He embraced Casey and kissed him quickly, "And I'll be wishin' you were fuckin' me, too! Come back some other time and give me a crack at showin' you what I can do, okay? You saw that big load I shot out in the audience?"

Casey grinned again, "Yeah—it was pretty impressive."

"Well, I was thinkin' of you when I did it—pretendin' your lips were wrapped around it." He stepped back slightly, and held Casey's shoulders. "And I can blow another one just as big any time you want—and damned near as often as you could want. I'm a fuckin' cum machine, cutie! But shit, with your looks, and your cock, you oughta be the star on that stage. I wish you were, 'cause we've got a tradition here at the T 'n B: every house dancer gets fucked by the guest star at least once while he's here. And I sure wanna get fucked by you, lover — just the way Gundo fucked me a couple a days ago, and the way you're probably gonna fuck him again tonight." He kissed Casey and whispered in his ear, "Gundo told me he really loved my ass — and you would too. Come back and give it a try." Then he went back into the auditorium.

With at least four hours to kill before Race's seven o-clock show, Casey was at loose ends. He went to a diner and ate a hamburger and fries. He strolled down to the waterfront and sat on a bench near Pier 20, listening to the seagulls, enjoying the breeze, watching the busy Bay traffic and glorying in the memory of having just fucked Race Rivera and sucked his cock. But he really couldn't keep his mind on much of anything except the upcoming meeting with the wonderfully hung, handsome Latino stud. Race ... no, Gundo. That was his real name? What kind of a name was that? He didn't worry about it though; what difference did it make what his name was, after all. From a classroom study of Romeo and Juliet he remembered Juliet's query, almost exactly, "What's in a name? That which we call a rose by any other name would smell as sweet." But to himself he was thinking, That which we call a big-dicked stud by any other name would fuck just as hard. Race, Gundo, whatever — he's gonna have his monster prick up my ass in a couple of hours!

He slouched on the bench, his legs spread out in front of him as he contemplated what "Gundo" had in store for him that evening. And the surprise he had promised? Casey wondered what that might be, but he felt sure it was going to be exciting. He was unaware of passers-by, and equally oblivious to the fact that his thoughts had given him such an erection that it looked like he had stuffed a salami down his left pants leg.

A couple of sailors walked by and goggled at him. They probably would have cruised him anyway; sailors are often attracted to gorgeous young blond boys sitting alone outdoors on a Saturday afternoon. But when this pair saw that this Adonis had a throbbing-hard prick of gigantic proportions, they altered their course and sat down on either side of their hoped-for prey. Casey immediately realized what a spectacle his posture and his condition presented, and sat up, pressing his legs together to conceal his erection to some extent.

One of the sailors said, "Shit kid, don't hide it. Be proud of it."

A flustered Casey began to speak, "Look, I was thinking ..."

The other sailor interrupted, "I hope you were thinkin' about what we're thinkin' about. You wouldn't be interested in sharing that big fuckin' ass-reamer with a couple a super-horny sailors with big dicks, would you?"

"Gee, I ... Look, I appreciate it, but I've got a heavy date in a little while, and I've gotta save myself."

"For her, or for him?" he asked.

Casey grinned, "For him, as a matter of fact."

"Lucky son of a bitch," the first sailor leered. "You wouldn't be interested in a foursome, would you?"

Casey shook his head, "No, but thanks for the offer. I'm sure it would be fun, but I don't think so."

"How much time have you got before you meet him? And you reckon he can take all of that huge dick of yours?"

"Oh yeah," Casey smiled. "He's already had it once today. And he's got just as much cock to give me as I can give him. And before you ask, I'm pretty sure I'll be able to take it," He added proudly, "I had it all down my throat, I figure I can take it all up the butt."

"God damn, thinking about it makes me horny as hell. But you didn't tell us how much time you have to kill until this stud is gonna fill your pretty little ass."

The other sailor interjected, "Yeah, maybe the three of us could go somewhere, and you could practice for later on." He grinned, "We always give good service. You ever fuck a sailor, kid?"

"Not yet," Casey laughed. "No. Wait—yeah, one. And thanks again, but I'm gonna pass, even though I know it would be fun."

"Fun? Shit, baby, you'd have a fuckin' ball—you'd have four fuckin' balls, in fact—and all four of 'em are really full of cum."

Casey shook his head. "Sorry."

The first sailor stood up. "Fuckin' tragedy."

"What a waste," the other said as he stood. "C'mon sailor, looks like we'll have to settle for each other. 'Bye, cutie. Good luck with that stud you've got lined up. Wish it was me." And they took off. Their uniforms were spectacularly tight; they had showed some promising bulges snaking down the legs of their pants, and their asses rolled seductively as they walked away—very, very fuckable, Casey thought. He considered that he should have arranged a meeting with them for another time. He'd never been in a threesome, and considering what he heard about sailors from some of his fuckbuddies who had gone to bed with them, it might have been fun to have his first one with the two who had just left. They were pretty cute, after all, and they certainly had been eager to fuck with him.

Casey had been blatantly cruised and publicly propositioned hundreds of time—a boy as beautiful and clearly hot as he could hardly expect less in San Francisco, after all—but seldom by men he found attractive, and almost never by boys near his own age. He had so far never yielded to the blandishments of those strangers seeking to have sex with him, but after his experience with the fuck-stud Hank, he was probably open to a new range of prospective fuck partners. And Hank was a sailor. Yeah, he should have at least got the two sailors' addresses!

There was a public phone booth across the street, at the Embarcadero, and Casey headed to it hoping he would find Joey Stone at home. He was bursting to share with someone his excitement about the day so far, and the promise of the rest of it. Joey was a huge Race Rivera fan, and besides, Casey had sex with Joey more frequently than with anyone else, and he was the second boy who had ever fucked him; who better to tell about his cumming adventure with Race Rivera, and his coming adventure with the porn stud?

Well, Dave Cotter might have been better. He was the first boy who fucked Casey. Dave was not available to talk with about sex, however, since he had recently moved overseas when his military family was relocated. Dave had been a tall, smolderingly sexy boy on the Serra High Swim Team, with a swimmer's body, but a horse's dick. The only reason Casey had been able to take Dave's cock the first time was that he so desperately wanted to please the cute, monster-hung swimmer.

For a long time, Casey had fantasized about sex with Dave while he masturbated—at least once every day, but often two or three times. He had studied Dave's body in swim meets, and had often seen his breathtaking prick when they stood next to each other at a urinal. He desperately wanted to suck that huge dick, and somehow—although he wasn't sure this was possible—he wanted to fuck Dave's cute ass with his own outsized prick. He certainly didn't imagine he could take Dave's prick up his own ass—but he fantasized about it anyway.

One unforgettable night they had gone to a movie, and were walking home when Dave suddenly asked Casey is he could come home with him and spend the night. Casey's heart suddenly began thumping so hard he almost trembled when he said, "You'll have to lend me some pajamas."

His heart went into overdrive when Dave replied, "You don't need pajamas. I always sleep naked. We both can."

Casey began to have visions of lying in a separate bed in the same room as his sexy fantasy partner, both of them naked, but ten or fifteen feet apart and doing nothing about fulfilling his fantasies. He thought he was going to be frustrated beyond belief, but he was thrilled to the same degree when they got to Dave's bedroom and he saw there was only one double bed! Even though it wasn't terribly late, Dave suggested they go to bed shortly after they got there. A good sign, Casey thought.

Dave stripped and threw his clothes on the floor, turning out the light as he got under the covers, even before Casey had finished undressing. Normally, Casey would have been glad that no one noticed his ten-inch raging hard-on, but he really wanted Dave to see it, hoping Dave would want to do something with it.

Dave said "G'night, Casey," and turned to lie on his side, facing away from him. Casey was so horny, he wanted to jack off, but was afraid to do so, knowing Dave would be well aware of it. Perhaps if he waited a while, he could slip into the bathroom and take care of his little problem — which, at ten inches, was not "little" by any stretch of the imagination. He turned and lay on his side, back-to-back with Dave, and tried to will himself to sleep, which was out of the question at the moment.

After about ten minutes — which seemed like an hour to the horny, frustrated Casey — Dave rolled over so that he lay front-to-back with him, with only a few inches separating their bodies. They lay that way for some time, and Dave's breathing seemed to indicate he was sound asleep. Muttering something unintelligible, Dave threw an arm over Casey's body and let it rest there, after which he resumed his deep regular breathing. Casey was afraid to move a muscle. Dave's arm over him felt so good holding him, as it were, that he didn't want to disturb his idol in any way, for fear he would move back to his side of the bed.

Dave didn't move his arm, but he did snuggle up so that his chest was pressed against Casey's back, and his arm moved down to cradle the blond stud's body. Casey was hoping Dave would move his arm down and meet his throbbing, fiercely hard erection. Perhaps ... but after a few minutes, Dave removed his arm and let his hand rest flat against Casey's hip. Casey felt Dave's breath on his neck, then Dave's mouth pressed against it and he soon was kissing it. That emboldened Casey to back up a little, snuggling more tightly against Dave while he reached behind to let his hand rest on Dave's hip. That was apparently a signal Dave had been waiting for. Instead of reaching around to take hold of Casey's hard-on, which Casey hoped was going to be his next move, Dave moved his hand so that he could stroke the rounded globes of Casey's ass. He whispered, "What a pretty ass," as his hand went between the boy's asscheeks and one finger began to toy with Casey's asshole, even penetrating it very slightly. "Feel good?" he asked. Casey murmured in obvious pleasure, and Dave whispered, "Can I fuck you, Casey?"

So excited he scarcely knew what he was doing, Casey reached down and grasped Dave's cock—feeling absolutely enormous, but also so hard it felt like warm skin wrapped around a fat steel rod. Without replying to Dave's question in words, he made his answer clear when he positioned the tip of Dave's prick at his asshole, and began to squirm around. He had no idea how he would take such a monster inside his ass, but he wanted desperately to try.

Dave told Casey to lie on his back and spread his legs. From somewhere he produced a jar of lubricant. He turned on the nightstand lamp so that Casey could watch him slather his throbbing cock with lube, and so that he could drink in Casey's beauty while he prepared him for the fuck. He lubricated Casey's asshole liberally, putting a finger deep inside as he did so, then two, then three—which was a challenge for Casey, but helped prepare him for the onslaught of Dave's wonderful cock, which was over nine inches long, and proportionally fat as well. That fat nine-incher would have been a real challenge for anyone, but as a cherry-buster, it was a cruel ass-reamer, anything but 'training size.'

Dave murmured encouragement and sweet words into Casey's mouth as he gradually, but insistently slipped his cock inside the eager boy, who had instinctively raised his legs and rested them on Dave's shoulders. Dave began kissing him sweetly at first, but with increasing passion until he was fucking Casey's mouth with his tongue while he started fucking Casey's ass in earnest. The pain was soon over for Casey, and in many respects, he had never felt anything more thrilling than the next fifteen minutes, while Dave fucked him unmercifully until he blew his load deep inside the deliriously happy blond's virgin ass.

A boy is to a considerable extent always in love with the first boy who fucks him, provided he wanted to be fucked, and Casey proved the rule. He had been dreaming of getting fucked for some time, and, miraculously, the boy he found irresistibly attractive was the one who gave it to him. From that moment he had been in love with Dave, even though Dave had never let him say it in so many words on the many occasions they had sex. Dave loved to suck Casey's cock, and never failed to swallow his load, but he never let Casey fuck him. Actually, he liked to get fucked, but having heard so many boys whimpering in pain when he began to fuck them the first time — and even the coach of the swim team had to muffle his cries of pain the first few times he took Dave's cock up his ass — he felt he couldn't endure the monster Casey wielded — the only one he'd had in his hands or mouth that was bigger than his own. Later in his life, Dave rode many cocks fully as big as Casey's, and a few that were even bigger, and he deeply regretted not having yielded to Casey's urgent pleas to take his dick up the ass — especially so since none of the enormous cocks he enjoyed belonged to anyone nearly as dazzlingly handsome as the Adonis to whom he had denied access.

Joey was home when Casey called, and was thrilled to hear every detail about his friend's good fortune. "Jesus, Casey, why couldn't it have been me? I would kill to get Race Rivera's dick up my ass — or down my throat, or anywhere he wanted to stick it." Casey told him about the two sailors who had just tried to pick him up, wanting a threesome. "Sounds hot as hell," Joey said. I wish I had been there to take 'em up on their offer. You think they woulda settled for me?"

"Christ, Joey, of course they would. You're cute as hell, you know that, and you woulda let 'em see just how fuckin' hot you are."

"Mmmmm," Joey groaned, "A threesome with two hot sailors. Sounds like heaven to me. Do you think you could … no, never mind."

"Go ahead, Joey, you know you can ask me anything. What is it?"

"Would you even consider asking Race if I could join you two guys in his hotel room tonight? Jesus, how hot would that be? A threesome with the biggest dick I've ever had and Race Rivera, with a dick that … well, his dick has gotta be as big as yours, Casey."

"I'm pretty sure it's even bigger," Casey replied.

"Oh my lord! Would you mind asking him, Casey?"

"Joey, you know I love you, and you're my best friend, and I enjoy fucking with you more than anybody I know. I've certainly told you that enough, but ... well, this is kinda special, you know? This is gonna be the most exciting thing that ever happened to me, and I don't wanna ... I don't know, dilute it, I guess. Can you understand, Joey?"

Sighing, but good-naturedly, Joey said, "Sure, I understand. I don't guess I'd wanna share a total fuck-stud like Race Rivera either if I had a chance to make love with him." He brightened up somewhat. "Not the first time, anyway. But would you ask him if we could maybe have a threesome later on? Or if he'd maybe fuck with me? Tell him I'm a great piece of ass. You've told me that enough, you know."

Casey assured Joey he was, in fact, a really terrific piece of ass, and he promised to see if there was some way he could arrange a threesome with him and Race, or a fuck date for Race and Joey alone. That was the second time considerations of a threesome had gone through Casey's mind in the space of the last half-hour. He decided he needed to examine the possibilities seriously sometime soon. But now, he had Race Rivera to look forward to.

3.

Bertha van Idea

The afternoon dragged on, but eventually it was time to return to the T 'n B. Casey arrived at about 6:45, and one of the house dancers he had not seen earlier in the day was performing. He was identified in the lobby program as "Carl." Carl was finishing up the naked half of his routine, and Casey stood at the back, not wanting to attract too much attention by going to the front row — where Race had directed he should sit. He wished he had been there to see Carl's performance in its entirety, though. The dancer was short, and although he wasn't cute, he was ruggedly handsome, and had a very muscular body, with the huge chest and massive, rounded tits Casey found particularly attractive — like those of porn star Brad Stone, pictures and videos of whose body and dark monster cock he had often used as aids in masturbation. Moreover, Carl's dick was nearly as fat and enticing as Brad Stone's, but oddly enough, it never seemed to be at full erection, even when several of the patrons handled it and stroked it. Judging by its length when it only jutted out partially, mostly hanging down and swinging like a toothsome flesh pendulum, it would be a deliciously challenging assful when it was fully hard — a thrillingly formidable ass-reamer. If he had already been seated in the front row when Carl performed, Casey thought, he would have done something to get that huge tube of semi-hard flesh throbbing in full glory.

Casey had only been to bed with one boy with a similarly mouth-watering chest and a physique to match: Rommel Chase, a classmate at Serra High. Casey had seen Rommel stripped to the waist, and had been very keen to get to "know" the very muscular boy. Although Casey had made several subtle overtures to Rommel, making it pretty clear he was interested in developing something more than just a friendship, they were either too subtle, or Rommel was straight — or perhaps simply not interested in Casey. So far, however, Casey had never met a boy who was gay, or even thinking about being gay, who wasn't interested in him. He later realized that the subtlety of his tentative propositions had apparently been too great, since out of the blue one day Rommel accosted him in a bathroom at school, with no one else around, and said, with admirable directness, "Casey, I just heard you like to suck dick. Is that right?"

Such a direct question deserved an equally frank answer, Casey thought. He replied, simply, "I love to suck dick—and I can do a helluva lot more with a dick that's even more fun."

Rommel leered, "Like takin' it up the ass?"

"That's what's really fun," Casey leered back, "but I generally expect to find a couple of places to put my dick when I do that. And I've got a mighty big dick. Not everyone can take it."

"Why don't we get together after school and see what we can do about my problem," Rommel said.

"What's your problem?"

"I'm so horny I could fuck a snake," Rommel said, groping his crotch.

Casey grinned, "You want me to hiss?"

"Nah, I wanna fuck you. How about it? But I oughta tell you, not everyone's able to take my dick, either."

"I guarantee I'll take all you wanna give me," Casey said, "and grin while you're doing it. But how about returning the favor?"

"I always return favors—and trust me, I can take whatever you've got."

"Meet me here after school. We can go to my house and see who can take what."

They went to bed that afternoon, and Casey spent as much time sucking Rommel's tits as he did sucking the muscle boy's cock—but Rommel seemed to enjoy either exercise equally. Getting his tits sucked while Casey fucked him in missionary position proved to be his favorite thing, however. Being held in Rommel's massive arms, pressed against his glorious body while they kissed, was especially enjoyable for Casey. Rommel's cock proved to be of good size, but not the monster dick he had implied he would bring to their play, while Casey's cock apparently proved to be a lot more than Rommel had anticipated, judging by his initial gagging and pains at being penetrated—both problems that cleared up very quickly. Rommel later said, with a certain amount of awe, and a great deal of satisfaction, that Casey's was far the biggest prick he had ever sucked or taken up the ass.

Later, after they had fucked each other a dozen or so times, Rommel apparently fell in love with a daintily beautiful young sophomore, whose adoration of Rommel's spectacular body amounted to utter worship. Now, Rommel only came to Casey occasionally, to get the kind of ass-reaming, lip-stretching sex that he missed with his young, almost epicene lover.

At the T 'n B, Casey watched Carl's muscular ass undulate marvelously as the muscleboy exited, and he made his way down to the front row to be ready for Race's show.

Race's appearance was announced, and he came out on stage, looking even sexier and more attractive to Casey than ever, knowing that he was probably going to get the porn stud in bed very soon. The on-stage portion of Race's 7:00 show was identical to the one Casey had witnessed earlier in the day. Casey had thought Race had improvised his sexy antics on stage that afternoon, but they were obviously planned out and rehearsed. There were almost twice as many in the audience as there had been earlier, so the part of the show where Race made the first circuit among the audience members, wearing his jockstrap, was cut out to allow him to visit everyone, however briefly, when he went out naked.

Race went all the way to the back row to start his circuit with the audience, and began working his way forward. He went down the rows treating everyone to a chance at seeing his fabulous cock and ass very close up, and allowing a bit of stroking and kissing, but less than he had earlier—again, probably because of time constraints: a house dancer was due to appear at 7:30. Race was not scheduled to perform again until 11:00 p.m. Thinking about his imminent meeting with the masterful stud now displaying his glorious equipment for all these men, Casey's dick was painfully hard; he dropped his pants and was ready in case Race wanted to sit on it again. By the time Race got around to Casey, however, it was past the time he should have finished his appearance, so he merely kissed Casey and stroked Casey's dick as he whispered in his ear, "I'm dying to get this up my butt again. Meet me out in the lobby when my show's over—but stay right here for the surprise I promised you."

Then he was back on the stage, and standing at the very edge of the apron, directly in front of Casey. He began to masturbate furiously, bending slightly backward, with his pelvis thrust forward. His head was thrown back, his eyes closed, and his ass bumping and grinding as it drove his huge prick in and out of his frantically pumping fist. After about three minutes, he straightened up, opened his eyes, and focused on Casey as he grinned and continued to stroke his dick wildly. As his right hand gripped his monster cock tightly, and drove frantically up and down the fat shaft. he pointed it right at Casey, like the mighty weapon that it was. He stretched out his left arm and pointed a finger directly at the boy, and shouted, "Just like Babe Ruth!" as massive jets of his cum began to erupt—accompanied by loud applause, whistles and cheers. His aim was pretty accurate, and Casey took almost all of Race's load on his face, chest and lap, except the last few, weaker spurts. A hand came out of the curtain at the side of the stage, holding a towel. Race went over and took the towel, wiped off the end of his dripping cock, then walked back and tossed it to Casey, with a wink, before he blew Casey—and then everyone else—a kiss before he exited.

Casey licked as much of Race's cum off his face as his tongue could reach, then used the towel to clean himself up further. He pulled his pants up and managed to get his throbbing cock stuffed in them before he stood, then walked back to the lobby to wait for his "date."

It took only a few minutes for Race to appear in the lobby, looking irresistible, Casey thought. "Ready to go?" he asked. "I didn't shower. I figured maybe we could shower together at my hotel." Putting his arm around Casey's shoulder, he grinned, "Okay with you?"

"Okay?" Casey laughed. "Sounds fantastic! Let's go."

The management of the T n' B leased an efficiency apartment in a building about a block away from the theatre—one very large room, a small kitchen and a fairly luxurious bathroom. Their visiting "star" was housed there as part of his contract. It was considered his home while he was there, and as long as no damage was done to it, the management didn't care what he did there. The building was fairly new and well-appointed, and the apartment was equally nice. There was a single bed in the room, as well as a queen-sized bed—which had undoubtedly had a greater number of famous, unbelievably hot men sleep in it than any other bed in the city. The single bed was to accommodate the star who was to succeed the one appearing at the theatre at the moment, for the night of his arrival. The upcoming star always arrived a day early to be ready for his tenure as guest star. The single bed was seldom used, in fact; during that one night when the two porn stars shared the same room, the queen bed usually got more action than at any other time of the week—even when one of the stars was one of those supposedly straight, gay-for-pay porn actors.

As they walked over to the apartment, the porn star and his young blond admirer introduced themselves formally—and Race immediately became Gundo to Casey after the sexy Latino explained the origin of his odd nickname. "Did you like my surprise?" he asked Casey.

"I loved it," Casey replied. "I was looking forward to getting your load, I just didn't expect it quite that way."

"Well, my contract with the T 'n B says I have to shoot a load on stage during at least one show a day—whichever show I choose. I wanted to give you a load earlier today when you were sucking my dick, but I had to save myself. There was a guy who I had promised to give one to after that show—and he was paying two hundred bucks for it, so I ... well, anyway, I would much rather have given it to you, but business in business."

"Jesus, how many loads can you shoot in a day," Casey asked.

"I dunno," Gundo laughed. "I suppose it depends on how inspired I get. Six? Maybe seven?" He stopped and took Casey's shoulders. "I think I'm really gonna be inspired today. Jesus, kid, you're fuckin beautiful! And you're just as hot as you are beautiful. I really enjoyed sitting on your dick today. Biggest one I've had in me in weeks. And then the way you took my whole dick down your throat? Wow! I definitely shouldn't be calling you 'kid.' God knows you're about as much man as anyone could want."

Casey smiled, shyly, "You just inspire me, that's all. You can't imagine how many times I've blown a load while I was watching your videos, pretending it was me you were making love with."

"Beating off? Or blowing a load inside some lucky fuckbuddy?"

"Both," Casey admitted, and grinned, "But usually with my dick down some guy's mouth or up his ass."

"Pretending it was my mouth or butt, huh?"

Casey admitted that was true, "But just as often pretending it was that big dick of yours in mine."

"Well, no pretending tonight, kid ... Casey. It's the real deal for Casey Lowe tonight—and for a lucky Gundo Lopez, too."

They arrived at the apartment building, and as waited for the elevator, Casey inquired, "Can I ask you something?"

"Anything at all, baby."

"Baby? Isn't that a demotion from kid?" Casey asked.

Gundo grinned, "For the next couple of hours you're gonna be my baby, okay?"

"Anything you want. Anything I can give you, you've got."

"I can hardly wait. But anyway, you can ask me anything you want."

"Well, the announcer at the theatre said it was against the law to touch the dancers' dicks or asses while they were performing, but … well, you know, you let me fuck you. Hell, you asked me to fuck you."

The elevator had arrived, and they entered it as Gundo grinned, "Yeah, a lotta guys tend to ignore that rule, and besides, it doesn't say anything about what the dancers can touch. We can do about anything we want, to ourselves or to the guys in the audience." He pressed the button for his floor, and kissed Casey tenderly, smiling into his face as the car began to rise. "We can fuck a guy's mouth, and even ride his dick until he blows a load, with everyone watching, if the guy is cute enough and really sexy enough to make us want to." He rested his lips against Casey's as he whispered, "And I never saw anyone cuter or sexier than the one I did that with today," and then he drove his tongue deep into Casey's mouth to initiate a protracted session of passionate necking. They broke their kiss when the elevator stopped, and they proceeded down the hall to the apartment. Actually, they could have kept kissing; no one on that floor would have paid any attention, had they been observed — they'd seen it all.

As soon as they closed the door behind them, Gundo put his arms around Casey, and they stood there while they necked and fondled each other for a long time, their cocks fully hard in their pants, humping against each other. Gundo was a deliriously fine kisser. As Casey was soon to learn, kissing apparently meant the same thing to Gundo that it meant to him: a kind of frantic, protracted mutual tongue-fuck that more-or-less continued until orgasm, followed by a leisurely, sensual mutual exploration of mouths and lips until the hormones kicked back in and threw the tongues into high gear again. Eventually, they stopped necking — far short of orgasm — and began to undress. Gundo offered a drink, but Casey declined.

Casey's heart beat like a jackhammer as the naked Gundo stood before him, prick fully erect and throbbing. And beautiful; my god how beautiful!, he thought. Race Rivera's prick! But Race's splendid cock was not any more beautiful than the glorious, golden, fat shaft that swung in front of Casey's perfect young naked body.

Gundo's prick was, perhaps, a tiny bit longer than Casey's, but Casey's was probably a bit fatter than Gundo's. Given the fact that Casey's body was something like four or five inches shorter than the Latino stud, his cock actually appeared to be a bit the larger of the two. Gundo only knew it looked absolutely irresistible, as beautiful as the boy himself. He knelt and murmured anticipation and admiration as his mouth opened wide to take it inside.

So many boys and men had praised Gundo's cocksucking ability that he had no doubt at all that he was unusually talented in that department, and Casey's groans and gasps of pleasure as Gundo sucked only added further testimony. A few minutes later, after they had moved to the bed and Casey took Gundo's cock in his throat so they could suck in sixty-nine, Gundo realized that his first assessment of Casey's talent, when he had swallowed all of his monster in the theatre, had been accurate: in spite of the gorgeous blond's youth, he was a master cocksucker—easily in his own league.

Gundo lay on his back on the bed, while Casey sucked his cock and lay over him, with his cock down the Latino's throat. Both sucked mightily and expertly, Gundo humping upward into Casey's mouth, and Casey fucking downward into Gundo's. The Latino stud had blown his load all over Casey in the theatre just a short while earlier, but Casey was ready to blow a load—*needing* to blow one, in fact. In only a few minutes he was gasping around the big prick filling his mouth, "I'm gonna cum if you don't stop sucking." The only answer he received was Gundo groaning an eager "MmmmHmmmm," as he cupped Casey's writhing buttocks in his hands and pulled down on them while he sucked the boy's dick all the harder. Casey's cum began filling Gundo's eager mouth with such a prodigious load, so violently delivered, that even with his vast experience, Gundo was barely able to take it all without gagging or losing some of it. But he managed, and swallowed every precious drop the young Adonis had given him as Casey continued to fuck his mouth, albeit more lazily now.

His orgasm inspired Casey to suck even more hungrily on Gundo's magnificent dick, eager to achieve what he had hoped for when he had sucked it in the theatre earlier that day. But Gundo stopped him, pulling his cock free and reversing his body so he could embrace Casey. With his lips almost touching Casey's, Gundo breathed, "What a fantastic load! And your cum tastes as sweet as honey. Check it out." With that he kissed the boy, driving his tongue deep in his mouth so he could savor the lingering taste of his own semen there.

They kissed for a long time, mostly sweetly and romantically, their hands fondling each other's bodies in appreciation of their physical perfection. While Gundo was using a finger to play with Casey's asshole, he stopped kissing long enough to say, "I do want you to suck me off, but this is where I wanna give you my load the first time." After another bout of kissing, he asked, "You ever get fucked in the shower?"

"Oh, sure," Casey replied. "My best friend, Joey, really loves it. We fuck each other in the shower a lot."

"Is Joey your lover? Is he cute?"

Casey laughed, "He's adorable, but he's not my lover. I don't have a lover. I don't want a lover. Too many other guys to make love with."

"How many cock-hungry worshippers do you have lined up waiting for a crack at that big thing of yours? And how many of 'em do you give it to?"

Blushing, Casey said, "I'm almost ashamed to tell you how many. There are a lot of 'em—and I let an awful lot of 'em have it."

"I'm not surprised," Gundo laughed. "You're fuckin' gorgeous, baby—and that dick would make any sane man crazy to get it. Well, maybe not the straight ones, but I'll bet you've fucked a lot of 'em who think they're straight—and probably a few who actually were straight. God knows I have. How about girls? You like to fuck pussy?"

"Yuck," Casey said. "No interest at all. How about you? You gonna do a straight porn flick some day?"

"They couldn't pay me enough. I've never fucked a chick, but I know I wouldn't like it. I'm like my dad, Tony Lopez the first. The only woman he ever fucked was my mother, and he only did that once, because she'd just been fucked by a guy he was dying to get into bed with."

"Is your dad hot?" Casey asked.

"Let's put it this way: if he was in bed with us right now, you'd probably go for him instead of me. If he wasn't my dad, I'd love to fuck with him. And he'd go nuts over you, believe me. Let's get in the shower and play Casey and …"

"Joey."

"Yeah, Joey." He kissed Casey and left the bed, extending his hand to pull Casey out as well. "Nah, fuck Joey—let's play Casey and Gundo."

"Okay. But you'd like to fuck Joey. He's hot."

"Well, maybe I will. You guys ever do threesomes?"

"I never have, but I think it would be fun. Joey thinks Race Rivera hung the moon. He'd die to go to bed with you, and as for me, I think a threesome with you and Joey would be unbelievably hot. Whaddya think?"

Moving toward the bathroom, Gundo said, "We'll see. Right now I wanna sink this big dick of mine in your pretty little butt. Oh, bring that lube dispenser by the bed when you come." He stopped and grinned "When you come! Mmmmm, that sounds good to me!"

Considering the apartment was a small one, the bathroom was unusually large—commodious, if a pun may be excused—and the shower easily big enough for two to play around in. They soaped each other up under the warm spray, taking ample time to kiss and fondle; rubbing their bodies together kept their dicks fully erect. Gundo used his hands to turn Casey's body away from him, saying. "Bend over, so I can get you ready."

Casey turned his head, and grinned over his shoulder. "Is this like that game, 'Drop the Soap'?"

"Something like that," Gundo said," and pushed Casey's upper body down so that the blond spread his legs and braced himself against the built-in seat. Gundo knelt behind him, pulled Casey's asscheeks apart, and buried his face deep in the cleft between them. His tongue penetrated Casey's asshole, and fucked it to a surprising depth, at the same time writhing and dancing inside so that Casey was murmuring and squirming with joy.

"Get me ready, lover," Casey moaned.

Gundo stood as he applied lube to his cock and Casey's ass. With his slick fingers massaging far up into Casey's ass, he growled, "You want it easy or hard?"

In a hoarse voice, Casey cried, "Hard! Shove it in and fuck me as hard as you can!"

Knowing how experienced this young man was—or, at any rate, said he was—Gundo happily took him at his word. He positioned his cock-head at Casey's sphincter, and threw his hips forward in one violent shove, sending his monstrous cock all the way inside Casey's hungry ass in one brutal thrust. Casey screamed – but more with joy than pain. "Yes! Give it to me, Race!"

"Gundo!" his fucker growled in his ear.

"Gundo," Casey gasped. "Fuck my hot ass, Gundo, I want that big dick. I need it! Slam it in me!"

And Gundo did just that. With his head thrown back and his eyes closed, his hands gripping Casey's waist, he fucked like a man possessed – pulling back and thrusting savagely, over and over, relentlessly. Considering that he was fucking with the kind of long strokes only a giant cock such as his would allow, the rapidity of his fierce plunges was amazing. Casey had been fucked hundreds upon hundreds of time, often by very accomplished young studs, but he had never have been fucked so excitingly. It wasn't surprising, of course: this was the biggest cock he'd ever had up his ass; it was a real man screwing him, not a boy – after the sailor Hank, the only other grown man to fuck him. But this was a man whose business was fucking – he was a professional fucker, for all practical purposes – and this was a man Casey had long dreamed of having sex with.

Gundo's fuck was wonderfully protracted, due to the fact that he had recently blown a load – but *on* Casey, not *in* Casey, where this one was going to be discharged. Though Casey's ass had never had such a workout, he gloried in Gundo's long, furious thrusts, alternating whimpers of joy, grunts of lust and shouts of appreciation, begging the Latino sex god to fuck faster and harder and deeper, and uttering cries of appreciation for his masterful technique. At the same time, Gundo was grunting his own rapture, praising the beauty of Casey's body and the tightness of his pretty ass, urging the boy to take it all, declaring him to be a fantastic fuck. And as his already wild fucking grew ever faster and even more ravenous, he gasped, in a crescendo of lust, "You're so fuckin' beautiful, and such a huge fuckin' dick! I can't wait to get it up my ass again! I want you to come in me again, like I'm gonna come in you. I want your cum!" Then finally, he screamed, "Here's mine!" just as he rammed his dick as far inside Casey as it would go, planting it there while his buttocks tightened and quivered, and he exploded inside the deliriously ecstatic blond Adonis, who had reached behind to hold Gundo's ass while he came, and who shrieked "Give me your load!" as he felt the violent eruption deep inside him.

After his joyous orgasm, Gundo began to fuck again, more gently and lovingly, but still in very long strokes, as he kissed Casey's neck and shoulders and cooed endearments into the boy's ear. Casey continued to hold Gundo's now gently undulating ass as the Latino reached around and stroked the boy's fiercely erect, throbbing prick.

"Better hold off," Casey said. "I'm close to coming, but I don't want to get my load yet. Keep fucking me — it feels so wonderful."

"Your sweet ass is full of my cum, baby, and my prick is swimming in it while I fuck you. Oh Jesus, you're such a great fuck, Casey." Gundo tongued Casey's ear as he whispered, "My sweet baby, so fuckin' hot."

"You're the one that's hot, Gundo. I've never even dreamed a fuck could be that wonderful." And it still felt wonderful, because Gundo was still fucking him, and although his strokes were less frantic now, they were still deep, and Gundo's cock seemed fully as hard and monstrous as it had when it was slamming away frantically, filling him with cum. He leaned over and braced himself on the seat again. "Don't stop fucking, Gundo. I'm still hungry for your big dick."

Casey worked Gundo's dick expertly; he had learned his lesson from Hank well. Squeezing it and pulling on it, riding it so expertly that Gundo again seized Casey's waist and began fucking in earnest, harder and faster until both were again lost in a frenzy of fuck-lust that culminated after a delirious ten minutes when Gundo cried out and blew another load in the ecstatic blond. As Gundo's frantic panting died down, Casey whirled around, causing the gigantic dick to slip out of him, and pressed down on Gundo's shoulders, gasping. "Get down there and suck me off. I'm almost ready to come!"

Gundo immediately deep-throated Casey's throbbing monster, and almost immediately the boy's cum began to fill his throat — while a thread of his own cum was still dripping from his dick. He fought against gagging, as he had when he had sucked Casey off before they got in the shower, and managed to contain in his mouth all the precious gift Casey had given him. Inside his mouth, he lapped at Casey's cock and bathed it in the boy's own load. Casey's gasps of thrill as he had ejaculated became murmurs of satisfaction as he fondled Gundo's head, whispering admiration for his skill and artistry as a lover.

Gundo released Casey's dick and stood, pressing his lips to Casey's. As they embraced, and Casey opened his mouth to receive Gundo's tongue, he was greeted by a flow of hot semen, which he passed back and forth with Gundo several times, finally telling him to swallow it. Gundo obeyed the injunction and grinned at Casey as they began a long, passionate kiss that gradually turned gentle and loving.

The shower had been running the whole time they had been in there. They soaped each other up again, once more kissing and fondling, relishing the sensual feeling of slick skin against slick skin, and turned it off. Surprisingly, it was still fully warm; the hotel obviously had a first class hot-water system. They dried off and Gundo put on a bathrobe. He told Casey to get in bed, under the covers, while he got them something to drink. Casey didn't drink alcohol at all, and Gundo rarely did, so the Cokes he brought back from the hallway dispenser were just fine.

Stripping off his bathrobe, Gundo got under the covers with Casey. Both of them were naked, but at the moment, each was sexually drained, so they merely fondled each other and cuddled tenderly and lazily as they talked.

Gundo said, "I sure would like to fuck you again before I have to go back to the T 'n B. You are a spectacular piece of ass, you know that?"

"Thanks," Casey grinned. "Comin' from the hottest buttfucker I've ever met, that's really high praise. But I thought you only had to blow your load in one show, and I'll bet ..."

Gundo cut him off, "I've got this guy in from Omaha that I have to spend the night with. I'll have to give him a load tonight, and probably another one in the morning—that's the usual deal. It's gonna be hard, but I can work up another load by midnight or so, when we go to his hotel after my eleven o'clock show. I don't much wanna do it, but it's five hundred bucks—and he's really not bad-looking. He even seems like a nice guy. Kinda old, about sixty I think, but clean, and in good shape. Hell, I'll think about being with you while I fuck him or he blows me—that'll keep me in the right frame of mind to earn my money."

"Wow, five hundred dollars! I wish I could earn money like that. It was all I could do to come up with the money to buy my ticket for the *Top 'n Bottom* today," Casey said. "Guess I'll have to get a job or something. My dad gives me an allowance, but it's not much. And I sure want to come back while you're here and see you again. And Michael Christopher's going to be there in a couple of weeks. I think he's really hot as hell. I sure wanna see him in person."

"Mike Christopher is hot as hell," Gundo replied. "I did a scene with him in a video, and that big ol' crooked dick of his fit my asshole just right—like my big ol' dick fit his. Man, I loved it when we were necking and he held me against that great big chest with those fantastic arms. He's not much for conversation, but who needs to talk when you're with a stud like that? Yeah, you've gotta see him when he's here. You'll flip—and he's liable to flip when he sees you, like I did."

"Well, I'll get the money somehow. My buddy Joey—the one I was telling you about—has been hanging around Polk Street, letting guys blow him, and he's making a bundle."

"That can be dangerous, Casey. There are a lot of really crazy guys out there, and you can't always tell who they are by talking to them for a minute or so while they offer you a few bucks to let 'em suck you off. I hope Joey's being very careful. He's the one I'm supposed to be thinking about you and me having a threesome with, right?"

"Yeah," Casey said. "Are you really gonna think about it?"

"Sure, baby. I think it would be fun, but I have to see how my schedule works out while I'm here. I know there's a local guy I agreed to spend tomorrow night with, but I think I'm clear the rest of the week."

"Another five hundred bucks?" Casey asked.

Gundo grinned. "Eight hundred. I told him a thousand, but he bargained a little bit—just not as much as the guy from Omaha did. Oh—speaking of money . . ." He got out of bed and went over to take something out of his pants, draped over the back of a chair, where he had flung them when they had torn their clothes off to make love. It was a stack of dollar bills. "Here," Gundo said, "I'm putting this with your pants. It's thirty singles, for when you go back to the T 'n B. Those guys dancing there really count on the money people stuff in their g-strings and boots. God knows they don't make much unless they hustle."

"Yeah," Casey said. "One of 'em told me I could have him for a hundred bucks."

"Well, that was just meant to open negotiations," Gundo laughed. "You probably coulda had him for twenty, if you wanted."

"Well, I really didn't want him," Casey said. "I've got at least fifteen or twenty fuckbuddies who are hotter than he was, and they don't cost me a thing. But anyway, thanks for the dollar bills. Somehow

I'll find the money to go see Michael Christopher, and I can use them then."

"What, you're not gonna come back and see me again?" Gundo asked.

"Well, I want to, but … Yeah, I'll get the money."

"Not by selling your dick on Polk Street, I hope."

"Well, Joey says it's usually not so bad."

"I have an idea," Gundo said. "What would you think about becoming a house dancer at the T 'n B? Do you think you could parade around naked and let a few guys grope you and kiss your dick or your ass now and then? You'd have to keep a hard-on, though; that'd be required. You'd be a knockout. A gorgeous blond like you, with that Dick of Death, they'd go crazy."

"Gee, I don't know," Casey said. "Actually, I always get a hard-on when I know people are looking at my cock and … well, admiring me, I guess you'd say. I don't think that would be a problem. But I have to go to school. This is my senior year, and my dad expects me to go to college, too. But I'm gonna have to look around a lot to find a college that will let me in with my grades."

"Bad?" Gundo asked.

"Nah, just so-so. I do okay, but only average. Tell you the truth, I spend too much time looking for guys to fuck with — and finding all I want. My teachers tell me I could easily be an 'A' student if I really wanted to."

"Well you wouldn't have to drop out of school to be a house dancer. One or two of 'em are college students, and they work their show schedule around their class schedule, so you could too. A high-school schedule would be less flexible than a college schedule, I guess, but you could dance after school, and on weekends. If you think you might be interested, I'll set up an audition for you, and even if you decide you're not interested, I'll be sure that at least you'll get in the theatre free that day. Of course, I guess it's possible they might not be interested in you doing shows, but unless your dick goes soft when you get in front of an audience, or your moves are really awkward, I'm sure Eddie will hire you."

"Eddie's the owner?"

"The Manager, Eddie Bliss. I don't know who owns the place. Eddie's a nice guy: totally gay, but not the least bit effeminate, and he's got one of the biggest pricks I've ever seen. But he says he never messes with the 'talent,' as he calls us, but I think he's lying. According to him, though, one of the most important rules of managing a business is, 'You can't fuck 'em and work 'em.' Besides, he's got a lover, but I don't know who he is. Richard, one of the house dancers is an old lover of Eddie's, from back in the days when Eddie was in the Army, stationed out at the Presidio. I'm not sure, but I think Eddie still fucks Richard once in a while. I couldn't blame him, and I'm not surprised; Richard really loves a big dick up his ass, the bigger the better, and from what I hear he's pretty fond of getting double-fucked, too."

"You mean two dicks in his ass at the same time?" Casey asked, actually just a bit shocked, but more than just a little titillated, too.

Gundo chuckled, "I can see we're gonna have to expand your horizons. Did you see Richard dance?"

"Well, except for you, I didn't see anyone really dance," Casey laughed. "I only saw two of 'em, and they just shook their dicks and their asses and strutted around."

"That's the kind of dancing you can expect at a strip theatre, but it's all that the guys out there beating off while they do it really care about."

"Anyway, I don't think I saw Richard. I saw two other guys, and they were okay, but nothing special. One was Carl, I don't know what the other one's name was."

"Well, Richard is an older guy, late thirties, I think, but he is really fuckin' hot! Handsome as hell, and really well hung. Be sure to check him out—and I'll bet he'll be checking you out pretty closely. He loves young guys, he loves blonds, but he loves big dicks above all else. And he'd love to fill that pretty little ass of your with cum almost as much as he'd want you to cram your prick up his ass and fuck him senseless. Just be sure to see him. You'll probably flip. Everybody has to blow a load on stage during one show every day, and if Richard is there when you're there, be sure you've got your dick out when he comes around, and be sure he feels how big it is.

"I can't wait to see him," Casey said.

"Does that mean you wanna audition for Eddie?"

"Sure," Casey said, "but tell me what's involved if he hires me."

"Well, the pay sucks," Gundo began. "You only get paid five dollars for each show, but you're guaranteed ten dollars for every day you work, even if Eddie only schedules you for one show. You'll probably do four or five shows during a full day—but if you have to work only after school, you'll probably only be able to do two on school days. No work on Mondays, 'cause the theatre's closed then. The amount of money you get in tips depends on you, for the most part. If you're really hot, and if you really please the guys out there in the auditorium, they're more generous. The size of the audience makes a lot of difference, of course: the more guys, the more money in your jock or your boots. You can probably average about twenty-five dollars with a so-so house, but probably fifty or more when there are a lot of 'em out there.

"The theatre keeps two small rooms in the basement, with only a washbasin and a single bed in each one, so that the dancers have a place to take a trick for a quickie."

"I guess that's where the first guy who I saw dance today wanted me to take him for a hundred dollars," Casey said.

Gundo laughed, "You can't blame a guy for aiming high, I guess. A dancer as hot and hung as you can probably figure on getting fifty, or maybe even that hundred bucks to let a guy blow you. If they wanna fuck you, or get fucked, you can figure a lot more, but I don't think fucking's a very good idea under the circumstances. Be sure you've got a bed in a decent place, and the guy is clean and seems to be okay before you fuck him or let him fuck you. An all-nighter oughta bring you at least two hundred bucks, but you could probably get three. I get at least five 'cause I've got the name and the videos out there that guys jack off to.

"The number of tricks you can turn in a day depends a lot on how often you can work up a decent load to give 'em. And you have to remember it's required that you blow at least one load on stage every day you work.

"The other dancers play around with each other when it's quiet, but less than you'd probably think. They're always thinking about having to save their loads for tricks."

"Carl said the visiting star always fucks all the dancers during the week he's there," Casey said.

"Not necessarily all of them," Gundo said. "There's always one or two of 'em who are straight—or think they are anyway—and don't suck dick or take it up the ass. I've noticed those guys are still usually willing to get a blow job or fuck butt when they get the opportunity, though—and they never seem to need much help in getting their dicks hard for those guys they fuck or get blown by. Then there's usually one or two who are in love, and want to be true to their lovers, but they frequently give it up to the visiting dancer. I fucked one of those yesterday—and one of the 'straight' ones I'd already fucked was fucking me while I did."

"Where do you do this, in the small rooms downstairs?"

"Oh no," Gundo laughed. "That happens in the lounge backstage, 'cause everybody wants to watch—that's part of the fun of working there. What the hell, there's no privacy at a strip theatre. But could you do that? Make love with a guy while another half-dozen sat around and watched?"

"I don't know," Casey said, "but I think so. The idea sounds hot as hell. As you can tell, my dick is getting hard from thinking about it."

Gundo kissed him, "Why don't you slip that big cock up my ass and fuck me while you think about it? I'm ready for it—haven't been fucked in five or six hours!"

"I think I might like to suck on that monster cock of yours for a few minutes before I do," Casey said.

"Great, but I've gotta hold off coming, and I want you to fuck me good and hard, so let's take it easy—just suck for the love of sucking dick," Gundo said as he reversed his body so they were in sixty-nine position.

It took only one or two licks before Gundo's cock was back to its fighting strength, and if Casey's delight in licking that big ass-reamer wasn't enough to bring his own cock to its very impressive full glory, the fact that it was deep in Gundo's throat certainly did the trick. They rolled over and over as they double-sucked, Gundo on top, then Casey, then Gundo again, their hands lovingly caressing each other, appreciatively fondling the gently undulating asses tenderly driving their glorious cocks into each other.

It was unfortunate that there was no one else there to see and appreciate the sheer beauty of two such phenomenally endowed, physically perfect specimens of manhood, equal in every way except age, making love purely for the sake of mutual worship. Thomas Gray expressed that tragedy best in his *Elegy Written in a Country Churchyard*: "Full many a flower is born to blush unseen, and waste its sweetness on the desert air."

Neither was working at release, so their restrained appreciation of the joy of cocksucking as a joy in itself, rather than as a means to an end, lasted quite a long time. Very reluctantly, because they were sharing such a special, almost holy and pure experience, Gundo finally released Casey's cock and reversed his body again, causing his cock to slip from Casey's mouth. "I really hate to stop, baby. I'd like to make love with you like that forever, but I've got to be back at the theatre before eleven, and I want you to fuck me again. I need you to fuck me like a demon, and fill my hungry ass with your hot cum again. You know, you've only fucked me once—and I need a lot more than that."

Gundo reached for the lubricant dispenser on the nightstand next to the bed, where he had placed it after they left the shower. But Casey stopped his hand. "Just a minute," he said. He rolled Gundo to his stomach and pulled on his hips, raising his ass slightly. He transferred his hands to the older man's buttcheeks, and spread them wide as he buried his face between them, beginning an extended tongue-fuck that had Gundo groaning and gasping in joy—until at last he raised himself to all fours and cried, "Fuck me, lover. Grease me up and slam that big prick in me as hard as you can!"

Never one to disappoint his partner, Casey did as he was told. Positioning his lubricated cock-head at Gundo's asshole, he thrust his hips forward violently, and his massive cock was completely buried inside the Latino stud, who practically screamed in joy as the younger man began an extended, savage, serious fuck. Halfway through, Casey pulled out and unceremoniously rolled Gundo to his back. Gundo automatically raised his legs, and almost without losing a beat, Casey's cock was back inside him, pistoning in and out like a jackhammer. He pressed his lips to Gundo's, and they practically ate each other's mouths in a frenzy of passion.

With both Gundo and Casey almost shouting their mutual thrill, the blond Adonis threw his head back and virtually howled in triumph as he planted his cock as far inside the Latino stud's wildly bucking and gyrating ass as it would go, and froze there while his cum shot forth in fiercely propelled spurts. Gundo had specifically said he did not want to shoot a load, but he was so completely seized with fuck-lust, that he grasped his prick to masturbate, but gave it only a few strokes before his own massive load spilled out onto his chest.

Casey fell over Gundo, and they resumed their frantic kissing, which gradually diminished in frenzy until they calmed down to the point that they were kissing romantically again. Gundo still had Casey's cock planted inside him when he asked, in sincere admiration, "Godamighty, how did a high-school kid learn to fuck like that?"

"Lotsa experience," Casey smiled. "I may be only eighteen years old, but I've been fucking for a long time."

"That, and a helluva lot of natural talent," Gundo said. He laughed, "Hell if aptitude tests scored fucking or cocksucking, your grades would be off the charts."

Casey rose to kneel on all fours, pulling his now flaccid cock out of Gundo. He lapped up the cum on Gundo's chest and Gundo licked his own cum off Casey's chest, where it had been transferred when they had been pressed together. They kissed again and shared the wonderful liquid until Gundo said, "That's it. I have got to get ready to go back to the theatre." He extricated himself from Casey's embrace and left the bed, heading for the bathroom. "Let's jump in the shower—but no fooling around." He grinned, "Not right now, anyway." Their mutual shower was relatively business-like, and both were so momentarily drained physically that their cocks were only semi-hard as they soaped each other up.

As they dressed, Casey had to refuse an invitation to return to the theatre. "My dad is probably already wondering where the hell I am."

"You want me to set up an audition with Eddie?" Gundo asked.

"Yeah, I think so."

"Can I call you and tell you when it will be?" Gundo asked.

Casey wrote his home phone number down. "I'll be home from school tomorrow about 3:45. You can call after that. It doesn't make any difference if my dad is home or not, he's great about letting me live my own life." He grinned, "In fact, he's great, period."

"I'll call you tomorrow, then. And I'll probably know by then if I'm gonna have some time when you can bring … what's-his-name over for a threesome."

"Joey."

"Yeah, Joey." Now give me a kiss and let's get the hell out of here. I dunno how I'm gonna keep my dick up for the eleven o'clock show, much less with the guy from Omaha."

"I'll bet you manage just fine," Casey grinned.

"Yeah," Gundo laughed, "I'll just think about Casey Lowe the whole time."

In the elevator going down, Gundo kissed the boy and said, "You're the best, baby—a fantastic lover. I can hardly wait to see you again."

"Same here," Casey said as the elevator doors opened, and they went their separate ways.

True to his word, Gundo called the next afternoon. "I described you to Eddie, and he's interested."

"What'll I have to do?"

"Bring some very sexy shorts or ... you have any Speedos?" Casey said he did. "Perfect. The smaller and tighter the better. And wear some boots if you have 'em—you gotta have something on your feet, and you need a handy place to put your tips."

"Sure, I have some boots. But, this sounds like he wants me to actually go out there and perform."

"Of course," Gundo laughed. "How else could he see how you'll do? He says he's had some guys who looked great, but who couldn't get it up in front of an audience, or who couldn't keep it up when they went out there and visited the patrons." He laughed again, "That's what the owner calls it when we go out and shake out asses and dicks in their faces: 'Visiting the patrons.' Even Eddie has to laugh, but he says the owner is the boss, so whatever he says, goes. Or maybe it's whatever she says. Who knows?"

"When does he want me to do it?"

"Well, he wants you to go for the first show of the day, noon. There aren't too many guys in the audience then—usually only a half-dozen or so."

"I've got school in the morning."

"Play hooky. Bug out in time to get to the theatre by—oh, eleven-thirty, I guess. I'll meet you there. Oh, by the way, Eddie wants you to blow your load on stage to end your act."

"I don't have an 'act'!" Casey said.

"Oh, hell. Nobody does, really. If you start working there, you'll want to pick some music to strut around to, but that's about all you need. Wriggle your ass and shake your dick—that's all they really wanna see, anyway."

"Okay, Gundo, I'll be there. And thanks a lot."

"You owe me big, baby. And you know what you've got that's big. That's what I want you to use when you pay me off." He laughed, "You can get me off to pay me off. How's that?"

"I can't wait, Gundo. My dick is so fuckin' hard right now, just thinking about you, I can hardly stand it."

"You know what to do about that—and just keep thinking about me while you do it. I just did my first show, and I was thinking about you most of the time. Okay, gotta go—there's a trick waiting for me. See you at the theatre tomorrow."

In spite of his assurances to Gundo, Casey was nervous about his upcoming performance. During lunch at the cafeteria that day, he had told Joey all about his experience with Gundo. Joey had been understandably green with envy: 'Race Rivera' was one of his favorites, too. Now Casey called his best fuckbuddy to share the news—and when Joey heard that Casey was going to strip at the theatre the next day, he vowed he was going to play hooky too, and be there in the audience. They agreed to go together, and Casey was relieved—having Joey there with him would make him less nervous. An added benefit was that Gundo would be able to see Joey, to help him make a decision about having a threesome with them. Casey would only tell Joey if it was good news.

At 11:30 the next morning, they were just opening the doors to the T 'n B as Casey and Joey arrived. Gundo met them in the lobby, eyeing Joey and asking "And who is this?"

"Gundo, this is Joey Stone, the guy I told you about."

"Oh yeah." He extended his hand. "Nice to meet you, Joey. You here to watch Casey audition?"

"Right," Joey replied, shaking Gundo's hand, his heart beating faster as he actually touched Race Rivera! "Where do I buy a ticket?"

Gundo turned to the man behind the lobby counter, "Mort, Casey, here, is gonna audition for Eddie this morning. This is his friend, Joey, so let 'em in free—for the morning, anyway." Mort agreed to admit them without paying admission—but not giving them dated tickets that would permit passage in and out of the theatre for the entire day.

"Let's go inside," Gundo said, leading the way. "Joey, sit anywhere you want while Casey goes back to meet Eddie. He's the manager." And Casey followed him through an unobtrusive draped doorway that led to the backstage lounge, where the dancers relaxed between shows. There were two men seated in easy chairs and another two on a sofa; one of them was Carl, whom Casey had spoken with on his first visit.

One of the men stood up, and Gundo introduced Casey to Eddie. He was not what Casey expected—kind of a quiet, friendly sort of guy with a warm grin, not at all the overtly "managerial" type. He was tall and lanky, nicely dressed, and an attractive man, although not conventionally handsome—certainly not 'cute.'

"Wow," Eddie said as he shook Casey's hand, " Gundo wasn't kiddin' when he said you were gorgeous. Let's see if what else he told me's true." Eddie had been raised in a small town near Athens, Georgia, and he had never lost his slight southern accent. "Take your clothes off and getcher dick hard." Eddie might not have appeared to be particularly businesslike at first blush, but he certainly knew how to cut to the chase.

"Go ahead," Gundo grinned. "You gotta leave all inhibitions behind if you're gonna work here.

Casey stripped off the T-shirt he was wearing over his Levi's; his bare chest brought a murmur of admiration from the three men still seated. He kicked off his boots and stepped out of his Levi's, revealing the fact that he wore a very skimpy red Speedo bathing suit underneath, stretched extremely tight over his rounded ass, and revealing an enormous bulge at the groin. Further, and more enthusiastic murmurs of appreciation greeted the sight of his fine young body and obvious endowments. He turned away from everyone, and pulled his Speedo down, revealing his adorable bare ass. Then he reached into a pocket of his Levi's and produced a jock strap, which he stepped into before he turned around, revealing the fact that the jockstrap was probably a size too small—certainly too small to sufficiently contain the bulging contents. He said, "Is that the way I should do it on stage? I figured it would look silly to wear a jock under that little Speedo." He stroked and groped his crotch as he said that, and the bulge in his jockstrap clearly began to expand. Then he pulled the jockstrap down below his balls, exposing his cock, which was already partially hard, and which began to erect further even before he gripped it and stroked it to full erection. With his magnificent prick standing straight out from his body, he stood with arms akimbo, thrusting his pelvis forward to emphasize the glory of his cock. "Whaddya think? He asked Eddie.

Eddie whistled appreciatively, Carl and the other two dancers—Casey assumed they were also dancers—whispered among themselves. One of those dancers, by far the best-looking one, was stroking his prick through his pants—and it was clearly a big one.

"I think you'll do jus' fine," Eddie said, patting Casey's bare ass, and allowing his hand to linger there for quite a while.

The handsome one, the one who had been stroking his dick stood, unaware—or, more likely, not caring—that his now clearly hard prick was tenting his pants, said "I think he'll be a fuckin' hit." He extended his hand, saying, "I'm Richard Austin—welcome to the T 'n B." He lightly caressed Casey's chest as he pointedly looked down at Casey's throbbing hard-on and added. "A really big hit."

One of the other dancers—not Carl—laughed. "Look out for that one, Casey, he'll be riding your dick before you can catch your breath."

Richard reached down and gripped Casey's dick, "I know I'm a pretty good rider, but I can offer a helluva ride, too." His grip felt electric to Casey. He really was a handsome man, and clearly well-hung He'd probably be fun to ride or give a ride to. "Gundo told me all about you last night,"

Eddie stepped in, "Save it, Richard. Almost time for the first show. Putcher clothes back on and get ready, Casey."

"I'm gonna go on first?"

"Sure, why not? Now you're probably gonna have to sit down to putcher boots back on after you take off your Levi's. It's awkward if you don't, so make it look natural. Gundo tells me you know the routine about visiting the patrons. Tease hell out of 'em and they'll give you the tips—but be sure you get around to ever'body. They all paid good money to come in here. There's never too many guys out there for the first couple a shows, anyway. And you can try to move around to the music, but don't worry about it. This ain't ballet, it's cock-teasin'."

Casey had been putting his clothes back on when Gundo spoke up, "You know, Casey, I wouldn't fool with the jockstrap at all. Go with only the Speedo before you show 'em your dick. Get it a little bit hard when you take off your Levi's, and the sight of that monster meat filling out one side of the Speedo is gonna be extra sexy. You can turn around once in a while and expose your bare ass for 'em—that'd be really hot, too."

"Thanks, Gundo, that's what I'll do. You gonna be out there watching?"

"I wouldn't miss, it, baby. I'll sit out there with Joey."

"Oh, what did you think of Joey?" Casey asked.

Gundo grinned, "I think we've gotta set up a threesome in the next day or so."

"I've gotta go back and make the announcements," Eddie said. "Okay, Casey, soon as I finish introducin' you, I'll start the music. Then tell someone to pull the curtain, and go out and show us whatcha can do. And don't forget, I wanna see you jack off and blow your load 'fore you leave the stage."

In just a few minutes, he heard Eddie's voice laying down the law about patrons fondling the performers. Then he said, And now, the *Top 'n Bottom* proudly presents the first appearance on any stage of the monster-cocked, gorgeous, super-hot young stud: CASEY!

The music began, the curtain opened, and Casey stepped out into the spotlight.

And that is where this story began

4.

Workers' Compensation

It wasn't necessary for Casey to get his dick hard when he removed his Levi's to show himself in the skimpy Speedo; it had started getting hard as soon as he began to strut around to the music, fondling his crotch and playing with his ass. There were probably only a dozen or so men out there in the auditorium; with the spotlight in his eyes, it was hard to see. He had removed his boots, then began to remove his pants suggestively, finally turning away from the patrons when he bent over to pull them away from his feet—at the same time projecting and presenting his ass. Before he stood up, he pulled his Speedo down to give them a good view of his luscious bare butt, which drew a faint round of applause. Hell, he thought, an ovation from this crowd would sound faint.

He sat down in the chair as he turned his body around, and after putting on his boots, he stood, his enormous prick gloriously filling out the left side of his Speedo, reaching almost all the way to his side, seeming to threaten escape. He stroked the fat tube provocatively and humped his ass as he leered at the men out there.

After a few more turns around the stage, he stepped down and began to visit the patrons. There were only three who were remotely attractive: Gundo and Joey, of course, but he also encountered Richard, sitting by himself. The others were considerably older, somewhat sad-looking, he thought. They all brightened up when he came around and pressed his bulging crotch into their faces. For each one, he turned around and leaned down over the row of seats in front of him as he pulled down his Speedo for a moment to give him a close-up view of his bare ass. His ass was fondled, his legs were fondled, several reached up to caress and tweak his nipples, and two of them put their tongues up his ass when he bared it for them—Gundo and Joey again. Richard had kissed his ass, but had reached around to grope Casey's covered cock, too. He also took Casey's hand and guided it to his lap, so the blond Adonis could feel that he had his cock out—and Casey fondled it appreciatively. It was, as Gundo had said, a really big one, rock-hard and throbbing.

He returned to the stage. He had fifteen or twenty bills—dollar bills, he assumed—stuffed into his Speedo. He pulled them out of the waistband and put them on the chair. He tugged his Speedo below his balls, allowing his now-fiercely erect bare cock to protrude, bobbing and swaying as he strutted proudly around the stage a few more times. He grinned at the audience as he masturbated for a minute or so with one hand, his eyes closed, licking his lips, the other hand rubbing his stomach suggestively. Then he turned away and bent to pull his Speedo completely off over his boots. While still bent over, he used his hands to spread his asscheeks far apart, so that his pink asshole was clearly visible as he wriggled it. Quite a bit of applause accompanied that part of his show. Then he returned to the auditorium.

The men were bolder this time. Most of them stroked his cock and caressed his ass. He slapped his prick against their faces, and all instinctively opened their mouths, hoping, no doubt, that the fat shaft was going to go inside. With Gundo and Joey, he realized their hopes for a few moments. Joey, in particular, sucked hungrily and fiercely, as he always did, and both he and Gundo deep-throated his huge shaft. Richard fondled him and kissed the end of his dick, murmuring, "God, I want this!" Then Casey turned around and sat down in Richard's lap. Richard's big dick didn't penetrate him, but he wriggled around on it, enjoying the thought of what a potentially enjoyable assful it was. Richard whispered in his ear, "That's where my dick belongs, Casey."

Casey stood and kissed Richard—quickly, but passionately—as he replied, "Maybe so. We'll have to see, won't we?"

When he returned to the stage, his boots stuffed with currency, he began to stalk back and forth at the apron, stroking his big dick fiercely. Then he seized it with both hands—something not possible for a man of lesser endowment—and began to fuck his fists. In a moment, his cum began to spurt—reaching the second row. Unfortunately, there was no one in that or the first row to benefit from the six or eight jets of pearly-white cum. Insofar as he was able to think reasonably while he was ejaculating, Casey thought, Why didn't Gundo sit there, so I could give him what he gave me?

The applause that greeted his eruption was intense and sustained. A few even stood as they applauded, continuing their ovation until Casey had picked up his clothes and money, and walked off the stage—grinning and waving, a thread of cum dangling from his bobbing cock.

Carl and the other dancer had watched Casey's performance from the wings. Carl had to go on himself in only about ten minutes. They were both effusive in their praise. Carl hugged him and groped Casey's dick while he tendered his congratulations. Richard, Gundo and Joey came in just a few minutes later.

"You were fantastic, Casey," Eddie said as he came backstage, grinning warmly and clapping him on the back—but also patting his ass again. "If you wanna be a T 'n B house dancer, you got the job."

Gundo kissed him as he complimented his performance, and Joey threw his arms around him excitedly. "I can't believe how incredibly sexy you were. You were absolutely great! Gundo and I were playing with each other's dicks while we watched—and he told me about the threesome. I'm so fuckin' excited, I can't wait."

Eddie told Casey to get dressed and meet him in his office, off the lobby, as soon as he had introduced Carl. Casey left and went in a corner to dress and gather his money together—mostly dollar bills, but he was excited to see several five-dollar bills, and even a few tens as well.

Richard, who had been standing back while Casey was receiving praise, approached him. "They're right, you know. That was totally, totally hot! And I wasn't kidding when I said my ass is where your dick belongs, you know."

"I wasn't kidding when I said 'maybe,' either—I think you're really hot, Richard. Apparently, I'm gonna be around, and we can talk about that—but after Gundo finishes his week, okay?"

"It's a deal," Richard said, and kissed Casey. He pulled back to look into the younger man's eyes. "Fuckin' gorgeous," he murmured, and put his arms around Casey as he pressed their lips together again. Casey responded passionately, and they stood there for several minutes, necking feverishly. Richard was a fantastic kisser, and Casey could feel the stud's hard cock pressing against him; it felt very good, and Richard struck him as among the sexiest men he had ever seen.

Gundo and Joey joined him, having held back while they watched his encounter with Richard. "He's beautiful," Joey said, watching Richard leave the lounge.

"He certainly is that," Gundo added, "and he's almost as good a top as he is a bottom, but ... Oh, I don't know. There's something about him. Just watch your feelings when you're around him, Casey. I know you're gonna fuck each other, even if you don't know it yet."

"I'll be fine," Casey said. "And look at all this money; there must be seventy-five bucks here." Later, when he counted it, he found he had sixty-three dollars in tips.

"You're worth it, kid. Oops... Casey," Gundo said, as Eddie could be heard, announcing Carl's appearance. "Go on and meet with Eddie. I'll talk with Joey here — we've got plans to make. See you in the lobby."

Arriving in the lobby about the same time Casey did, Eddie opened his office door and said, "C'mon in, Casey. Have a seat."

Eddie outlined what was going to be expected of him as a house dancer, and what he could expect from them in return — almost exactly as Gundo had set it forth for him. They agreed that Casey would do two shows on weekdays — Tuesdays, Wednesdays and Thursdays, starting at 5:00, and finishing by 7:00. Casey was not so dazzled by the prospect that he failed to realize he had to keep his schoolwork in mind. He also didn't plan to abandon his activities with his fuckbuddies, although he knew they would have to be curtailed. On Fridays and Saturdays he could come in at 7:00 and work until 11:00. On Sundays, he could come in at noon and work until 5:00, or later, if he wanted. "We get much bigger crowds for shows on Sundays than any other day," Eddie explained.

"You're gonna be propositioned to go off and fuck with a lotta guys while you're workin' here, but be careful, kid, there are a lotta crazies out there. Take my advice, and limit yourself ta gettin' blowjobs, here in the theatre. You can make plenty a cash doin' that. You won't make any money fuckin' around with the other house dancers or the guest stars, but you'll have plenty of fun, and you'll be safe.

There was paperwork to be filled out, of course. Since Casey had learned he only had to be eighteen to be in the strip theatre, he showed Eddie his actual identification papers, rather then the fake ones Hank had secured for him.

"I was afraid you were gonna show me somethin' that said you were twenty-five or so," Eddie said. "I see a lotta phony I.D., believe me." Casey laughed, and brought out the cards that showed he was a twenty-one year-old sailor. Eddie whistled, "Jesus, you look adorable as a sailor." He studied his face, and said, "Even more fucking edible than you do right this minute—if that's possible. Well, I think that's all then, Casey. We're set to go—and you start work tomorrow at 5:00; we expect ya to be in the lounge at least a half-hour 'fore you're scheduled to go on."

Eddie hesitated a moment, and then said, "And this is somethin' you don't hafta do, 'less you want to. And for god's sake, keep this strictly between us if you're gonna keep workin' here. Okay?"

"Sure," Casey said. "What is it?"

Eddie grinned, and his grin was warm and infectious. "I wanna fuck that pretty ass of yours now and then—if you can take it, that is. I've got a helluva big cock."

When Gundo had first told him about the size of Eddie's dick— 'one of the biggest I've ever seen,' if Casey remembered Gundo's words correctly—his first thought was, I wanna see that, and his second was, I'd probably like to suck it and get fucked by it. Practically all gay men are impressed by, and hungry for, big cocks ("There are only two kinds of gay men: size queens and liars."), and Casey was no exception. If anything, he may have been more impressed with outsized cocks than most, given the fact that he was, himself, so exceptionally well-endowed. Given that Eddie was physically attractive and clean, with a friendly personality as well, it took Casey no time at all to decide how to reply to his proposition. He stood, and began unbuttoning his Levi's, smiling crookedly and saying, "You wanna seal the deal right now?"

"Oh, yeah," Eddie replied as he stood and began to remove his own clothing, while Casey disrobed completely. "Jesus, you're somethin', ya know? I don't do this with the guys who work here. That's why you can't tell anybody about it, but my God," he panted, stroking the smooth, golden skin of Casey's sublime ass. "you're jus' fuckin' perfect." He put his arms around Casey from behind, kissing his neck and panting, "I want you so fuckin' bad I almost shot my load when I watched you jackin' off on the stage." He was still wearing his shorts, but even so, Casey could tell that Gundo had not exaggerated: the cock Eddie was proposing to fuck him with was epic.

There was really no need to keep silent about what was going to happen. All the house dancers knew, in spite of what he had just said, that Eddie got around to fucking virtually everyone who worked at the theatre, although he normally did so only occasionally.

Eddie turned Casey's body around and studied his face. He was smiling, but at the same time he was clearly consumed with lust; it made for an odd expression, but one that made him seem more attractive. "Oh hell, Casey, I shouldn't be doing this. You got the job, You don't hafta let me fuck ya." He said this to all interviewees, but none had ever declined when they learned how much cock Eddie had to give them.

Casey reached down to grope Eddie's prick, which was protruding from the leg of his boxer shorts. It was gargantuan! "Eddie, I don't think I've ever felt a cock I wanted more than I do this one. I want you to fuck me—and it doesn't have anything to do with working here."

Eddie's smile turned into a grin, and he pulled down his shorts. As the elastic band cleared his prick, it bobbed up to meet Casey's awe-struck gaze. It has to be a foot long, he thought, and it was fat and perfectly formed as well. He knelt and began to suck it. He could deep-throat Gundo's cock, which was slightly longer than his own ten inches, but he couldn't quite take all of Eddie's, no matter how hard he tried. He had to restrain himself from gagging as Eddie held his head and fucked lazily into his mouth. "Jesus, Casey, that feels fuckin' great!"

Casey stood and bent down over Eddie's desk, wriggling his ass seductively. "Fuck me, Eddie. I don't even know if I can take all of that cock, but I sure wanna try."

Eddie fondled Casey's undulating asscheeks as he said, "Seems like everybody wants ta try, once they see it—and most of 'em can take it if they try hard enough." He knelt and said, "Lemme get ya ready," and began to eat out Casey's hungry ass.

Squirming with pleasure as Eddie's tongue explored his asshole, Casey gasped, "I'll try hard enough—I promise you. I want that dick up my ass." Eddie licked, sucked, and tongue-fucked Casey's ass for several minutes, reaching between Casey's legs to play with his rock-hard cock at the same time. Then he stood and produced lubricant from somewhere, which he slathered over his cock and into Casey's asshole. He positioned his cockhead at Casey's twitching sphincter and held the boy's waist as he gradually began to penetrate him.

Casey had always felt a thrill of joyous anticipation as a prick began to enter his ass, and the larger the shaft, the keener the expectancy. As Eddie began to fuck him, the incredible feeling of warmth and completeness Casey had felt when Gundo had filled his ass with over ten inches of cock was soon reached, and even greater thrill excited him when Eddie groaned, "You got it all, baby. You want me ta really fuck ya now?"

"God yes, Eddie. That feels so fuckin' good! Just hammer my hot ass with that big thing." And Eddie filled Casey's urgent request as he filled his voracious ass — joyfully, ecstatically, eliciting moans and groans of pleasure and desire from the deliriously happy blond youngster.

Although apparently seized with complete fuck-frenzy, Eddie restrained the volume of his rapturous cries, knowing that his office was insulated from the lobby only by a door. After all, this was far from the first time he had fucked someone in his office during hours when the theatre was open; he regularly fucked an equally vocal and appreciative Richard there at least once a week. Several years earlier, he and Richard had fallen in love with each other in a small town in Alabama, when they had fucked each other in a relatively small orgy. At the time, Eddie was a soldier, stationed in San Francisco. Richard had moved out to be with him, and they had become lovers for a time, until Richard left to make porn films in Los Angeles. Recently, most of his porn films had been issued on videocassettes, and he was enjoying a renewed popularity.

Although both Eddie and Richard had moved on with their sexual and emotional lives, they still loved each other, and still loved to fuck each other. Richard was especially eager to get Edddie's monster meat up his apparently insatiable ass. He maintained a very nice apartment not far from the theatre, where he and Eddie usually met, but mood and circumstances often dictated that Eddie's office was the scene of their lovemaking.

After about five or ten minutes — or fifteen? Time meant nothing to the delirious pair — Eddie pulled out of Casey and turned him around, pressing his back down on the desk. "I wanna look at that beautiful face while I make love to ya," Casey automatically raised his legs, and Eddie re-inserted himself. He resumed his attack, with only a few beats lost in the rhythm of their impassioned fuck. Casey rested his legs on Eddie's shoulders, and used them to lever his ass up to meet and counter Eddie's savage thrusts. Casey had blown a large load on the stage of the theatre less than a half-hour earlier, but he was very near coming again as Eddie's labored breathing and hoarse cries signaled an orgasm. Just as Eddie slammed his glorious cock all the way inside Casey and froze there while his orgasm erupted in violent spurts, Casey shot another load, on his belly. He had never—never—been fucked more magnificently.

Eddie leaned down and kissed Casey—surprisingly, the first time they had kissed—with his prick still buried deep inside the boy. They necked for a long time; Eddie was almost as superb a kisser as he was a buttfucker. Finally, Casey said, "Eddie, they're gonna wonder what's taking so long. We'd better quit."

"Only if you promise I can fuck ya again," Eddie grinned.

"That's a condition I'd like to make for my employment at the *Top 'n Bottom Theatre*: I get fucked by the boss—at least once in a while."

"At least," Eddie said. "And next time the boss gets fucked, too, okay?"

"Oh, yeah!" Casey exclaimed as the two resumed their passionate kissing for several more minutes.

Gundo was gone when Casey emerged from Eddie's office. But Joey was there, waiting for him. Casey's face was flushed, and Joey studied him for a minute before he said, "Eddie fucked you, didn't he." It was more of a statement than a question.

"No," Casey said, "we were just talking."

"Bullshit," Joey said, grinning. 'That's okay, I won't say anything. "We're gonna meet Gundo at his apartment building lobby tonight a little after 7:30. If you can't make it, I guess I'll have to see if I can't entertain him by myself—which I would love to do, but I really want you there. A threesome with you two sounds fantastic. Let's see now, what can I do with twenty inches of hard dick?"

Casey laughed, "You'll figure out a way to deal with it. And I wouldn't miss it for anything. You wanna go back to school? We can still make the last two periods."

"Fuck it," Joey said. "Let's go back to my house and watch Race Rivera videos and make out."

"Okay," Casey said, "but I'm not gonna blow a load. Gotta save it for our hot threesome tonight."

Joey and Casey had only been waiting in the lobby of Gundo's temporary apartment building for five minutes that evening when the porn star appeared. "Two hot studs," he exclaimed as he came through the door, smiling broadly. "I blew my load for the 3:00 show today, so now I'm ready to suck some high-school dick and fuck a couple of hungry high-school butts."

Casey grinned, "And a couple of hot high-school cocks are ready to fuck some hungry porn star ass!"

"Starving porn star ass is more like it," Gundo said.

When they got to the apartment, Gundo told Casey and Joey to make themselves at home while he took a quick shower. When he returned to the main room, wearing only a towel wrapped around his waist, he found the two boys lying on the bed, naked, kissing and fondling each other, and apparently unaware that he had come back into the room. He walked over to the side of the bed nearest Joey, dropped the towel and stroked his dick while he watched them for a few minutes. "This look good to either of you?" he asked, his huge cock standing straight out and bobbing.

Both boys turned to look at him. Joey grinned and said, "Good enough to eat," as he scrambled to sit at the edge of the bed. Reaching out and pulling Gundo's body in to him, he opened his mouth wide and took the challenging gift inside, licking and sucking hungrily while the big-dicked Latino stud held his head and fucked his mouth.

"You're good, kid," he told the feasting Joey. Then he grinned at Casey, "And I'll bet you know that." Casey rose to his knees behind Joey and reached out to put his arms around Gundo. The two did a mutual tongue-fuck over Joey's head, and Casey's fiercely hard cock pressed up against Joey's back while he humped it up and down.

Joey rose to his feet, abandoning the monster cock in his mouth and causing Gundo and Casey to break their embrace. He held Gundo's face in his hands as he said, just before pressing their lips together, "Your dick is fuckin' fantastic. I've wanted to suck it for so goddamned long."

"I'm glad your dreams finally came true," Gundo said, "I love the way you wrap those fuckin; hot lips around my big prick." He opened his mouth wide and thrust his tongue deep into Joey's eager mouth. Casey had moved to sit on the edge of the bed, behind Joey; he pulled the boy's buttcheeks apart and tongue-fucked his ass while Joey and Gundo necked.

Breaking his embrace with Joey, Gundo said, "Let's all get in the bed."

The three rolled around, generally kissing, fondling, sucking and licking each other for some time, until Gundo said, "Joey, get on top of Casey, and you two sixty-nine." The two eagerly complied.

While he was lying on his back, sucking Joey's dick, Casey looked up at Joey's eagerly humping ass, and watched as two of Gundo's fingers, glistening with lubricant, entered the boy's ass and drove in and out for a few moments, until they were withdrawn, and Gundo's cock-head replaced them. As Gundo began to slide his prick slowly into Joey, the boy gasped, "Hard! Shove it in and fuck me hard!" Gundo gladly complied, and Casey watched as Gundo's fat shaft assaulted Joey's humping and hungry hole, his balls lightly sliding over Casey's forehead while he fucked. Fucker and fuck-ee groaned and cried in passion. Joey was so animated, it was all Casey could do to keep the boy's prick from pulling out of his mouth while he sucked. Shortly before Gundo shouted, "Take my load," Joey's delicious cum began filling Casey's mouth, and at almost the same moment Joey's expert sucking brought Casey to orgasm. All three blew their loads within a period of less than fifteen seconds. Casey and Joey continued sucking, and Gundo continued fucking for several minutes after their discharge They finally broke formation and collapsed over each other, moaning in satisfaction,

At Gundo's request, Casey went to the kitchen and returned to the bed with Cokes for all of them. He had stocked the small refrigerator. Joey seemed unable to quit praising Gundo's beauty, sexiness, endowment, and fucking expertise—both in person and in videos. Finally, Gundo told him to take it easy, the feeling was mutual, even though it was based on a single, in-person fuck. "After a while, I'm gonna suck you off while Casey fucks me, so you can check out what kinda cocksucker I am, too." He kissed Joey for a long time before adding, "And I'll bet you're a helluva good buttfucker, too. And I expect you to prove it to me."

An ordinary mortal would have had to wait a while before he was able to fuck again after blowing a load, but Gundo was no ordinary mortal. He rolled Casey to his back, put the boy's legs on his shoulders, and slipped his enormous cock inside the eager blond. He administered a very long and very intense fuck to the joyous Casey, while Joey eagerly fondled Gundo's body and ate his ass out. By the time Gundo had blown his load, Casey was sufficiently worked up that he pulled out from under him, telling him to get on all fours and take it doggie style. Gundo was more than happy to comply, and Joey ate Casey's ass this time, while Casey slammed into Gundo at length, finally rewarding him with a sizeable load, very explosively delivered — and at a depth where only a gloriously hung stud like Casey could deliver it.

Everyone had been fucked, and a bit later, after Joey managed to suck a load out of Gundo's prick, all had been sucked off as well. They continued to fondle and kiss generally, until it was nearing time for Gundo to return to the theatre for his 11:00 show. He needed to shower again, and he took Joey in with him, where he fucked the boy another time, but without reaching orgasm.

As they parted company back down on the street, Gundo kissed an elated and grateful Joey at great length, then kissed Casey and said, "See you at the theatre tomorrow, I guess."

Casey declared his first threesome had been extremely enjoyable, and Joey decided it had been the most exciting thing that ever happened to him.

Richard Austin was the oldest of the house dancers, by several years. He said he was thirty-two, but according to his driver's license he was born on September 2, 1945 — the day World War II ended — and was thus thirty-eight, but he didn't look a day over the age he claimed, if that. His last name was actually Harper — Austin was his middle name — but he almost never used it, and even most of his closest friends didn't know he wasn't Richard Austin — and never Dick, Rick, Ricky, Rich, Richie, or any other diminutive. However, his time was so consumed by sexual pursuits that he had little time for friends — and he had few of those, since those who came to know him well realized there was something cunning and selfish, about him; most knew he could not be counted on to tell the truth about many things. One of his few close friends once said of him, "Richard would tell a lie when the truth would sound better."

If his personality traits were not particularly attractive, his physical attributes were quite the opposite. He was remarkably handsome in addition to being cute, and he fairly exuded sex. He was tall and his build was somewhat slim — something of the classic 'swimmer's' body — but his cock was perfection: about nine inches in full erection, circumcised and unusually fat, with a lightly plum-colored head that was unusually large in proportion to the perfectly smooth fat shaft. His prick was a show-er, not much of a grow-er, so that even when it was completely flaccid it was almost eight inches long. Hanging down from his groin, the beautiful big column of flesh looked like it would probably grow to at least twelve inches when he had a hard-on. Such was not, alas, the case—but when it was erect it was still a very formidable weapon, one that Richard wielded masterfully and often savagely.

He was born and raised in a suburban town on Long Island, to relatively affluent parents. He was never a good student, but he had a natural ability to convince people that they wanted to do what he wanted them to do. That, combined with instinctive cunning and a determination to get what he wanted at any cost—however amoral or even immoral the methods or consequences—got him through school as it later got him through life. His charm, his physical attractiveness, and in most cases, starting almost immediately at the onset of puberty, his huge prick and sexual voraciousness were the major factors in his successes in life,

He had fucked and sucked his way through high school—not limiting his activities to students, but interfacing more often with teachers whose favors he needed to pass and to graduate. He picked up an older man named Paris Williamson, who was the band director at Dowd College, in Alabama. Richard and Paris so impressed each other that Richard enrolled at Dowd, where their tempestuous affair was short-lived. Later, he continued to use sex for success, but less successfully than he had in high school. He was barely managing academically, but succeeding mightily in the area of satisfying his rapacious sexual appetite. He was living with the school's Choir Director—he seemed to specialize in music professors, having also had an affair with a third—when one of the director's former lovers visited, bringing along a soldier with the biggest cock Richard had ever seen. The soldier was Eddie Bliss, who fucked with Richard and fell in love with him almost at once. Richard fell in love also—but more in love with Eddie's gargantuan cock and his prodigious sexual technique than with Eddie himself. Eddie returned to his Army post in San Francisco, and convinced Richard to join him there—where Richard abandoned all pretense at further schooling. He left Eddie when he was lured to Los Angeles to pursue a successful career as a nude model and porn "actor," but his most significant source of income there proved to be that of almost all porn actors: prostitution.

He had made a very successful series of porn videos when he was in his twenties and early thirties, He had even appeared several times as the guest porn star at the T 'n B a decade earlier, but as his age had increased, his porn fame diminished He was still remembered, however, by ever-older men who masturbated to his movies

Many of older patrons of the T 'n B recalled him from his porn-star days, and his performances there were sufficiently sexy that it was not unusual for him to actually collect the hundred—or even two hundred—dollars he initially asked of patrons for some private time in the small rooms the management of the theatre provided for quickie assignations. He frequently went to patrons' hotel rooms for all-nighters, which typically brought him four or five hundred dollars. As a place of contact to arrange such trysts, the T 'n B was ideal, so he didn't mind having been 'demoted' to house-dancer status. Besides his position as a house dancer meant that by tradition he would get fucked by the visiting porn stars, many of whom he lusted after—and his looks, charm and endowment were sufficiently attractive that he got to fuck a lot of them in return.

He continued to advertise his services as an escort—a prostitute, of course—in a national gay magazine that printed classified ads, emphasizing his porn-star status, but not mentioning that those days were in the past. As a result, he often flew all over North America, and occasionally to Europe and the Caribbean—and, on rare occasions, even to Japan and Hong Kong—to have sex with well-paying admirers, but more frequently he entertained those who flew in to San Francisco to be with him. Unless it was a regular client—and he had a considerable number of those—Richard met with visiting men in their hotel rooms, rather than at his own apartment. Normally, the only men he led to his own bed were those he personally wanted to have sex with: the unusually young or beautiful or well-built, or those with particularly large cocks. Given how frequently he was having sex for money, he was still able to satisfy a rather astonishing number of those he bedded because he found them attractive.

Richard was happiest, of course, if a paying john showed up looking like a young Adonis, with the physique of a bodybuilder and a prodigious dick, particularly interested in fucking butt. Surprisingly, there had been quite a few who met one or more of those qualifications, and even one who had scored very high in all four areas. That one was Charlie Jackson, a married man living in Columbia, South Carolina, who had answered Richard's magazine advertisement and booked the stud-for-hire's services for the first night of his planned week-long stay in San Francisco. Richard had turned on the charm and figuratively 'pulled out all the stops' in his sexual technique, which convinced Charlie to leave his hotel room and move into Richard's apartment for the rest of the week—with no additional charge for sexual services rendered. Actually, Richard admitted to himself that he would be glad to pay Charlie for sex. He had gone to bed with better-looking men, ones with bigger dicks or more exciting bodies, and ones who fucked more excitingly, but they had not exceeded Charlie's individual qualifications by much, and no one else had brought such an incomparable combination of those factors. As a wonderfully exciting bonus, Charlie seemed indefatigable: he could literally fuck all night, and it was not uncommon for him to blow four or more loads during one of their marathon sex sessions. There was often a fifth or sixth to enjoy the following morning, and a final mutual fuck in the shower invariably capped each session they shared.

Richard didn't normally meet Charlie load-for-load, but he came close, inspired not only by Charlie's performance as an unflagging, cum-filled top, but by Charlie's vocal expressions of hunger to suck Richard's massive cock or to get fucked by it. Richard's obvious appreciation for Charlie's tireless excellence was matched by Charlie's eager expressions of mutual admiration and gratitude. In essence, their encounters were like cum-filled meetings of a mutual admiration society.

When Charlie returned to San Francisco, as his architectural business occasionally required, he invariably stayed with Richard, and no money ever changed hands. On one occasion, Charlie called to say his wife was going away for a week, and Richard flew to Columbia to spend that week in Charlie's bed. He had flown to Columbia several times before, hired by a South Carolina state senator, but those trips had only been financially rewarding.

Any male prostitute soon learns that the vast majority of his clients want mostly to suck dick and get fucked. Perhaps one of the key factors leading to that fact is that a great many of them pretend to be straight: they have wives and, often, children; they date women or are involved in relationships with them; or they have sex with other men, but, through some feeling of machismo pretend to be straight when they do so—and sucking dick or taking it up the ass tends to contradict an assertion of heterosexuality. In their regular sexual relationships, those straight-pretenders tend to have either pussies or asses to fuck and have no trouble getting their dicks sucked, but that does not satisfy them.

Married men constituted Richard's principal clientele, so more of them were fucking pussy than ass. When the pretenders go to a male prostitute, they do so to enjoy what they can't normally get—or are afraid to ask for—in their regular sex lives. Fortunately, Richard loved to use his enormous cock to fuck butt, with a kind of mastery and fierceness that never failed to satisfy, and he adored getting blown, so he never had trouble meeting his clients' desires. Still, what he really liked was the bottom role, and he almost always convinced his clients, if they were attractive or, especially, if they were well-hung, to fuck him. Clients seeking to get fucked or suck cock often realized after they came away from a session with Richard, that they had fucked and got blown more frequently than they had blown and been fucked. Richard's astonishing good looks, and the amazing charm he was able to turn on at will, made it easy for the stud to accomplish this. Moreover, he was a virtuoso cocksucker, and he provided an amazingly satisfying experience for those who fucked him, so none of his clients minded. The well-hung and indefatigable Richard was an extraordinarily fine top and bottom, and he very rarely entertained a client who didn't want to come back for more.

He was making a lot of money, and he was smart enough to save and invest most of it, on the advice of a canny local financial adviser who frequently utilized his services as an escort in lieu of his usual fee. The adviser thought he was getting the better deal in those sex-for-advice encounters

Given his very crowded sex life, it was not surprising that Richard was often absent from his duties at the *Top 'n Bottom*, but Eddie didn't mind. Not only did Eddie still love Richard, but Richard always more than made up for his absences by sharing with Eddie the kind of sex that had caused them to fall in love with each other many years earlier.

# # # # #

When Casey arrived at the theatre for his first day as a regular house dancer, he got there a full hour early, hoping to meet, and become acquainted with some of the other dancers. One dancer was performing, and two others were in the backstage lounge, Richard and one he had not met. Richard greeted him warmly, kissing him passionately, as if they were old fuckbuddies, and then introducing the dancer who was scheduled to go on next. He was Steve Renard, a tall, nice-looking, if not outstandingly handsome man, who had an absolutely glorious body.

Steve spent a couple of hours in the gym almost every day, building and maintaining his magnificent physique: a chest that was vast, with unusually large nipples surmounting glorious rounded breasts; abdominal muscles clearly defining a 'six pack'; a waist that was extremely narrow for one so strongly built; huge, bulging muscles on his arms and legs; and an adorable ass—small, but very well-rounded. Steve's body was perfect, save for one failing: his prick. On a slim, willowy boy or man, Steve's prick would have been attractive and at least fully adequate, but with his breathtaking body, it almost seemed small, out of place.

The kind of "oohs" and "aahs" that were normally heard when a dancer revealed a big, hard dick were heard when Steve bared his chest. He always began his performances wearing a loose shirt over a skin-tight T-shirt. As he doffed his outer shirt to reveal the outlines of his glorious chest, he invariably received a round of applause, and when he removed the T-shirt presenting his golden, molded flesh to view, the applause grew enormously. His tight, leather breakaway pants went next, leaving him in a very revealing g-string, basically a pouch containing his cock and balls, held on his body by near-invisible cords at his waist and between his buttocks. When he circulated among the patrons, most of them concentrated on fondling his well-defined six pack and his luscious breasts and nipples, but not ignoring the golden twin globes of his voluptuous ass. Later, when he returned with his cock bare and erect, the fans still focused mainly on his muscles. Steve knew that on another man, his cock would be perfectly fine, but he wasn't embarrassed at the apparent disinterest the patrons displayed; he knew where his attractiveness lay, and he was more than satisfied with that. When he blew his required once-a-day load on stage, he spent most of the time working up to his orgasm by clearly fucking himself with a dildo, which he enjoyed doing as much as the patrons enjoyed watching the act, and which greatly increased the trajectory of his explosions of cum. He made as much in tips as any of the other house dancers, until Casey came on the scene, and went downstairs for a paid session with an individual patron after almost every performance. Casey later asked him how he could go for so many private encounters in a day, and Steve explained that he rarely got a load when he went with them; they seemed content to play with his body, instead of his dick, and he always encouraged them to shoot their loads on his chest or belly. All but a few would follow that up by licking Steve clean.

Casey would have been blown away by Steve's body, if it hadn't been for the fact that he was still occasionally having sex with his classmate, Rommel Chase, who was almost as mightily built, and who was much cuter. Nonetheless, Steve was impressive, and Casey made a mental note to get his cock in between those tight little asscheeks at the earliest opportunity. Judging by the way Steve eyed Casey's cock as he stripped off his underwear, threw it into his assigned locker and put on the Speedo he would wear for his show, Steve was as interested in playing around with Casey as Casey was with him.

The dancer who was performing when Casey arrived at the theatre finished his show, and came backstage. Richard introduced him to Casey as Mikey—no last name. Mikey was reasonably well-built and attractive, and he seemed like a nice enough person, but he had no special 'selling points' for this work, as far as Casey could tell.

Muscle-stud Steve Renard was on next, and Casey watched his on-stage performance from the wings. Richard watched with him for a while. "Fuckin' impressive body, huh? Sucks a mean cock, but not much of a fucker. I love to fuck him missionary or have him ride my dick so I can play with his tits while I give it to him." He had been fondling Casey's ass as he spoke, and said, "When're you gonna give me a crack at this pretty little butt of yours?"

"Still thinking about it," Casey laughed, and he was not kidding; he was seriously contemplating sex with Richard.

Richard left and Gundo appeared at his side. "Hey, cutie," he said, and he, too fondled Casey's ass. "That's some body, huh? I'd just as soon suck his tits as fuck him." He laughed, "And I think that's the way Steve prefers it—but he does like to take it up the ass, too. When do you go out there?"

"I'm next," Casey said.

"Nervous?"

"No, it's actually kinda exciting," Casey replied.

"I gotta get ready," Gundo said. "I go on after you. C'mon back and talk to me. You've still got fifteen or twenty minutes."

"Be there in a minute," Casey, said, his attention still riveted by Steve's mighty body.

Back in the lounge, Richard greeted Gundo, who said, "This is my last night, so I'm gonna do a double for the 11:00 show. You wanna double with me?"

"Sure," Richard said, enthusiastically. "You want me to hold my on-stage load until then?"

"Nah. But listen, why don't you make sure Casey sees you do your special 'thing' when you blow your load tonight? I'll bet he'll get a kick out of it, like I do. It's damned impressive,"

"Sure, Richard said. "I hope it'll get him in bed with me. I want that incredible dick of his in the worst way.

Gundo laughed, "Get it in the best way instead—up the ass. The kid fucks as good as he looks!"

"That means he's a fantastic fucker."

"Yeah, and he's just as good as a bottom. He'll go ape over your dick," Gundo leered, "just like I did." He groped Richard as he kissed him passionately, feeling Richard's cock grow hard and huge within his pants. "And just like I will again, when we double tonight."

A 'double' act at the T 'n B was typically reserved for fairly special occasions, like the last show of a visiting porn star, or an overflow crowd. It meant that one of the dancers—normally the visiting star—would invite another performer to share the stage with him at the end of his act, after he had finished his circuit of the audience. He would have saved that day's mandatory public ejaculation for the occasion. The two performers would fondle, kiss, suck and fuck each other in full view of the audience, with the stipulation that orgasms would be seen by the audience. Usually, that meant the star would be fucking the other dancer, and would pull out just before shooting his load, to blow it all over his partner. Occasionally a third partner, or even another couple, would appear on stage and join in the fun. One memorable New Year's Eve, a 'double' was in progress when midnight struck, and all the house dancers, who had been pretty freely drinking champagne backstage, joined the star and his fuck-partner for an out-and-out orgy in front of the audience. By the time they finished, most people in the audience were having sex with other ones; couples fucking and engaged in sixty-nine filled the aisles, while others stood around watching them and masturbating.

As Gundo went to his locker and began to prepare for his show, Casey came into the lounge. The sight of the fat cock 'tent-poling' Richard's trousers was not lost on him, and renewed his contemplation of sex with the fascinating older man. It also helped get him in the mood for his upcoming show as he dressed for his entrance.

Casey's dance went well. The audience was quite large—almost a full house. The larger audience turned him on much more than had the handful of patrons that had watched his debut. His show was more-or-less exactly what it had been on that occasion, except that he didn't blow a load at the end. He was going to hold that for his last show. His performance was received very enthusiastically, his tips were very generous, and several of the patrons propositioned him to go with them somewhere for private sex—either downstairs, where they apparently knew about the private rooms, or to their homes or apartments. One asked him to spend the night with him. The money offered was tempting, but Casey declined all offers. He was more than a little nervous about going along with that part of the job as a dancer—just yet, anyway.

Back in the lounge, Casey counted his tips, and learned he had made well over a hundred dollars. He voiced his pleasure, and Gundo said, "I'm not surprised, Casey. You're gonna do well. Just a matter of time before some porn scout spots you. You can make a few movies, and you'll be visiting here as the star."

It was time for Gundo to go on, and Eddie was already making the announcement, but he took Casey by the shoulders and looked very seriously into his eyes. "But you listen to me. You finish high school and go to college. You can dance here and do some porn films while you're doing that, but keep enough time with your dick in your pants to train yourself for something you're good at. You're great at sex, but you'll probably only have ten or fifteen years when you can make a living at it—and you're gonna have forty or fifty years where you have to make a living. Okay?" He kissed him tenderly, and added, "Seriously. Think that over carefully."

"I will, Gundo. I promise," Casey replied, and they kissed passionately for just a few moments before Gundo hurried out to the stage.

Casey overheard Richard telling Carl, who had just come into the lounge and was getting ready to go on after Gundo, that Gundo had asked him to double with him for the last show. Richard left to watch

Gundo's show from the wings, and Casey asked Carl what doubling with Gundo meant. Carl explained the traditional practice, that it meant Gundo and Richard were going to fuck for the audience as part of the porn star's last performance. Casey's initial thought was, *Why Richard, instead of me?* He felt a twinge of jealousy when he heard the news; he had come to feel that he and Gundo had some sort of special relationship, yet Gundo had selected Richard to share the honors with him that night. Then he felt hurt. He knew, intellectually, that there was probably nothing special about the time he and Gundo had spent together, but emotionally, he couldn't think otherwise. In spite of his mind telling him to forget it, he was still somewhat upset. Remembering how sexy and gorgeous Richard was, however, he also had to admit Gundo had chosen a very hot guy to share the final public moments of his visit.

He had a couple of hours to kill before he had to perform again, and he planned to go to a nearby diner for a hamburger. But Richard had made him promise to watch his show from the audience when he went on in about forty-five minutes, and see his special 'thing.' Even though Casey was resenting Richard at the moment—for no good reason, he had to admit—he was curious about Richard's 'specialty,' which he had promised to perform just so Casey could see it. His curiosity won out, and he elected to go eat after he had satisfied it.

He sat in the audience for the last part of Gundo's performance, and his hurt feelings were somewhat mollified by the special attention Gundo paid him when he circulated through the audience naked, kissing him passionately before he shoved his cock into Casey's mouth and fucked it for several moments, withdrawing before orgasm, of course. *He's saving his load to do his "double" with Richard,* Casey thought, but with les bitterness than he had felt when he first heard of the plan.

Carl performed next, and also paid special attention to Casey, but there was nothing unduly exciting about it. Again, Casey felt that he had hotter numbers to have sex with back in his high school.

Then Richard came on, and he looked stunning, Casey had to admit. He virtually oozed sexiness in every movement, and his cock looked huge and mouth-watering. With the large crowd, he forewent the non-naked circuit of the audience, and first went out wearing nothing but his boots. His boots were full of bills when he got around to Casey, who was sitting near the back. He kissed Casey hungrily, then reached down to grope his cock, saying, "Don't forget where I told you this thing belongs," just as he turned around and leaned over the seats in front of them, presenting his very succulent bare ass for Casey's admiration. Casey immediately forgot his resentment, and buried his face deep between Richard's buttocks and ate his ass out eagerly while he reached up between Richard's legs to play with his huge, throbbing prick. He was going to miss Gundo's attentions, but he was looking forward to some hot times with this beautiful stud. Let Gundo fuck Richard tonight; Casey felt sure he would be fucking him very soon.

Back on stage, Richard strutted around, brandishing his prick and finger-fucking himself to the applause of the audience. He walked downstage and stood at the apron as he began to masturbate in earnest. Just as he was about to blow his load, he thrust his hips as far forward as they would go, forcing his erect cock into an almost vertical position. Smiling dreamily and murmuring satisfaction, he rubbed his belly sensually and pinched his tits as the cum began to flow from his throbbing prick, without his touching it. Rather than shooting out in jets, the semen welled up and oozed out in a generous flow, which varied in volume as his cock throbbed and bobbed up and down slightly with each spasm of his discharge. An actual continuous column of gushing, pearly cum flowed over his balls and reached for a few seconds all the way to the floor, revealing what a huge volume of semen he had produced. As his orgasm was ending, several shorts spurts shot from his cock, leaving only a trickle that soon became a thread hanging from his prick and swaying as it continued to bob. All this time, Richard's hands had continued fondling his upper body. His hands-free orgasm was inordinately sexy, particularly stimulating to watch. The audience went wild, not just applauding furiously, but also stamping and whistling their appreciation and admiration. Casey joined in; it was one of the sexiest things he had ever seen.

Richard blew a few kisses to the audience, and exited, a drop of cum still glistening at his bulbous cock-head.

That was not the way Richard normally blew his load. If he had an orgasm while he was being fucked, a common occurrence in Richard's lovemaking, the cum didn't well up and ooze out of his big dick; it could shoot with considerable force and for a very impressive distance, and usually did. And like any sane gay man, except the most committed bottom, he especially enjoyed blowing his load explosively in a hungry throat or voracious ass, but he also enjoyed demonstrating his unique, ultra-sexy, hands-free orgasm, especially if there were a number of people to enjoy watching it. But he was happy to give a private performance if there was an individual from whom he especially wanted something. Exactly what he wanted might vary: perhaps a fuck from an unusually well-hung, muscular or studly boy or man who for some inexplicable reason was withholding his sexual favors, or, more likely, someone who had something more material to offer him. Richard often used sex to get what he wanted — especially, in recent years, money. Normally, on those occasions, he would have his admirer lie on his back while he straddled the man's upper body, with the tip of his cock-head positioned directly over the man's open mouth, so that the column of cum ended in it, and the lucky recipient could watch the flow of pearly-white love-juice filling his mouth.

Most of his admirers wanted to know how Richard achieved his special kind of orgasm. He explained that very delicate, split-second timing was needed as one masturbated: he needed the ability to sense exactly when the semen would begin to discharge, and the discipline to release his prick about one stroke before that happened — and it took a lot of practice to get it just right. (Surely there can be few other kinds of talent in which the practice necessary to achieve mastery is more enjoyable!)

Much of Richard's novel sort of display would later become a unique feature of the inordinately erotic fuck films produced and directed by the enduringly handsome Kristen Bjorn.

Backstage, Casey congratulated Richard for his performance. "I damn near blew my load just watching you come that way," he said. "I'm really looking forward to seeing you double with Gundo tonight, and I don't know who I'm gonna be more jealous of when I watch — you or Gundo."

Richard said, very solemnly, "Gundo's gonna be fucking the hell out my ass tonight, but would you believe me if I said I wish it was gonna be you?"

"I don't think so," Casey said, "I've been fucked by Gundo, and I can't imagine thinking about someone else fucking me while he did it."

"That's 'cause you can't believe how fuckin' gorgeous and sexy you are, and how much I want your huge dick inside me. You sit in front and watch while Gundo's fucking me tonight. When I look out and wink at you, you'll know I'll be wishing it was you plowing my ass. If I see you wink back at me, it's gonna mean you want to do exactly that some time, but in private. And if you grin while you wink, it's gonna mean we've got a date to do just that tomorrow some time. Deal?"

Richard was still wearing only his money-stuffed boots, and his cock was now only semi-erect, but when he put his arms around Casey and kissed him, he guided the young blond's hand to his prick; Casey felt it stiffen and grow as he held it. Richard whispered into his mouth, "I sure hope I see you winking and grinning later tonight. I can't wait to make love with you." Then he detached himself, and strode to his locker, his splendid, now fully erect cock swaying as he walked, and his ass looking magnificently fuckable to Casey. He was ready to wink and grin at Richard later on, and he hoped to conduct some personal research tomorrow to determine just exactly how fuckable Richard was—and he looked forward to demonstrating his own fuckability to Richard as well.

"What a sexy sonofabitch," he heard someone behind him exclaim, and he turned to find Carl also studying Richard's ass. Then he turned to face Casey. "You have time to get something to eat before your next show?" Casey was happy to join Carl at the diner.

Casey's show was extremely successful, and when he blew his load out into the audience, standing all the way downstage, he wished Richard was sitting in the front row, so he could receive the same kind of salute Gundo had given him when he sat there. The crowd was large, and he was worried that there might not be an empty seat in the front row when Gundo and Richard doubled. He would worry about that when the time came.

Steve Renard went on next, and although his performance was not nearly as sexy as others' had been, his stunning body more than compensated. He had already blown his required public load for the day, but he still fucked himself with a large dildo, to the delight of the audience, but without coming; the dildo appeared to be even larger than the one he had used on himself earlier in the day. Casey was able to catch only the last few minutes of Steve's performance, watching from the wings, and he fantasized about using his cock in place of the dildo in a private performance with Steve some time soon. Or perhaps in a double on the stage? Who knew? There was no doubt, Steve was extremely foxy, a term that inevitably came to Casey's mind, since he had taken French for a year at Serra High, and knew that "Renard," Steve's last name, meant "fox" in that language.

As Steve exited, he ran into Casey in the wings, who said, "Great show, Steve." Steve thanked him, and Casey added, "And I gotta admit, I really envied that dildo."

Steve grinned, "Well, we gotta do something about that. I'm always open to new experience. Soon, Casey, I promise—but I gotta hurry and get dressed so I can see Gundo's last show. Richard's doubling with him—wish it was me!" He kissed Casey and went back toward the lounge.

Casey thought, I wish it was gonna be me doubling out there, too—but I'm not sure which of the two I'd rather be doing it with. Maybe with both? Tripling? Wow, what a thought!

The auditorium was filled when Casey went out into it; in fact, a dozen or so patrons were standing, their backs to the side walls. Sunday night—the night when the visiting star made his last appearance and traditionally invited someone else to double with him—was very popular. Few places in "The City"—as San Francisco was popularly known by its denizens—had Sunday worship services with worshippers as avid as the communicants at the T 'n B.

There was a fairly attractive older man, probably in his forties, seated in the middle of the front row. Had it not been for his experiences in this very theatre in the last few days, Casey would have been too timid to do what he did, but this was not the same Casey Lowe who had first come here to drink in the sight of Race Rivera. Casey knelt in front of the man, obviously surprising him. The flustered man stuttered out a compliment about Casey's performance. Casey thanked him and said, "Listen, what could I do to get you to give me this seat for the next show?"

Than man thought for a moment, and collected himself. He looked Casey in the eye and said, "You could let me suck you off."

"Okay," Casey said. "Stand over there by the wall, but when Gundo—I mean, Race—and Richard are almost finished, come back and kneel here where I am. I'll have my dick out for you." The man agreed eagerly, and yielded his seat to Casey.

Gundo's show progressed as usual, but he had no time for the first circuit of the audience, and because of the full house, even his naked circuit was perfunctory. Back on stage, he paraded, at times masturbating, at times stopping and grinding his hips so that his enormous hard cock flopped up and down, swaying from side to side. He ended up center-stage, where he faced away from the audience, leaning over so that his ass was displayed for their appreciation. He spread his legs and from his front he reached up between his legs to finger-fuck himself, deeply and very vigorously—to warm applause. The music has been faded out completely by that time, and his grunts and pants and exclamations of "Oh, yeah!" were clearly heard by everyone.

Straightening up and facing the audience, Gundo extended a hand toward the wings and said, "Here's Richard," and a naked Richard came on stage, his big prick already hard, swinging from side to side and bobbing pendulously as he walked out to join Gundo. The audience applauded wildly; they knew what was coming—and who was going to be coming!

Richard and Gundo embraced and kissed feverishly while they fondled each other with equal passion, grinding their bodies together, their long pricks jutting out from their sides as they did so. Gundo pressed down on Richard's shoulders, pushing him to his knees. Richard immediately deep-throated Gundo's challenging shaft, to renewed applause, and began driving his lips all the way up and down its entire length while Gundo fucked his mouth and fondled his head, gasping and moaning in pleasure. Every gasp and moan either one emitted was clearly audible to the audience, which was enrapt and completely silent. Soon Gundo was holding Richard's head tightly, and pulling it in toward him forcefully to meet each savage thrust of his dick. Finally, Richard relinquished the prodigious mouthful of dick, looked up at Gundo, and cried out, "Fuck me!" He dropped to all fours and wriggled his ass expectantly. Gundo swiped his hand through a large container of lubricant on the table just behind them. He greased up his cock and Richard's asshole with a few practiced movements that consumed only a few seconds before he had his cockhead positioned for entrance. With a fierce thrust, Gundo slammed his monstrous prick all the way inside Richard with a savage grunt, accompanied by a triumphant shout of joy from the grateful and—every gay man would no doubt agree—lucky recipient.

Although he had watched many men and boys being fucked in videos and films, and in spite of his own precociously vast experience in fucking and getting fucked, young Casey had actually only seen men fucking in the flesh on three occasions before he came to the T 'n B to work. The first time had been in his sophomore year, when he was hiking along a trail in San Francisco's Lincoln Park, on the cliffs overlooking the Golden Gate, west of the Bridge. He had stumbled into a glade, and saw a naked boy—who looked, Casey thought, no older than he was—standing next to a tree and bracing himself against it, his upper body arched inward so that his ass protruded seductively, while behind him a uniformed sailor, with his pants around his ankles, was holding the boys waist and fucking him wildly. The sailor spotted Casey and growled, "Get the hell outa here, kid, or I'll fuck you next!" While that proposed scenario would have probably pleased Casey quite a bit—he was far from inexperienced, even at that age, and knew very well what he liked—the sailor scared him, so he retreated. But the sailor also aroused him, so he sneaked back and watched from behind a tree, masturbating as he did so. The sailor clearly blew his load in the boy, and the boy turned around and kissed him before pressing him down to his knees and fucking his mouth. The sailor sucked happily for a while, then got on all fours and presented his ass to the boy, who fucked him as intensely as he had been fucked. The boy and Casey reached orgasm at about the same moment.

The second occasion was when he had watched Gundo and Joey fucking each other in Gundo's apartment, and the third time only the day before, when he had watched Gundo fucking muscle-boy Steve Renard, in the backstage lounge. The only dancer Gundo had not fucked was Adam, the muscular blond dancer who was married and claimed he was straight; Gundo had sucked him off instead. Casey had watched himself fucking other boys in the mirror in his bedroom, and one of his fuckbuddies had a mirror on the ceiling over his bed, but that was different.

Watching the ecstasy of a live fuck in action was extremely stimulating, and watching two such hugely handsome and accomplished fuckmasters at work was especially inspiring: Gundo and Richard were absolute virtuosos in the art of lovemaking. Although he had blown a load less than an hour earlier—and it had been his third orgasm of the day—Casey unzipped his pants and freed his dick so he could masturbate. The men on either side of him were already stroking their cocks, and when one reached over to stroke Casey's as well, Casey let him continue for a while, until the man was jacking him off so eagerly he was afraid he was going to blow another load. He made the man stop, because he didn't want to do that for a while yet—and besides, he had promised the guy who had given up his seat that he could blow him.

The fuck Gundo was giving Richard, only ten or twelve feet from where Casey sat, was probably as brutal, savage, rabid and unrestrained as any Casey had ever seen in a film or video—wilder than the three he had seen live by a huge margin—and, not surprisingly, the most exciting. It was the kind of fuck Casey dreamed of throwing into Dave Cotter, the first boy who ever fucked him, the only one he had ever fallen in love with, and still the only one who had consistently refused to take Casey up the ass. Someday, if Dave ever came back to San Francisco, Casey swore he would re-open his campaign to fuck him until he succeeded—and when he did (not *if*), the fuck he was watching was going to serve as a model.

Both Richard and Gundo were grunting and gasping their thrill, interspersed with Richard's fierce, unrelenting moans of *Fuck Me!* and Gundo's triumphant cries of *Take it!* and *Yes!* Gundo often panted Richard's name while he fucked the deliriously happy stud, and Richard often used Gundo's name when he enjoined him to fuck as hard as he could. Many members of the audience were by then too worked up to continue their rapt silence, and began calling out, urging the two studs on and complimenting them—and no doubt wondering why Richard kept using the name "Gundo" when he screamed his joy at the way Race was fucking him.

Although he was completely caught up in the action on stage, and unthinkingly thrilled by the feeling of a complete stranger jacking him off while he watched the most exciting fuck he had ever seen or even imagined, Casey was still rational enough to realize that Gundo wasn't really Gundo at that moment: he was Race Rivera, a demigod of gay sex, and he was not just fucking Richard, he was performing for a wildly appreciative audience, actually feeding on their excitement as well as his own. He determined he was going to give Richard a fuck that was fully as intense—and do it the next day if he got the signal from him. Casey had to wonder if the fascinating man kneeling on all fours, apparently lost in the delirium of fuck-lust that Gundo's mastery had so clearly inflamed in him, would remember to wink at him, to give him the cue for the signal they had agreed on—and to have the presence of mind to apprehend Casey's answering signal. Casey was somewhat frustrated by often having to watch for Richard to wink, when he wanted to be looking elsewhere—at the sight of Gundo's glorious cock ramming in and out of Richard's frantically undulating ass, for instance. Nonetheless, looking at Richard's strikingly handsome face was a pleasure in itself, especially when it was suffused with such added beauty while he was obviously experiencing incomparable, utter joy.

Richard's head was flopping up and down uncontrollably with the brutal slamming his body was receiving, and the loud slaps of Gundo's belly hitting his ass were as loud as Gundo's feral grunts and Richard's accompanying gasps.

Almost without losing a beat in his ravenous lovemaking, Gundo suddenly withdrew his cock, rolled Richard's body over roughly, slamming his back against the floor while Richard's legs automatically rose to circle Gundo's waist, and the Latino stud shoved his cock back inside Richard's ass in one ferocious plunge to resume his ecstatic fuck. For five minutes, Gundo's splendid ass humped frantically while he jackhammered his gigantic cock in and out of Richard's hungry ass— more rapidly than would have seemed possible, given the amazing length of his strokes—and Richard's heels beat a tattoo on the apparently fuck-crazed Gundo's buttocks. Then Gundo seized Richard's legs and raised them, so they rested on his shoulders while he continued to fuck, now driving his prick almost straight down into Richard for a few more minutes.

Gundo had already shown he was a complete master of fucking; now he showed he was also a master of timing, a true professional. One second he was fucking like a maniac, the next he had pulled his cock out of Richard and reared up on his knees as Richard's legs fell to the floor on either side of his body; at the same time, he seized his prick and aimed it at Richard's belly, like the lethal weapon it was, just as his cum began to erupt and he howled in triumph—but not so loudly that it drowned out Richard's repeated scream of admiration and appreciation: "Yes!"

And still Richard had not looked at Casey or winked.

Gundo's orgasm was massive, coating Richard's chest and belly in ropes of thick, white cum before it was exhausted. Grinning, Gundo swiped his right hand over Richard's chest and stomach, scooping up his own cum—and doing it slowly, allowing everyone to see what he was doing. Then he displayed his hand so that all in the theatre could see it was literally covered with his cum. Richard rose to his knees, took Gundo's right wrist in his hand, and brought it to his face. He very slowly lapped up and licked cum from Gundo's hand, exaggerating the motions to provide a clear view of what he was doing. He faced the audience, with his tongue protruding so that the coating of white cum was visible to all before he swallowed, and then he lapped and licked further until Gundo's hand was clean. Richard again stuck out his tongue to show its cum coating, but this time he looked directly at Casey before he swallowed—and winked!

Casey winked back at Richard, of course, and grinned hugely—not just to signal the amazingly sexy stud that he ready for sex with him tomorrow, as agreed on, but because he was so pleased and excited with anticipation that he couldn't *not* have grinned!

With his cum-covered tongue still protruding, Richard held out his arms to Gundo, who enfolded him in his own, opening his mouth widely so that everyone could see Richard's tongue enter it before they sealed their lips and kissed passionately, fondling each other feverishly as they did so. The audience went wild with approval, and their ovation drowned out whatever it was Richard said to Gundo that caused the Latino fuckmaster to look surprised, then turn around and kneel on all fours, his beautiful ass presented to Richard. Richard lubricated his formidable cock, and massaged his lube-covered fingers into Gundo's asshole. He rammed his huge prick home in one fierce thrust, and this time it was Gundo who screamed in thrill, and it was clearly audible above the sound of the continuing applause.

Richard began a fuck as savage and satisfying as the one he had just received, and Gundo registered his joy and appreciation just as clearly as Richard had shown his when he was the object of Gundo's frenzy. As Richard rammed his monster cock in and out of Gundo's ass, and Gundo slammed his ass back to meet every thrust, the audience gradually grew quiet again, in awe of the breathtaking majesty of the display they were witnessing. Again, Gundo and Richard's grunts and gasps of ecstasy were clearly audible throughout the theatre.

Richard's head was thrown back and his eyes were closed as he fucked, but in the throes of his crazed fucking, he slowly turned his head and opened his eyes to look directly at Casey again, to wink sexily, wearing a crooked, confident smile that seemed to say more than just, "This is what I want to do to you tomorrow." Instead, it was apparently saying, "This is what I'm going to do to you!" The appearance of sexual delirium returned to Richard's face and his attention went back to the world of the savage fuck he was administering.

Casey's heart was racing. He couldn't remember having looked forward to anything more eagerly than he now hungered to be making love with the breathtaking man pounding Gundo's ass like a sex-crazed maniac.

Just a few minutes later, Richard backed up slightly, pulling his cock out of Gundo. He grabbed it and aimed it downward so that his load began to splash on Gundo's back. And it was a generous load — amazingly large, considering that he had performed his "no hands" orgasm less than an hour earlier, while this same audience had watched. The applause erupted again as Richard reached down and scooped some cum from Gundo's back; the audience knew what was coming. As he had done when he ate Gundo's load a few minutes earlier, he slowly licked and lapped his hand clean, then stuck out his tongue to show it covered with cum before he directed his gaze at Casey to wink again before he swallowed. Casey returned his wink and grinned, of course. Richard grinned back at him, then scooped the remaining cum from Gundo's back. By this time, the applause had died down, so Richard was clearly heard when he asked Gundo, "You want some of this?" Gundo rose to his knees, licked Richard's hand clean and embraced him while they kissed.

Like most in the audience, Casey was masturbating, and he knew he was nearing orgasm as Gundo and Richard started to kiss. He was too lost in the rapture of the moment to remember he had promised the man whose seat he had taken, that he would let the man suck him off. It wasn't necessary: the man had already knelt in front of Casey, and suddenly, his mouth engulfed Casey's cock and his lips sank down all the way to the base; he was clearly an accomplished cocksucker. Casey seized the man's head and pushed it down as he fucked upward into his mouth, rewarding him only a few minutes later with a huge explosion of cum, which the man swallowed eagerly, continuing to suck and lick until Casey had expended every last drop and began to calm down.

Casey pulled the man's head away from his cock, and whispered to him, "Great job, man!" The man looked up, and replied, "Great load, stud. And what a cock!"

On the stage, Gundo and Casey were still kissing, but instead of the frantic fondling that had marked their kisses before, they were now caressing each other gently and lovingly. They finally stood, and holding hands, they bowed to acknowledge the audience's frantic applause. As they turned to leave the stage, Richard looked directly at Casey and slowly mouthed the word "to-mor-row," his quizzical look clearly adding a question mark to the word. Casey eagerly nodded, and Richard smiled before he and Gundo exited.

Still sexually stimulated from what he had just witnessed, but emotionally drained from just having been sucked off, Casey was ready to go home and go to bed—prepared to dream about meeting with the fascinating, exciting Richard tomorrow. He was eager about getting fucked the way Richard had fucked Gundo, but equally keen to fuck Richard's beautiful ass the way Gundo had. What he was not prepared for that evening was further sexual activity. The man who had sucked him off watched wistfully as Casey pulled his pants up, concealing his cock. He thanked Casey profusely for letting him blow him, and begged for a chance to meet with him sometime to fuck. "Whatever it costs," he said. Casey was not interested, and politely dissuaded the man.

He went backstage, ostensibly to congratulate Gundo and Richard on their magnificent performance, but also to arrange with Richard for a meeting the next day. He found Gundo and Richard still naked, lying on the couch and necking as passionately as they had on stage. He cleared his throat, but they either didn't hear, or were so wrapped up in each other that they were unwilling to be interrupted—Casey guessed the latter was the case. Perhaps they were simply ignoring him, but Casey thought not: his relations with Gundo that week had been very warm, and Richard was clearly lusting after him—as, he had to admit, he was lusting after Richard, especially after having just witnessed his show with Gundo. He found a scrap of paper and wrote a note to Richard: *I'll be home from school tomorrow by 4:00. Please call me between then and 6:00, so we can set up a time to get together. You were fantastic tonight, and I can't wait to be with you.* He added the number of the private telephone in his bedroom and wedged it in the door of Richard's locker, so he couldn't miss it.

As he turned to leave. he saw that Eddie has entered the lounge, and was looking at Gundo and Richard making out on the sofa. Eddie turned his head to look at Casey, and said, "I need to see ya."

"Sure," Casey said.

"C'mon back to my office," Eddie said, and turned to go. Casey followed him, casting a final glance at the two naked men, still kissing and fondling each other, humping their bodies as they writhed—obviously still very aroused. He was dying to see Richard alone the next day, but he realized Gundo was leaving in the morning, and he probably wouldn't see him again any time soon—if ever.

In the office, Eddie locked the door behind Casey. Casey happened to glance down, and saw that Eddie's prick was tenting his left pants leg, bulging two-thirds of the way to the knee. Eddie was breathing hard, and to Casey, he looked haunted somehow. "I've gotta fuck ya, baby," he panted, beginning to unbuckle his belt. "Getcher clothes off."

Casey was really not in the mood for any more sex at the moment—an unusual condition for the young fuckmaster—but he responded to the urgency in Eddie's voice, and began to disrobe. By the time Casey finished undressing, Eddie was also naked, stroking his cock—which looked even more enormous than it had the last time Casey had seen it in this office. Even though he thought he was not interested in sex just then, the sight of the gargantuan meat caused Casey's own cock to fill out and rise.

Eddie stepped in front of Casey and said, "Get down there," as he pressed on Casey's shoulders, driving him to his knees, the big head of his throbbing prick at Casey's lips. It took no further invitation for Casey to open his mouth wide—very wide, of necessity—and drive his lips as far down the fat shaft as he could, and begin to lick and suck greedily while Eddie fucked his mouth—so urgently that Casey proudly realized he was soon deep-throating the monster dick all the way. Eddie groaned his pleasure for several minutes before he rudely hauled Casey to his feet, turned him around, and bent him down over the desk. "Gotta fuck this pretty ass," he gasped, as he lubricated his cock and began to enter Casey.

He had thought he was done with sex for the night, but the thrill of Eddie's massive penetration changed Casey's mind quickly. He sensed that if he resisted, Eddie would fuck him anyway, but with such a glorious cock inside his ass, why would he resist? If he did, it would be rape, he supposed, but what wonderfully enjoyable rape it would be. Why not relax and enjoy it? And enjoy it he did!

As Eddie's dick began to slide in and out in deep, very long strokes, Casey picked up the rhythm of Eddie's fucking, and worked with him to give him the same degree of pleasure Eddie was bestowing on him. He worked Eddie's prick the way Hank, the sailor, had worked his that day he learned how to be a better bottom. Clearly, he was doing a good job of it, judging by the way Eddie was praising him and moaning his pleasure.

Soon, Casey realized that Eddie had been calling him "Richard" while he fucked. Casey didn't bother to correct him; if Eddie wanted to pretend it was Richard he was fucking, so be it; just as long as he continued to hammer away with that magnificent dick, Casey was happy. Eddie was administering an epic fuck, similar in intensity to the ones Casey had just watched Richard and Gundo share.

Finally, with a loud cry of "Take it, baby," Eddie sank his cock as far inside Casey as it would go and froze there for a moment, shuddering as his load began to explode. Then he resumed fucking rapidly and violently as he cried, "I'm comin', I'm comin' … God, Richard … love you so much!"

After his orgasm, Eddie's fucking gradually abated, and he fell over Casey, pinning the boy's belly against the desk. "That was … was incred'ble," he panted in Casey's ear. They lay like that for about thirty seconds, while Eddie kissed Casey's neck and purred his contentment. Then he said, "You gotta fuck me now, baby … need it."

"Jesus, Eddie, I blew my load on stage about an hour ago, and a guy just sucked me off while I was watching Richard fuck Gundo."

"Yeah … Richard … gonna fuck me now," Eddie panted, pulling Casey to his feet and stepping between him and the desk. With one hand he grasped Casey's now fully erect cock, and with the other he pulled the blond's head in so they could kiss. "Beautiful fuckin' big dick," he muttered into Casey's mouth, "beautiful fuckin' man … all man!"

With their first kiss, Casey realized his suspicion was true: Eddie was drunk. The way Eddie was slurring his words should have tipped him off, but the taste of whiskey in his mouth was unmistakable—one of his supposedly straight fuckbuddies always fortified himself with it before he kissed Casey or took Casey up the ass. Well, what the hell, maybe Eddie was drunk, and maybe he had just blown two loads, but he was ready to fuck again. And if Eddie thought it was Richard fucking him, fine. He only wished it was Richard getting ready to fuck him.

Eddie bent over the desk and used his hands to spread his asscheeks. "Fuck me, Richard … need … beautiful big cock in me again. Please, baby." The lube was close at hand, and Casey prepared Eddie's ass, while Eddie continued to mutter incoherent pleas to get fucked. Casey slammed his entire monster cock deep inside Eddie with one furious thrust and began a serious fuck inspired by the ultra-serious one he had watched on stage only a short while earlier. He fancied it was Richard he was fucking, just as Eddie's gasps of pleasure made it clear he was fancying it was Richard who was fucking him.

It took a long time before his orgasm arrived, the third one in less than two hours; it was not a new record for Casey, but it did tie his previous record. He cried "Take my load!" as he finally came inside Eddie, who was frantically bucking and gasping with joy.

Casey fell over Eddie, and stayed plugged in as he savored the moment. Eddie muttered, "Love you so much … fell in love with you firs' time we fucked … Richard, my sweet baby …"

Richard a sweet baby? Casey laughed to himself; the big-dicked, raging stud he had just watched fuck Race Rivera was no baby! And although he was by then sexually exhausted, and his cock was still inside a different stud, Casey couldn't help but think of tomorrow, and the promise of making love with Richard.

Casey had trouble getting Eddie dressed, but he managed. He offered to call him a cab to take him home, but Eddie somehow made it clear he would sleep on the sofa in his office. It wasn't much of a sofa, and it didn't look comfortable to Casey, but he was glad to accede to Eddie's request. As soon as Eddie lay his head down on the sofa, he was out like the proverbial light.

In a way, Casey felt flattered that Eddie had confused him with Richard—the comparison was a considerable compliment, after all. *Eddie is still head-over-heels in love with Richard,* he thought. *That's sweet, but as totally hot as Richard is, I don't think I'd want to be really in love with him, unless I just wanted to get my heart broken.* Then he chuckled as he thought further, *But I'm looking forward to being heels-over-head in love with him.*

Leaving the theatre, Casey encountered a middle-aged man standing outside the door. The man asked, "Have you seen Race Rivera? He's supposed to meet me here, but I've been waiting almost an hour."

"I'm sure he'll be along any minute." Considering what a professional Gundo was, he probably would show up and give the man the thrill of his life.

"Thanks," the man said. "Oh—you were incredible, by the way. Do you ever ... well, meet clients after a show?"

"Maybe someday," Casey replied, and smiled as he said good night to the man. *Yeah, maybe someday*, he thought. He had already been propositioned quite a number of times, for 'quickies' or for 'all-nighters'—twice that very night, in fact. He hadn't made up his mind if he wanted to go that route yet. It was good money, but ...

He decided to take a cab home. It was almost 1:30 in the morning, and he had school tomorrow—no, today! Besides, his tips had been extremely good tonight, and he could easily afford some luxury. In the back of the cab, wondering if he should start 'escorting,' he remembered Scarlett O'Hara's famous line, "I'll think about that tomorrow. After all, tomorrow is another day."

Tomorrow! Richard! He could hardly wait, and the luscious cock that had performed so well and so often that night, stirred in his pants.

5.

Trixie Spills the Beans

Bill Lowe was waiting for his son when he got home at 1:45 in the morning. Casey was surprised to see the lights on and his father sitting in the kitchen, reading a newspaper. Had he known which newspaper, he would have been even more surprised.

"Awful late to be getting in on a school night, buddy," Bill said.

Casey was gratified that his father didn't seem angry or accusatory. "I know, Dad. I just got caught up in some things, and lost track of the time."

"I think we need to talk. Sit down," he said, gesturing to a chair across the table from him.

As he passed Bill and went to sit down, Casey was startled to see that the newspaper his father had been reading was the *Golden Gate Nation*, a local publication aimed at the gay population of the Bay area. *This can't be good*, he thought.

In addition to news of national and regional gay interest, the *Golden Gate Nation* featured want ads and advertisements that appealed to the local gay community. A very popular feature of the want ads was the "personals" listings, where local hustlers and 'escorts' publicized their availability for sex with men willing to pay for sex with other boys or men. Oddly enough, there didn't seem to be any lesbian prostitutes—certainly none advertised their services.

"Read this," Bill said, opening the newspaper and pointing to an article as he passed it across the table to Casey. The article in question was actually a chatty column of local gay events and gossip, called *Trixie's Tricks*. The photograph of 'Trixie" at the head of the column showed that "she" had a very bushy moustache! Casey took the paper, and Bill said, "Read the third and fourth paragraphs."

Casey said, "Aloud?" Bill nodded, and Casey began:

Mary, if you haven't seen the latest dancer at the Top 'n Bottom Theatre, you owe it to yourself to get your buns parked in one of their sticky seats, but right away! This girl caught his act the other night, and my heart hasn't settled down yet! He's blond (well, OF COURSE he's blond, you know what

Trixie likes), but I mean REALLY blond – and absolutely, downright, all-out, certifiably GORGEOUS: high cheekbones, pouty lips, he-man jaw line, broad shoulders and a tiny waist, with an adorable bubble butt I could get lost in! But – get this – his most striking feature would hang down to his knees if it hung down at all, but it seems to stand up all the time! Ooh, I used that word, 'hung,' and as you know, that always makes the inside of Trixie's knees sweat – and they never sweated more than they did while she watched this dishy blond Adonis dance the other night! It's probably not his real name, but they call him "Casey" (nobody, but NOBODY at the City's premier jack-shack has a last name). Anyhoo, Trixie would love to be the ball when THIS Casey is at the bat!

And as if all that weren't enough, he's young, young, young! I still don't know if I believe Eddie, the theatre manager, when he says he checked Casey's ID. Trixie is REALLY hoping Casey will also offer those discreet 'appointments' most of the other dancers offer to the well-heeled patrons at the T 'n B. If so, this girl is saving her money! And it took oodles of detective work, but we learned that Casey is not one of those "gay for pay" numbers that give our sisterhood what they have to offer only when we grease their palms, and almost never let us grease anything else they have (our hard-earned money is all they're usually willing to take). But we learned Casey is definitely a player on our team, and enjoys real give AND take with a string of young admirers as long as his ... well, you know!

While he was reading the article, Casey's voice gradually became hoarse, and his breathing more troubled. He could hardly finish reading; his heart was pounding, and he was filled with dread. His father knew! By the end of the account, his voice was almost a whisper. He stared at the paper for a very long minute, then slowly raised his eyes to meet his father's as he asked, dully, "How did you find out?"

"A friend called my attention to this article at the office yesterday. He'd seen your picture on my desk, and he knew your name, but he honestly thought it was just a funny coincidence that there was another gorgeous blond named Casey – that was his word, gorgeous – who was dancing in a strip theatre. It wasn't hard to put two and two together – after all, this Trixie's description is pretty accurate. Then, you're gone practically all the time lately, and you come in late, and you obviously have found some way to make money. I wanted to be sure, though, so I called the *Top 'n Bottom* to find out when Casey would be performing last night. I got there in plenty of time for your show."

"But, I didn't see you when I was ..."

"I was sitting all the way to the side in a row half-way back, wearing a hat, and when you got to me, I waved you away." Bill said.

"Dad, I don't know what to say," Casey said, his voice breaking. "Did you ... did you see the whole show?"

Smiling crookedly, Bill said, "Yeah, I did. You were pretty goddamned amazing, too. I watched all of your show, and I stayed and watched until Race Rivera had finished, with the other guy, Richard."

"You watched that? But Dad, why? If you were there to spy on me ..."

"Son, I wasn't spying on you. I just needed to know. I know you're eighteen, and you're a man now, but you're still my son, and I care very much about what's happening to you. Look, I'm not ranting and raving and telling you what you can and can't do, am I?"

"No, of course, Dad, you never have."

"Well. I'm not going to start now, but we need to talk about where this is going to take you."

"But, I don't understand why you stayed and watched Gundo's ... Race Rivera's show."

Bill smiled again, "Casey, there are a lot of Race Rivera fans, you know. Actually, I had considered going to see him while he was appearing here, anyway, but I just hadn't got around to it. Then, when I saw that article—well, I figured, what the hell, if I was going to pay twenty-five bucks to get in, I might as well get my money's worth. And, I stayed because I was wondering if you were gonna appear again. I know that the visiting porn star usually brings someone else on stage with him for his last show, and ... well, I wondered if it might be you."

"But, Dad ..." Casey was at a loss for words, "how did you know that? You've been to the T 'n B before?"

"Quite a few times, actually."

"But ... but does that mean you're a ... that you're ..."

"Queer?" Bill asked. Casey nodded numbly. "The answer is yes, Casey. I always have been, always will be, I guess."

Casey was dumbstruck, but he eventually asked, "But what about you and Mom? You . . . you are my father, aren't you?"

Laughing, Bill replied, "Son, look at me and look at you. There's no question I'm your father. Your Mother and I had a decent marriage for a long time; I wanted a family and children, and things worked for quite a while. She finally learned the truth, and took off almost without a backward look."

"She never told me why she left," Casey said, wistfully.

"She told me she figured you were going to turn out gay, too, and she thought you'd be better off with me."

"In other words, she deserted me because I might be a queer. That's mighty hard, Dad."

"I know it is, Casey, and I'm sorry."

"But what did you do about ... what do you do about ..."

"Sex?" Bill asked. Casey nodded. He went on, "Look, son, no parent wants to discuss his sex life with his child, and no child wants to discuss his sex life with his parent. Most parents don't think their children even have a sex life, and most kids don't think their parents have a sex life. Am I right?"

"Yeah, I guess you are. I gotta admit, Dad, the thought crossed my mind that you might be gay—like me. You never dated after Mom left, after all, but I really didn't think you were."

"Well, I am," Bill said, "and I guess it's high time I told you the truth." He stood. "This is a pretty important subject, and we'll talk about it all we need to, but it's after two o'clock, you have to be in school in the morning and I have to be at work early, so let's get to bed." Casey stood, and Bill embraced him. "I love you more than anything in the world, Casey. I don't want to run your life. I want you to be happy, but I also want you to be safe, and I wonder how safe working at the *Top 'n Bottom* is—in many ways. And, you've gotta think about your future. You're due to graduate in six months or so, if you're going to college—and you really need to, you know."

"I know, Dad."

"Well, let's talk about this at a reasonable hour, and see if we can't figure out how you can reconcile your school work with what you're doing, if you still want to continue doing it. I'm not going to forbid you to dance at the theatre, but I have to admit I'm pretty far from thrilled about it."

"Dad, I'm having fun doing it. And I know it's temporary, but— well, it's really exciting, too."

Bill laughed, "Yeah, I can see it's exciting. That Richard who was paired up with Race Rivera was almost more exciting than he was."

Somewhat shamefacedly, Casey said, "Richard wants to get together with me tomorrow some time after school—well, today, after school. It's Monday, and the theatre is closed."

"Here's a shocker for you: I envy you—and if you weren't my son, I'd envy Richard even more."

Casey was finally able to grin, "You want me to tell you about it?"

"NO!" Bill thundered, but he also managed a grin. Then, more seriously, he said, "I'm curious. Would you have agreed to appear with Race tonight, if he had asked you? I'm assuming he didn't."

"Sorry to tell you, Dad, but since we're being honest here: I would have been thrilled to do it. Actually, I was kinda hurt when he didn't ask me, but I don't blame him for asking Richard. I think Richard is unbelievably hot. I'd be more than happy to do it with either Gundo— Race—or Richard.

"I can't say I blame you, Casey. I'd probably agree to do it in public for a chance with either of those two, myself."

"Whoa, Dad! Too much information."

Bill laughed, "Okay. Now—bed!"

Casey kissed Bill on the cheek. "I love you, Dad. You're the best!"

"And I've always thought you were the best, son—and after seeing you perform tonight, it's clear you're pretty goddamned hot, too!"

"Dad!" Casey cried, and went into his bedroom. Bill chuckled, then sighed, and went into his.

# # # # #

The next morning, Casey was very pleased that there seemed to be no awkwardness between him and his father as they snagged something like a breakfast on the run, and headed for their separate days' obligations—promising to have an all-gay father-son talk very soon.

It was Monday, and the theatre was closed, so Casey didn't have to go to 'work'—if that's what you wanted to call something that was so much fun. During lunch period at school, Casey and Joey sat on the bleachers at the deserted football field, and Casey told his fuckbuddy about the previous evening at the theatre, especially the ecstatic pairing of Gundo and Richard—but he didn't say anything about his encounter with Eddie after that; he had, after all, sworn to Eddie earlier that he would tell no one about any sex that they shared—but he really did wish he could tell someone about Eddie's phenomenal cock. Joey was flabbergasted to learn about Casey's meeting with his father at the end of the day, but Casey failed to tell his friend about his father's revelation that he himself was gay. Casey wasn't at all sure how that was going to sort itself out in his mind; in the meantime, he didn't plan to discuss it with anyone but his dad.

If Joey had been excited when Casey described Gundo and Richard's fuck in great detail, he was even more so when he learned that Casey was going to get together with Richard later that day. "I wanna hear every little detail about that," Joey had said, "Rommel Chase was talking about getting together with me tonight. Apparently he needs to get fucked, and that young number of his isn't giving it to him. I'm gonna fuck his muscle-bound ass silly tonight, thinking about what you're doing to Richard, and whether he knows it yet or not, he's gonna fuck me silly while I think what Richard is doing to you. And by the way, it's been a long time since you did anything to me."

Casey snorted, "What, three or four days since we had that threesome with Gundo?" He kissed Joey warmly, and at length; there didn't seem to be anyone around to observe. "Don't worry, fucking with Joey Stone is still very much an important part of my permanent agenda," Casey said, "and you can tell Rommel that sucking his fabulous tits while I fuck him is still high on my agenda, too."

It was hard to keep his mind on schoolwork that day. For one thing, he hadn't had enough sleep the night before. He had partially solved that problem by putting his head on the desk in Study Hall, and the teacher let him sleep. Actually, although Casey didn't know it, his Study Hall teacher would have let him get by with almost anything; he was one of a number of Serra High teachers who fantasized about sex with the gorgeous, golden senior.

His mental unease over the encounter with his father the night before was relatively—surprisingly—mild, but still it was nearly impossible to shake. It made it hard for him to concentrate on Chemistry and Government, and may have contributed to what he felt sure was going to be a failing grade in a pop quiz his Trigonometry teacher had given that morning. The fact that his Dad was gay was not really a shock, but he was surprised that his father had been so forthcoming about it. He wouldn't have been surprised by his father's easy acceptance of his own homosexuality under any circumstances— his Dad was a very fair person, tolerant and supportive of a myriad of people and causes—but the fact that his Dad was gay himself made it even more logical. What had surprised Casey, however, was how broad-minded Bill had been about what his son was doing at the T 'n B – prancing around and lap-dancing naked for a room full of complete strangers, and jacking off so those same men could watch and get their rocks off. The anticipated discussion with his father, and whatever changes in his life that might bring about was what was worrisome to him.

Then there was the proposed meeting with Richard later in the day. In spite of his weariness and his concern over relations with his father, his dick was at least partially hard most of the day, thinking about the handsome, impossibly sexy stud, and what he hoped to be doing with him that night. It was strange that Casey didn't think of Richard as being much older than he, since, in fact, Richard was only five years younger than his father, but at thirty-eight (he only admitted to thirty-two of those years, of course) Richard's sexual endurance and athleticism were characteristic of a much younger man, even a perpetually horny teen-ager like Casey.

Casey got home from school shortly before 4:00, and sat in his bedroom waiting for Richard's call. The telephone rang promptly at 4:00, and he snatched it up. Richard's voice was soothing and sexy, his words were stimulating and wonderfully frank: "I can't wait to suck a load of cum out of that huge cock of yours, so that when you fuck me it'll take you a really long time before you come again. I didn't leave Gundo's apartment until five this morning, and I just woke up a couple of hours ago – and I'm so hungry to get fucked, I can't stand it."

Casey was almost gasping with desire as he replied, "I feel the same, and I hope you're gonna fuck me the way you did Gundo last night. That was the hottest thing I ever saw!"

"Baby," we'll make last night look like a warm-up. When can you come over?"

"Right away," Casey said, and took down Richard's address and telephone number. He lived on Hartford Street, near Nineteenth – just a block away from Castro Street and the center of the Castro District, the gayest neighborhood in a city noted for its large gay population. It was a short bus ride on the Divisadero line from Casey's house, which was off Divisadero on Jackson Street, near the Presidio.

The apartment where Richard lived was the first floor of a converted Victorian two-story, in extremely good condition. Richard answered the door wearing only a towel wrapped around his waist; he had just finished a shower, and smelled wonderful as he engulfed Casey in his arms, kissing him as hungrily as Casey kissed back. A gorgeous blond necking with a man wearing only a towel rated nothing more than an admiring glance from several men walking by on the sidewalk; this was the Castro, after all.

Casey had looked forward to this moment from the first time he had spoken with Richard, when within ten seconds of being introduced, the startlingly handsome stranger had grasped Casey's hard prick and declared he wanted to have sex with him.

"Maybe we'd better go inside," Richard suggested when they broke their kiss. He followed the young blond through the door, his cock obviously fiercely hard now, tenting his towel as alarmingly as another passer-by's cock tented his pants when he visualized the magnitude of Richard's 'tent-pole.' Inside the door, Casey pulled the towel from Richard's waist as they kissed again, and he fondled Richard's writhing bare ass while Richard unbuttoned Casey's shirt. Richard's hard cock was poking into him, and Casey reached down to encircle it and stroke it as Richard groaned excitedly into his mouth.

"Your dick feels so fuckin' big and hard," Casey gasped, as he broke their kiss and sank to his knees to take it in his mouth. It wasn't as big as Gundo's or Eddie's—or his, for that matter—but it was a challenging mouthful: fat, and probably over nine inches long. The challenge was compounded by the ferocity with which Richard fucked Casey's mouth as he held the boy's head tightly. Casey was fondling Richard's eagerly driving buttocks while he sucked, and when a finger found its way into Richard's asshole, the handsome stud's mouth-fuck turned almost savage.

"Suck my big dick, baby, I love it," Richard panted, and Casey responded to the injunction eagerly and expertly. Even though Richard was ramming it in and out of Casey's mouth with fierce intensity, the enormity of Richard's wonderful—and quite beautiful—cock presented no obstacle to the boy's expert technique. His lips were buried in Richard's pubic hair, and Richard's balls slapped against his chin each time the stud drove his cock inside. "I've been wanting you to do this since the first moment I laid eyes on you," Richard gasped. "You're the hottest fuckin' guy I've seen in years. Hell, I don't think I've ever seen a man I wanted more." He dragged Casey to his feet and kissed him again, saying, "If you don't stop, I'm gonna shoot my load in your throat, and I wanna blow my first one all the way up that cute little ass of yours."

Casey broke away and began to shed his clothes. "I can't wait." His dick was fully hard, throbbing, standing parallel to the floor when he finally shed his shorts and stood there completely naked. Richard whistled in appreciation and sank to his knees to afford Casey the same form of admiration the boy had shown him. As Richard had done to him, Casey fucked his mouth unmercifully, and Richard had no trouble at all in accommodating every inch of Casey's ten-plus inches, licking and sucking so hungrily that Casey brought a halt to his blowjob until they could get in bed together. Without saying anything, Richard took Casey's hand and led him into the bedroom. Casey eyed Richard's splendid, rolling ass hungrily as the older man preceded him. As they approached the bed, Casey pushed Richard's upper body down onto it, so that he was bent over, his face on the mattress and his ass presented for Casey's admiration. Casey knelt behind Richard and pulled the stud's buttocks apart, burying his face in between them, his tongue immediately penetrating the tight ring of Richard's sphincter—and it was really quite tight, in spite of the fact that literally thousands of pricks, and quite a few pairs of pricks, had slammed through it over the years, many of them wonderfully ample in girth. Richard gasped and humped as Casey ate his ass for several minutes, moaning his pleasure, and declaring he couldn't wait to do the same for the young blond Adonis.

Pulling away and falling to the bed on his back, Richard extended his arms to Casey, who fell into them, and they ground their cocks together while they kissed and groped each other passionately. Then Richard rolled Casey to his stomach, and ate out his ass hungrily before he reversed the boy's body so they could suck cock in sixty-nine, rolling around so that at times they lay on their sides, other times with Richard on top, and more frequently with Casey on top. It was while Casey was on top that he cried around the mouthful of Richard's prick, "I'm coming," and he shoved his monster cock all the way up into Richard's throat while Richard sucked out a delicious mouthful of creamy, hot semen. Richard continued to nurse gently long after he swallowed Casey's generous offering. Finally, he broke their embrace, and reversed his body again, so they could kiss. He said, "Your cum tastes as sweet as your body looks—and so does your ass. Jesus, Casey, you're fuckin' perfect! I'm dying for you to fuck me, but I just had to taste your cum first—I've been dreaming about it for a week. I made Gundo tell me everything you guys did.

"How did you know I fucked with Gundo?"

Richard laughed, "Hell, you told me he'd fucked you, and besides, I could see the way you guys looked at each other. I knew you screwed him, too—but I didn't know about the threesome with your fuckbuddy. That sounds like it was really hot. You suppose he'd be interested in repeating it with you and me?"

Casey assured Richard he felt Joey would be interested, but he didn't plan to ask him. He didn't mind sharing Gundo with Joey, but somehow, with Richard … he seemed to feel something special about Richard: he was so beautiful, and if he didn't have the body of Rommel Chase or a dick quite the size of Eddie Bliss's, he was still probably the most attractive guy Casey had ever seen. He knew he didn't want to share him with anybody.

Casey loved Joey, and was very fond of Rommel and some of his other fuckbuddies, but the only boy he had ever felt he might be *in love with* was Dave Cotter, the boy who had taken his cherry. The relationship with Dave had not been given time to ripen fully, so Casey was basically inexperienced in actual love, and didn't realize that he was probably falling in love with Richard—even though it was based only on Richard's looks and his own perception of the unparalleled sexiness of the older man. He really knew nothing about Richard's personality or character.

There was no question that Richard was unusually attractive physically, or that he was prodigiously talented in the art of lovemaking, but he was also as vocally persuasive as he was physically irresistible. He was what an earlier generation called, "a smooth talker." Many boys and men, younger and older, had fallen under the spell of Richard's charm as they had fallen in love with him. He had given most of them good reason to feel he returned their love, too, indicating by words and deeds how totally wonderful he found them, and how much he loved them.

To give Richard the benefit of the doubt, he was perhaps sincere in some of his overt and implied protestations of love, but the fact remains, that except for his love for Eddie Bliss, which Eddie returned, and which had lasted for quite a number of years, his love was invariably short-lived, and he would forget about it and move on to someone else with apparent ease and lack of regret. Such was his beauty and the efficacy of his lovemaking that few of those whose love he abandoned were easily able to abandon their love for him—if they ever did. The enduring nature of his love affair with Eddie was perhaps explained by two facts: Eddie loved fucking butt with the biggest prick that Richard had ever personally encountered, and Richard's favorite thing in the world was getting fucked by the biggest dick he could find. There had been numerous other lovers along the way for whom Richard had not actually felt anything, but to whom he had declared his love for some kind of gain: financial, usually, but also for provision of housing, promotion at work, better grades in school, and even a deferment from the draft. The last was owing to a smitten, closeted cardiologist, an avid fan of porn star Richard Austin and a regular client of escort Richard Austin, who lost his heart to Richard and falsely attested to his supposed lover's supposedly weak heart.

It is significant, and doubtless no coincidence, that none of those whom Richard 'loved' solely for some personal advantage were especially well-hung. In fact, a statistician might have observed that the degree of Richard's genuine 'love' varied directly with the size of the cock his 'lover' fucked him with.

With Casey, Richard was virtually pouring on the charm: the boy was breathtakingly beautiful to him—exactly the blond 'preppy' type he especially favored—and, of paramount importance, Casey's cock was enormous. Even with his vast sexual experience, Casey's naïveté didn't stand a chance against Richard's experienced, persuasive magnetism.

"Did you enjoy my show with Gundo last night?" Richard asked.

"It was probably the hottest thing I've ever seen," Casey replied warmly. "I went backstage to congratulate you, but you and Gundo were on the sofa, making out, so I left you to it. Besides, Eddie wanted to talk with me."

Richard laughed, "I'll bet Eddie wanted to talk with you while his dick was up your ass. Any time he watches me making love with someone else, he kinda goes crazy until he can fuck me. See, he and I were lovers a long time ago, and it still bothers him to see someone else fucking me. He usually goes home and takes it out on his little boyfriend until we can get together, but if you were there … well, I know he thinks you're hot as hell. I hope you fucked him back—he needs more than his boyfriend can give him."

"He fucked me and I fucked him back, but most of the time he called me 'Richard.'

"He's still in love with me—and I sorta love him, too, even after all this time. And he is a fantastic fucker," Richard said, "but I'm told I am, too."

"Remember, I saw you last night. I think you're just as fantastic."

Richard kissed Casey and thanked him, "Before you leave here today, you're gonna know I'm just as good as Gundo. But what a stud he is! He can throw a mean fuck into you."

"Looked to me like you threw a pretty mean fuck into him, too," Casey laughed.

"Yeah, and he wasn't expecting it, but he told me he loved it. We went to his apartment when we left the theatre last night, and spent another four or five hours screwing around. There was some poor guy waiting for Gundo in front of the theatre. He was paying Gundo for an 'all nighter,' and he'd been waiting for an hour. Gundo took him along, and he got a lot more than he paid for—two big dicks for the price of one. Gundo was still fucking him when I left to go home. And I'm dying to fuck you. You ready for me?"

"I don't think I've ever wanted anything more in my whole life," Casey said, sincerely.

Richard replied, looking very deeply into the young blond's eyes, "And I don't think I've ever seen anyone I wanted more than you. I've been dreaming of this since I first saw you—Jesus, is it only a week ago? Seems like I've wanted you forever. And I'm so hungry to get your dick up my ass, I can hardly wait. But you've already shot one load ..." he kissed Casey again, "and I can still taste your cum. I've gotta get my first load or I'll explode."

"Explode in me," Casey murmured. "Fuck me, Richard, I want you!"

While he was kissing Casey, Richard lubricated the boy's ass and his own prick. He rolled Casey to his back, and the boy's legs automatically rose to receive the throbbing prick; Richard pressed his cock against Casey's asshole as he knelt between them. Richard reached over and retrieved a bottle of amyl nitrate 'poppers' from the bedside table, and took a deep sniff. He offered it to Casey, who declined; then his eyes glazed over as he seized Casey's shoulders and shoved mightily, sending his prodigious cock deep inside the eager blond, and beginning a wild, almost brutal fuck. He leaned down and

Casey's arms went around his neck while they kissed as rabidly as Richard was fucking. The effect of the poppers wore off after a few minutes, but if it had been the inspiration for the ferocity of Richard's fucking, he found resources elsewhere, as his joyous assault on the beautiful blond boy continued unabated for a delirious ten minutes, while Casey gasped and whimpered his complete submission to Richard's mastery. Soon—all too soon, Casey thought—Richard slammed his cock as far inside Casey as it would go, and held it there as he shouted in triumph, "Take my load, Casey," and just as his cum began to erupt deep inside Casey, he added, "I love you, baby!"

The words thrilled Casey almost as much as the exploding cock did, and he gasped "I love you, too," just before Richard sealed their mouths in a voracious kiss that very gradually turned gentle and romantic as Richard's frantic humping little-by-little became slow and tender—but still profound and insistent—and his big prick remained the same hard and wonderfully filling assful it had been from the first moment his fuck began.

They continued to kiss and caress for a very long time, muttering sweet endearments, with Richard's prick sliding in and out of Casey's ass the whole time, having apparently lost none of his erection in spite of his orgasm. He whispered, "I loved fucking you, Casey, but I think I love making love to you this way even more."

"Just keep fucking, lover," Casey groaned. "My ass is so full of your hot cum, Nothing has ever felt better."

"I know it's crazy to fall in love with you so soon," Richard said, "but I know what I feel."

"I feel the same way, Richard. I can't help it."

Richard had continued to fuck all the while, and he began to pick up the pace of his stroke, and the intensity of his thrusts increased accordingly. He pulled out and had Casey kneel on all fours. Then he immediately rammed his ravening prick back inside the boy, holding Casey's waist in a vise grip while he gasped and grunted in fuck-frenzy, driving into Casey with full force. Casey, completely lost in ecstasy, whimpered with lust and begged Richard to fuck even harder.

And although he didn't fuck any harder, since he was slamming Casey's grateful ass as fast and as violently as he was able, Richard did continue to fuck for another ten or fifteen minutes until he actually shouted his joy when he blew a second load in Casey's already cum-filled ass. Casey's cries of joy matched the intensity of Richard's rapturous exclamation. Immediately, Richard collapsed on top of Casey, driving him flat onto the bed. "I love you, Casey," he panted.

Casey knew he had just received what was possibly the fuck of his life, and was too thrilled and excited to do more than echo Richard's sentiments.

After a few minutes of recovery, Richard pulled his cock from Casey—amazingly, still hard—and rolled the boy to this back. "I don't think I've ever enjoyed fucking any more than I just did. You are so goddamned beautiful and so … God, I love you so much."

They necked passionately for some time, Richard lying on top of the boy, and then slipping off to the side while they continued to kiss, so he could fondle Casey's monster cock—which was so hard Casey was almost in pain with desire. "I've got to fuck you, or you have to suck me off again," Casey said. Then he raised his head and smiled crookedly at Richard, "Or I could just jack off, if you're not interested."

"What a waste that would be," Richard laughed. "Don't be crazy," he added as he took Casey's prick in his mouth and began to suck it. "He stopped to admire it and lick it, saying, "So fuckin' big, and so fuckin' beautiful!" After a few minutes of eager licking and sucking, he said, "I'd love to suck you off again, but I've just gotta get this beauty up my ass, where it belongs. Gundo told me you throw a mighty mean fuck yourself."

"I'm ready to throw one. I'll pitch, if you're ready to catch. How do you want it?"

Richard got on all fours, facing away from Casey and smiling back over his shoulder as he said. "I like it this way best. Eat my ass first, and get it ready for that big dick, lover. I need it."

Although Richard was twenty years older than most of Casey's regular fuckbuddies, and a bit older than that in a few cases, his ass was as attractive to Casey as he could have desired—not surprising, since Richard, and everything about him, seemed to be more attractive to Casey than anyone he had ever met. While it was true that he still loved Dave Cotter, and making love with Gundo had been the realization of a dream, this gorgeous stud kneeling in front of him, begging to be fucked, appealed to him as no one ever had before. One could call it puppy love, and insofar as age itself was concerned, that would be an accurate description, but in spite of Casey's youth, he was no 'puppy' when it came to lovemaking: he was a widely experienced, naturally talented, superbly equipped, full-grown stud 'dog.' In any event, love, not just the usual lust, was an additional factor in the eagerness with which Casey addressed taking this gorgeous stallion the way he, himself, had just been taken.

Richard was wriggling in anticipation as Casey feasted on his hot asshole, and moaning his pleasure at the boy's obvious expertise. "Oh, baby, you're so good. Eat my ass — get that hot tongue in there and fuck me with it!" Casey's tongue writhed and twisted as deeply as he could penetrate inside the obviously appreciative Richard, until his brain, inspired by the urgency his cock was communicating to it, told him to get on with it — give him what you're both dying for! After having observed Richard's obvious joy while Gundo was hammering his ass the night before, Casey knew the sexy stud wanted to get fucked as much as he wanted to fuck him.

Reluctantly, Casey stopped servicing Richard's asshole with his tongue, and reared up on his knees so he could prepare to service it with his dick. While he was slathering lubricant on his cock, Richard was applying it to his own asshole, and finger-fucking himself, panting, "Give it to me, lover, I need your prick!"

Casey positioned his cock-head and took Richard's waist in his hands as he slowly began to penetrate him. He was feeling as amorous as he was horny — understandably, he was very horny — and he enjoyed the sensation of wooing this beautiful stud by gently entering him, savoring the joy of being inside a man he so wanted, showing him he wanted to make love, not just fuck. He panted, "Oh, baby, you're so fucking beautiful," as he gradually began to slip his dick back and forth, entering incrementally until it was finally seated all the way inside.

The magnificent cock Casey was feeding him was not just prodigiously long, it was wonderfully fat as well, and Richard reveled in the feeling of great warmth and utter fullness it provided him. The suggestion of appreciation and even honor that Casey's slow, romantic entry and words of admiration implied gave Richard a kind of happiness he seldom experienced when a stud began to make love to him; most of them thrust their dicks in to the hilt and began to fuck fiercely — which was a thrill, of course, but this was a different kind of thrill, and Richard actually felt that Casey was going to make love to him, not just fuck him.

And making love, rather than just fucking, was what Casey unconsciously intended to do, but with over ten inches of fat cock all the way up his ass, Richard decided he'd rather get fucked, and make love later. He reached for the bottle of poppers and took two deep sniffs, one in each nostril. Almost immediately, he turned into a wild, voraciously hungry fuck-bucket, fiercely anxious to be filled with cock and cum. He slammed his ass backward to slap it against Casey's stomach, and began to hump with frenzied speed and writhe around the blond Adonis's dick eagerly, joyously, irresistibly. Casey's mood changed at once, and he began to deliver the kind of fuck Richard obviously craved.

This was the kind of bottoming Casey had discovered, and admired so when he had sex with the sailor, Hank. But he had only found Hank attractive (well, very attractive once he discovered what a satisfying lover he was), but he was stunned by Richard's sexiness and was by this time completely in thrall to his potent sexuality. He didn't need the added stimulus of poppers to become the raging fuckmaster Richard clearly wanted and, Casey thought, deserved.

With Casey's huge prick ramming in and out of him, Richard virtually shouted, "Oh God, I love to get fucked!" It was pointless to tell that to God, who knew that fact only too well, along with at least a few hundred others who knew it from first-hand experience—to say nothing of the many thousands who had deduced it from watching Richard's films. Surprisingly, there were a few dozen others strewn along the rocky path of lovemaking with Richard Austin Harper who were not aware of his keen enthusiasm to take it up the ass. He occasionally liked to feed the mildly sadistic pleasure he took in not giving to selected sex partners what they desperately wanted and often begged for: the privilege of fucking him the way he fucked them. Possibly, it gave him some momentary feeling of power, or perhaps denying access to his otherwise insatiably hungry ass to this or that loving admirer made him feel superior somehow. But he wasn't really cruel to those he disappointed that way: he invariably told them he wasn't able to get fucked, for some trumped-up reason, and mollified them somewhat by kissing them and sucking them off with the same eagerness and expertise he tendered all his lovers. Significantly, and not surprisingly, the ones to whom he refused access to his ass were never among his better-hung admirers,

In general, Richard felt it was better to receive than to give, but he never failed to give. He invariably bestowed the ultimate gift he could offer on his sex partner: he fucked him, expertly, at length, and with the right tool for the job—and over the years he had often given that gift to a boy or a man who didn't know he wanted it until he had received it, and who, on realizing what a precious gift he had been given, almost always petitioned Richard to give it to him again and again.

Casey hammered away at the deliriously appreciative Richard for several minutes before Richard rose to his knees, arched his spine inward and turned his head, so that Casey could kiss him while he continued to fuck. Then Richard fell forward onto the bed, rolling to his back and disengaging Casey's cock, but he immediately raised his legs, presenting his twitching asshole, pink, glistening with lubricant, and distended from Casey's assault. Casey lost no time in crouching between Richard's legs and filling that tempting target again. Richard's knees were locked against his shoulders by the force of Casey's body pressing down as he resumed his by-now savage attack. Their mouths met, and they kissed as wildly as Casey fucked, Casey occasionally being able to gasp an appreciative comment, but Richard only being able to grunt bestially, lost completely in animal lust.

With a cry, Casey's body stiffened into a straight line and jerked with each spurt of his orgasm as he filled Richard's wildly thrashing ass with the cum the stud eagerly called for. With his load completely spent, Casey's body relaxed, Richard's legs encircled his waist, and they resumed kissing—still wildly at first, but gradually subsiding into a romantic, mutually appreciative sharing. Richard straightened his legs out, causing Casey's monster shaft to slip from his ass, and they lay on their sides, caressing and necking for a long time in post-orgasmic afterglow.

Finally, Richard murmured, "My god, best fuck ever! Jesus, baby, you're the stud I've always been hungry for." Looking sincerely into Casey's gorgeous green eyes, he had said it with a straight face—although 'straight' is hardly an adjective to be used in describing anything about Richard's lovemaking. But it was complete bullshit: Eddie had plowed him just as wildly and satisfactorily on any number of occasions, and with even more dick—and if Richard were really looking for a special stud, it would have been one who was able to offer something more personally or financially advantageous than Casey's stunning looks, monster cock, youth and sexual virtuosity. Smiling, he added, "I think I need a break—but just a break, okay?"

They shared a quick shower, which was much shorter and more efficient than it would have been had they not blown their loads so recently. Their sexual appetites were appeased for the moment, but they had both worked up a considerable appetite for something to eat other than cum, or cock, or asshole, so Richard called to have pizza and Cokes delivered. "Be sure to have Carlos deliver it," he said as he placed the order. They had a half-hour to kill, so Richard showed Casey around his apartment, which was very nicely furnished, and started to play one of his own videos on the living room television. Casey had never seen one, and thought the younger Richard was hot as hell—as top and bottom—but no more attractive than the mature Richard who sat next to him on the sofa.

The doorbell rang, and as Richard got up to answer it, Casey asked if they should stop the video and put on some clothes—both were still naked. "Nah," Richard said, "it'll be Carlos—he won't be shocked. He's seen it all before." Surprisingly, in spite of the video they were watching, neither Richard nor Casey had a hard-on, thanks to the exhausting sex they had just been sharing. Actually, although Casey's cock looked formidable in spite of its flaccid state, Richard's cock looked considerably bigger than Casey's, though his, too was flaccid. The opposite of Richard, Casey was a grow-er, not a show-er.

It was Carlos at the door, as expected, He entered and put the pizza and drinks on the dining room table. He glanced at the television, where Richard could be seen getting fucked by a rather hairy man with the physique of a bodybuilder. "I like this one," Carlos said, grinning.

The pizza boy was young and very cute: a Latino, with a mop of straight, coal-black hair parted in the middle, and snapping black eyes. He was not very tall—about Casey's height—but in spite of the fact that he was wearing a fairly loose uniform, it was clear he had a nice build.

Richard introduced Casey to Carlos, and Carlos' grin, combined with his firm, lingering handshake and unconcealed scrutiny of Casey's prick made the latter stir a bit from its flaccid state. Carlos did not miss the growth, and grinned even wider. He asked, "You go to Serra High, don't you?"

"Yeah, but how did you know?" Casey replied. "I'm pretty sure you don't go there, or I'd have seen you." It was Casey's turn to grin. "I would remember seeing someone around who looks like you."

"No, I go to Sutter High. My boyfriend goes to Serra, and he's got a picture of you in his bedroom."

"Who's your boyfriend?" Casey asked.

"Thom Nelson. You know him?"

"Sure, I know Thom," Casey said, but he thought, *You'd be surprised if you knew how well I know him.* "But why does he have my picture in his bedroom?" *As if I don't have a pretty good idea.*

"I don't know," Carlos said. "He just said you were a good friend. I told him you had to be about the best-looking good friend I ever saw. But shit, you look better in person than in your picture." He again looked pointedly down at Casey's dick, which had grown a bit more — and began to swell even further as Carlos focused on it. "And it's nice to see all of you."

Turning his attention to Richard, Carlos said, "I can see you're busy," he flashed a quick grin and a wink at Casey before he turned his gaze back to Richard, "but do you want your usual extra topping?"

Richard moved to stand behind Casey, and reached from behind to fondle Casey's chest and belly as he asked Carlos, "You have time for two extra toppings?" By this time, Richard's prick was hard again, and it poked between Casey's legs, causing Casey's cock to reach its full glory.

Carlos looked at Casey's mammoth prick and whistled. He reached down and encircled it with his hand as he said, "Jesus, I wish I did, but I've gotta get back. My boss'll fire me if I'm gone as long as I was last time I gave you two extra toppings."

Richard stepped out from behind Casey and kissed Carlos as he unbuttoned the boy's shirt and removed it, while Carlos unbuttoned his own pants and dropped them, and his shorts, down to his ankles. His prick was hard, and was good-sized — probably about eight inches. He was uncircumcised, but that was not evident in his aroused state. His body was well-formed, lightly muscled, with copper-colored skin, and his ass was nicely rounded. He was definitely a hot kid. *Thom Nelson is lucky*, Casey thought; remembering Thom, he thought further, *but so is Carlos.*

"Who gets the topping," Carlos asked, leering seductively as he stroked his prick.

Richard knelt on the side of the bed, with his toes hanging over. Looking back over his shoulder, he asked, "Who always gets the topping?" Carlos shuffled over, walking with his pants puddled around his ankles, to stand behind Richard and fondle his pretty ass while he reached into the jar of lubricant and began to grease up his dick.

"I can tell you're not gonna need any lube," Carlos laughed as he ran his hand up and down in Richard's asscrack while he positioned his cock for entry.

Taking a big hit from his bottle of poppers, Richard held it up for Carlos while the stimulant began to do its work. As Carlos was inhaling the poppers, Richard began to wriggle his ass and breathe harder. "Fuck me, stud,' he gasped, about the time the effect of the amyl nitrate hit Carlos, who shoved his hips forward violently, and buried his cock all the way inside Richard's ass. Carlos put his hands on his buttocks and pressed his pelvis far forward as Richard fucked himself violently on the boy's cock for a few minutes while Carlos threw his head back and gasped, "Yeah, ride my dick!" Soon Carlos grasped Richard's undulating ass and held it fast while he fucked it savagely, grunting in lust until the effects of the poppers had diminished to the point where fucker and fuck-ee were better in control of their actions, but still having an obviously wonderful time.

Casey was standing next to the bed, stroking his cock and admiring Carlos' busy little ass, thinking about eating it while the boy fucked Richard, when Carlos grinned at him and said, never ceasing the fervor of his fucking, "Man, his ass is so full of your cum. You gave him a really big load, I can tell."

"I need a big load from you now," Richard gasped.

"Let me suck another big load outta you," Carlos said to Casey. "Get up on the bed."

At that moment, fucking Carlos' mouth sounded just as good as eating Carlos' ass, so Casey did as he was told. He knelt on the bed, straddling Richard's body, and Carlos held Casey's waist while he swallowed his mouth-stretcher in a single gulp, and began to suck profoundly, sucking out a mouthful of cum about the same time he blew his own load inside Richard.

"Man, that tasted good," Carlos said.

"Hey, I gotta come now," Richard said. How about riding my cock, Carlos?"

"I got a better idea," Carlos said. "Lay on your back here, Casey, and get those legs up. I guess I've got time to deliver a quick second topping. And Richard, you can fuck me while I fuck him."

It took Carlos quite a while before he blew his load inside Casey, considerably less time than it took for Richard to come inside the boy's driving ass. Richard had often fucked someone who was fucking someone else, and it was tricky, but he had mastered the rhythm needed to allow for general satisfaction to all parties. Certainly by the time Carlos exploded his second load inside Casey, all were thoroughly satisfied.

As Carlos was dressing to leave, he exacted a promise from Casey that he would not tell Thom Nelson about their meeting. Casey assured Carlos he would say nothing when he saw Thom at school. Richard gave Carlos fifty dollars for the pizza, which basically included something like a forty-dollar tip, but Richard wanted to be sure the boy knew he appreciated the extra toppings he had delivered.

While they were eating their pizza, Richard asked Casey if he knew from experience that Carlos' boyfriend, Thom Nelson, was gay. Richard replied, "I started to suspect it when he propositioned me in the bathroom at school, and sucked me off, but I was almost sure after the first couple of times we fucked each other. He's on the basketball team. There are several gay guys on the basketball team, but Thom is by far the cutest. I know the basketball coach thinks so, anyway — he and Thom have been fucking each other for at least two years. Funny about Thom having my picture in his bedroom, 'cause he told me the coach has my picture in his bedroom. I don't know where either of 'em got it — out of the annual, I guess. I don't suppose Carlos knows about Thom and the coach, or Thom and me. Do you ever fuck him?"

"Oh, sure," Richard said, "when he has time — but if he doesn't, he almost always has time to give me a quick blowjob after he fucks me."

Changing the subject, Casey confessed that he had been a little bit hurt that Gundo had chosen Richard to double within his final show. "I can sure as hell see why he wanted it to be with you, but he had paid so much attention to me right up until then, I guess I thought ... well, anyway, I was disappointed. But after watching you and him on stage, I think he made the right choice. I wouldn't have been nearly as good a partner as you were."

"Well, Gundo fucked me the first day he was here, in the lounge," Richard said, "and after he blew his load, I turned him around and fucked the hell out of him. I think it surprised him — I know it surprised all the guys in the lounge — but he loved it. I guess it impressed him, too, 'cause later that day, when I was coming off stage after my show, he was waiting there, and asked me if I would double with him for his last show on his last day. With a dick like Gundo's, who wouldn't say yes? Anyway, you came along a day or so later, and once I got a look at you, I figured Gundo would change his mind and ask you to double— hell, I would have, if I'd been him. But he still wanted me, and I was flattered—and Jesus, it was fun. You know, sometimes the house dancers do doubles without the porn star being involved. I'd love to double with you some time. Whaddya think? I doubled with Adam about two weeks ago."

"Adam? The straight guy with the fantastic body?"

"Yeah, him. I guess he might really be kinda straight, since he wouldn't let me fuck him—but he sucked me off and spit my cum on my asshole to lube me up before he ate it out and then fucked me. The crowd went fuckin' nuts."

Casey promised to double with Richard any time he wanted.

They fucked a little bit more, but Casey had to get home. It was a school night, and his father already thought he was staying out too late. And that reminded him of the "big talk" he and his dad were going to have. He didn't know if he was dreading it or looking forward to it. Certainly he was curious about it.

Richard was flying to Amarillo, Texas the next day for a two-nighter with a client there. "He's an older guy, but he has this really young lover, and he wants to videotape me having sex with the kid in a couple of scenes—like a homemade porn video. And then the second night he's having eight or ten of his friends in, and all of 'em are gonna gang-bang me."

"Jesus," Casey said, "I don't know if that sounds exciting or horrible."

"Sounds exciting to me," Richard grinned. "Now get outta here, or I'll personally gang-bang you, and I won't have enough cum left to fuck the kid tomorrow night."

"I can't see you running outta cum any time soon," Casey said.

It had been a helluva night, and if earlier in the day Casey had wondered if he was falling *in love* with Richard, he was almost positive he was as he boarded the Divisadero bus and headed for home. Tomorrow night he'd be dancing at the T 'n B, and there'd be a new porn star guest. He didn't know who it was going to be—if Eddie had told them, he had missed it—but he knew that whoever it was, he was going to have to be unbelievably hot to keep him from thinking of his gorgeous lover fucking that lucky kid back in Amarillo. And how was he going to feel the next night, when eight or ten complete strangers were going to be fucking his lover?

A couple of weeks after Dave Cotter became the first boy to fuck him, Casey heard that Dave was also fucking someone else. The feeling of hurt and emptiness he had experienced when he discovered that had been offset by the fact that at the moment he learned of it, he was, himself, fucking the 'other' boy that Dave was giving it to. That was as close to jealousy as he had come. So, he'd never been really jealous before, but he'd never had a lover before. Now he did.

His lover! Richard!

6.

A Tale of Two Daddies

Bill Lowe had a problem. It wasn't that his son was gay; that only bothered him insofar as it meant that the boy's life would undoubtedly be more complicated than it might be if he were straight—not that straight life was all that goddamned simple, judging by his experience. He himself was gay, always had been, and couldn't honestly say he regretted it. He had tried the straight life for over fifteen years, and also he couldn't honestly say he regretted that—Casey was the happy result of his heterosexual union, and he adored the boy. He knew he should be appalled that Casey was dancing naked in a theatre, and masturbating for the delectation of a bunch of—probably—dirty old men, and he suspected that would not be as far as his appearance there would go.

But he wasn't appalled—quite the contrary.

Watching Race Rivera fucking with 'Richard' on the stage of the *Top 'n Bottom* had excited him greatly, even though he had come to the theatre concerned about what his son might be up to. He had not developed a hard-on when his son performed; he admired his son's appearance and great sexual power, but it didn't turn him on (thankfully, he thought to himself). However, Steve Renard's body and his hungry use of a dildo to fuck himself had excited Bill tremendously, and like the man sitting next to him, he had his pants open and was masturbating when Race Rivera came around to give him a very close-up view of his mighty cock. Race had reached down and groped Bill's cock; he said, "Fantastic dick, man," and with his other hand he pressed the tip of his own prick against Bill's lips, which opened wide to permit Race to fuck his mouth for what Bill regarded as a tragically short period—only three or four thrusts before the handsome stud moved on to the next man. He only saw Richard from a considerable distance, but it was obvious he was both gorgeous and a virtuoso fuck machine. Although Bill thought Richard was very handsome, and extremely sexy, he wondered why Race had chosen him over his son for the double fuck on stage; he thought Casey was better looking, better built, and even better hung—and if Casey's solo show was any indication, he was probably as great a stud as Richard. What am I—a Jewish mother? he asked himself, inwardly laughing in spite of the seriousness of the situation.

It seemed inevitable that if Casey continued working at the theatre, sooner or later he would be up there on stage, fucking and getting fucked by some other porn star. Intellectually, he knew that prospect should horrify him, but as a highly sexed, very active gay man, he had to admit that emotionally, he was proud that Casey was so handsome, so accomplished, and so desirable.

What Bill was concerned with was Casey's future, and his safety— both physical and emotional.

Bill Lowe was born in San Diego in 1940, and grew up there—a sailor town, with a generous sprinkling of Marines mixed in. Long before he had his first orgasm, or became sexually active, the sight of swaggering sailors in their tight uniforms or the controlled and serious-looking Marines excited him. He knew he was attracted to those sailors and Marines long before he began to understand what that attraction meant, and when his friends began fantasizing about girls, he began wanting to see those sailors and Marines naked, to see their bare dicks hard and watch those sailor asses roll and swagger without being concealed by uniforms. When his friends began to pass around pictures of men and women having sex, he longed to see pictures where it was other men sucking those cocks, and other men being penetrated by those hard dicks. With the full onset of puberty, he began dreaming about sucking dick and fucking ass, and getting sucked and fucked in return. At the same time, he began to realize that he was unusually gifted in the cock department: at mutual jack-off sessions, his dick was always by far the biggest, and few of his friends shot bigger loads than he, or blew them more frequently. The blond Bill Lowe was not only gorgeous, he was sexy as well, and all the girls in his class were flocking around him, which did not interest him. And as his reputation as the best-hung king of the circle-jerk grew, he found that other boys whose fantasies were similar to his, were irresistibly drawn to him for fulfillment—and he took complete advantage of that attraction. Long before most of his friends got laid the first time, Bill was having full-blown sex with a variety of other boys.

By his senior year in high school Bill graduated from sex with his peers, to an amazingly active sex life with those sailors and Marines he had desired for years.

In the spring of his senior year in high school his father came into his bedroom unexpectedly, and found Bill kneeling naked on the bed, with his best friend, equally naked, kneeling behind him with his face buried between his son's buttocks. Had Bill's father entered only a few minutes later, he would have found his son fucking the boy—as he had done many times by then. Mr. Lowe unceremoniously threw his son out and, as he said, 'washed his hands of him.' When many years later, his wife surprised Bill in a similar situation, the irony was not lost on him.

Bill went to live with his best friend until his graduation. Since there was no extra bedroom in his friend's house, Bill said he did not mind sharing his friend's bed. The arrangement provided a great deal of fun for both of the boys.

He graduated shortly before his eighteenth birthday, and joined the Navy for a 'Minority Enlistment,' which would end with his twenty-first birthday. The closeness of living in Boot Camp and lack of freedom kept his sexual exploits relatively restrained—for him—but he still managed to score enough dick and ass to stay fairly well satisfied.

Upon graduation from Boot Camp, he was assigned to the aircraft carrier *Lexington*, where he stayed for the remainder of his enlistment. The ship was based in San Diego that entire time, although she made several Far East deployments while Bill was a member of her crew. The three-or-so years he was assigned to the ship marked a period of wonderful, freewheeling sex, bookended by an unforgettable first night aboard, and an equally memorable last night there.

During the years of his service, Bill formed many ongoing and easygoing relationships with sex partners, but only one romantic attachment, and that was with Tony Lopez, a sailor he met the first day he came aboard. Tony set Bill's dick tingling immediately because he was so handsome and sexy. He was a ridiculously good-looking Latino from Los Angeles, only one year older than Bill, who slept in the bunk above the one Bill had been assigned, the bottom in a stack of four. That first night, Bill thought about the gorgeous Tony, lying less than two feet above him, and he got so horny he began to jack off— surreptitiously, he thought, but he apparently got sufficiently active that Tony's head popped into view from above and he whispered, "You just tryin' to make me horny?"

"Sorry," Bill whispered back, "I'm just horny myself."

"I can give you some help, if you want."

"Here?" Bill asked, surprised, and a little bit apprehensive—but definitely interested.

"Roll over so you're facing the bulkhead," Tony said (a bulkhead, in Naval parlance, means the wall of a ship's compartment). Still stroking his cock, Bill rolled over as directed, and Tony's arm came down from above, between the bunk-frame and the bulkhead. His hand closed over Bill's cock, and Bill heard a gasp. Then the hand was taken away, and Tony climbed out of his bunk to kneel next to Bill. "Jesus, how big is this thing?" he whispered, as he again took hold of Bill's prick and stroked it. With his other he took hold of one of Bill's hands and guided it to his own prick, protruding from his skivvies, his boxer-shorts underwear. It was Bill's turn to gasp: Tony's cock was almost as big as his own, and wonderfully fat and hard. "If you want it, follow me," Tony said.

Tony stood and began to walk to a passageway leading from their berthing compartment. He apparently assumed Casey would follow him; it was a reasonable assumption—so far no one had ever declined when he had made that same offer. Casey was more than merely interested, of course, and he climbed out of his bunk, tucking his cock into his skivvies with considerable difficulty, and following the Latino stud. "In here," Tony whispered as he unlocked a door, using a key hanging next to his 'dog tags' on a chain around his neck. Casey followed him through the door and Tony closed it behind them.

Tony switched on the light, revealing a room apparently used as storage for linens and bedding—towels, pillows, blankets, bedcovers and the like. A piece of cardboard was taped over the grillwork on the door, so no light would be visible from the passageway outside. What else was revealed was Tony's prick—standing straight out from the flap in his skivvies; apparently he hadn't bothered to stuff it back in while they walked to the storage room. And, in truth, it would be a shame to conceal such a beautiful thing at any time. It wasn't quite as long as Bill's stunning ten inches, but it appeared to be at least nine—and it was fat and beautifully formed.

Seeing Bill goggle at the sight of his prick, Tony whispered, "Like what you see?"

Wrapping a hand over Tony's endowment, Bill replied, "I love what I see," whispering as Tony had, clearly understanding that they needed to keep their voices down to avoid detection. While Bill stroked Tony's prick, Tony put his hand behind Bill's head and drew it in close so they could kiss. It was a long kiss, sweet when they first embraced, but growing more passionate as they began to fondle each other. Each slipped a hand in the back of the other's skivvies to caress his ass. Tony's ass was rounded, firm, and satin-smooth to Bill's admiring touch, and it undulated enticingly while Tony humped it as he fucked Bill's fist. At the same time, Tony stroked the outline of Bill's cock, pressing against the tightly stretched constraints of his skivvies.

Breaking their kiss, Tony moved his head down to suck Bill's nipples, then knelt in front of him. He kissed Bill's stomach as he unsnapped the blond's skivvies. He leaned back and sat on his heels as he slowly—reverently—pulled Bill's undershorts down to the deck. Bill's cock was raging hard when it cleared the waistband, and it bobbed up forcefully, causing Tony to whistle quietly and breathe, "Jackpot!" just before he leaned forward and opened his mouth very wide to admit it. It was clear the Latino beauty was no novice; his lips slowly traveled the entire length of Bill's enormous shaft and nestled in his pubic hair as he licked the challenging fat shaft inside his mouth, exerting suction all the time. Bill held Tony's head in his hands and started to fuck his mouth as Tony increased the suction and murmured his pleasure.

After only a few minutes, Tony rose. He unsnapped his own skivvies, and stepped out of them. Bill quickly fell to his knees and engulfed Tony's beautiful monster in his mouth with one swoop as he began to suck profoundly. Tony put his hands on his ass and leaned back, projecting his pelvis outward as he humped into Bill's mouth to counter each forward dive Bill's lips made down his cock. Tony whispered, "Jesus, baby, you can really suck dick!"

Bill relinquished Tony's cock for just a moment as he grinned up at the stud and whispered, "You're pretty fuckin' good at it yourself. And who wouldn't want to suck a beautiful monster like this?" Then he returned to his work.

After reveling in Bill's masterful blowjob for a few more minutes, Tony said, "Let's get on the deck so we can sixty-nine." He spread a couple of blankets out on the steel deck, and they lay down on them end-to-end as they began to feast on each other.

Tony abandoned Bill's dick momentarily in order to eat his ass, which brought a moan of pleasure from Bill. Tony said, "I sure hope you like taking it up the ass." Bill assured Tony he liked nothing better, and proceeded to feed on Tony's twitching asshole, eliciting a confession that the Latino beauty was also addicted to getting fucked, and that he would be particularly delighted to play host to a colossal dick like Bill's—was, in fact, eager to welcome that very cock as soon as Bill could ram it inside him.

Within seconds, Bill had Tony kneeling before him, with his cock firmly planted inside the Latino stud, who writhed and humped his ass around it while Bill hammered away like a pile driver until he exploded a huge load. Tony was delirious with happiness, and lost no time in throwing Bill to his back, so he could return the favor. With Bill's legs resting on his shoulders, Tony fucked like a maniac until the last moment, when he pulled his dick out and spewed thick ropes of cum all over Bill's face and into his open mouth. Tony licked up what cum Bill couldn't reach with his tongue, and spit it into Bill's mouth as he grinned, "Welcome aboard, sailor!" Then he shoved his cock back inside Bill and did it all over again—but this time shooting his load deep inside Bill's hungry ass. As Bill soon came to learn, Tony Lopez always blew two loads at the beginning of a sex session, usually without taking a break of any kind—and a brief break frequently yielded a third.

The two horny sailors lay there necking for some time, trading compliments for each other's looks, dicks, asses, and sexual power. Tony said that as far as looks, dick, and fucking ability were concerned, Bill was the answer to his dreams. Bill assured him he'd be happy to keep fulfilling the stud's dreams. He grinned, "But you don't like my ass?"

Tony assured Bill his ass was absolutely choice, that he had loved eating it and fucking it, and was looking forward to doing so again and again and again. He told Bill that a young sailor had just shipped aboard who had the roundest, cutest, most edible and fuckable ass he had ever seen. "I've eaten it and fucked it, so I know what I'm talking about." He kissed Bill and added, "I'll introduce you to him." He filled Bill in on what sexual activity he might expect while he was aboard the *Lexington*.

Since Tony worked in the Ship's Laundry, one of his duties was stocking the half-dozen linen supply lockers around the ship, so he carried a key that fit all of them. As Bill had just learned, those lockers provided opportunities for privacy in making love—a rare commodity aboard a ship. Tony promised to get a key for Bill to use—in exchange for a promise to keep using a locker with him, the way they had just used the one they were in.

"The showers are a great place to make contacts," Tony said, "but it's pretty dangerous to do too much there; you can get caught. I got caught getting a blowjob in the shower once, but fortunately the guy who caught us was willing to keep his mouth shut after he opened it wide enough to suck me off, too. You could keep guard for me, or I could keep guard for you while we were getting it on in the shower with some other guy, but that can be pretty hard to arrange. But anyway, even if you don't get to suck or fuck in the shower, you can check out who's got a hot body or a big dick. You can watch how they look at you, or talk dirty with 'em, and you can usually tell if they're interested in getting together with you someplace else. If they grope you or get a hard-on and don't hide it from you, you can be sure they're interested. The guy who runs the hobby shop at night closes it up at twenty-two hundred," Tony continued, "and every night he has sex with at least one guy after he locks up—usually more than one, from what I understand. And there's a lot of action in the gun tubs when the weather is right."

'Gun tubs' are locations aboard a ship where certain classes of guns are fixed, fenced in by a circular steel enclosure about four feet high. On the *Lexington*, there were twelve gun tubs located along both sides of the ship and on the fantail—the rearmost part of the ship— below the level of the flight deck, housing batteries of 5-inch and 40-millimeter guns.

"There's not a lot of room in a gun tub," Tony explained, "It's hard to find a place to lie down, but you can kneel in front of somebody to suck 'im off. Mostly, guys stand up to fuck each other, since you can bend over and rest your belly on a seat, and be at about the right level to get fucked, or get your ass eaten. Sometimes there'll be eight or ten guys in a single gun tub on a warm night—especially out at sea. See, there're a lot of guys who are straight—or think they are—who want to fuck butt or get a blowjob when they're out to sea, with their girlfriends or wives back ashore. Funny how much some of those straight guys like a tongue up the ass, though—get to whimperin' like a girl—and I've eaten out quite a few of 'em out who decided they wanted something bigger than a tongue in there—like nine inches of fat dick."

"And I'll bet you were happy to give it to 'em," Bill laughed.

"Oh, yeah," Tony said, "fucked practically every one of 'em."

When Bill wondered about the danger of being caught having sex in the gun tubs, Tony went on to explain that he had never encountered any Marines on watch around them," Marines acted as sentries throughout the ship. "The Marines have gotta know about what goes on," Tony said. "God knows I've screwed enough of 'em there." He laughed, "Anyway, from what I know of Marines, they wouldn't want to break up the parties in the gun tubs, knowing there's always plenty of sailor dick on hand, anxious to fuck jarhead butt." (Marines were universally known as 'jarheads' as well.)

It was late, and they returned to their bunks. Just before Bill drifted off to sleep, Tony's hand came down from above and crept into his skivvies to fondle and stroke his cock. Bill reached up to find that Tony was lying so that his cock hung down over the side of his cot, providing Bill the opportunity to salute it and 'say good night' the way Tony was. That began a tradition that went on almost every night until Tony left the ship, three years later. Occasionally, one of them gave the other a full hand-job that way, masturbating him all the way to orgasm, in which case the one being jacked off blew his load into his palm, and reached down (Tony), or up (Bill) to feed his fuckbuddy a late-night, going-to-sleep snack.

Bill's relationship with Tony was an ongoing joy for both of them. They not only fucked and sucked each other regularly, they spent countless hours in mutual kissing, trading endearments, and growing genuinely fond of each other. Each told the other, truthfully, that he loved him, and although it was definitely an ongoing romance, neither fell *in love* with the other—they were far too busy in the excitement of sex with a variety of shipmates and shoreside fuck partners.

It was not long before Bill's golden good looks and outstandingly huge prick were noticed by his shipmates, many of whom subsequently managed to shower at the same time as he. Bill was able to get in some very limited sucking and fucking in the shower, usually with Tony standing guard, but mostly it was a place he could make contacts to meet his shipmates elsewhere for sex—both onboard and ashore. He always had at least one of them along when he went on liberty, hoping to have sex with him without the dampening furtiveness that on-board sex entailed. Often two or three went on liberty with him, with the same goal in mind, and none of his liberty companions were ever disappointed.

He was especially popular with the Marine detachment aboard ship. Like any section of the ship's crew, men transferred in and out of the unit regularly, but at any given time, Bill would have fucked at least half of the detachment. Usually, when Bill went on liberty with a Marine, a few other Marines joined them. For some reason, the Marines seemed to take special delight in having others of their number watch while they took it up the ass—especially if they got fucked by a really big dick. But, stranger still, they didn't want to be seen getting fucked by another Marine. Even though they tended to look down on sailors as inferior beings, they particularly liked to get fucked by them if a fellow Marine was on hand to watch. Bill figured it was some screwed-up masochistic tendency on the Marines' part, where they could show each other how tough they were, and how much punishment they could take. The *Lexington* Marines mostly agreed that the handsome, golden-blond sailor Bill Lowe had more cock to give them than any of their other regular fuck-mates—and really big cock was what they all seemed to crave. God knows, a cock like Bill's can deal out punishment—but of the most enjoyable kind!

When Bill was ashore, in his uniform and unaccompanied, other servicemen and civilians often tried to pick him up, but unless he found them sexy for some reason, he usually resisted their blandishments. He got paid very little as a sailor, but he didn't actually need much money. When money ran out, however, he occasionally acceded to propositions from reasonably attractive civilians or servicemen. He could easily get twenty dollars or more to allow someone to give him a stand-up blowjob in an alley, a men's room, or a secluded section of Balboa Park. Going to a prospect's hotel, where Bill's prodigious equipment could be given free rein, he usually got a hundred dollars to fuck the 'client' or swap blowjobs with him—but if they wanted to fuck him back, and were either well-hung or attractive, he was usually happy to grant them access to his hungry ass without further charge.

Many of his 'civilian' clients were actually sailors and Marines in civilian clothes, usually officers who had an itch for enlisted dick. Without knowing it, Bill once fucked a Rear Admiral who picked him up in the lobby of the El Cortez Hotel. He was equally unaware that he had fucked several junior officers in the anonymity of the gun tubs, officers who kept enlisted uniforms hidden away to wear when they craved some exciting action with enlisted men.

Friends who are also shipmates are very, very close friends—whether or not that friendship includes sex, as it did with Tony and Bill. And yet, oddly enough, when shipmates are transferred to assignments that separate them, the friendship often stops at that point. Shipmates usually swear they will keep in touch, but in fact, few manage to do so, in spite of the best intentions. It is simply a fact of life in the military service, and does not mean the closeness that the status of 'shipmates' brought about was any less meaningful at the time of that association. So it was with Tony and Bill.

Tony was separated from the Navy when Bill still had six months remaining on his enlistment. Bill got a 72-hour liberty beginning the day Tony left the ship, and they rented a nice hotel room for the next three days—nothing like the cheap ones they had rented on regular liberties when they wanted to expand their usual sexual twosome into a threesome or even a foursome or, occasionally, a fivesome. They only left the room for meals during the entire time, and spent their last three days together wisely: they had sex almost constantly. After ducking into the men's room at the railroad station for a goodbye kiss, Tony whispered "I love you" to Bill and boarded the train for Los Angeles. Bill returned to the *Lexington* alone.

Bill was exhausted as he boarded the liberty boat to go out to North Island, where his ship was moored. For several days, any time he tried to whistle, he found he couldn't—his lips were so stretched or tired from three days and nights of kissing Tony almost non-stop, and sucking the Latino beauty's fat prick for gloriously long stretches, that his pucker needed time for recuperation.

A new sailor was assigned Tony's old bunk after two days, but he didn't interest Bill sexually He did seem to be a nice guy, however. In particular, Bill missed Tony's hand coming down from the bunk above him to squeeze his dick as a loving way to say good night, as it had for almost three years, and he missed being able to reach up and tender the same salute to his shipmate/lover.

They exchanged occasional letters at first, but their correspondence dried up within a few months. Bill had no way of knowing, nor would he ever learn, that in a year or so, Tony Lopez would sire a son who would become the famous porn star Race Rivera, the one he would watch fucking on stage the night he would also see his own son perform a sex act for the same audience. In fiction, such a coincidence would be hard for the reader to accept, but since this is a factual account, it simply reports the real-life peculiarity.

For some reason, sex didn't seem to be as much fun for Bill with Tony gone. He did far more than simply go through the motions, of course. He still had sex at least three or four times a week, but no one he fucked or sucked with meant anything to him, as Tony had. In spite of the exciting sex life he enjoyed, he began to look forward to leaving the Navy and getting on with his future—as a civilian.

He had managed to save a considerable amount of the money he had earned by allowing men to suck him off or for going to their homes or hotel rooms for more intense sexual activity

He knew that all that activity had been nothing but prostitution, but he never felt the slightest pang of guilt over the fact. He was comforted by the knowledge that he never acceded to requests for sex from anyone he didn't find at least reasonably attractive. He knew other sailors who would fuck any guy, or let any guy blow them who could come up with the money. At any rate, he had his nest egg, and since he was now entitled to educational assistance through the "G.I. Bill," he would be able to go to college.

Architecture had always appealed to Bill, for some reason, and he applied to a number of good schools for acceptance into that field of study. The best of those schools that accepted him were Clemson College, in South Carolina, and Georgia Tech, in Atlanta. Clemson was located in a tiny town, and Bill assumed (rightly) that he would have only limited opportunity for a rewarding sex life there, so he opted for Georgia Tech and the urban environs of Atlanta—where there had to be a plenty of available dick and a rich supply of hungry butts waiting for a gay ex-swabbie with a ten-inch dick.

His last night aboard the *Lexington*, the end of his last full day in the Navy, Bill decided to turn in early; the next day was going to be a long one, and his plane for Atlanta left at ten in the morning. Just as he was getting ready to undress and hit the rack, he heard someone ask, "Which one is Lowe?" and someone answered, "Over there." In a moment, a very large Marine Master Sergeant appeared and asked, "You Lowe?"

"That's me," Bill said. The Marine said nothing further, but beckoned him to follow as he headed for the forward hatch. Curious, Bill followed, wondering what he had done.

Just inside the passageway, the Marine stopped Bill with a hand to his chest, and said, simply, and without any preamble, "I hear you like big dick and a tight asshole, and they say you got a big one too, and a sweet little ass."

At about 6'5" tall, with a chest around two axe-handles wide, the Marine dwarfed Bill Lowe. He was older—probably in his late thirties—but his close-fitting uniform showed he was in perfect physical shape. Given the sergeant's rank, age, size, and the directness of his question, Bill was very slightly apprehensive, but he was much more aroused than he was alarmed. The man was not only imposing, he was also quite attractive, and seemed to exude the kind of ultra-masculinity that makes gay men's hearts flutter. Bill couldn't look the Marine 'straight in the eye,' as they say, since he was so much shorter, but he looked up at him and simply said, "You heard right."

The Marine smiled grimly, and said, "I'm your man."

Taking hold of one of Bill's hands, the Marine moved it down to his crotch, where an enormous tube of firm flesh snaked down the left side of his trousers. It wasn't hard, although it began to stir and grow somewhat as Bill held it and stroked, but given its size when flaccid, it promised to be a mouth-stretching, ass-reaming monster of incomparable proportions. "You can tell; I wasn't lyin' about the big dick," he said, "and if you wanna check out the part about the tight asshole, meet me up on deck, and I'll prove it to you."

Bill still carried the key to the linen lockers. He hadn't turned it in as he saw to the myriad of details his separation from the Navy entailed, since it had never been officially issued to him. Normally, he would have taken the Marine stud to one of them, but it was a beautiful, hot August night and the prospect of *al fresco* lovemaking, in full view of his home town before he left it—possibly for good—sounded romantic as well as exciting. He agreed to meet the Marine, whose name he never learned, at the fantail railing, one deck below the flight deck, at eleven thirty—well after 'lights out.'

In hot weather, when below-decks ventilation was a problem, many of the crew carried blankets and pillows up to the flight deck and other open-air parts of the ship to sleep under the stars, wearing only their skivvies; officers were never identified among those seen sleeping in those open areas—presumably, they had better ventilation in 'Officers' Country'. Bill knew that there would be hundreds of sailors topside that night who would be clad only in skivvies when he went up to meet the Marine, so he knew he wouldn't look out of place dressed the same way, and he was glad to be almost naked and ready to make love.

The only illumination at the fantail was from the very bright moon and the distant lights of the city of San Diego, but although there were quite a few sailors at the railing—mostly in pairs, smoking or talking, or clearly making love, Bill had no trouble spotting the horny Marine in the dim light: he was the giant leaning against the railing alone, also clad only in his skivvies, his bare arms, chest and thighs making him look like a much taller Steve Reeves—the extremely muscular stud named "Mr. Universe" in 1950, who soon after that played Hercules in a well-know series of movies. Bill's heart was beating very rapidly as he approached the statuesque sergeant, and he felt something like a small child reporting to the teacher as he looked up and said, "I'm here." The dizzying prospect of being held in those massive arms, pressed against that stupendous chest, made even the ultra-masculine Bill's voice quiver slightly.

The Marine was backlit, so Bill couldn't tell if he smiled, but his voice sounded like he did when he said, "I'm glad," and wrapped his huge arms around Bill, pulling him close and bending his head down as Bill raised his to receive a long, very tender kiss.

Bill was surprised, and very pleased to receive the kiss. A few of the Marines he had sex with had never kissed him, no matter how extensive their sex play became, even the ones who eagerly sucked his cock, swallowed his cum, and took his monster prick up their asses—of course, virtually every Marine he had gone to bed with had done all those things. Quite a number of others had resisted kissing until they were fully impaled on Bill's cock, taking the kind of fierce thrusts only a stud hung like Bill could give them. The rest of them—perhaps the majority, actually—were as eager to kiss with him as they were to fuck or suck with him. Still, Bill was pleased to discover that the breathtaking Marine holding him in his arms that night was one who was clearly open to making love, not just fucking.

The feeling that suffused Bill was one he had never experienced with another man. No man who had embraced him had been so tall, so muscular, so wide, so potentially exciting. He felt almost like a child—

not really daunted by the Marine's awesome proportions, but somehow feeling safe and protected. He felt wonderfully vulnerable, pressed tightly against the most colossal chest he had ever encountered, held there by muscular arms roughly the same girth as his own legs. He was literally in the Marine's arms, but he also knew he was figuratively in his hands; at that moment he was willing to submit to anything this glorious giant wanted to do with him, or to him.

Bill was not only willing, but extremely eager to submit to what the Marine made it perfectly clear he wanted when he put a hand in the back of Bill's skivvies, fondling him and murmuring "Sweet ass" into his mouth, and then gradually insinuating a huge finger inside him. Bill's ass began to undulate and work the finger, and the Marine responded by gently driving it in and out as far as it would go. The Marine stopped kissing to whisper, "You want me to fuck you?"

"More than anything I know," Bill replied. He had managed to extricate the Marine's prick from his skivvies as they kissed, and it grew as he stroked it until it promised to be the high-water mark in Bill's vast experience with pricks. His own cock was still inside his skivvies, but it was throbbing painfully, needing release. He unsnapped his skivvies and let them drop to his feet as he took their two dicks in one hand and stroked them together—not an easy task for one hand, given the amount of engorged flesh it encompassed.

"Can you take it all?" the Marine asked. Bill kissed him fervently, and promised to take every inch he was being offered. "I just hope I can take all of this," the Marine added as he fondled Bill's cock, having released him from his embrace in order to do so. Then he sank to his knees and easily deep-throated Bill's dick. Bill held the Marine's head in his hands while he fucked his face and the Marine provided the kind of licking and suction that were the hallmarks of a first-class cocksucker. After a few minutes, he rose and kissed Bill, "Yeah, if I can take it down my throat, I can take it up the butt—and I'm really looking forward to that." He was no longer backlit, and Bill could see he was smiling as he said it—and looking very handsome, too. "You wanna try the same test on me?"

As he knelt, Bill kicked off his skivvies and dragged the Marine's down to his ankles so that he could step out of them. The cock throbbing at his lips looked unbelievably huge: it was an inch or so longer than Bill's extremely impressive ten inches, and quite a bit larger in girth as well. He opened his lips wide as he began to take it in his mouth, and had to stretch them as far as he could before the cock-head passed inside. He instinctively knew that whistling was going to be out of the question again, for at least a few days!

Bill hadn't yet met a cock he couldn't take all the way down his throat—although a few of them had taken some practice before he could master them. The Marine's monster meat finally made him 'come a cropper.' Try as he might, he gagged with the last inch of dick still not inside his mouth. The Marine told Bill he was doing a fine job, that so far he had only met one guy who could deep-throat him, although something like a thousand or so had tried. Bill moved his lips a couple of inches up the fat cock so there would be room in his mouth for the Marine to fuck it, which he did for several minutes before raising Bill to his feet and saying, "Gotta fuck that pretty ass. Hope you can take all of it that way."

Bending over and bracing himself on the railing, facing the harbor, Bill gasped, "Yeah! Give it to me."

"Shit," the Marine said, "I forgot the Vaseline."

"Here," said a sailor standing nearby, wearing nothing but a white hat and a hard-on, stepping closer and offering a jar of the lubricant. Neither Bill nor the Marine had been aware of it, but several of the other sailors and (presumably) Marines had left off their lovemaking and gathered to watch the giant muscleman fuck the cute blond. Both Bill and his partner were too horny to care if they were being watched, and continued as if they were alone, although the Marine thanked the sailor who proffered the Vaseline, dipping into it and slathering it on his dick and Bill's asshole as he said, "Hang around, we'll need more later." Poised to enter Bill, the Marine asked, "Ready?" as he began to press his cock-head against the hungry sailor's ass.

"Give it to me hard!" Bill gasped, and pressed his ass backward as he began to wriggle it around the fat shaft starting to enter him.

The Marine had long before stopped slamming his cock all the way to the hilt when he began to fuck an ass. He had too often sufficiently hurt someone so that it spoiled the fuck—or the beginning of it anyway—so he pressed steadily into Bill's undulating chute while Bill moaned and gasped in pleasure, without calling a halt until the Marine had his entire cock buried inside. "You okay?" he asked.

"Never better," Bill cried. "Now just fuck the hell out of me."

And the Marine began a frantic, epic, unforgettable screwing such as Bill could not remember having been given before. Hanging onto the steel railing, he looked out at the water of the harbor, glistening with moonlight and the reflection of the colorful lights of San Diego, from Point Loma up into the hills behind the city—a scene he had often contemplated quietly in off hours. Now he did not consider the beauty of the scene, romantic as it was. The Marine held Bill's waist as his huge body slammed against Bill's ass with brutally jarring force, over and over, endlessly pounding the hungry sailor's ass mercilessly, making his head actually flop up and down too much to allow him to focus on the scene even if he had not been delirious with lust. Finally, with a near scream of triumph, the Marine reached forward and grasped the railing on each side of Bill's body, pulling his own body violently in toward the railing, and forcing Bill's body upright, flat against the railing just as he erupted inside the ecstatic sailor. Bill threw his head back and echoed the Marine's cry of passion with an animal-like howl of equal force. They froze there, lit by the moonlight, and clearly visible to the dozen or so standing there watching, almost all of them masturbating as they did.

For several minutes, Bill and the Marine stayed still while their bodies gradually relaxed. The Marine backed out of Bill's ass and turned the sailor's body around to they could kiss. Bill raised his face so he could meet the Marine's as he bent his head down. Neither said a word; nothing needed to be said, as each was fully aware of the magnitude of the lovemaking they had just shared. Again, Bill was enfolded in those massive, protecting arms, and his face was pressed against the muscular roundness of the Marine's enormous breasts — and he glowed in the knowledge that this magnificent giant had filled him with his essence. They kissed for a very long, hushed time, until the Marine finally whispered, "I can feel how hard that big dick of yours is—and I want it really bad. I need it!"

Bill lowered his head even more so that he could lick and suck the Marine's succulent nipples while he caressed the powerful shoulders and arms. The Marine purred his satisfaction, tousling Bill's hair while he enjoyed the sailor's worship of his body. Then he again sank to his knees to take Bill's prick in his mouth and provide it with the same kind of reverent adulation. The Marine again showed he was a superb cocksucker, and Bill began to fuck his mouth, gently and lovingly at first, but soon his mood of quiet reverence morphed into an urgent need to fuck this raging satyr the way the satyr had fucked him.

"On your feet and bend over," he said roughly, pulling up on the Marine's shoulders, "Gonna fuck you now."

The Marine eagerly stood and bent over the railing. Bill knelt behind him and growled, "Gonna get this hot ass ready." He buried his face between the Marine's generous, muscular ass cheeks and began to feast.

The Marine thrashed about and bit his hand to mute the almost girlish squeals he could not help but utter as Bill's tongue writhed and danced inside him. Finally he gasped, "Stick your dick in there!"

Bill stood, and the jar of Vaseline was again extended by one of the admiring onlookers, Bill prepared himself and the Marine but found there was a problem: there was so much disparity in their relative height that as he stood behind the Marine, Bill found that only the tip of his prick reached its target comfortably. The Marine tried spreading or bending his legs enough to alleviate the problem, but both he and Bill knew instinctively that was not going to allow for a satisfactory fuck for either of them.

"Anybody got a blanket we can use," the Marine asked. "Right here, Sarge," one of the bystanders said, and stepped in to spread a blanket on the deck. "Thanks, Jonesy," the Marine replied, and lay on it, on his stomach, raising his ass and saying, "C'mon, Lowe, get that big dick in here where it belongs." Bill fell over the horny giant and positioned his cock. The Marine cried, "Do it!" and Bill shoved it inside in one fierce thrust, eliciting a gasp of pleasure from the Marine, who began to wriggle his ass around the monster prick filling it as Bill began to fuck in earnest.

While Bill was pounding his ass, the Marine gradually rose to his knees until he was on all fours, panting and groaning in ecstasy, his head hanging down and thrashing from side to side. Much of the time, Bill gripped the Marine's waist and pulled his body in toward him to meet each forward thrust, but he also rested his belly on the Marine's back and reached underneath him to play with his magnificent tits while he continued his fierce assault.

After he had knelt and taken Bill's savage fucking for nearly ten minutes, the Marine reared up on his knees and began stroking his enormous cock frantically. Bill continued to fuck and play with the Marine's tits with unabated enthusiasm, and in only a minute the Marine cried, "I'm coming!" As he did so, the bystander who had provided the blanket knelt in front of the Marine just in time to receive on his face the copious jets of cum that shot from the Marine's dick.

Within a few seconds, Bill threw his arms all the way around the Marine's waist and yelled, "I'm coming, too!" and blasted his load deep inside the ecstatic sergeant.

"Oh, baby, give me that big load," the Marine cried, "but don't stop fuckin' me—your dick is amazing."

Bill had frozen in place to deliver his cum, but he gradually returned to the profound jackhammer fuck he had been giving the Marine, and as he did so, the Marine again knelt on all fours to take it. Unlike his beloved Tony Lopez, who routinely delivered non-stop, back-to-back loads to those happy, lucky men who bottomed for him, Bill usually needed at least a bit of rest before blowing a second load. But tonight, many thoughts swirled around in his mind that made him unwilling to stop fucking the god-like stud, in spite of having already filled him with cum: this was his last night in the Navy, and he was fucking one of the most exciting men who had ever fucked him; the Marine continued to beg for more, and he was as talented a bottom as he was a top—a total joy to fuck; a dozen or so shipmates stood around urging him on and voicing appreciation for his technique; it was a beautiful, warm night, romantically lit by the lights of his home town, which he was leaving tomorrow; and he was saying goodbye to the *Lexington*, which had been a beneficial home for over three years, providing him with Tony's love and the hundred-or-so other shipmates who had shared their love with him on a more temporary basis.

It took another fifteen minutes before Bill's delirious fuck yielded its second payload, during which time quite a few more 'treasures' were produced by the spectators, most of whom managed to fuck and suck with each other while they continued to watch Bill and the Marine in awe. Those who weren't fucking or sucking were masturbating enthusiastically, and quite a few loads of cum splashed off the sergeant's back and Bill's ass while he was fucking. Bill finally produced his second load as he uttered a muted shout of triumph. The Marine sergeant was unable to cry out, since one of the bystanders was lying on his back in front of him, with his legs wrapped around the sergeant's neck and his prick buried completely in the sergeant's mouth.

Bill and the Sergeant stood and kissed for a long time, fondling each other lovingly. Still kissing the blond sailor, the sergeant grasped Bill's buttocks and picked him up, off the deck. Bill's arms went around the Marine's neck, and his legs around his waist as the sergeant used a hand to maneuver his cock back into Bill's asshole. Still holding the Marine's neck, Bill leaned back as far as he could, his head hanging down and flopping as the giant stud began to fuck him again. After a surprisingly short time, the Marine gasped, I'm gonna come, and began a series of short, fierce jabs into Bill's ass as Bill pulled himself inward and locked lips with the giant stud just as he began to blow his load. They kissed a long time, until Bill's legs gradually slipped from around the Marine's waist so that he was standing on the deck, and the Marine's cock wilted somewhat and slipped from Bill's ass. They continued to kiss while the sailor who had provided the Vaseline knelt behind Bill and sucked the Marine sergeant's cum from his ass.

When the Marine expressed his eagerness to repeat lovemaking with Bill, he was dismayed to learn that the sailor would be gone in the morning. "You're the best," the sergeant told him—high praise from one who was clearly, in Bill's opinion, 'the best' himself. However, both were accustomed to the transitory nature of military friendships and sexual relationships (some might call the latter 'romances'), and they parted without regret—but each with the fond memory of an unforgettable encounter.

Atlanta was already a major city in 1961, when Bill arrived there to begin his studies at Georgia Tech. Unfortunately, it wasn't crawling with tens of thousands of horny sailors and Marines, as San Diego had been. Or perhaps it was fortunate that sex wasn't so readily available to Bill; he needed to apply himself as he had never done before. Architecture was a tough major, a stern mistress, and he didn't have the luxury of devoting endless hours to the pursuit and consummation of his ravenous sexual appetites, as he had while he was in the Navy. Moreover, he had to work to help pay his expenses, and much of the time he could spare from schoolwork was devoted to the long hours he spent flipping burgers at The Varsity, a popular fast-food restaurant near the Tech campus.

If there were a significant number of other gay students on campus or in his dormitory, Bill wasn't aware of it, although he felt sure they must have been out there. He found a few to play with, but none of them as freewheeling and eager as his shipmates on the

Lexington had been. He found two active gay bars: *Mrs. P's* on Ponce de Leon Avenue, across from the huge Sears and Roebuck's building, catered to middle-aged and older men, although young gay men and hustlers who sought partners in that age range could be found there; and *The Cove*, on Monroe Drive, where the younger, mostly college-age gay crowd gathered. Bill drank very little, and did not smoke, so the gay bar scene did not appeal to him, although he occasionally dropped in to one when he was in real need of release — and, given his looks, he never had any trouble picking up attractive, willing partners. Gradually, however, the strong sex drive that had fueled his wild days in high school and the Navy was at least partially sublimated to his academic ambition.

In his Junior year, he worked on an architecture project with Faith Casey, a girl who decided Bill was the husband she had been looking for: handsome, good-natured and thoughtful, dedicated to his education, and not gay — or so she thought — like several others she had considered as husband material. Bill had never dated a girl regularly, much less fucked one, but when Faith pushed her agenda, he found himself dating her regularly — which was pleasant, because she was smart and fun — and eventually going to bed with her. When Faith discovered what a huge, extremely pleasant surprise hung between Bill's legs, her agenda went into overdrive, and by his senior year, Bill had impregnated Faith, married her, and in 1965 become father of the boy who bore his mother's maiden name as his own Christian name.

Taking his marital vows and fatherhood seriously, Bill was for some time reasonably faithful to his wife. His final years of architectural studies — a five-year-program — found him very busy. At the same time, Faith increasingly depended on him for seeing to the needs of little Casey, a duty he found very enjoyable — more rewarding than she, apparently. Then he joined an Atlanta architectural firm on graduation, and was busier than ever. He managed to appease Faith's fairly undemanding sexual appetite by fantasizing about his own hunger for sex with men while he made love to her. Fortunately, Faith greatly enjoyed anal sex, which helped feed her cravings and make his fantasies seem more real at the same time. Holding her waist and fucking her eager ass, Bill was able to pretend it was one of those hot young sailors he had so often serviced that way. Nonetheless, he could not completely ignore his true desires, and managed to conduct a discreet, secret sex life with a few men — mostly other married men who, like him, were far more interested in sucking dick and fucking butt than they were in making love to their wives.

In 1970, Bill received an offer to join a prominent San Francisco architect in his firm. San Francisco seemed far more attractive than Atlanta to both Bill and Faith—particularly Bill, who rightly suspected he could indulge his homosexual life more satisfactorily in a city becoming noted, whether rightly or not, as the gay capital of the country. They moved to 'The City' and found a modest house near the Presidio, but had to pay an immodest price for it. However, with Bill's new salary, they could afford it.

The opportunities for gay sex in San Francisco were vastly greater than they had been in Atlanta. At thirty years, Bill was still a very attractive man, and he was cruised constantly, often by men considerably younger than himself, and if they were attractive enough and circumstances permitted, he took advantage of offers to have sex. His huge dick and stunning sexual virtuosity always satisfied, and he went to bed with many who urged him, in vain, to engage in an ongoing relationship.

A turning point in Bill's sex life came in 1972, when the movie *Boys in the Sand* opened in San Francisco. It was a hardcore gay fuck film, starring the very hot young blond, Casey Donovan. Instead of being shown in one of the city's seedy porn movie theatres, the normal venue for erotic films, it played in a regular movie house, as it was doing in most major cities around the country. It became a cultural phenomenon, as the straight porn film *Deep Throat* would do very shortly after that. *Boys in the Sand* played to packed houses, attracting both women and men—almost as many women and straight men as it did gay men, for whom it was obviously intended. Many of the straight men who went to see Casey Donovan sucking and getting fucked did so because their wives or girlfriends wanted to see the film, but many of them went—alone or with a female companion—because they were secretly anxious to watch men getting it on with each other. It no doubt opened many closet doors.

The thing that set *Boys in the Sand* apart from other hardcore gay fuck films, aside from the fact that it played in regular movie houses, was that it featured really attractive actors, had a plot—admittedly a very sketchy one, at best—and had production values miles ahead of the typical porn film. It was even reviewed in the New York Times— the first and only pornographic movie to be so honored until then.

Faith Lowe was curious to see the fashionable new porn film, and Bill was delighted to escort her when it finally opened in San Francisco, since he was actually anxious to see it, and had planned to do so on his own at the earliest opportunity. Bill was blown away by the movie, and especially by Casey Donovan, but Faith thought it was disgusting, and insisted they leave halfway through the film. Fortunately, it was a rainy night, so Bill had his raincoat along to conceal the almost painful erection the movie had inspired in him. Faith was mildly surprised at the unusual ardor Bill showed that night when he fucked her. Their love life hadn't been very satisfying in the last couple of years, and she was seeing a very young man on the side who was clearly more interested in sex with her than her husband was. She was pleased with the fierce fuck Bill gave her that night, but while she would have preferred he fuck her pussy than her ass, that was obviously what Bill wanted, and she always enjoyed it, too. She had no idea that as Bill was slamming his huge cock into her, he was fucking the beautiful Casey Donovan's hot ass in his mind.

Bill left his office early the next afternoon, and went to see the movie all the way through. Even though it was a matinee, the theatre was crowded, and the audience was almost entirely male. Almost entirely gay, Bill thought.

He had never seen a porn film that could compare to *Boys in the Sand*, and he had never seen a porn actor as handsome and sexy as Casey Donovan. All the actors seemed to be as joyous as they were horny—especially appealing to Bill. The hard-on that had plagued him though the entire movie had not subsided in the least as he went up the aisle to file out of the theatre at the film's end. It was clearly tenting his pants, but he didn't care; the movie had made him extremely horny, and if some cute guy saw the size of his dick and was moved to proposition him, he was ready,

There was a bottleneck in the aisle at the exit door, and the line was moving very slowly. Two attractive young servicemen stood in line just ahead of him. They were not in uniform, but their shoes and haircuts gave them away—probably sailors or Marines, since soldiers and airmen were far less commonly seen in San Francisco. The taller of the two turned, and smiled at Bill. "Helluva movie, huh?"

"Best I've ever seen," Bill replied. "You guys Navy or Marines?"

"The haircuts give it away, right?" Bill nodded. "He's a swabbie and I'm a jarhead."

"Interservice cooperation?" Bill asked, smiling crookedly, obviously insinuating something more than that was probably going on.

"Yeah, we like to cooperate a lot, right, Owen?"

"Oh yeah," the sailor agreed, and extended his hand. "I'm Owen. This jarhead who has no manners is Haynes."

Bill introduced himself, and they shook hands all around. Haynes and Owen were both on liberty from the aircraft carrier *Ticonderoga*, which was visiting San Francisco.

Haynes, the Marine, had checked out Bill's box while Owen was speaking to him, and was impressed by the huge sausage hanging at least halfway to Bill's knee, obviously straining for release. Looking pointedly at it, he said, "I can see you enjoyed the hell out of the movie."

Owen, alerted to the Bill's erection, whistled lowly and added, "Yeah, that's a lot of enjoyment! You wouldn't be lookin' for someone to share the enjoyment, would ya?"

"Yeah, we've got a hotel room just around the corner," Haynes said, "and it's got a big bed—but only one."

Bill grinned, "I can't see why we'd need more than one. But who gets to play Casey Donovan?"

"We'll take turns," Owen said, "if that's okay with you."

Sounds great to me," Bill said. "Let's go."

As they walked to the hotel, Bill admitted he was an ex-swabbie, and described some of his sexual adventures while he was serving on the *Lexington*. Owens and Haynes remarked that action on the *Ticonderoga* was hot, but perhaps not as much so as Bill described. "But we're workin' on it," Owen laughed.

Once inside the hotel room, Owen began to grope Bill's cock through his pants, exclaiming appreciatively about its size, saying "You're gonna love this, Haynes." To Bill, he said, "Haynes likes 'em big. That's why he likes me. Right, baby?"

"No shit," Haynes laughed. He had begun to undress, but took time out to fondle Bill's cock and agreed he was going to enjoy it. He told Bill, as he folded Owen in his arms, "That's not the only reason I like this swabbie, though." They kissed lovingly, then Haynes added, in a bantering tone, "It's what he does with that big dick of his that I like."

"I hope you like to fuck butt, Bill," Owen said. "Of course it'd be mighty fine if you liked takin' it up the butt, too."

Bill began to strip, saying, "It's been way too long since I fucked any swabbie or jarhead butt, but I'm ready to make up for lost time. And nothing ever feels quite as good to me as jarhead or swabbie cock up my ass."

"I promise we're gonna make you feel good, then," Haynes laughed, as he left Owen's arms and kissed Bill.

They all finished undressing. Bill's erection had faded during their walk to the hotel, but had returned in force while the two fondled his cock, and when it sprang out of his shorts as he dropped them to the floor, Owen whistled in awe, saying only "Oh, yeah!" while Haynes sank to his knees and took it in his mouth—all of it. Bill had mentally echoed Owen's sentiment when he saw the sailor's own prick; it wasn't as big as his own, but it had to be at least nine inches.

With one hand, Bill held the head of the Marine who was sucking his dick so eagerly, and with the other he held out his hand for Owen's cock. The sailor moved in so that Bill could play with it and they could kiss, after which he suggested that Haynes stop sucking long enough so they could all move to the bed, which they did, whereupon Owen began sucking Bill's cock, while Bill sucked Haynes's, and Haynes sucked Owen's. Later, they reversed their daisy chain so that each had a chance to suck the other two for a time. While Haynes was sucking Bill's dick, Bill said, around Owen's cock, "You'd better stop, unless you want me to come. I'm getting near."

Haynes stopped sucking long enough to gasp, "Give me your load—then it'll take you longer to come when you fuck me," and returned to the excellent service he had been rendering Bill's cock.

Owen added, "Save some of his cum for me, Greg." It was the only time either the sailor or the Marine used the other's first name. In a minute, Bill cried out as his load filled Haynes' throat. Haynes murmured his satisfaction as he continued to nurse, savoring Bill's cum and bathing Bill's cock in it for a few minutes.

Owen abandoned Haynes' cock and moved his body so he would be in a position to share Bill's cum when Haynes was ready to give it to him. The second Haynes let Bill's cock slip from his mouth, Owen moved in and locked his lips to Haynes' so they could share the generous mouthful of precious fluid Bill had delivered. While they were passing it back and forth, Bill began to eat the Marine's ass.

After several minutes kissing Owen while they shared Bill's load, Haynes broke to gasp, "Jesus, Bill, your tongue feels so fuckin' good in my ass. Eat me out, baby!"

"He's gonna like your dick in there even better," Owen said.

"Yeah, fuck me, stud!" Haynes gasped.

"Jesus," Bill laughed, "give me a minute. I just gave you a load in the mouth. Why don't you fuck me, first?"

"Why don't we both fuck you first?" Owen asked.

"Great idea," Bill said, abandoning Haynes' ass and kneeling on the side of the bed.

The lube was at hand, and Owen greased up Bill's ass. "Give it to 'im, lover," he enjoined Haynes as he greased up the Marine's cock. Bill reached back to separate the cheeks of his ass, exposing the pink target Haynes' cock immediately sought. Without ceremony, the Marine grasped Bill's waist and pulled hard as he seated his prick firmly inside, producing a grunt of satisfaction from Bill.

While Haynes was savagely and very expertly fucking Bill's ass, Owen greased up Haynes' ass and his own prick, and was soon fucking Haynes at the same time Haynes was fucking Bill. Haynes did much more than grunt his satisfaction; he almost yelled out, "Yeah, fuck my hot jarhead ass, baby!"

Such exclamations were not at all uncommon in this particular hotel, and the walls were sufficiently flimsy that they were widely heard. Another Marine, two rooms down the hall, clearly heard Haynes' shout, and repeated it verbatim to another Marine, who was already engaged in doing what Haynes was enjoining Owen to do.

Haynes was able to coordinate his fuck perfectly with Owen's—it was tricky, but he'd had considerable experience doing so—and both he and Bill reveled in their respective fucks until Haynes screamed "I'm coming," and froze with his exploding cock buried deep in Bill's hungry ass.

Owen pulled Haynes' body away from Bill, and drove his larger prick deep inside Bill almost without missing a beat. He grinned at Haynes, saying "Your cum is hot as hell in here, Baby!"

"Give him some more, lover," Haynes said. "Fill his pretty ass the way you do mine." Bill enthusiastically encouraged Owen to do just that, and Owen obliged only a few minutes later.

The three took time out to drink the sodas Haynes had brought from the drink dispenser. After a pleasant respite, Bill said he had to leave very soon, to get home. Haynes said, "You promised you were gonna fuck me, Bill. Lemme ride your dick before you go." Bill smiled and lay on his back on the bed, holding his enormous, still-hard cock up as he said, "Mount up, cowboy."

Haynes squatted over Bill, face-to-face, and positioned the tip of Bill's cock at his asshole as he sank down heavily and impaled himself. He groaned with pleasure as he rode up and down the considerable length of the shaft inside him. He leaned over and began to kiss Bill at the same time, and soon Bill felt the tip of Owen's cock pressing against his shaft where it entered Haynes, and slipping inside Hayne's chute alongside his own. With two pricks inside him—one, Bill's gargantuan monster, and the other the formidable weapon the sailor wielded— Haynes cried out wildly for the two studs to fuck him as hard as they could. Both Bill and Owen were fairly well experienced at double fucking—Owen especially so, since Haynes always managed to get double-fucked if there was a third party to their lovemaking, as there often was—and they had little trouble establishing a rhythm and coordination that provided all parties maximum pleasure. In a relatively short time, considering both fuckers had recently blown a load, Owen gasped, "I'm coming!" and Bill felt the sailor's hot cum flow over his prick inside Haynes' ass. It was enough to bring him to orgasm, and soon the two pricks inside Haynes were bathed in a double load of considerable volume.

Only a few moments later, Haynes blew his own load, on Bill's chest, and all three collapsed for a few minutes of post-coital afterglow. Finally, Bill said, "That was incredible, and I wish I could stay. You haven't got fucked yet, Owen, but I've gotta get home."

Haynes laughed, "Oh he's gonna get fucked, you can bet on that. I'll see to it."

Bill gave the two the telephone number at his office, and urged them to call if they were going to be on liberty and wanted to repeat their adventures of the afternoon. He took the bus home, the memory of an afternoon spent with a big-dicked sailor, a fuck-hungry Marine stud, and Casey Donovan vivid in his mind. He wondered if his son Casey was going to be as sexy as Casey Donovan; he decided he probably would be, since he was his son, after all! And he knew his Casey was going to be as beautiful as the porn star Casey.

Bill met with Owen and Haynes a number of times—usually together, but occasionally with only one of them. He also found it very easy to pick up other sailors and Marines on Market Street, near his office, and his gay sex activity blossomed as sexual activity with Faith ground to a near halt. He was almost relieved when his wife found him fucking with two sailors in their bedroom. It simplified his sex life considerably, and he also realized that his marriage had already ended, for all practical purposes. His responsibility for taking care of Casey was a joy, not a problem, and he managed the tightrope act of balancing his work, his active gay sex life, and seeing to the needs of his son with surprising agility while Casey grew into a gorgeous, hung, horny young stud with a thriving gay sex life of his own.

7.

Cockboys and Indians

Bill was probably more nervous than his son when they sat down to have their promised father-son talk about sex—although this one would not be about the traditional "birds and bees," but about "the bees and bees."

The discussion was a short one. After all, it was clear Bill needed to explain nothing about the sexual process or sexual technique to Casey; the boy's technique was, as his father had observed, not only masterful, it was enviable—and very likely more sophisticated than his own. So, their conference was mostly admonitory on Bill's part, the gist being basically summed up in two words: be careful. Sexual predators and disturbed people were out there, as well as sexually transmitted diseases—even a new "gay virus" that was apparently targeting gay men seemed to threaten. Little was known about the gay virus at that point, but some people were becoming convinced that it, too was sexually transmitted, and had the potential for being the worst of all. As Bill frankly told Casey his own sexual history, his son's fascination with his father's experiences and his filial pride in what a stud his father was, overcame his natural discomfort in hearing about his own parent having sex. He came to admire and envy his father in new ways. And Bill was astonished to learn the vastness of Casey's experience, and many of the details of it.

From Bill's standpoint, what did emerge from the talk was the fact that although Casey was physically accomplished in sex, he was still relatively naïve, emotionally. A teenager's heart is usually a fragile thing, regardless of the extent of his physical experience, and Bill sensed his son was no exception to the rule. Casey had confessed that although he had sex with several dozen partners, he had fallen in love with only two of them: Dave Cotter, the first boy who had fucked him, and, newly, Richard Austin—coincidentally, the last one who had fucked him.

Bill had also fallen in love with the first boy who fucked him—a high-school classmate who, by the time of their graduation, had fucked about half the boys in the class, but who married the Homecoming Queen in their senior year—and he still harbored that futile, long-past affection. Quite a number of boys whose cherries he had taken had fallen in love with him, so he understood the apparent principle, and well understood how Casey was still in love with Dave Cotter. Having seen Richard Austin in action, he could as easily understand how Casey had also fallen in love with him. He knew he, himself, would love to have sex with Richard Austin, and if love and extreme physical attraction were the same thing ... but he well knew they were not. Apparently, Casey knew that as well, intellectually, but he seemed emotionally unprepared to deal with the strength of his attraction to Richard.

Casey had told his father every detail about his relationship with Richard—bubbling over with the excitement of it, as he was. There was something about the whole business with Richard that set off alarm bells in Bill's head. To be sure, Richard was gorgeous, hung, stupendously sexy, and an accomplished fuckmaster, but Bill sensed Casey was being subjected to a 'snow job" calculated only to feed Richard's ego and his voracious sexual appetite. In Bill's view, Richard was an older man who should be far more responsible in dealing with a teenager's heart, however experienced that same teenager's body might be. Bill felt sure the affair would lead to heartbreak for his son, but he knew that he couldn't criticize Richard while Casey was so clearly under his spell. So, when he cautioned Casey about being as careful emotionally as he was physically, he did not mention Richard specifically. But in the back of his mind, Casey knew his father was warning him about Richard.

Casey grudgingly admitted to himself that he harbored an uncomfortable suspicion that his relationship with Richard was too good to be true. To him, it seemed impossible that anyone as unbelievably attractive as Richard would be as in love with him as he was with Richard. And so he decided he needed to heed his beloved father's advice about guarding his love even more than his libido—at least for the time being.

When he appeared at the theatre the next day, Casey learned that Al Parker was the new porn star guest. Al Parker was very well known, having done a huge number of fuck videos, many of which he also directed. He had a really fat, big dick, and he fucked like a demon, but he was also a ravenously hungry bottom. But he just didn't appeal to Casey: he was very hairy and stocky, the type of guy who would come to be called a 'bear'—not the sort that the boy found attractive. Still, he was friendly, and seemed to have little 'attitude,' in spite of his renown. Keeping alive the tradition he had honored in his several earlier engagements at the *Top 'n Bottom*, Al fucked all the house dancers—except for Adam, the one who was supposedly straight. Casey enjoyed getting fucked by Al's really filling dick, clearly wielded by an accomplished fuckmaster, but he wasn't interested in fucking him in return, although Al made it clear he would be glad to welcome Casey's big cock any place he wanted to put it. Several of the dancers did return Al's fuck, and the straight Adam fucked him at least twice. Al seemed fascinated by Adam's assertion of heterosexuality, especially since Adam had sucked Al off on one of those two occasions.

Richard got back from Amarillo a few days after Al Parker began his appearance. He had enjoyed his trip, and brought back copies of the videotapes his client had made. One showed him fucking the client's young lover—who was very cute, but looked to be about fifteen years old, although the client swore he was nineteen. The other tape, shot the following day, showed eleven older men gang-banging Richard relentlessly for almost two hours, some of them fucking him twice, and one of them, three times. By the end, cum was flowing out of Richard's ass and down his legs, and he was hoarse from screaming his enjoyment. Almost the entire time he was being gang-banged, the young lover was sucking his prick; Richard was not sure how many loads he shot down the young man's throat—three, certainly, perhaps four.

Viewing the first videotape with Richard, at his house, Casey was intensely aroused as he watched the stud's enormous cock and busy ass at work on the young lover. His arousal was intensified because as he knelt on all fours to watch, with Richard kneeling behind him, that same enormous cock was savagely fucking his own ass while Richard kissed and bit his neck and ears, panting his lust, his appreciation, and his love.

They reversed positions to watch the second film, so that Casey fucked Richard while they watched the tape of all the other men fucking him. The first half-hour of the second tape was as exciting to Casey as the first tape had been—perhaps even more so, given the unrestrained fuck-lust that Richard evidenced while he was being so relentlessly, and often brutally fucked by the eleven men in the video.

Richard's gasps of joy and appreciation for the huge cock and the savage fuck he was receiving at any given moment added to Casey's enjoyment. Before the video ended, however, Casey had come twice inside Richard, as a result of which his own fuck-lust had diminished to the point that he began to feel the whole procedure he was watching was somewhat sick and debasing. By the end of the video, when the camera zoomed in to show the river of cum flowing from Richard's gaping asshole, and down his legs, Casey was almost feeling that he was one of those who had contributed to Richard's debasement, and he felt somehow ashamed.

Long before the nearly two-hour tape ended, Richard rose to his knees, and turned around, causing Casey's now-flaccid cock to slip from his ass. Seizing the back of Casey neck, he pressed their lips together. He was masturbating wildly as his tongue invaded the depths of Casey's mouth and he grunted his passion while his prick shot a fiercely propelled load of cum onto the boy's chin and chest. Casey's erection had returned while Richard stroked it as he was bringing himself to climax. Casey returned Richard's kisses, and his hard-on was throbbing in Richard's fist, but his heart was not in it.

Richard licked his own discharge from Casey's chin and chest, and shared it with the boy. Then he knee-walked behind Casey and put his cock back inside. He fucked Casey as he reached around to masturbate him until the boy shot yet another load, most of which Richard captured in his hand. Licking the cum from his hand, Richard moved back in front of Casey and kissed him again so they could share it. A beaming Richard stood, raised Casey to his feet, and led him to the shower. The tape presumably played on out to the end in the living room.

Under the soapy spray, with an incredibly handsome, sexy, marvelously hung stud kissing him, fondling him and pressing their bodies and cocks together, Casey was astonished to realize he was no longer in love with Richard. He echoed Richard's sentiments of "I love you" mechanically, but he realized he was merely being polite.

Al Parker greeted Richard at the theatre that night like a long-lost friend. They had worked together on a fuck video a few years earlier, and Al had directed another one in which Richard appeared. Clearly, Richard shared none of Casey's reservations about having sex with the hairy 'bear.' They fucked each other in the backstage lounge while quite a few of the house dancers watched. Casey was one of those who watched, and he envied neither Al nor Richard while he did so. In fact, when Richard doubled with Al for his last performance, Casey did not stay around to watch the encounter.

Casey was disappointed, as were many of the dancers, when Eddie announced that Michael Christopher's appearance at the theatre was postponed for two weeks. Christopher was an exciting, massively hung star, with a breathtaking body. In his place, Eddie had engaged a little-known bodybuilder who had made only two fuck films, Greg Marcus, and for the following week, Miguelito Santos, equally little-known and also a bodybuilder. It was no surprise to the T 'n B veterans that the last-minutes replacements were muscle boys. Eddie clearly had a penchant for those broad chests, big arms, and luscious tits. House dancers Carl, Adam and Steve fit that description, and it was generally known by the employees that Eddie watched their performances more regularly than those of any other dancers, except for Richard's.

Richard was not particularly muscular, but he was a special case among the house dancers. When he and Eddie first met, years before, in Alabama, Richard was blown away by Eddie's gargantuan cock, and went overboard getting it. Turning on his prodigious charm to make Eddie fall in love with him, Richard was, in a sense, caught in his own trap, since, unlike so many other times when he had wooed a guy who was either rich, well-placed, or unusually desirable sexually, he not only got Eddie to fall in love with him, he also fell in love with Eddie. It was understandable that Richard fell; in addition to Eddie's monster endowment and persuasive lovemaking, he was a sweet, loveable guy. Richard, in typical fashion, moved on to another man in a few months, but Eddie was still in love with him.

Given Eddie's tastes, and since he did the hiring at the T 'n B, it was not surprising there were no blacks or Asians or real 'bears' among the dancers, but odd that there were almost no Latinos, since Eddie was drawn to them.

Both bodybuilder guests were good dancers, and entertained the patrons extremely well. Their bodies were much more impressive than their dicks—which were of barely average dimensions, at best—and the patrons seemed happy to fondle their chests and arms in lieu of surreptitiously playing with their cocks. Backstage, the pattern was similar: more body worship than actual fucking and sucking, although there was still plenty of the latter activities.

Miguelito Santos, who performed under the single name "Santos," may not have been particularly well hung, but he was a raving fuck machine with the house dancers — especially the muscular ones. He had to settle for fucking the straight Adam only in the mouth during their lounge encounter, with several other dancers watching, Later, however, after having spent an ecstatic half-hour eating Santos' ass and sucking his tits, Adam went back to the Latino stud's hotel room to spend the night with him. Adam claimed he had never been fucked before, but by the next morning, he been fucked at least three times.

The fact was, Adam loved getting fucked as long as the cock wasn't too big, and no one he knew would learn about it. He often used a modest-sized dildo on himself while he fucked his wife, and she loved fucking him with a strap-on dildo of more impressive dimensions when he was sufficiently in need of getting fucked that he welcomed it. He also worshipped Greg Marcus' body as he had Santos', and he also sucked him off as well. He probably would have gone with him to get fucked if Greg had pushed for it. Strangely, Adam still considered himself straight, even when he was savoring and swallowing the cum he had just sucked from a cock, or screaming *Fuck me harder. Fuck me!* while his wife hammered his ass with a strap-on.

Both of the muscle boys, Greg and Santos, doubled with the equally muscular Steve Renard for their final shows.

Michael Christopher was a disappointment to Casey. He had a huge body, with a thrilling, vast chest, and his stupendous, crooked dick was as impressive in person as it was in his videos. But other than those physical attributes and the passion he brought to sex, he didn't attract Casey in any way. To be sure, those qualities were sufficient to make fucking with him very exciting. Casey treasured the time he spent sucking Michael's colossal cock while he played with the porn stud's succulent tits, and being held in those massive arms while Michael's incomparable ass-reamer plowed him mercilessly and gloriously. Michael singled out Casey to fuck him, the only one of the house dancers who were accorded that 'honor' — granted, probably, because Casey's cock was the biggest among the dancers. Judging by the groans and gasps coming out of the theatre office one night that week, Michael Christopher and Eddie Bliss swapped fucks with their stupendous dicks. Still, Casey didn't relate to Michael at all. He neither liked nor disliked him; he felt no kind of connection with the man, although he admitted he was a great fuck.

Richard campaigned shamelessly—and successfully—to double with Michael for his last performance, often sucking on his cock during the week, and relentlessly sucking up to the giant stud. Casey didn't know how many times Michael fucked Richard that week, but he watched it happen twice, and heard reports of two other occasions. Watching the man he thought he had loved virtually delirious with lust as the giant Michael's prodigious cock pounded his ass ferociously, Casey felt no emotion except envy.

During the double in Michael's last show, Michael bent Richard over a table and plowed his ass so savagely that shortly before Michael blew his load, Richard rose with Michael's huge arms encircling his chest and, without his touching it, his prick shot a load about four feet into the air. The audience went wild, and Michael slammed Richard's upper body back down onto the table, withdrew his cock, and blew his own copious load on Richard's back. While the audience cheered, Michael licked the cum off Richard's back, hauled him to his feet and turned him around, so they could kiss and share the visiting stud's emission. Their kiss was long and very passionate, accompanied by delirious groping and caressing, and when it ended, Michael dropped to his knees and sucked Richard's still-erect cock for a few minutes before he kissed him again and led him off the stage. It was the only time during the week that Michael publicly sucked dick, although he frequently demonstrated to everyone backstage that it was something he greatly enjoyed.

The next two guests at the theatre were both more interested in getting fucked than in fucking, and although the house dancers weren't all treated to their traditional plowing by the stars, both stars got plowed by all the house dancers. Casey and Richard, as the best-hung in the company, were special favorites, of course.

The first of these guests, Derrick Stanton, used very large dildoes to fuck himself while he was dancing, and blew his load for the audience three or four times during each day he appeared. He normally blew a load as far into the house as the third row, but with a dildo up his ass, he could make it to the fifth row—as he did when Casey fucked him while they doubled during Derrick's final show.

Jon King was the other visitor more interested in receiving than giving. He was fairly diminutive, but well muscled, with an unusually fat dick—a prototypical 'beer can dick.' He also had an adorable round ass that all the dancers were eager to fuck, and which all of them did at least once during the week. Jon was especially attracted to the muscle boys in the company, Carl, Steve and Adam, and they were the only ones he wanted to fuck in return. Carl and Steve enjoyed Jon's monstrously fat cock up their butts, but Adam declined, of course, opting instead to stretch his lips extra wide to get Jon off in a way they both enjoyed.

During his shows, muscle boy Steve Renard had been having trouble with his erection for a couple of weeks, although his body was so spectacular, no one much cared. He doubled with Jon King early in the week, and with King's dick up ass, he came to full erection and blew a tremendous load involuntarily — which for some reason seemed subsequently to solve his erection problem.

For Jon King's final show, he doubled with Casey on stage. During the time he had Casey's glorious cock planted deep in his cute ass and hammering away relentlessly, he blew two loads, much to the delight of the audience. Casey had actually blown a load inside Jon's ass while he fucked him, but he continued to fuck until he was ready to deliver his second load, and he pulled out in time for the audience to watch it splashing over the worshipful Jon's face and into his mouth.

And then the legendary Casey Donovan came for a four-day appearance. He had spent most of his time recently acting as a tour guide to foreign cities, and appearing in a few unsuccessful theatrical ventures in New York. With a few days to kill, he yielded to Eddie Bliss's plea to return to the T 'n B, where he had made guest appearances several times in the past. .

Casey had retained the notoriety his appearance in *Boys in the Sand* bestowed for well over a decade by that time, and he drew the largest crowds the theatre had ever seen. He was still gorgeous, and his body was in the same great shape, but up close he was showing signs of advancing age and the sexual wear-and-tear of eleven years of considerable debauchery. He was very friendly and polite, and was well liked personally by all the house dancers, who, at his insistence, called him by his real name, Cal. All agreed to call him Cal, and usually did so, but everyone had seen *Boys in the Sand*, and thought of him only as Casey — the golden sex god of the film.

Like his two star predecessors at the T 'n B, Cal was more interested in getting fucked than fucking. But the famous Casey Donovan was besieged with offers to meet with patrons for private sessions, and he commanded top dollar for the many he accepted, so

Cal had to save some of his sexual energy for them. To get in the mood for each appearance on stage, he wanted to get fucked for a few minutes — preferably while someone was also sucking his dick — and he never had trouble finding house dancers more than willing to oblige. Richard had Eddie adjust his schedule so that he was slated to dance immediately before each of Cal's shows. He was, as a result, always on hand to 'get Cal in the mood' to go on, and by the end of Cal's brief tenure, he and the blond sex-god were hanging out together outside the theatre when Cal could fit Richard into his schedule. According to Richard's reports, and doubted by none who knew him, Cal was also "fitting him in" regularly in other ways.

Bill Lowe was anxious to see the famous Casey Donovan in person, remembering well how *Boys in the Sand* had been something of a catalyst for his sexual emancipation from marriage. He told his son he was going to the theatre to see the famous blond porn god, and Casey Lowe promised to introduce his father to Cal.

Casey Lowe's monster cock had attracted Cal, of course, and Cal had enjoyed it enormously on a number of occasions when it had been planted to the hilt inside his hungry ass. Cal declared he was anxious to meet Bill Lowe when Casey asked if he could bring his dad around to meet someone who had thrilled and influenced him so much. Cal was clearly attracted to Bill when they met, and Casey asked no questions of either Cal or his dad following the period of a few hours the two spent together in the nearby apartment provided for the guest star. When Bill began to tell Casey about his private meeting with Casey Donovan his son made him stop — but he was secretly glad for his dad, and proud of him as well. That evening, as he was fucking Cal's ass briefly before he went on stage, Casey wondered if he might not be fucking the porn star in his own father's cum. It was unnerving, and, for some perverse reason he didn't understand, exciting as well.

Cal's final performance began as a double with Richard, but soon several other house dancers — including Casey Lowe — joined them on stage, and it turned into a gang-bang of the endlessly hungry Casey Donovan ass. Eventually, after six of the house dancers had fucked the star and two members of the audience came on stage to join in, Eddie called a halt and closed the theatre, leaving an exhausted Casey Donovan bent over a table, with cum dripping from his distended asshole and down his legs.

The first half of Casey Lowe's senior year wore on, and by Thanksgiving he knew he was in academic trouble. He had spent so much time at the theatre, often necessitating quite late hours, that his grades had slipped badly, and with final exams for the semester not far away, he began to fear he would fail several, if not all of the classes he was taking. Moreover, he had largely neglected his lovemaking with his 'regular' classmates and fuckbuddies, Joey Stone and Rommel Chase, and both had complained they missed the magnificent reaming they had become used to from Casey's glorious cock. Quite a few other boys Casey had fucked regularly at Serra High also expressed their disappointment at seemingly having been cut off from his lovemaking. Casey felt guilty about his failure to satisfy his former sexual playmates the way he had before he began dancing at the theatre, but even a young fuckmaster like him had his limitations. Furthermore, after his experiences with Hank, Richard, Eddie, and the porn stars, lovemaking with many of his old fuckbuddies seemed rather immature.

In addition to the shows at the theatre — including his required daily public orgasm and frequent doubling with porn stars — there was the backstage cocksucking and fucking that was so wonderfully unavoidable, and he still had sex regularly with the exciting Richard. He was certainly no longer in love with Richard, but he still loved sex with the handsome stud. Richard seemed not to have noticed that Casey no longer replied in kind to his declarations of love when they were in bed together. Richard continued to tell Casey he was in love with him, but Casey knew it really meant nothing.

His time and energy were further drained by those occasions when he would accept requests from audience members to meet with them privately in the downstairs cubicles the theatre provided for the dancers to make extra money. Many of the house dancers actively solicited people in the audience to meet them downstairs for private sex or to take them to their homes or hotel rooms for extended sessions — and many of them were quite successful. Dancers who went for quickie sessions downstairs usually allowed patrons only to play with their bodies and suck their cocks while they masturbated — and the patron's orgasm brought an end to the session. The dancers were adept at making sure the patron blew a load before they did, so they could save their own orgasms for those they wanted to have them, or for patrons who sprang for a costly off-the-premises session.

The number of patrons who wanted to meet privately with the dancers varied directly with the degree of handsomeness the dancer possessed, the size of his prick, and the massiveness of his physique. Casey was literally besieged by requests, as was Richard; neither of them had to solicit requests. The muscle boys were almost equally popular. Casey rarely acceded to requests, limiting them to the men he found reasonably attractive. Richard accepted quite a few, as did the muscle boys, who loved receiving the body worship the patrons accorded them. The allegedly straight Adam received almost as many requests as Casey did—and he went for a paid 'quickie' after almost every one of his shows.

On only one occasion had Casey agreed to an off-the-premises sexual tryst. A very dark, foreign-looking man with a shaved head offered a hundred dollars if Casey would meet with him for a few minutes outside the theatre to listen to a proposition—no strings attached. Accepting the man's offer, Casey met with him on the sidewalk out front. The man had a limousine waiting for him there, but Casey was naturally uneasy about the situation, and declined to sit inside it with him to discuss 'something.' Instead, they talked while standing under a lamppost a few yards up the street.

The man produced the promised hundred dollars and introduced himself as Jandura Singh, a citizen of India. He was extremely wealthy, and not only had a passion for sucking off blond boys, but was equally eager to watch his son, Kumar, fucking blond boys. He thought Casey was the most exciting blond boy he had seen, "uncommonly beautiful and well-endowed," and he felt sure his son would find him equally fascinating. He produced a photograph of Kumar, who was dark-skinned like his father, but whom Casey thought was amazingly handsome. The boy did not look to be more than fifteen, but Singh swore he was twenty—and, if that was a consideration, he had a cock about the same size as Casey's. Singh offered to pay Casey a thousand dollars if he would meet with him and his son for not more than two hours, while each satisfied his cravings with the blond.

Seeing that Casey was clearly hesitant about accepting the offer, Singh told him he could bring a friend along to 'stand guard' in the living room of his hotel suite while he and his son met with Casey in the bedroom. Casey agreed to the arrangement, and went back into the theatre to find someone to accompany him. Adam had just finished dancing, and he had some time on his hands. Casey promised him a hundred-dollar share of the promised thousand-dollar fee if he would act as a sort of chaperone while he met with Singh and his son at their hotel. Adam agreed to help out.

Meeting the blond, very muscular Adam, Singh immediately offered to engage his services as well as Casey's, for the same thousand-dollar stipend. "Perhaps after I suck you off, and Kumar fucks you, you and Casey can fuck each other while my son and I watch,"

"But Adam doesn't … " Casey began.

'That will be great," Adam interrupted. In an aside to Casey, as they got into the limousine, Adam grinned, "Maybe I can make an exception for you,"

"You know how big my dick is?" Casey whispered.

Still grinning, Adam groped the object in question, and said, "Believe me, I've been checking it out for a long time now. We'll work it out. No — we'll work it in."

"You're gonna lose your hundred-dollar share of my fee," Casey said.

"I'm gonna lose my load inside that hot ass of yours. It'll be worth it." And they took off for the Mark Hopkins Hotel, where the Singhs were staying.

The suite at the prestigious hotel was nothing short of opulent, but the two blonds had little time to appreciate its quality. Singh ordered them to strip naked as soon as they came in; he, himself, stayed fully clothed, as he would throughout the encounter.

A very large man, apparently also Indian, had accompanied them in the limousine. Singh explained that the man was his bodyguard. He also accompanied them into the suite, and sat very quietly and unobtrusively in a corner of whatever room they happened to be in. There was no one else in evidence, but as soon as both boys were naked, Kumar Singh entered from the bedroom, wearing a floor-length silk paisley dressing gown. He was fully as handsome as his picture, Casey thought, although he appeared slightly older.

Singh introduced his son to Casey and Adam, and as he walked around them, studying them and caressing their asses, Kumar paid special attention to Adam's magnificent chest, causing Adam's cock to come to full attention. The thought that he was finally going to get a crack at the muscular Adam's splendid ass brought Casey's cock to full erection at the same time. Kumar whistled in appreciation at the sight of Casey's glorious prick, and he wrapped his fist around it, stroking it. His dressing gown parted when his own erection poked out between the folds. Singh had not exaggerated much: Kumar's prick was nearly as big as Casey's—at least nine inches in length, and fatter than the blond stud's. It was as dark in color as Kumar's complexion, and only a slightly pinker area below the cock-head revealed him to be uncircumcised. The boy might be young, but he was certainly equipped like a man. Taking Casey's throbbing meat in his hand, Kumar said, "Suck this one first, father. It is really magnificent."

"It certainly is, but I believe I am looking forward to sucking these just as much," Singh said, as he stroked Adam's magnificent tits.

Adam smiled, and fondled Singh's head as the man bent to lick and suck his nipples. Looking at Casey, he grinned, "My hot tits trump your monster cock, hotshot."

"I'm gonna trump that cute little ass of yours with ten inches of hard dick," Casey laughed. "And I think you better be prepared for that ass-reamer Kumar is getting ready for us." The younger Singh had abandoned Casey's cock to doff his dressing gown, and stood there nude, stroking his enormous prick as he savored the beauty of the two blond studs.

Indicating Adam, Kumar said, "I want to watch you suck him off, Father, and then I will fuck him while you watch." He smiled crookedly as he added, "And be sure to lubricate his ass the way we like it."

The elder Singh sank to his knees and opened his mouth wide to admit Adam's prick inside. Adam held the older man's head tightly as he fucked into his mouth, bucking wildly. Singh's hands frantically caressed Adam's clenched and driving buttocks, and he murmured his delight around the mouthful of cock he was servicing. Adam's head was thrown back, and he gasped, "Yeah, take my big dick! That's so fuckin' good! You're a great cocksucker!"

Casey was amused by Adam's show. The prospect of a thousand-dollar fee was apparently a real inspiration for Adam. He had watched the muscular blond getting sucked off countless times, and he had never been so vocal, or showed such delight, even when being blown by a really consummate cocksucker.

Using Casey's cock as if it were a handle, Kumar led him so they could stand next to his father and Adam to watch them from up close. Abandoning Casey's cock and using his hand to caress the blond stud's ass, Kumar whispered hoarsely into his ear, "Your ass is almost as beautiful as you are. I can't wait to fuck it. You want it?"

At the moment, Casey was thinking how much he was looking forward to fucking Adam's frantically busy ass, but he reached down to stroke Kumar's dick as he muttered in reply, "Oh yeah, I want you to fuck me really hard with this monster." Even as he said it, he knew that the enthusiasm of his reply was inspired by the thought of the fee he was going to receive, but he also knew that he would probably be willing to fuck with the handsome, nicely built and well-hung Kumar under most circumstances.

Kumar transferred his hand to Adam's busy ass. He used the other hand to scoop a generous glob of Vaseline onto his fingers, which he used to lubricate between Adam's buttocks. Then, forming three fingers into a tube, he penetrated Adam's ass forcefully with it and began to drive it deeply in and out. Clearly, Adam enjoyed the sensation, as he projected his ass backward to better receive the penetration and yelled, "Yeah, fuck my ass!" The prospect of a thousand dollars was apparently a real inspiration to him, for he eagerly rode Kumar's probing fingers, humping and rotating his ass in obvious enjoyment. Soon he gasped, "I'm gonna come!" as he drove his cock as far into Singh's mouth as it would go, and froze in position while he obviously began to unload.

Singh was clearly exerting as much suction as he could, and he groaned his excitement at the receipt of Adam's cum. Adam panted, "Fuck! Suck that cum outa my dick and eat my big load." He seized Singh's head and held it tightly while he continued to fuck fiercely into his mouth, in short, rapid jabs. The cheeks of his ass were so tightly clenched, that Kumar's hand was forced out from between them.

As Adam calmed down, he drew Singh's head in against his belly, and his ass continued to grind, but it now rotated gently and humped slowly as he continued to feed his dick to the hungry Singh, who was murmuring his satisfaction.

When Singh released Adam's cock and stood, it seemed clear he had retained Adam's load in his mouth. Kumar put his hand on Adam's shoulder and led him to the bed, telling him to lie face down on it, saying, "And now you get fucked. Father, are you ready?" His father only nodded his assent, clearly unable speak with his mouth full or Adam's semen.

Kumar removed a condom from a saucer on the bedside table and tore the package open, rolling the sheath down his big, fiercely hard cock. At the same time, Singh knelt on the bed, between Adam's legs and drooled his mouthful of cum into the crevice between Adam's buttocks. "Such a beautiful ass for you, Kumar," he said when his mouth was empty and he was again able to talk. He stepped off the bed, and his son took his place.

Casey had seen many condoms in his life, of course, but oddly enough, it was the first time he had ever seen one put into use.

"On your knees," Kumar commanded, and Adam positioned himself as he was directed. Holding Adam's waist, Kumar moved in and positioned his cock-head at Adam's asshole, then gently began to hump until his shaft started to enter the kneeling blond.

Adam had been well lubricated with Vaseline when Kumar finger-fucked him, and his own cum added to it made entry of Kumar's cock even easier. Still, Adam grunted and moaned, "Take it easy. It's so fuckin' big!" And Kumar was fairly gentle, but he was also unrelenting. His cock continued to slide in until it was completely buried. Adam's groans became gasps of pleasure as he panted, "Fuck my ass. Fuck me hard!"

As Kumar complied with Adam's request, it became clear to Casey that although Kumar may have been young, he was a masterful, experienced, and very fierce fucker. If he had earlier entertained any doubts about sex with Kumar, Casey cast them aside as he watched his superlative technique and Adam's rapturous enjoyment; he was looking forward to getting fucked by the young Indian. Looking at Kumar's beautifully rounded ass writhing and pumping while he fucked Adam, Casey also hoped somehow he would get to fuck Kumar. Of course, he had been wanting to fuck Adam's ass for a long time, but he had thought his hopes would never be realized—even though the allegedly straight Adam had fucked him twice; they had also sucked each other off several times, and they had enjoyed fondling each other's bodies as they did so. Now, under the term of their arrangement with Singh, he and Adam would soon be fucking each other. Casey determined he would fuck Adam in the missionary position, so he could play with those magnificent tits while he plowed his tight little ass.

After a fairly long time, protracted by a careful rationing of his savage fucking, Kumar seized Adam's shoulders and drove his cock as deeply as he could, while his buttocks clenched tightly and he screamed "I'm coming!" Adam wriggled his ass, shouted his enjoyment, and worked Kumar's exploding cock like a widely experienced, ravenous bottom, which he claimed not to be. Kumar and Adam complimented each other for their respective roles in the fuck.

During the Kumar-Adam fuck, the older Singh had been standing behind Casey, watching along with the big-dicked young blond, fondling Casey's body and gently stroking his cock—fully hard, of course, considering what they were watching. Kumar disengaged from Adam, stripped off the condom he had been wearing, and threw it into a wastebasket. It was clear he had shot a very generous load into it. As Kumar and Adam left the bed, Singh told Casey, "Lie on the bed, on your back."

Casey lay on the bed as directed, and Singh climbed onto it from the foot, spreading Casey's legs and kneeling between them. He had shed his coat, tie and shoes, but was otherwise still fully clothed. He took Casey's fat, hard shaft in his hands and bent down to take it in his mouth.

Literally hundreds of different boys and men had sucked Casey off, but when Singh began his blow job, it was clear to the blond stud that this was possibly the most accomplished and satisfying cocksucker he had yet encountered. No wonder Adam had been so enthusiastic. Given the excellence of Singh's service, Casey blew his load in a relatively short time—too short, in Casey's estimation, to fully savor the Indian man's wonderful talent.

As he proclaimed his orgasm, while Singh murmured his enjoyment around the huge tube of hard flesh still driving in and out of his mouth, Casey grinned at Kumar, Kumar grinned back, promising to grant Casey the same pleasure he had just afforded Adam—and in the same way. Accordingly, Singh retained Casey's load in his mouth as Casey rolled to his stomach on the bed and used his hands to spread his buttcheeks wide to accept Jumar's lubrication and to provide a better target for Singh to further lubricate with cum. At the same time, Casey watched Kumar rolling another condom onto his monster erection, still grinning at him.

"On your knees," Kumar commanded, as he had with Adam, and Casey obeyed, eager to accept the master services Kumar had just rendered Adam—using such a glorious tool. "What a fine ass," Kumar cooed as he lubed Casey's asshole and coated his condom-clad prick generously with Vaseline. Singh drooled Casey's cum into the boy's asscrack just before his son positioned the tip of his dick at Casey's sphincter. "You ready?"

Rather than replying to Kumar's question, Casey violently drove his ass backward, burying the prodigious cock deep inside him while he fairly shouted, "Fuck me hard," and began to exercise the technique he had learned from the sailor Hank. Surprised at the ardor Casey displayed, and the excellence of the boy's skill as a power bottom, Kumar began an earnest fuck that clearly demonstrated his equal artistry as a power top.

Since he had blown a load in Adam only a short while earlier, Kumar's fuck proved to be a very long one, but it was in no way anything but the dedicated, fierce, ecstatic one such a beautiful, exciting bottom deserved. Both participants grunted and panted their eagerness and enjoyment for some twenty minutes until Kumar screamed, "Take it," while his buttocks froze in position and he obviously emptied his cock into the condom buried so deep inside Casey. As he accepted Kumar's offering, Casey rose to his knees and cried out wordlessly in joy as his enormous cock shot a load all the way across the bed, without his touching it, in spite of the fact that Singh had sucked him off only a short while before.

Kumar clasped his arms around Casey's chest, and he pulled them down on their sides, his prick still buried inside the blond Adonis. He began humping again, continuing his fuck in spite of the interruption of his orgasm, his copper-colored ass humping eagerly. Casey murmured, "Yeah! Keep fucking me, Kumar."

And Kumar responded to Casey's urging with a wildly enthusiastic, very prolonged follow-up fuck in spoon fashion, Both gasped and groaned their pleasure for another half-hour or more, until Kumar blew yet another load inside his partner. In spite of the delirium of Kumar's magnificent fuck, Casey retained the presence of mind to refrain from masturbating while he was being plowed so masterfully; he knew he had to fuck Adam when they finished—and he was very anxious to do a particularly fine job of nailing the muscular man who had been the sole holdout against the blond stud's conquest of all the staff asses at the *Top 'n Bottom*!

At the same time Casey was contemplating fucking Adam while Kumar continued his fevered fuck, he could see, out of the corner of his eye, that Singh's bodyguard was kneeling in front of his employer, sucking Singh's cock as Singh drove it in and out of the man's distended mouth while he watched his son fuck. It was the first time Casey had seen Singh's cock—the only time he would, as it turned out—and the older man was equipped with a very fat, lip-stretching monster.

With an exultant cry, Kumar blew another load inside Casey and held the boy's body very tightly as he cooed his post-orgasmic satisfaction. Singh's bodyguard had apparently finished his service to his employer, who had restored his cock to his trousers, and beamed as he watched his son luxuriating in the afterglow of very satisfying sex with the blond Adonis.

Kumar withdrew from Casey and rolled him around so that they faced one another, still embracing. The Indian kissed Casey's lips, gently and lovingly, with none of the passion he had displayed while fucking. It was the only time either of the Indians displayed any tenderness during the evening's encounter. Kumar smiled at Casey and said, "And now we watch Adam fuck your pretty ass."

Singh stepped forward. "I would suggest we take a brief respite so that Adam and Casey can rest a few minutes before they fuck each other. I want to see both at their best, and they have had quite a workout in the last hour or two. I promised you we would only take two hours of your time, but that was when Casey was going to be our only active guest. Is that agreeable with everyone?" It apparently was.

Singh sent his bodyguard out for drinks as the quartet went into the living room and seated themselves around the roaring fire in the fireplace.

The older man was not much for small talk. He elicited from Casey and Adam the particulars of their lives, and filled them in on the facts of his and Kumar's situations. So far, Adam and Casey knew only their names and their sexual appetites.

Singh was a surgeon, trained at the Stanford University School of Medicine in Palo Alto, who had returned to his homeland and was presently on the faculty of the Bangalore Medical College. Kumar was a medical student at Stanford, following in the footsteps of his father, but he planned to remain in the United States to practice medicine when he finished his studies. Singh had a wife and a total of seven children back in India. All the children were female except for Kumar, his fourth child, and Singh clearly did not plan to say anything past that basic information. Casey suspected that the older man's 'bodyguard' was actually his lover when they were in India, but he never raised the question.

That evening at the theatre, Richard Austin had danced alongside Steve Reynard at one point, and the two ended their part of the show with Richard cramming his monster cock up Steve's ass, and fucking the ecstatic and clearly appreciative muscle boy until he blew a load inside him. Kumar commented on how very hot he thought Richard was, and how well-built he found Steve, but he smiled at the two house dancers seated next to him, noting that Casey was even better hung than Richard, and Adam was fully as well built as Steve. "And you're both blond—and as far as I'm concerned that alone tips the scale in your favor."

"I, too, am very partial to blonds, as you know," Singh added. "But I'm not exclusively attracted to them. For instance, I thought Richard was exceptionally attractive. I surely would like to watch Kumar fucking him, and I would be more than happy to suck him off."

Both boys had often blown Richard and fucked him, and both attested at first hand to his sexual power. Adam confessed he had never been fucked by Richard, as Casey had been so frequently. "But I've wanted to get that big prick of his up my ass for a long time now" he added, and offered Casey a big grin and a wink in answer to the question implied by Casey's raised eyebrows. "And I've been wanting to take this monster from the minute I saw it," he laughed as he reached over to fondle Casey's prick—uncharacteristically flaccid at the moment.

"Why have you never said anything," Casey asked Adam.

"My wife looked in on a few of the shows at the T 'n B right after I started dancing there, and she didn't mind if I did anything that was going on except getting fucked. If I'da had as many dicks stickin' outa me as I already had stickin' into me at that point, I woulda looked like a porcupine, but she didn't know that, and nobody at the theatre knew that either. So, I decided that if it made her happy, I'd give up takin' it in the ass. I figured she was being pretty forgiving, since she didn't mind my sucking dick and fucking ass—and even eating ass now and then—so I made that concession. But I'll tell you, it's been getting harder to keep my promise all the time. Like I said, I've been wanting to get Richard inside me for a long time, and then you came along, and I wanted you that way even more. Coming over here tonight, I decided, What the hell? What she doesn't know won't hurt her. So at last I'm ready for that big dick of yours right where I most want it."

"You want me to give Richard the good news?" Casey asked.

Adam laughed again. "I'll give Richard the good news one night when we're on stage together. I'll enjoy seeing the look on his face almost as much as I'm gonna enjoy his fantastic dick in my ass."

"Well," Singh said, "it's time for us to watch you getting it, I believe. But, I must insist that each of you uses a condom when he fucks the other. I noted that Richard used none at the theatre when he fucked the muscular boy."

"Oh yeah, I meant to ask you about the rubbers," Adam said. "What's the deal?"

"The deal, as you put it," said Singh, "is that there is a very serious disease, mostly attacking gay men, called Acquired Immune Deficiency Syndrome. They call it by its acronym, AIDS."

"I've heard something about a gay cancer," Casey said. "Is that the same thing?"

"Yes," Singh said, "but it's not a cancer, it's a virus, and it's not strictly gay. Anyone can get it if they are careless about having sex. We actually know very little about it, except that it is sexually transmitted, and mostly through anal sex—which probably accounts for the fact that people think of it as a gay disease. We are reasonably sure it is fatal, and at this point we have no prospect for a cure, or even for reasonably successful treatment." He looked pointedly at Casey and Adam. "Does that frighten you?"

"With all due respect, sir, it scares the living shit out of me," Adam said.

"It should," Singh replied, and went on to outline some of the horrors carriers of the HIV virus might anticipate. By the time he had finished, both Casey and Adam were firm believers in what came to be known as "safe sex," which should have been properly called, "safer sex." They wondered about the safety of sucking someone off, since Singh clearly wasn't worried about contracting the virus that way. Singh said that the virus was a very fragile one, and oral saliva was almost surely a hostile environment for it. The medical community had not officially declared oral sex to be safe, but he felt sure it would, and that he was not risking his own health.

When Singh called for the two T 'n B dancers to perform their final contractual duty—viz., fucking each other—both were somewhat daunted by what Singh had just told them. Casey agreed to fuck Adam first, and the thought of the dangers of AIDS and donning the unaccustomed condom worked together to make it difficult for Casey to get an erection. However, when he began playing with Adam's round and sexy ass and thinking about how much he had been wanting to fuck it, his monster cock began to grow, and attained its usual size and rigidity when he buried his face between Adam's buttcheeks and tongue-fucked the eager muscle boy. He lubricated his cock and Adam's ass, and held Adam's waist in his hands as he poised the head of his cock at Adam's asshole. "How bad do you want it?" he asked.

Adam grunted a feverish "I want it bad! Fuck me, Casey. Give me that monster cock."

Casey honored the request with a savage thrust of his big prick into Adam's asshole, sinking it to the hilt while Adam screamed his joy at receiving it. Both boys grunted their thrill, lost in a kind of fuck-lust as Casey pounded away. Some time during the fuck, Casey rolled Adam to his back—without withdrawing from him—so that he could play with Adam's magnificent tits while he continued to hammer away at his hungry ass. Adam put a hand at the nape of Casey's head and drew it down so that their lips met. Adam's mouth opened, as did Casey's, and they began to kiss hungrily and passionately. Casey had never seen Adam kiss anyone at the theatre, and he was surprised—but gratified—at the ardor of his supposedly straight partner's technique. Considering the joy Adam was evidencing at ten inches of cock fucking him while he was feverishly tongue-fucking his partner's mouth, Casey knew he would never again accept the muscle stud's claim of being straight.

Singh had given Casey such a masterful blowjob, that it was only after a very protracted period that Casey shouted his exultation as he blew a load inside Adam's ass—the first time he had ever come in a condom—and Adam worked his ass ecstatically to drain as much of Casey's orgasm as he could.

Adam had a fierce erection, and had no trouble in sustaining it as he rolled a condom onto his cock—the first time he had ever done so in earnest—and driving it brutally into Casey's lubricated asshole. Fucking Casey was not a new experience for Adam, but with an ass full of the young blond stud's cum, he was especially inspired to make it a memorable one for both of them—and for their paying audience as well.

Both Adam and Casey agreed, to their surprise, that fucking with a condom, or getting fucked by a condom-covered dick, was not substantially different from what they had been used to, and agreed to honor the promise they made to Singh before he called for the limousine to deliver them to their respective homes. They had sworn they would not only practice 'safe sex' in the future, but would insist their partners do the same. They also swore they would spread the gospel of safe sex to their friends and fellow sex-workers.

Singh shook their hands after giving them their thousand-dollar fees and bidding them goodbye, but Kumar was moved to kiss them and express his admiration for their performance. Kumar also made sure each had his telephone number and address in Palo Alto, so they could come to visit him if they wished. No suggestion had been expressed at any time that either of the boys would get to fuck Kumar, but as they left, Kumar whispered into Casey's ear, "I don't usually take it up the ass, but I would make an exception for you any time we can get together. Call me."

In the limousine, Adam asked Casey to say nothing around the T'n B about what they had experienced with the Singhs.

"You still wanna pretend you're straight?" Casey asked.

Adam replied, "Yeah, but not around you. Any time you wanna fuck me, I'm more than eager—almost as eager as I am to fuck you again, and often. We can go to my apartment when my wife isn't around. But for some reason, I like having the guys at the theatre thinking I'm straight." In fact, of course, Adam often took a cock up his ass, and the bigger the more enjoyable to him, but always secretly. Since he was married, and engaged in an active sex life with his wife, he nonetheless still thought of himself as something like straight.

"Okay by me," Casey said, and Adam expressed his thanks by kissing the blond stud very passionately, and at great length.

They arrived at Casey's house first, and they were still necking. After a minute o two, the driver laughed and said, "You guys take all the time you need. Lookin' at you two, if I wasn't straight, I'd wanna get back in there and join in the fun."

If Casey and Adam hadn't been sexually exhausted, they might have really given the driver something to watch, but they parted company without so much as a grope. The next day each of them bought a generous supply of condoms.

Joey Stone, Rommel Chase, and the majority of Casey's fuckbuddies had no objection to adopting safe sex practices with him, especially when Casey gave them his version of the lecture Singh had delivered in his suite at the Mark Hopkins Hotel. A few who demurred were told that Casey's ass and cock would only be available to them under those conditions, and they came around. In fact, all agreed, once they became accustomed to condom usage, that it made little, if any, discernible difference in the level of their enjoyment.

Casey's crusade carried over into the *Top 'n Bottom* as well, reinforced by Adam's new subscription to the practice. Most of the dancers had heard rumors about AIDS, and were willing to switch to the use of condoms, but a few of the older or more experienced pooh-poohed the idea. The oldest of them, however—Richard—was surprisingly willing to insist that a condom always be used as a condition of fucking him. It was Richard adoption of the practice that convinced Eddie to rule that all dancers use a condom when they fuck in the theatre, whether backstage with each other, onstage, or in the private rooms downstairs. Casey had denied Eddie access to his ass unless Eddie sheathed his gargantuan cock, and Eddie had refused to do so—denying himself the huge pleasure he took from fucking the young blond stud, and also denying Casey the great pleasure he took from Eddie's expert and thrilling fucking. But it was when Richard refused to grant Eddie his greatest pleasure in life—viz., fucking his beloved's ass—that Eddie came around. When he realized it made little difference in his enjoyment, he acceded to Richard's and Casey's ultimatum, and even became something of a crusader for safe sex. Patrons of the *Top 'n Bottom* were subjected to subtle propaganda in the cause through observing condom usage in the theatre, as well as posters extolling the virtue of safe sex and the dangers of AIDS. About that time the San Francisco Health Department closed down the bath houses of the city for notorious, unsafe sex practices on their premises, and San Francisco's Eagle Productions, the country's most successful and prestigious gay porn studio, eventually followed suit after several other major video producers adopted condom usage in all their films.

It was a long time before Adam bottomed for anyone at the theatre (except for Casey, and that always in private), but he continued to top many there, now insisting on wearing a condom—sometimes in spite of the objections of those he fucked. Eventually, as he had told Casey he would, Adam took Richard up the ass—on stage, in front of a large audience—much to Richard's surprise and pleasure. All but one of his fellow workers at the theatre—Casey, of course—were pleasantly surprised as well. His wife learned about it, and she was equally surprised, but nothing like as pleased as Richard and the others were. She sued Adam for divorce, and left him. The blond muscle stud was happy to be free to practice his sex life as he wanted—much to the enjoyment of his fellow workers and guest performers at the T'n B— but he was very fond of his wife, and was sorry to lose her.

Casey was making a lot of money. The thousand dollar fee that Jandura Singh had paid him was a windfall, but he was also regularly making several hundred dollars a week from tips at the theatre, and at least a few hundred more from theatre patrons who met with him for private sessions. He was saving virtually all his earnings, in cash, but he kept it in a secret stash, not at a bank. He didn't want the tax people to know about it.

During the holiday season, patrons of the theatre were unusually generous, and Casey added another two thousand dollars to his savings during the period. The dancers were equally generous with their distribution of sexual favors for their co-workers.

Perhaps the sexual highlight of the season was the night Casey and Richard met their boss, Eddie, in the T 'n B guest-performer hotel suite for a private pre-Christmas celebration. The guest performer of the week—the temporary resident at the hotel—was the famous Steve York, a good-looking and reasonably well-built porn star whose claim to fame was an absolutely gargantuan prick. Both Casey and Richard had been fucked earlier in the week by Steve, backstage at the theatre, but Eddie had not sampled Steve's most salient feature. Unfortunately, Steve was doing an all-night session with a wealthy local man, and would not be present, so Casey and Richard were unable to enjoy his formidable talent again, and Eddie—who had been seriously considering having sex with Steve—was unable to realize his ambitions vis-à-vis the monster-cocked guest.

Eddie fucked both of the dancers, and watched while Richard fucked Casey. Following Eddie's directions, Casey lay on his back, his fiercely erect cock standing straight up, while Richard positioned his asshole over it. The older dancer drove his ass downward as he impaled himself on Casey's formidable instrument, then leaned forward to kiss Casey while Eddie gradually inserted his titanic prick into Richard's asshole, alongside the challenging bulk of Casey's dick. Richard gasped in ecstasy as he gloried in the most challenging double fuck he had ever taken, often crying out the names of his fuckers in his joy, expressing his gratitude to them and his admiration for their masterful technique. It was the literal climax of the season for all three men.

8.

Advice about Vice

On the second day of classes for the spring semester — supposedly his last at Serra High — Casey was called to the school counselor's office. He was not surprised. While his bank account had been growing exponentially in the last few months, his scholarship was declining at a similar rate. Working at the T 'n B, along with its corollary activities and trying to maintain his sexual activities with his regular fuckbuddies had taken its toll. His report card for the fall semester of his senior year showed he had failed two courses, and barely passed three others with grades of "D." His highest grade was a "C," in a Sociology course, and he felt pretty sure he only escaped failing that course because the teacher was hot for his body; according to his test scores, he had clearly scored a failing grade.

The Serra High School Guidance Counselor was a thirty-five-year-old man named Hallie Teegerstrom. A native San Franciscan, he had himself attended Serra High, graduating in 1969. He had served a two-year hitch in the Navy after his graduation from San Francisco State University, with bachelor's and master's degrees in counseling. After three years as a counselor at a high school in Nevada, he returned to his alma mater as a faculty member, in 1980. He was attractive, but not strikingly handsome, well built or unusually well endowed, and his sex life had been unspectacular, but surprisingly satisfactory. He had never made love with a female, nor had he ever seriously entertained a desire to do so. By the same token, he had never disappointed any of the dozens of boys and men with whom he had affairs. His success was due to his pleasant personality, his considerable versatility in making love, and a talent for employing his ordinary physical attributes in extraordinary ways.

Hallie was not a stranger to the offerings at the *Top 'n Bottom*, and had recognized Casey as a Serra High student when he first saw him dance there. He was not sure Casey would recognize him, but he used a San Francisco Giants baseball cap to conceal his face sufficiently that when Casey circulated among the patrons the boy would not know who he was, in any event. He had had no contact with Casey at school, although he had seen him around and thought the young blond was probably the most attractive boy there. He never had any sexual contact with students, not only for ethical reasons, but also because he was mostly attracted to men his own age, or a bit older. Still, he was professionally interested in Casey's case: the boy was a Serra High student, and thus his concern, and he was in academic trouble. Furthermore, he was gorgeous, dazzlingly sexy, almost indubitably gay, and hung like a horse. Hallie was not overwhelmingly a 'size queen,' but neither did he exactly negate the old adage that 'there are two kinds of gay men: size queens and liars.' He thought that no sane gay man could look at a naked Casey and not want to wrap his lips around that colossal cock or ride it joyously while he studied the boy's magnificent body and face.

Checking out Casey's records, Hallie could see that he had been a decent student for several years, but lately had slipped academically to the point that he would not graduate with his class, and would even have to attend summer school to graduate this year. As nearly as he could tell, the sudden decline in Casey's scholarship had begun when he started dancing at the strip theatre.

Hallie welcomed Casey into his office during Casey's study-hall period. After a few exchanged pleasantries, the counselor told Casey he was worried about his ability to graduate that year. "After your fall semester, I can't see that happening without your working hard to get much better grades this semester. I know you can do it; you used to make perfectly satisfactory grades, but even then you will also have to make up a few courses in summer school."

They discussed Casey's plans for college. In essence, Casey had no real plans. He assumed he would be going to college, but had made application to no institution yet. Surprisingly, his father had not pressed him on the subject.

Hallie was exasperated. "Why have you not come to me to talk about this? Your applications should have gone out well over six months ago, at the latest. But Casey, I have to be honest with you. Your grades have never been unusually good, even though I can see by your various aptitude and intelligence tests, there's no reason you shouldn't have been getting better ones. Any major college that looks at your grades from last semester is going to turn you down. Any college you apply to is going to see them. So, if you are going to go on with your education, what you have to do is pull your grades up drastically this semester, and graduate in summer school. You will need to apply to a school that isn't very selective, one that can accept you for almost immediate admission this fall. Then, if you can do well there, you can apply for transfer to a better school."

Casey was properly humbled. "I know I should be doing better, Mr. Teegerstrom, but I've been so busy the last year, something had to give. And I guess it was my academic work that gave."

"You want to tell me what it was that kept you so busy?"

"Well, I guess it was a lotta things" Casey replied. "No one thing in particular."

"I think it was one thing in particular, Casey: your performance with the strip theatre, and all that probably goes along with it."

Casey was astonished. "But…but how did you know about that, Mr. Teegerstrom?"

Hallie assumed a very grave air, and asked Casey to keep what he was about to tell him in strictest confidence. "Just as I will keep anything about this discussion strictly between you and me." Casey agreed, beginning to suspect where their conversation was headed.

"Okay," Hallie said. "I know you've been dancing at the *Top 'n Bottom* because I've seen you perform there several times."

"I…I don't know what to say," Casey stammered. Hallie's declaration was what Casey had expected by that time. "Does that mean …"

Hallie completed Casey's question."…that I'm gay?" Casey nodded. "Of course it does. And just because I'm telling you this doesn't mean I'm going to make a pass at you, or anything like that. Frankly, Casey, I think you are one of the most attractive and sexy young men I have ever seen. And after watching your performance at the theatre, I think I can say that unless you're one of the great actors of your generation, you're also gay. Right?" Casey nodded—but not with any suggestion of apology or shame, Hallie was glad to note. "You have everything going for you as an 'adult performer,' as they call it. But I'm sure you realize that sort of thing only lasts a few years, and then where will you be if you haven't prepared for a career that will see you through your later years?" Casey had no answer to that, of course. Naturally, those considerations had surfaced in his mind, but he had always deferred them.

Hallie said, "No one worried about what would happen to Scarlett O'Hara at the end of Gone with the Wind, when she declared how she would address her problems. In case you don't know, what she said was, 'I'll think about that tomorrow. After all, tomorrow is another day.' "

Casey grinned, "No, I know what she said. I've seen the movie several times. You gotta remember, I'm a gay boy! In fact, I thought about that line just a few days ago."

Hallie laughed, but added, "Anyway, you're not Scarlett O'Hara. You're Casey Lowe, and you have to plan."

The exchange about Scarlett O'Hara lessened the seriousness and formality that had marked their interview to that point, and their interaction now seemed more that of friends, rather than teacher and student. Casey agreed he needed to limit his T 'n B activities considerably, and reassured Hallie that he was aware of the HIV problem, and was practicing safe sex.

Hallie cautioned Casey that the principal factor necessary to bring about the boy's academic improvement was spending much more time on serious study in all his courses—and that was going to take a lot more time than he had been devoting to it. Casey agreed, and the meeting ended with both parties feeling they had made progress.

Casey had no idea how much Mr. Teegerstrom knew about the off-stage activities regularly associated with dancing; at the *Top 'n Bottom*: the private meetings downstairs and the arranged off-site sexual meetings with patrons—in short, the prostitution. He suspected the counselor was aware to some extent of those activities, but he was glad the subject had not been raised; it was somewhat embarrassing to Casey to know he was selling his body for cash, even though he felt no guilt about it.

How a sexually sophisticated man like Bill Lowe had failed to learn anything substantial about AIDS, much less grasp its implications for his, and his son's, sexual activities, is a mystery. But the word was circulating very slowly in the gay community, probably attributable to its reluctance to accept such alarming news. Furthermore, Bill did not circulate freely in the San Francisco's gay scene. When Casey sat down one night to talk about safe sex with his father, Bill was basically flabbergasted, and, like Casey, he resolved to adopt condoms when fucking or getting fucked. Casey also broke the bad news about his grades and his failure to graduate in the spring with his class. Casey resolved to follow his father's admonitions: he would cut down on the time he devoted to the theatre and his corollary encounters there, and he would start to 'hit the books' seriously.

Casey discussed the situation with Eddie, who was sympathetic, and agreed that Casey could cut back his hours and participation as much as he needed. Casey had become the most popular dancer with the theatre's patrons, and Eddie agreed to schedule his performances at the most advantageous times so that he could make extra tips to compensate for some of the revenue the boy would lose from scheduling fewer private, extracurricular meetings.

If any of the other house dancers noticed the newly favored schedule Casey was assigned, none but Richard said anything about it to Eddie. Not only was Casey the most popular dancer with the patrons of the T 'n B, he was also probably the best-liked among the other dancers—likely owing to his genial nature, his physical beauty, and more than likely, his generosity in sharing with them backstage the fabulous cock and beautiful, hungry ass they all admired and wanted. Even the muscular Adam, formerly regarded by the dancers as straight, no longer hid his lust for the young blond fuckmaster. Lately, Adam had been surprised a few times by his fellow employees while he was taking Casey up the ass, and loudly exhorting the blond to fuck him faster, harder and deeper, so he no longer bothered to protest his supposed heterosexuality. If the other dancers were willing to be charitable to Casey, Richard was not. He thought that he, himself, was the one who deserved better treatment, not the newcomer Casey, however admittedly hot he might be. He decided to broach the subject with Eddie in the way he knew would dispose Eddie most favorably to his situation.

Richard was doing a 'double' with guest porn 'artist,' "Big Bill" Eld, a somewhat over-the-hill, but monstrously hung and still popular star of the late seventies—good-looking, with a trademark helmet of dark hair and very full lips. Bill fucked Richard on stage at the conclusion of their show, with Richard bent over a table and practically squealing in pleasure as the porn star pounded his ass unmercifully with his monster cock, pulling the condom from it only at the last split second before his orgasm, and blowing his load explosively all over Richard's ass and back—all to tumultuous applause. The applause increased when Richard stood tall and, with Bill's cum oozing down his back and onto his ass, he seized his cock, turned around, and after only a few strokes his own cum erupted, hitting Bill's chest and belly.

Backstage, as the audience filed out, Bill and Richard had necked for a long time, watched by the last two of the remaining house dancers. Bill praised Richard's exciting bottoming as some of the best he had ever enjoyed, saying he wished he could take Richard back to the hotel so he could fuck with him all night. "And I wanna do plenty with this gorgeous cock of yours," he said as he fondled Richard's throbbing big prick, "I'll bet it tastes as good as it looks. But I've got an all-nighter waiting out on the street who wants to invest five hundred bucks in a night of getting fucked the way I just plowed your pretty ass." He grinned as he opened his locker and began to dress, "Maybe tomorrow night, huh?"

Richard began fondling Bill's ass as he said, "Maybe you'll give me some of what I just gave you? You've got mighty pretty ass yourself, you know. I sure would like to fill it for you."

Bill turned to kiss Richard, and replied, "You know I'm a top, but who knows? Maybe I'll make an exception for you. That dick of yours is mighty fine; takin' that up my ass might be a helluva lotta fun. I can tell you'd really fill it good!" He had not put on his underwear yet, and as he said it, he backed up to press his bare ass against Richard and wriggle it around the end of Richard's cock—which was standing straight out, throbbing in full erection.

"I'm gonna hold you to it," Richard said, humping his dick against Bill's ass and reaching around to fondle his tits.

"Now, it's not a promise, Richard," Bill grinned, "but we'll sure see what we can do tomorrow. How does that sound?" It sounded extremely good to Richard!

Bill finished dressing, and left the theatre to meet his 'all-nighter.' The two remaining dancers also left—for home, or wherever they were going. Richard again put on the tiny pouch g-string and boots he had been wearing when he had started his double with 'Big Bill.' Dressed in that skimpiest of ways, he went through the empty auditorium and into the lobby—which had been locked for the night, He went into Eddie's office, where the manager was reckoning the day's receipts

Richard had decided to confront Eddie with Casey's newly diminished, but preferential schedule, which he, but apparently none of the other dancers had seemed to notice—or, if they had, they had not remarked on it to the best of Richard's knowledge.

Eddie smiled as Richard entered and said they needed to talk. Part of the reason for Eddie's warm greeting was the fact that Richard was nearly naked, and his cock was hard, standing straight up and protruding from the g-string, pressed by the waistband against his belly. Richard knew very well the power he had over Eddie, and as he walked up to the office, he had stroked his prick until it made the kind of impression he knew Eddie would most appreciate.

"God, you look fantastic," Eddie grinned. "What do we need to talk about? I hope it's got something to do with that beautiful big hard-on."

"We'll talk about my hard-on in a minute." He slipped the waistband of the g-string down, beneath his balls, so that his erection stood out in its full glory. He leered and smiled crookedly as he added, "We can talk about this, and we can talk about that monster hard-on you've probably got." Casey was right; Eddie's prick was throbbing, and he was stroking it beneath the desk. "And we can do a lot more than talk, if you want, but before we do, I wanna talk about Casey."

"What about him?"

"I can see what you're doing for him," Richard said, "and I don't think it's fair."

"Whaddya mean,?" Eddie asked.

"You know perfectly well. You're giving him all the best times for his shows, and pretty much scheduling him only for the good ones. You've always been more than fair to me. I know that, and I appreciate it, but what's Casey got on you? You have the hots for him? I can't blame you for that, but I assume you still want me, too?"

"You know I still want you and I love you, Richard. I have for all these years. But Casey is having trouble at school, and I don't want him to quit. The audiences love him, you know that. He's gorgeous, he's hung like a horse, and he's a complete turn-on. You know that, too. From what I've seen, you know that as well as anyone does—from experience."

Richard approached Eddie, brandishing his erection. "Yeah, we've played around a lot, but I know you've had him, too. Do you want his dick more than this one? Is his ass hotter than mine? "

Eddie stepped out from behind his desk, his enormous prick tenting his pants. He enfolded Richard in his arms and kissed him passionately as Richard responded with equal fervor. Eddie fell to his knees, and reverently took Richard's cock in his cupped hands. He planted a kiss on the cock-head and whispered, "More than anything in the world, I want this beautiful dick in my mouth and in my ass." As he spoke, he unzipped his trousers and freed the monstrous erection straining for release. He stroked it and asked, "You still want mine the same way?"

Richard put his hands under Eddie's armpits and raised him to his feet. He kissed Eddie lovingly and spoke, very seriously, "You know I do, Eddie. I always will. He undid Eddie's belt and dropped his pants to the floor. "Get out of that shirt and give it to me right now." He pulled the g-string down and stepped out of it, then leaned over Eddie's desk and used both hands to spread his ass cheeks. He panted, hoarsely, "I want you now, lover."

Eddie shucked out of his clothes, and was reaching for the jar of lubricant he always kept on his desk, when he remembered to find a condom and roll it down the long, fat shaft Richard was begging for. He greased up Richard's ass and the condom, then positioned his cock-head at Richard's asshole. Richard began to press backward to accept the gargantuan offering Eddie had for him.

Eddie had no trouble in entering Richard, whose ass was still distended from the fierce fuck Bill Eld had given him only a short while earlier. Once he was completely inside, Richard began to moan, "Fuck me, Eddie. I love your cock." Eddie complied, as he always did when he invaded his beloved, the ravenously fuck-hungry stud impaled on his dick: he fucked with a strange mixture of love, tenderness, and delirious, almost brutal lust. Richard's response to Eddie's fuck was, as always, complete joy and ecstasy.

Eddie blew a load inside Richard, panting and heaving, almost shouting in seemingly victorious passion. Richard groaned, "Don't stop, lover. Keep fucking my hot ass!" Without slowing his stroke, or lessening the intensity of his feverish rapacity, Eddie kept hammering Richard's thrashing, humping, voracious ass for another fifteen minutes, until Eddie cried out in wordless victory as he filled the condom inside the object of his love with another load. His body fell limply over Richard's as he kissed Richard's ear and whispered his satisfaction into it, "God, I love you so much, baby!"

"I love you too, Eddie. You're always the best." Richard's declaration of love was not completely untrue. He had honestly been in love with Eddie when he moved to California to be with him, many years earlier, but after a few months, he had transferred his love to a big-dicked porn movie producer, and moved out to make fuck films in Los Angeles. Still, he retained considerable affection for Eddie, especially for Eddie's gargantuan prick and his stamina as a buttfucker, two characteristics Richard prized more than any others in a sex partner. They were the same qualities Richard had employed to win Eddie's love, and which he regularly offered a partner if he was moved to do so — and he was moved to do so almost daily.

Eddie had remained steadfastly in love with Richard since the first night they went to bed together, back in Alabama, and though he ostensibly had a partner at home, who admired those same things Richard loved about Eddie, his young partner did not have the same outsized cock and fierce fucking technique that Richard could offer in return. Eddie was fond of his young partner at home, but he loved Richard — even though over the years Richard had done much to test that love, or perhaps destroy it. He had never met anyone who was such an insatiable, voracious bottom as Richard, but one who could also match Richard's ability to kiss, suck dick, eat ass and fuck with such glorious intensity.

Eddie continued to nibble Richard's ear as Richard declared his continuing love, and then whispered, "Get on your back now. I'm gonna fuck you senseless. Then I want you to fuck me again, okay?"

"God, yes," Eddie gasped, "anything you want!" He stood, causing his cock to slip form Richard's ass. Richard stood, faced him and kissed him passionately and at length.

"What I want," Richard finally said as he ended the kiss and began to press Eddie's back down onto the desk top, "is for you to give me an even better kind of deal than you're giving Casey."

Eddie ripped the condom from his prick and threw it to the floor as he lay on the desk top and raised his legs. He looked intently at his lover and panted, "Anything you want, lover, it's yours. What I want right now is that beautiful cock inside me again." Richard reached for the ashtray full of condoms, but Eddie added, "Don't put on a rubber. I want you to fill my ass with your hot cum — not a rubber." Eddie was normally careful about condom usage, but he was not thinking clearly with *The Love of his Life* positioning his big prick to fuck him.

Richard had blown a load on Bill Eld less than an hour earlier, so he knew he would have plenty of time to fuck Eddie senseless before he had another orgasm, as promised. And he virtually kept that promise.

While Richard hammered Eddie's ass with brutal, relentless thrusts, Eddie moaned and groaned in an apparent delirium of fuck-hunger, gasping Richard's name, hoarsely declaring his love and need for him, and his gratitude for his masterful fucking. Finally, after fifteen minutes of savage near-frenzy, Richard cried loudly, "I'm gonna come. Take my big load, lover!"

Eddie cried, even louder, "Don't stop fucking, baby. Fill me with that hot cum, but keep ramming that big dick up my ass. I love you so much, Richard!"

"I love you, too, baby," Richard gasped as he froze momentarily while he exploded his load inside the delirious Eddie. Then he resumed his rapturous work with undiminished ardor, continuing to fuel the obviously ecstatic thrill Eddie was experiencing.

After another quarter-hour of savage fucking, Richard knew he could not continue without a rest — a long one — but he chose to retain the thrill for Eddie by faking an orgasm. He almost screamed a passionate "I'm coming again, baby!" as he thrust his prick as far inside Eddie as he could, and wriggled his ass wildly in simulated orgasm while Eddie groaned his thrill.

Keeping his cock in Eddie still, Richard fell over his lover's chest, and they kissed feverishly, their kisses gradually turning to tender affection while they continued necking for five or ten minutes. Finally, Richard whispered, "I have to go soon, lover, but you promised you'd fuck me again."

"I'll always keep my promises to you, baby," Eddie said as he stood, causing Richard to stand also, and pulling Richard's now limp cock to slip from his ass. Richard turned and bent over the desk, groaning, "Give it to me again!"

Without thinking about putting on a condom, Eddie positioned the head of his fiercely hard, gargantuan prick at his lover's fuck-hole. He grabbed Richard's shoulders, and used them for leverage as with one ferocious shove he plunged his monster deep inside. Richard yelled with thrill as Eddie began to fuck like a pile driver. He had come close to blowing another load while Richard had been fucking him, and the aborted orgasm, oddly enough, seemed to make it take longer to arrive at another one — which was fine with Eddie, and even more fine with Richard. Eventually, however, Eddie erupted inside Richard, and both stood facing each other, panting their satisfaction, kissing and fondling affectionately, both at long last sated. Not surprisingly,

Richard retained the presence of mind to remind Eddie of the promise he had made to try and make his work at the theatre as advantageous as Casey's.

As it turned out, Bill Eld wound up having another lucrative overnight engagement to fulfill the next evening, so while the next-to-last show was going on — with the muscular Carl dancing and offering his big cock and succulent tits for the enjoyment of an enthusiastic audience — Bill told Richard he would give up his ass to him, as he had more-or-less promised the night before. Bill, the putative top, lay in the missionary position on the backstage sofa and put his raised legs on Richard's shoulders while Richard knelt between them and fucked Bill's ass unmercifully. While he was getting fucked, Bill gasped his pleasure and masturbated himself, blowing a huge load on his chest and face just as Richard exploded what seemed to be an equally large load deep inside the grateful porn star's wildly bucking ass. Richard had not put on a condom, but if Bill had noticed, he said nothing about it, welcoming Richard's cum inside him with ecstatic enthusiasm.

Fortunately, Bill — who was in a few minutes due to make a solo appearance for the final act that night — had already blown his obligatory on-stage load earlier in the day, and did not have to produce another orgasm on stage. This allowed him to be better prepared for his all-night, paid client. "He asked Casey, "You gonna watch my dance, hot stuff?" as he was getting ready to go on stage. "That big load of cum you just gave me is gonna be sloshing around inside my ass while I wag my dick for the paying customers, and I'll be thinking about how it got there!" As he performed following Carl on stage, he was remembering the masterly fuck Richard had just given him, and he had no trouble in maintaining the famous monster erection that had given him his nickname of "Big Bill." In fact, he came fairly close to blowing yet another load on stage as he played with his cock for the delectation of the patrons, and very close when a few of the bolder members of the audience briefly sucked it. When he finished and went backstage, Richard, who had watched his performance from the wings, congratulated him on the sexiness of his 'dance.' Instead of replying in words, Bill turned Richard's body around and bent him over, panting, "Gonna fuck your hot ass one more time." Following Bill's example, Richard said nothing, but reached behind himself to spread his buttcheeks until Bill's throbbing cock was inside, after which he braced himself against a wall while the porn star seized his waist and clasped it tight as he savagely plugged Richard's hot ass again. Richard was so turned on that after Bill had exploded inside his ass, he continued to work Bill's cock for several minutes before he turned around and shoved Bill ruthlessly against the wall where he had been braced. Bill knew what was coming; he bent over and wriggled his ass while Richard drove his cock inside, with one fierce thrust, provoking a loud cry of joy from Bill, followed by subsequent gasps of thrill at the ferocious fuck he was enjoying.

Richard sent Bill out into the night to meet his 'date' with yet another load of cum inside him. Such was Bill's mastery and staying power that the client never suspected his lover-for-the-night had been fucking, and being fucked, by a hot stud only minutes before they met.

9.

A Walk in the Park

By the time Spring Break rolled around, in March, Casey had already improved his scholarship to the point that if he could maintain his new academic performance level he would easily be able to graduate at the end of summer school. He had "A" averages in all his classes, something he had never achieved before. He had accomplished this through rigid budgeting of his time, and very serious study outside of class. He continued to dance at the T 'n B, albeit on his new, more limited schedule, and had accepted only a very limited number of offers for outside, private engagements there. Still he had been able to budget time for enough fucking with both Joey Stone and Rommel Chase to keep them reasonably well satisfied—and to keep himself satisfied as well. His other regular fuckbuddies were not happy with the fact that Casey was no longer feeding them his fabulous dick and luscious ass, but the young blond stud managed to direct them to each other for satisfaction.

Hallie Teegerstrom was so impressed with the vast improvement in Casey's work that he felt the boy might even be able to gain entrance to a fairly decent college in the fall if he were given a recommendation pointing out how much he had improved after his junior- and senior-year academic slump—and Hallie was more than willing to write letters of recommendation to that effect.

Monday of Spring Break week was a beautiful, sunny day, much warmer than usual in "The City." Casey had no school, and no work to occupy his time, since the T 'n B was closed for the day. He felt wonderfully free, and planned to spend the day pretty much by himself, although he had promised Joey they could get together fairly late that night for one of their usual torrid fuck sessions. He had promised his father they would go out for dinner together earlier in the evening. Bill laughed when Casey told him he had plans with Joey for after dinner. "I can't think of a more attractive dessert than that." Knowing that Joey was not getting as much fucking as he had been used to before he started working at the theatre, Casey was tempted to tell his father that he thought Joey might be amenable to substituting father for son now and then; he thought both Joey and his dad would enjoy such an arrangement. Joey had often told Casey, "Your dad is really hot," and Joey was clearly attractive to his father. Actually, Casey rather thought he liked the idea of Joey and his dad making love, but he would want no part in it—no threesome welcome if his dad were involved!

After sleeping late, Casey decided he would spend a few hours at his favorite spot in the city: atop the bluffs in Lincoln Park overlooking the western side of the Golden Gate Bridge. He knew plenty of gay sex action took place in the thickets that lined the main trail; it was, in fact, the place where, three years earlier, he had watched a sailor and a boy fuck each other, the first time he had watched someone get fucked "in the flesh" when he was not himself a part of the equation. He had frequently been propositioned there, but only once had the man soliciting sex with him there been attractive enough that he took him up on it—and then the man had wanted only to suck him off.

But Casey was not looking for sex this day; he simply wanted to enjoy the beautiful weather in a favorite location.

Deciding to kill two birds with one stone, he decided to take the new Stephen King book along with him, to read both for pleasure and for his English class, where his report on it would be due after Spring Break. Casey was reading King's *Different Seasons* as an assignment for his English class. Normally, his English teacher would have disdained a book by the wildly popular so called horrormeister, King, but he felt the new book—a collection of four novellas, actually—was far the best thing King had ever written, and worthy of a student's time. Casey was enjoying the book far more than he had anticipated—he was not, in fact, much of a reader. He thought the stories would make wonderful movies, and he conjured up those would-be films in his mind as he read. Subsequent developments would prove Casey's prescience: three of the novellas were made into movies, one of them good, and two of them superb.

He dressed in walking shorts and a sweatshirt. He knew the winds at the Lincoln Park cliffs would make it much cooler than it was around his home, where only a T-shirt would have been sufficient for the warm temperature. He was hoping it might be warm enough, though, that he could shed the sweatshirt at the park and begin working on his spring tan. He walked the nine short blocks to Geary

Boulevard, and boarded the bus to the end of the Geary line, near Cliff House at the ocean.

Passing through the ruins of the Sutro Baths, Casey ascended the fairly steep path leading to the bluffs, where he ambled along, enjoying the beautiful weather. It was still fairly early in the day, and he saw no one sucking dick or fucking in the thicket—not his normal experience up there. One or two other guys had eyed him suggestively as they crossed paths, but none had openly propositioned him. There was, strangely, no breeze at all, and it seemed to be as warm there as it had been back at his house. He came to a bench with an especially spectacular view of the Golden Gate, the bridge and the boats and ships wending their way out to sea. There seemed to be no incoming traffic at the moment. He pulled off his sweatshirt and laid it on the bench, where he sat and began to read.

He finished reading the third novella in *Different Seasons*, which he found wonderful, and was well into the final story, which he was finding inferior to the other three—so far, at any rate. Then he thought he heard a voice calling him from a distance. But who knew he was going to be there? Only his dad knew where he had planned to go this morning. but he was working. So who could be calling him?

Then a large Irish Setter bounded into view—sleek, red, and absolutely beautiful. The dog appeared to be looking around, and when Casey said, "Hey, boy. Where did you come from?" the dog trotted over to him and allowed him to pet his head and to stroke his back. Casey looked down to check, and ascertained the dog was, in fact, a male. Then he heard the voice calling "Casey!" again, his time closer.

Confused as to who was calling him, he nonetheless called out, "Over here." The dog put one paw on Casey's leg and looked up at him, wagging his tail majestically. When the voice called "Casey!" again—this time very near—Casey stood and looked around, calling "Right here." Just then a very tall man came into sight around a bend in the trail, dressed in very tight walking shorts and an equally tight T-shirt.

"Casey! There you are, boy!" the man called, and approached Casey and the dog, whose tail went into overdrive. Casey did not recognize the man, but since he was calling him, it seemed they must know each other in some context. The young man was grinning a very attractive grin, and was, in fact, very attractive. He came up to Casey, but it was clear he was looking at the dog. He knelt next to the setter, saying, as he tousled the dog's fur, "I've been looking all over for you,"

"You're looking for me? Casey asked. "I don't think I ..."

"No," the man said, looking up, "I was looking for Casey, here."

Casey laughed, "Wow, that's funny. I thought you were calling me." He extended his right hand and said, "I'm Casey, too. Casey Lowe."

The man also laughed, then stood and took Casey's hand. As they shook hands, he said, "This Casey is Casey Seymour, my cousin Mike's dog. I'm just taking him for some exercise. I'm Luke Henson, by the way." He smiled again as he said the last, this time a huge grin, and when he did, Casey thought his entire face lit up like a Christmas tree—a dazzling Christmas tree, a dazzling, tall Christmas tree—dressed in clothes that emphasized a very fine body to go with the grin.

Luke Henson had one of the most engaging smiles Casey had ever seen, and his heart seemed to be acting like a complete cliché: it skipped a beat or two, accompanying the strange, but pleasant, feeling he got in his stomach—as though the cliché butterflies had flapped their wings inside. He finally realized he was still shaking Luke's hand, and reluctantly released it. "You and Casey live near here?" he asked.

"Well, Casey does. I'm visiting my cousin, He lives a few blocks away from here, but I'm from a little town in South Carolina." He gestured toward the book, which Casey had laid there when the dog appeared. "Whatcha reading?"

"Oh, the new Stephen King book. I'm reading it for my English class."

"Where do you go to school? San Francisco State? Berkeley?" Luke asked.

Casey laughed. "Thanks for the compliment. No, I'm still a high school student—but if all goes well, I'll be going to college this fall."

"Wow," Luke said, "you sure look mature for a high school student." And then the magic grin appeared again. "In fact, you look like you're all man."

The sensation that had caused Luke's butterflies and irregular heartbeat had drifted a bit south, and was swelling the crotch of his shorts. He didn't know if Luke's comment about his supposed manhood was because the tall boy had noticed his swollen shorts, but he hoped so. Luke's swollen T-shirt displayed a very fine upper body, massive shoulders, large breasts and a washboard stomach. His muscular, and divinely long legs were showcased by the tight shorts, and Casey was hoping to get a glimpse of Luke's ass in those shorts; he was betting it was as divinely swollen as the T-shirt was. Casey was soon to see he won his bet: Luke's ass was beautifully rounded—and the shorts were so tight they clearly revealed the cleft between his buttocks. He took time to gaze unapologetically up and down Luke's fine body, then said, "You're a helluva man yourself, if you don't mind my saying so."

Luke's grin was clearly embarrassed as he said, "Thanks, Casey. I apologize for this shirt and these shorts. I didn't bring clothes for really warm weather this trip, so I borrowed some of Mike's—and he's a lot smaller than I am."

"They do a lot for you," Casey said, with a crooked grin—almost a leer—as his gaze traveled up and down Luke's body again. His tone of voice made it clear that he intended the remark as sexual innuendo. "Don't apologize."

"You look mighty goddamned fine to me, too," Luke said, looking Casey seriously and unflinchingly in the eyes. Then he smiled again, and asked, "You wanna walk with Casey and me for a while? This Casey, I mean," he added as he ruffled the fur on the dog's head. That Casey's tail made it clear he was ready for further adventures.

"Sure," Casey said, and you can tell me about how they raise 'em like you in South Carolina."

"How's that?"

"Tall, and built, and hot" As he said the last, Casey gentle palmed one of Luke's swelling breasts.

Luke put his hand over Casey's, and held it to his breast. "I may be taller'n you, but I'm damned sure not as built or as hot as you are."

"Sez you," Casey said, and they both grinned

Casey picked up his book and sweatshirt, saying, "Let's find someplace nearby where we can stash these until we get back."

"Yeah, and I can find someplace to take a leak, too," Luke said.

"Believe me," Casey said, "you could take a leak anywhere around here without having to hide. But a guy with his dick hanging out will probably get propositioned before he finishes pissing."

"Yeah, Mike said I might see just about anything up here."

"Cousin Mike knows best, I see," Casey said. "Is Mike … is he gay?"

"Oh yeah," Luke laughed.

"Have you two ever …"

Luke laughed again, "Not since yesterday. He's in bed with his landlord right now — paying the rent, so to speak — and I'm dog-sitting with Casey."

Luke's cousin was really named Kenneth, but had always been known as Mike. He was a few years younger than Luke, but when Mike's mother visited her sister in South Carolina, the two boys played together as equals, and were very close. On Mike's last visit, two years earlier, when he was 18 and Luke was 20, they got about as close as two guys could get. Mike and Luke had always been "into" each other, in the figurative sense, but this time they literally got into each other — and at least once daily, but usually several times. This was the first visit Luke had made to San Francisco, and the first time he had been with his cousin since he and Mike had connected so memorably in 1981.

Mike had been born and raised in northern California; after his high school graduation, he had served in the Army, and moved to Los Angeles. His wholesome, 'boy-next-door' sexiness had soon landed him a place where he got paid for what he had been doing so frequently in the Army for free. It was a gay 'escort service' called Pete's Pals, actually a wide-ranging male prostitution ring employing mostly gay porn stars — current and veteran — and others who were clearly at the porn-star level in looks and sexual talent. Gorgeous, well-built, fairly well-hung and talented as both a top and bottom, Mike was a natural — and proved to be quite popular with the clientele.

For his work in the sex industry, Mike had adopted an alias, using his sobriquet as a first name, and taking his uncle's last name. Thus he was "Mike Henson," a name that would become very well known in porn circles within a few years.

Although Mike was very successful as an 'escort' — one of the most popular of Pete's Pals — he found the work demeaning more often than it was enjoyable. Furthermore, given the percentage of his wages as a prostitute that he had to share with his pimp (euphemistically called the proprietor of Pete's Pals, and not, incidentally, named Pete), Mike decided to strike out on his own, He accepted an offer to appear in a porn video, to be shot in San Francisco. Like most of his colleagues, he had received other such offers while working as a Pete's Pal, but, unlike his colleagues, had declined, since he would have had to share the money with his pimp; now he could keep all of what he was paid — which wasn't that much to begin with.

The new porn video Mike had just finished shooting when Luke encountered Casey in the park had been filmed by Eagle Productions, arguably the classiest of the many gay porn producers that were springing up. Most were based in Los Angeles, but Eagle called San Francisco home. The head of Eagle had been so impressed with Mike's work that he had convinced the newcomer to move to San Francisco so he could be ready for many more films to be shot there; several were already 'in the works' or in the planning stage.

San Francisco was a very expensive city in which to live, and Mike accepted the offer of a wealthy older client to live rent-free in his house, with the understanding that Mike would come to the older man's bed at least twice a week while he lived there—to 'pay the rent' in his very special way. The house was large, almost palatial, situated on a hill near the Sutro Heights Park, overlooking the ocean at the Ocean Beach Esplanade. The older man was fit, surprisingly athletic and intense in his lovemaking, and Mike actually enjoyed their sexual encounters. Furthermore, Mike was permitted to entertain other sex partners in his own room from time to time, using his own private entrance, as long as he was discreet and selective about whom he brought there.

"I wonder if Casey realizes what a hot man is talking care of him," Casey Lowe mused. "No offense, Luke, but do you mind if I ask you a personal question?"

"Of course not," Luke replied. "Would it have to do with seeing to the needs of some other Casey?"

"Oh, yeah," Casey replied, "and hopefully to taking care of Luke's needs at the same time. But let's find a place to stash this book and piss; then we can discuss it while we walk Casey some more."

As the two walked, Casey tried to analyze what was so overwhelmingly attractive about Luke. He was very tall—six feet, five inches, actually—and that was imposing. His tight clothing made it abundantly clear he also had a fine body: broad chest, muscular shoulders and arms, a distinctive washboard stomach (what years later would come to be called a 'six pack'), a cute, rounded butt (later, a 'bubble butt,' of course), fairly small waist, and long, long, muscular legs. He had dark hair, cut in a very short 'buzz cut." Facially, he was not remarkable: his eyes were black, and they seemed a bit to small for his face; his nose was long and very straight—a patrician nose; he was amiable-looking, with a broad, open face and an unusually wide mouth; and when that mouth smiled it revealed large, very white, even teeth, and completely adorable dimples. The total physical package was what Casey was reacting to, but as he chatted, Luke gave the impression he was fairly quiet, just a tiny bit shy, and quite sweet, further cementing the powerful impression he was making on Casey.

They strolled up the trail, heading toward the Golden Gate Bridge, and came to a particularly dense growth of short trees and tall shrubbery. "This looks like somewhere we might find a hiding place," Casey said. They brushed aside some low-hanging branches and entered a secluded opening. "Perfect," Casey said as he wrapped the book in his sweatshirt and secreted it under some branches growing near ground level. "Now if we can just find it when we come back," he laughed. He unbuttoned his shorts and pulled out his dick. "Good place to pee, also." He began to do so.

Luke whistled his admiration as he saw the mighty organ Casey was wielding. "Wow, that is some cock! And it's not hard. Jesus, how long does that thing get?"

Grinning proudly—justifiably so—Casey said, "A little over ten inches." He began to stroke his fat shaft as he added, " And looking at you, it's probably gonna get there before I stuff it back in." His prophecy began to come true as he stroked, and as Luke goggled, reaching down to cup Casey's crotch and helping him hold his own dick—still streaming with piss.

"I'm already so hard I'm not gonna be able to get my cock out without pulling these damned little shorts down," Luke said, seemingly a bit embarrassed, "and my dick is gonna look pretty small compared to yours." As he said this, he began tugging the shorts halfway down his legs, and then began peeling off his underwear. His hard prick sprang out when it cleared the elastic band.

"Shit, there's nothing wrong with that cock," Casey said. "Very nice, in fact." Luke's cock was about eight inches long—a very impressive one, well above normal size, even if it didn't compare to the monster weapon Casey was holding. He began stroking it as he said, "I'm gonna have to get off before I can get it back in my shorts. You wanna help me with it?" he asked Casey, while he tied the dog Casey's leash to a tree trunk.

Casey replied by kneeling in front of Luke and pulling Luke's underwear and shorts down to his ankles. Then he took Luke's hard cock inside his mouth in one hungry gulp. Luke gasped his satisfaction and gripped Casey's head in his hands while he fucked the blond boy's mouth as he licked and sucked expertly. Casey fondled Luke's busy ass, and he ran his hands up, under Luke's tight T-shirt, feverishly fondling his chest and sides. Luke pulled off his shirt and threw it on the ground, providing Casey with greater freedom to caress him. Both moaned their satisfaction for ten minutes until Luke gasped, "I'm gonna come! Stop, or I'm gonna blow my load in your mouth." Casey simply sucked harder, and was soon rewarded with an ample flow of thick, hot cream, which he savored while he bathed Luke's cock in it, and then swallowed.

After continuing to nurse for several minutes, while Luke's erection wilted somewhat, Casey released his cock and smiled up at the boy. "Wonderful!" To Casey, the sight of Luke's answering grin was almost as enjoyable and rewarding as his load of hot, sweet cum had been. Casey could stand it no longer; he had to kiss this boy! Luke was feeling much the same sort of thing: looking down at the face of the golden-haired Adonis; with his prick resting on the chin and his cum glistening at the lips, he had the same overwhelming desire to kiss. He was also burning with desire to blow the Adonis's monster cock — but he wondered how well he would be able to properly suck what was probably the biggest prick he had ever encountered in person. Casey stood, and their arms instinctively went around each other. He turned his face up as Luke bent his head down; their lips met while their arms pulled their bodies tightly together, and they kissed passionately for a very long time.

Finally, Luke whispered, "My cum tastes good on your tongue, but now I wanna taste your cum." He kissed Casey again, briefly, and sank to his knees. Casey held Luke's head tightly as the boy opened his mouth very wide to accept the challenge of Casey's enormous prick.

Casey gently began to thrust his cock in and out of the welcoming heat of Luke's mouth, a little deeper each time. Luke's lips locked around the fat shaft and he sucked profoundly, welcoming the forward thrusts with inward plunges. In his mind, he felt he would never be able to take all of this golden boy's magnificent cock in his mouth, but gradually his nose came to be nesting in Casey's pubic hair. Casey groaned "Yes!" as he began to fuck Luke's mouth, and Luke groaned in wordless thrill as he feasted hungrily. He had never sucked a cock this big, and he was amazed that he was virtually deep-throating it — but he was inspired: he had never sucked a cock he wanted more, nor had he ever made love with a more beautiful boy. Casey's hands continued to hold Luke's head firmly as he drove his prick in and out, so that Luke wasn't so much blowing Casey as he was getting fucked in the mouth,

Luke's hands played over Casey's busy ass, and as one of his fingers teased his asshole, Casey groaned, "Yeah, give me that finger!" With that encouragement, Luke began fucking Casey as furiously with his forefinger as Casey was fucking his mouth. Soon—far too soon— Casey cried, "I'm gonna come!" and his hot discharge began to fill Luke's mouth. So copious was Casey's load, and so violently discharged, that Luke had to back off about an inch on his cock so he could accommodate it without gagging—and he didn't want to lose a drop of it. After savoring it while he continued to finger-fuck Casey, Luke swallowed all of the precious discharge, and rose to his feet so he and Casey could kiss again.

Casey panted into Luke's mouth, "Your finger felt so goddamned good inside me, baby. You gonna put that hot cock in there next?"

"Only if you promise to ram that monster of yours up my butt," Luke grinned.

"That's a promise I can't wait to keep," Casey said, kissing him again. "But we don't have any lube or rubbers here, and we don't wanna fuck on the bare ground."

"We'll figure out a place and time soon," Luke said. "Real soon. I'm only gonna be here until Friday. Then it's back to South Carolina and school. But we'll definitely figure it out. C'mon, let's finish walking Casey, and we can talk about it."

Luke's erection had faded, and he peed, which he had needed to do all along, but had been unable to since he first got a hard-on when they entered the thicket. They put their clothes on, although Luke left his T-shirt with the hidden book and sweatshirt. They untied Casey the dog—who had been remarkably well-behaved, lying there quietly while they had been blowing each other.

As they emerged from the thicket, they almost ran into a sailor. He was leaning against a tree, smoking a cigarette. His white hat was on the back of his head, and his jumper cuffs were rolled up, showing embroidered dragons inside. A patch on his shoulder read "U.S.S. *Enterprise* (CVN-65)." The flap on his thirteen-button pants was open and hanging down, revealing the fact that he was wearing no underwear and showcasing his balls and a long, very fat prick that lay against his pants flap—not erect, but clearly massive meat. He was good-looking, if not especially handsome, but his tight uniform showed he had a fine, muscular body. He held a rolled-up blanket under one arm. There was no doubting what he was there for, and the sight of two such handsome young men coming out of the brush, both naked to the waist, raised his hopes for success in his quest. Raising one eyebrow and leering suggestively at Luke and Casey, he said, "You guys lookin' for some action — or did I just miss it?"

"You just missed it, I'm afraid," Casey said, but he reached down and fondled the sailor's cock — which grew as he did so, and began to stand out. "Too bad. This coulda been fun."

Luke reached down and held the sailor's prick for a moment, feeling it reach its full, impressive potential as he said, "Yeah, a lotta fun."

"Maybe next time," the sailor grinned, now stroking his massive shaft — a delectable one.

Casey and Luke waved goodbye to the sailor as they started up the trail, the dog Casey wagging his tail — very happy to be moving again after the boring business of having to watch his handler sucking cock and getting sucked off. They marked the bench where they had met, so they would be able to locate the thicket where Casey had hidden his book and sweatshirt when they returned, and headed east on the trail

As they walked, they chatted easily. Both felt a kinship far past what simple traded blowjobs would normally engender. Casey filled Luke in on all the details of his life — including his wild sex life at school, but omitting his work at the *Top 'n Bottom* and the concomitant prostitution. For some reason, he didn't want this apparently sweet boy to know about it — at least not yet — and he somehow sensed that he was going to have a future with him; certainly he wanted to have a future with him. Not since Richard had he felt this way — and the feeling was not so overwhelmingly based on sexual attraction this time. God knows, however, there was plenty of sexual attraction involved — and why was he thinking of a guy who was a few years older than he and who could deep-throat a ten-inch-plus cock and give it such a splendid blowjob as a sweet boy, anyway? But there did seem to be a trusting naïvete about Luke — refreshing and charming, and, in its own way, very sexy. Plus, Luke was built, and cute. Feeding him a load, and sucking one out of him had done nothing to allay the butterflies flying around inside him.

Luke responded by relating his story.

He was 22, and was visiting from South Carolina, where he had been born — in the town of Irmo, near the state capital, Columbia.

Casey remarked on Luke's lack of a southern accent. Luke explained that both his parents were Midwesterners, so he naturally adopted their accent — or, rather, their lack of accent, as some would have it. His father had died in Vietnam when Luke was only thirteen, a highly-decorated hero in the Air Force. His high-school career had been interrupted for two years while he cared for his mother, who had become increasingly remote and distraught following his father's death. She rallied somewhat, and Luke returned to school, where he graduated in 1981, but his mother had failed again, and died just weeks short of his graduation.

His father had graduated from Farrar University, a medium-sized college in the northwestern corner of South Carolina, and had often expressed a wish that Luke would also go to Farrar; Colonel Henson had very fond memories of his Farrar days. Luke almost felt it was his duty to attend Farrar, but after visiting the school in the small town of Oconee — the country seat of Foothills County — he liked just about everything he saw there. One of the things that impressed him at Farrar was an unusually high percentage of cute boys and hot young men.

Luke always knew he was gay, and by the time he was ready for college, he was decidedly interested in expanding and exploring his homosexual nature, which he had hitherto been able to indulge only in a very limited way. His sexual experiences had largely been limited to the "Boy, was I drunk last night; I don't even remember what we did" variety, following sleepovers with friends whom he found sexy. The pseudo-amnesia adopted by those boys he fucked and sucked off, and who invariably returned his ministrations in kind, was not attributed to alcohol, however, which Luke almost never used. His partners protested something like "Boy was I tired last night, I don't even remember what we did." Luke remembered it all, however, and treasured it, but somehow he felt like he was the only queer in South Carolina. He assumed all those boys who kissed him, sucked him off, and took him up the ass were straight. He felt that way — intellectually, at any rate, but emotionally, he didn't believe it for a moment.

His mother had been insured, and she had wisely invested the money left from his father's insurance. Luke inherited all that, and he was able to sell their very fine house on the shores of Lake Murray for a handsome sum. He paid for sound advice from the same financial adviser who had done so well with his mother's money, and he was, himself, now well-fixed financially. He could have easily attended Farrar University without student aid, but he was awarded a scholarship that had been established in his father's name, not just because he was his hero-father's son, but because he was a Farrar 'legacy' and a good student as well.

Since he had sold his family home, he now lived in a small house he rented in Oconee, but he usually spent extended vacation periods with relatives—of whom he had many. Normally, freshmen at Farrar are required to live on campus, in a dormitory, but an exception was made for Luke, since he was not only a legal adult, but also had no other actual home to go to. He had never traveled as far to visit family as he had this spring, when he visited cousin Mike, whom he had often wanted to visit, not just because he was his favorite cousin, but because he also hoped to re-live in San Francisco some of the intense sexual experiences they had shared back in South Carolina. He also hoped to find new sexual experiences in a city famed for its tolerance of homosexuality.

He was in his second year at Farrar University, and, like Luke, was on spring break. He was majoring in Business Administration and doing pretty well academically—on the Dean's list, although barely so. The cute boys and hot young men he had seen when he visited Farrar as a high school student were not as available or as amenable to sharing sex as he might have hoped. Most of them seemed irretrievably straight, but he knew from experience how some solidly heterosexual guys often enjoyed indulging homosexual fantasies or even giving in to their hidden gay orientation. He was finding enough sex to keep him well satisfied, mostly with a few 'regulars.' He had even had a few short-lived relationships, but he had never met anyone with whom he thought he might share a permanent liaison.

As they talked, Luke was afraid to intimate to the dazzling blond Adonis that he had a gut feeling that Casey could be "the one," for fear he might jinx it, if it actually was possible. It seemed too good to be true, anyway.

After walking east about a half-hour, Luke and the two Casey's reversed their course and determined to find a place where they could share lunch. The nutritive value of the high-protein sustenance they had fed each other in the thicket was wearing off. They reached the marked bench, and headed toward the thicket, where they found the sailor still there, still smoking, with his cock and balls still on display.

"No luck?" Casey asked the sailor.

"A really cute kid came by, with an even cuter butt, and really hot to get it fucked. I didn't want to disappoint him, after all. He took it like a man, and went away, but I'm in the market for some more action. Changed your minds?"

"Nah," Casey began, "we're gonna …"

"No, wait," Luke interrupted, putting a hand on Casey's arm. Speaking to the sailor again, he said, "I see you've got a blanket, and I was wondering if you might have some lube and some rubbers rolled up in there," He smiled at Casey, and raised an eyebrow inquisitively. Casey grinned, and nodded to him.

"I'm not a Boy Scout, but I'm always prepared," leered the sailor. "Got plenty of lube, and even some rubbers if you insist on 'em. The kid I just fucked didn't want anything standing between my cock and his ass, so I loaded him up with plenty of cum, and he was mighty happy to get it."

"How about letting us use your blanket and lube, and giving us a couple of condoms?" Luke asked.

"You two gonna fuck each other back in there?" the sailor asked, indicating the clearing in the thicket.

"We want to," Luke said. "Right, Casey?"

"Oh God, yes!" the blond stud replied.

"Tell ya what," the sailor said, "I'll give you that stuff, but there's a condition. I'll do it if you let me watch."

"Just watch?" Luke asked.

"Well, yeah, but if you wouldn't object to a tongue or a cock goin' into someone's butt when it's not in use, that would be even better," the sailor replied. "I promise you, no one has ever complained about the way I use this," he added, stroking his generous, and by-then fully erect cock.

"Casey?" Luke asked, looking at him with a grin.

"I don't see why we should object," Casey answered. "I'm not in the habit of passing up sailor dick when I can get it." *And I don't wanna start now, even if I'm getting ready to fuck the guy I think I'm falling in love with,* he thought. Luke was thinking something along the same lines, even if he had never had the opportunity to avail himself of any sailor dick—but he had often fantasized about sex with sailors, wondering if their alleged appetite for, and superior artistry in, gay sex was deserved.

The sailor surprised Casey by seizing his head and drawing it in as he locked their lips together, kissing him passionately, expertly, and at great length. When he released a breathless Casey's head, he grinned, "Let's go fuck."

Casey took Luke's hand in one of his, then with the other he grasped the sailor's throbbing cock, using it as a handle while he led the sailor and Luke into the clearing in the thicket.

Inside the clearing Luke again tied the dog Casey to a tree, then he and Casey shed their shorts and underwear, while the sailor stripped off his pants, leaving his blouse and hat in place. Neither Luke or Casey said anything, but they were both glad the sailor had stripped only from the waist down—the sight of the tight, always sexy Navy uniform blouse and hat made them well aware they were in a sexual situation with a sailor—one of that legendary breed of hot men who are reputed to glory in sucking and fucking with other hot men and boys. Furthermore the blouse served to accentuate the bareness of the sailor's ass, which proved to be particularly appetizing—generous, muscular, and beautifully rounded.

Casey whistled when the sailor stepped out of his pants and hung them on a bush. "Wow—what a sweet ass! Have you ever met another sailor who didn't want to fuck it?"

The sailor grinned. "Not many—and there's been damned few who didn't get a chance to do just that if they let me know. And looking at you guys, I'm hoping you're gonna want to join the always-growing list of guys who have fucked this tight sailor butt." Both Luke and Casey had roaring hard-ons, and the sailor wrapped his hand around both as he looked into Casey's eyes, adding, "Jesus, kid. This is a real monster. I sure hope you wanna bury it up my ass."

"I'm hoping the same thing," Luke told Casey, eagerly.

"We'll hafta see about you," Casey said, and kissed the sailor for a moment before adding, "but right now, get that blanket spread out for Luke and me. He's gonna get his wish for sure." Then he kissed Luke for a much longer time, while the sailor spread the blanket out on the ground.

The blanket was the standard Navy-issue, single-bed-width gray blanket, designed for use on those single-width shipboard bunks that historically had so often been used by sailors in pairs, and used so masterfully, according to legend. Wrapped within the blanket roll had been a large tube of K-Y Jelly lubricant and an unbroken strip of a dozen single-pack rolled condoms. Luke laughed when he saw the long strip of condoms. "Man, you really are prepared for action today, aren'tcha?"

"Shit, I've already not used one of 'em today, and if I get the opportunity, I can use at least half of what's left," the sailor said, grinning. "I just hope I can line up enough guys to use the other half on me."

"Like Casey said," Luke put in, "we'll hafta see how far he and I can help you meet your goal. 'Course you realize, we're gonna be using some of 'em on each other."

"Well, I can probably find some other guys to not use rubbers on," the sailor leered.

Luke lay down on the blanket, on his back, and Casey lay on top of him. They embraced and kissed for a long time, humping their erections into each other's bellies. After a few minutes, the sailor said, "My god, you two guys are so fuckin' hot!" Soon, Casey felt the sailor's hand fondling his busy buttocks and then felt the sailor's tongue licking them, then zeroing in on his asshole, where it began flicking and lapping.

Casey and Luke's kisses were sweet at first, but soon became passionate and hungry. Casey disengaged and reversed his body, so that his cock hung down over Luke's face, and his mouth was positioned over Luke's prick. At the same moment, each opened his mouth wide and began to feast. The sailor's tongue had been displaced in the move, but soon Casey felt two lubricated fingers massaging inside him, followed by the sailor's cock-head pressing against his hole. He rested from sucking for a moment to say to the sailor, "You better have a rubber on that thing." The sailor said, "Oops," and withdrew his cock for a couple of minutes while he rolled a condom onto it, then positioned it again at Casey's asshole.

From below, looking up at Casey's beautiful ass while he sucked Casey's even-more-beautiful prick, Luke watched as the sailor's cock entered his partner's ass in a slow, but unrelenting thrust. Casey groaned in pleasure around Luke's cock as the sailor began to fuck him in earnest. Casey's balls rested on Luke's nose, and the sailor's balls slid back and forth on Luke's forehead as he slammed his dick savagely in and out of Casey.

Luke and Casey had sucked each other off something like an hour earlier, so their sixty-nine was a long one. The sailor had fucked someone even more recently, but he apparently had a shorter 'fuse'; he pulled his prick from Casey's ass and stripped the condom from it. He began to masturbate furiously, reaching down to pat Luke's cheek and saying, "Gotta give you something, too" just as he began to spray hot cum on Casey's asshole—still gaping from the fuck it had been receiving. The sailor directed his cock a bit downward, and blew the next several spurts over Casey's balls and Luke's mouth where Casey's cock continued to drive in and out of it. Luke opened his mouth very wide to allow the sailor's cum to enter it alongside Casey's prick.

"God, that is so fuckin' hot," Casey cried as he felt the cum splashing on his ass and then on the shaft of his prick inside Luke's mouth. He relinquished Luke's cock to lower his head and begin eating the boy's ass. After a few minutes of relishing the tongue darting in and out of him, Luke cried, "I'm gonna come," which caused Casey to resume sucking his cock just in time to receive the generous load he blew inside his mouth. That, in turn, brought Casey to orgasm, and before Luke had stopped ejaculating, Casey's cock was exploding inside Luke's mouth.

The sailor assumed, judging by the moans of satisfaction both civilian studs were murmuring, that each had blown his load in the other's mouth. He stroked his still-hard cock and smiled at the thought and the sight of the two beautiful young men enjoying each other in such an agreeable way. He had sucked a load of cum out of the boy he had fucked while Luke and Casey had been gone, but he was hungry for more—and he hoped he was going to get some when the two were fucking each other, an eventuality he was absolutely sure was going to ensue. And he was right, of course, but he was going to taste their cum earlier than he might have hoped.

Casey and Luke sat up and began to kiss, their arms around each other. They accompanied their very extended kiss by further murmurs, which made the sailor assume—rightly—that they were mingling their loads and passing them back and forth before swallowing. "Hey, how about sharing a little bit with me?" he said. Casey broke the kiss, and put his lips to the sailor's as he passed into them a portion of the cum mixture he had been sharing with Luke. He looked meaningfully at Luke, and Luke kissed the sailor, giving him some of what he head been retaining in his mouth. All three studied each other as they savored the precious fluid they were sharing. Luke was the first to swallow, and he grinned at the others, panting "Fantastic!" as his adorable dimples lit up his face. After he had done so, Casey and the sailor quickly followed suit, displaying equally delighted grins.

"Why don'tcha take off the rest of your uniform, and let us see what you're hiding in there," Luke asked the sailor.

"Yeah, and why don'tcha tell us your name," Casey added.

The sailor pulled his jumper, neckerchief and T-shirt over his head. His hat had long since rested with his uniform pants. He was left wearing only socks and shoes, as were the two hot young civilians. He revealed a flat stomach and a nicely chiseled chest, with large nipples on his rounded breasts—which engendered an enthusiastic "Nice tits!" from Casey. As he sat with Casey and Luke on the blanket, he said, "The name's Gunther. Steve Gunther." Luke and Casey supplied Gunther with their names, and they shook hands all around, which seemed a little formal, since they had so recently been sucking and fucking each other.

The sailor, Gunther, told the boys a little about his gay life in the Navy, He'd only been aboard the *Enterprise* for a short while, and was only beginning to find shipmates with like interests in sex, but he had found a great many of them. Prior to his deployment on the carrier, he had been in the submarine service of the Navy, and he declared it had been hard to find shipmates in the subs he had served on who did not want to fuck and suck with him. "I got more cock and ass than I knew what to do with," he laughed, "but I don't think I ever failed to give plenty of satisfaction."

"This is the first time I've ever had sex with a sailor," Luke said, "but I've always been fascinated by them."

"Don't let it be your last," Gunther joked. "And I hope the next time you have sex with a sailor is gonna be in about ten minutes. But when you're with a stud who looks like this," here he indicated he meant Casey, "and has a cock like his, I can see how you might not be interested in anyone else. How long have you guys been a couple?"

Luke actually blushed as he answered, "Oh, we just met this morning. We're not a couple."

"Hmm," Gunther said. "It just seemed to me like you … well, never mind. My mistake."

Casey rose to his knees, his hands on Luke's shoulders and said, looking intently into Luke's eyes, "Not yet, anyway." He bent down and kissed him tenderly.

With a look that could only be described as adoring, Luke simply breathed Casey's name when they broke their kiss, in a tone that combined wonder and hope.

Gunther watched the two gazing into each other's eyes wordlessly for what seemed a very long time, but was probably only twenty or thirty seconds. Finally he broke the spell by putting his hand around Casey's cock and asked, "You ever share this beauty with a swabbie?"

Snapping back into the moment, Casey replied, turning his attention to the sailor and smiling, "Oh, yeah." He instantly remembered the glorious, wild sex he had shared with Hank, the sailor who had provided him with fake I.D. In his 'escorting' encounters he had a number of times discovered the man he was fucking or being fucked by, was in the Navy, although none of them had been in uniform.

"Who gets first crack at fucking this cutie?" Gunther asked Casey, indicating Luke.

"Do I have anything to say about it?" Luke laughed.

"You've got everything to say about it," Casey said. "Do you want me to fuck you?"

"More than anything."

"You want Gunther to fuck you, too?"

"Well, I … yeah, Casey. I do."

"I don't blame you, He can throw a mean fuck—a damned fine fuck' you'd be crazy not to want him. Who do you want to fuck you first?"

Luke reached for the strip of condoms, and tore one packet off the end. He put a hand around Casey's cock and began to stroke it. It took only a few strokes before the blond Adonis' prodigious cock began to grow, and only a few more before it reached its breathtaking, even wonderfully alarming state. Using his teeth, Luke ripped the wrapping from the condom, and began to roll it over the stupendous shaft. Looking into Casey's eyes he said, "For one thing, I can't wait if I don't have to." Then he directed his attention to the sailor, stroked his throbbing erection, and added, "For another, you can rest up while he's fucking me. Then you'll be ready to fuck me before he shoves that monster of his up your ass."

Gunther was stroking his prick while he said to Luke, "Oh man, I'll be dreaming about getting that beauty of his inside me while I hammer that sweet ass of yours." Then he kissed Luke, and said, "And I'll be dreaming of you fucking me, too."

Luke now lay on his back on the blanket, and he spread his legs. He watched as Casey spread lube on his condom-clad cock and then worked more into Luke's ass. He raised his legs when Casey knelt between them. "What a sweet ass," Casey murmured as he positioned the tip of his huge dick at its target, eliciting only a deep sigh of satisfaction from Luke as Casey began to penetrate him. Gunther whispered, "Man, that's beautiful," as he watched more and more of Casey's gargantuan shaft entering the ever-more blissful man on the bottom.

Luke gasped a fevered "Fuck my ass, lover" as Casey's pubic hair pressed up against his balls, and he raised his legs higher, resting them on Casey's shoulders. Casey moved forward, raising Luke's lower back from the blanket as he began to fuck in earnest. Luke moaned an ecstatic litany as he thrilled to his invader's penetration: "So fuckin' big! Give it to me! I love it! Fuck my hot ass," and even "I love you!" (that final declaration was becoming more true with every thrust of Casey's magnificent tool inside him). Further, similar vocal ejaculations preceded the impending other, more meaningful kind of ejaculation. Casey responded with his own litany of fuck-frenzy talk.

Gunther crouched behind Casey, and watched Casey's asshole appear and disappear as the crevice between his asscheeks opened and closed while he thrust his cock in and out in glorious ten-inch strokes. The rapidity and intensity of Casey's fuck grew, and both fucker and fuckee groaned, wordlessly now, in a delirium of sheer lust. Gunther caressed Casey's smooth ass, and put a lubricated finger up his asshole. He held the finger motionless as Casey's fucking drove his sphincter-ring back and forth on it. Gunther had been thinking of both Luke and Casey as "boys," but what he was watching made it clear to him that both of them were men, in every sense of the word. He wanted to put his face into Casey's ass and eat it while he was fucking Luke, but the fuck was too savage, and Casey's strokes too long, to permit the sailor to properly coordinate a rim-job on the blond stud while he was plowing the fortunate boy—man—below him. He felt sure Casey would collapse over Luke after he reached his inevitable orgasm, and he would probably have a chance to feast on Casey's asshole at leisure.

Luke screamed, "I'm gonna come!" Casey continued to fuck with savage abandon while, without his touching it, Luke's prick erupted, spraying cum onto Casey's face and neck. Casey opened his mouth, wide and actually managed to catch a part of Luke's orgasm. Still, cum dripped from his face and neck, coating Luke's chest. He leaned down to kiss Luke hungrily, and Luke licked his own cum from Casey's lips and face. In a moment, Casey drove his cock as deeply as it would go, and his buttocks clenched very tightly as his orgasm exploded inside the condom, and holding Gunther's finger in a vise grip.

In a moment, Gunther's expectation was realized, and Casey collapsed over Luke, unclenching his buttocks and freeing Gunther's finger, which the sailor replaced with his tongue. For a long time Luke and Casey feasted on each other's mouths while Gunther feasted on Casey's ass.

Luke and Casey reversed their positions and Luke began to fuck his partner with as much ardor as Casey had shown him. The anatomical equipment Luke brought to the fuck was not as titanic as Casey's, but the blond appreciated it as much as if it had been greater than his own. Both were bringing emotional equipment into play that made their lovemaking ever more meaningful and enjoyable—and more truly lovemaking than simply fucking. Luke labored for a very long time, if such delightful activity could be characterized as labor; he had, after all, blown a load just minutes before it began. The increased duration was greatly appreciated, as neither really wanted it to end. They kissed fervently during almost the entire time, and Casey did not have another orgasm. As he had before, Gunther finger-fucked and tongue-fucked the top man in the encounter, and looked forward to replacing his tongue in Luke's asshole with his cock—which had been throbbing with need for release for quite a while.

Luke ramped up the already furious pace of his fuck until he shouted with exultation as he filled the condom inside Casey's ass, while Casey gasped his pleasure and Gunther licked Luke's asshole for all he was worth—preparing it for him to fuck. As eager as he was to fuck Luke, Gunther was touched by the tenderness with which Casey and Luke kissed and fondled each other following Luke's orgasm. In turn, Luke was touched by the tenderness in Gunther's voice as he whispered in his ear. "You love him, don'tcha?" Still kissing Casey, Luke nodded. "You still gonna let me fuck your pretty ass?" Luke nodded again. "How do you want it?"

Breaking his kiss, Luke turned his head. "You can fuck me while I'm sixty-nining with him—the same way you fucked him when we were doing it before."

"Sounds like a great plan," the sailor said, eagerly. "But I'm so fuckin' ready, I'm about to pop. How about now?"

Luke pulled his cock from Casey's ass, stripped off the condom, and drained it over his cock, coating it with his thick, white ejaculate, and then threw it into the bushes. Casey relaxed his legs and while Gunther was rolling a condom onto his dick, Luke reversed his body so that he knelt on all fours over Casey, his cock hanging down into Casey's mouth and dripping his cum into it. Casey opened his mouth eagerly, and nursed on the thing that had just been giving him such pleasure elsewhere while Luke eagerly engulfed Casey's cock in his mouth—still hard from Luke's fuck, and still tasting of Casey's cum from their fuck.

This time it was Casey who lay below, and watched the sailor's excellent and near-brutal fuck from very close-up. It was Luke's balls on his chin and Gunther's balls sliding back and forth on his forehead. Unlike the outcome of the fuck he had administered when Casey was on top, the sailor remained inside his fuck-ee while he blew his load. After several moments of decompression from his orgasm, Gunther pulled out of Casey's ass. Casey and Luke were still sucking each other when the sailor stripped off his condom, and drained part of it on Luke's lips where they met Casey's cock, and the rest on Casey's lips while they were traveling up and down Luke's shaft.

"I hope neither of you guys got your load while you were blowing each other," Gunther said. "I am so goddamned ready to get fucked by both of you studs I can hardly stand it." He laughed, "On the other hand, maybe I oughta wait until you suck each other off—then you can fuck me a lot longer. Fine by me, come to think of it." Both apparently thought that was a good idea, since they didn't slacken the pace of their sucking. Soon Casey grunted loudly as he drove his hips upward and froze while his cock erupted inside Luke's mouth; only a few minutes later, Luke grunted and slammed his ass downward, forcing his cock deep inside Casey while it exploded. Gunther applauded, "All right!"

Luke and Casey abandoned their sixty-nine, then sat up, embraced, and kissed for a long time. Their cocks were considerably less rigid than they had been before. Finally, Casey threw himself on his back and gasped "Time" as he held his hands up, forming the classic "time-out" signal. Luke lay next to him and nestled against his side, under Casey's protecting arm. They smiled at each other — looking more like two purely chaste angels, rather than two young men who had each been recently fucked, who had fucked each other, and who had sucked each other off.

Gunther sat cross-legged, in tailor fashion, as he watched the two beautiful studs, marveling at his good luck in encountering them today, and anticipating getting fucked by both of them. He had not had a cock up his ass yet today — well, technically, he had, if you counted the unknown, but very well-hung and talented one that had plowed him on an after-deck of the *Enterprise* shortly after midnight last night — and he was itching to get fucked. After watching for a while, he grew impatient and stretched out so he could suck Luke's and Casey's cocks to get them primed again, ready to satisfy his craving. He wanted Luke to fuck him first, leaving Casey's colossal cock for last.

After watching Casey and Luke snuggling and necking while their cocks returned to a state of full erection, an impatient Gunther knelt on the blanket, on all fours, saying, "Now it's my turn to get fucked. Luke, you first." As Luke prepared to tear another condom off the strip, Gunther stopped him. "Fuck me bareback. I wanna feel your cum blasting inside my ass." Luke began to remonstrate with him, but Gunther waved aside his objections. "I'm sure you guys are healthy, and I don't want anything standing in the way when you fuck me. I know you can't be absolutely sure, but I'm betting neither of you guys has the virus." I'll bet that stud who fucked me last night wasn't wearing a rubber, he thought. Safe sex was not a practice widely adopted yet in the Navy, in spite of the lectures advocating it that were delivered to all sailors. Besides, he considered, these two guys are so fucking young and pure — they've gotta be safe. Not a wise practice to assume such, although the assumption was valid in this particular instance.

Actually, the sailor didn't care so much if Luke used a rubber or not, but he sure as hell wanted Casey to blast a totally unimpeded load ten inches inside him. He might have reconsidered had he known how extremely active the innocent-looking blond's sex life was. To Luke, he said, "C'mon, stud, slam it in and fuck my ass as hard as you can."

Luke took Gunther at his word. He rammed his cock unceremoniously up the sailor's ass in one savage thrust and began a serious, fierce assault while he held Gunther's sides tightly, pulling his body in to counter each forward thrust. *He may not be hung like the other one*, the sailor thought, *but he fucks like a bull.* Luke was muttering incoherently, completely lost in lust. His brutal thrusting was so exciting that Gunther came close to blowing his load without touching his dick. Soon—too soon, Gunther thought, no matter how eager he was to get around to taking Casey's prick inside him—Luke slammed his cock as deeply as it could go, and fell over the sailor, driving him face down on the blanket while Luke continued to fuck as his orgasm filled the sailor a few moments later.

When it had become obvious that Luke was about to blow his load inside the sailor, Casey lubed his cock, and was prepared for what came next. The minute Luke began to show signs of relaxing after he screamed "I'm coming!" and clearly filled Gunther's ass, Casey pulled back on Luke's shoulders, and shoved him aside, unceremoniously separating him from his prey—for such Gunther seemed to be, considering the rapacity of the fuck Luke had just given him. Without any hesitation whatever, Casey rammed his monster prick inside the sailor in one brutal thrust, impaling him on more than ten inches of fat, throbbing cock. Gunther literally screamed in surprise and delight, but was soon babbling in thrill while Casey pounded him mercilessly. Gunther had been fucked by Marine Corps drill sergeants who rightfully regarded themselves as extreme examples of ultra-masculinity, but he couldn't remember ever having been fucked more savagely, or more satisfactorily—and by a high-school boy, of all things! He rose to his knees while he enjoyed the rest of the glorious assault on his ass in dog style, culminating in a wild cry of triumph from Casey as he erupted inside in several fierce blasts, generating an equally excited cry from their recipient. When the fuck was over, and Casey withdrew his cock, Gunther rolled to his back and studied Casey through eyes gleaming with satisfaction, gratitude, and respect. "God damn, you're lucky to have a lover like this," he said to Luke.

"But we're not ..." Luke began, but Casey cut in: "If that's true, he's not the only lucky one." Luke was thrilled by the fact that Casey allowed Gunther's attribution of their status as lovers to stand.

It had been an incredibly exciting morning and afternoon for all concerned—although the dog Casey had no doubt found it pretty dull. They dressed, although Gunther still left his pants flap open, "showing off the merchandise," as he put it. Clearly he meant to stay up on the trail and cruise for further sex. How he could still be horny was unimaginable to Luke and Casey, who were completely satisfied, sexually, and sought no further activity along those lines for the time being. They did want to seek some food, however—neither had eaten anything since breakfast except cock and ass and cum—great feasting, but not nourishing. They all dressed—the flap of Gunther's pants left open to 'display the goods,' as he put it—and Casey retrieved his book. Then the two boys said goodbye to Gunther with thanks for a wonderful time as they set out together to find a place to eat.

The sailor rolled up the tube of K-Y Jelly and the remaining condoms in his blanket, and went back out on the trail to troll for other playmates. He had six condoms left out of the original dozen, and still held out hope he might have occasion to use them all. He came very close to meeting his goal. He was sitting on a bench and smoking when he heard footsteps approaching. He stood, fluffed up his exposed cock and balls and struck a sexy pose. In a moment, two men came into view. Looking at their haircuts and shoes, Gunther pegged them immediately as Marines, jarheads. They were obviously interested in what the sailor had on display, and were not in the least embarrassed to express interest in sharing it with him and between themselves.

They retreated to the same clearing Gunther had shared with Luke and Casey, and all were fully naked in a few minutes. Gunther sucked off both the Marines, and then watched while they fucked each other. After a brief respite, each Marine watched while Gunther fucked the other, and then the smaller, better-hung Marine fucked the sailor. When they had finished, the Marines departed, leaving a Gunther who had finally to admit to himself that he was tired—for the moment, anyway. He had only one condom left, which he took back to his ship, where that night he would put it on the cock of a massively-hung shipmate/fuckbuddy, who would plow his ass in the shower after "lights out"—at the end of one helluva day!

Casey and Luke decided to go to a hamburger joint near Cliff House. They would have preferred to go the Cliff House restaurant, but the dog Casey would not be allowed. So, they got their burgers and drinks "to go," and ate while they sat on the patio of the Cliff House, overlooking the sea and the seal rocks. By that time, each knew there was something special at work between them, even though they had only known each other for five or six hours.

Casey had to work the next day, and he had not yet told Luke anything about his job. It was obvious that in spite of the shyness and innocence Luke's looks suggested, he was sexually experienced and sophisticated, but Casey wondered if he would be interested in being the boyfriend of a guy who wriggled his ass and cock to tease other men, and actually sold them for others to use personally. He had to tell him, of course, but decided it could wait a day or so.

They made a date to meet the next morning, to bum around the city for a while, and to have lunch. A bench in Union Square, facing the St. Francis Hotel was set as their meeting place. They kissed for a long time before Luke took off for cousin Mike's house, leading—or, rather, being led by—the dog Casey. Casey Lowe boarded the Geary bus and headed home.

Casey spent the rest of the afternoon around home, catching up on the reading he had missed after Luke showed up—entered his life was the way he was thinking of it. When his dad, Bill, showed up, they went out to dinner. Returning home, Casey called Joey Stone and arranged for him to come over to spend the night. Waiting for Joey to appear, Casey told his father virtually none of the sexual details about his experiences in the park earlier that day, but he could not seem to stop talking about the wonderful guy he had met that morning: Luke.

Bill knew the signs of 'puppy love,' and it was clear that his son had been smitten with it—even though it was obvious he was now a full-grown 'dog.' He only hoped it would prove more satisfying that the one other time Casey had been so infatuated with someone, and he hoped this "Luke" would be a much better person than Richard had proven to be. In a roundabout way, he cautioned his son to be wary, to guard his heart.

When Joey showed up, Casey took him into his father's bedroom, where Bill was changing into comfortable, after-dinner clothes. "Here's Joey, Dad. Don't bother getting dressed. I'm turning him over to you. You both know what to do. That okay, Joey?"

Joey was dumfounded, but quickly recovered. A small smile formed as he looked at Bill, saying, "Yeah. Sounds great to me. Okay with you, Mr. Lowe?"

"If you promise to call me Bill. It sounds very exciting."

Bill began to strip, and Joey quickly followed suit. Casey closed the door to his father's bedroom, and went to his own room, where he lay in bed, mentally reliving the wonderful day he had shared with Luke, and looking forward to Tuesday morning at ten o'clock in Union Square.

The next morning, Casey slept until about eight o'clock. He went into the kitchen, and found Joey sitting there, reading the newspaper and drinking coffee. "Well, how was it?"

Joey looked completely happy as he replied. "It was fantastic. Now I know where you get your talent!"

"Well, if you and he get married, I am not calling you Dad!"

10.

Working Can be Fun

Casey arrived at Union Square at 9:30, a full half-hour before the time he had promised to meet Luke. To his joy, he found Luke already there, apparently as anxious to meet Casey as Casey was to meet him. They shared a kiss, which surprised Luke, since back at home, one never saw two guys kissing unless they were in a gay bar. Casey assured him that no one in San Francisco would be much put off by it. They had only spent part of a day together, but they both felt they were old friends—completely comfortable with each other.

Their easy conversation covered all manner of topics, and after the ultimately personal nature of their first day together, almost no topic was off-limits. Luke still didn't know about Casey's work at the *Top 'n Bottom*—and out of it. For some reason Casey was still reticent about telling him, but knew he had to do it before he left for the theatre, where he was scheduled for a 4:30 show.

Casey told Luke about his fuckbuddies at Serra High, and even about falling in love with Richard, while Luke revealed some of his past crushes and short-term relationships back in South Carolina, mostly at Farrar University. Luke apologized for having been so sexually forward the day before. "I'm not usually that aggressive; I tend to let the other guy make the first move. But you're just so incredibly attractive and hot, and I didn't want to miss out on doing everything with you because I held back."

"I sure am glad you didn't," Casey grinned, and they shared another kiss—a very long and passionate one this time.

As they talked, they strolled down to the waterfront, took the ferry out to Sausalito and had coffee while they were waiting for the return ferry. Back in the city they walked up the waterfront to the Fisherman's Wharf area, where they had lunch, and after lunch, they sat on a railing, looking at the fishing fleet. It was almost three o'clock, and Casey knew it was time to tell Luke about the theatre before their relationship went any further—and he knew he desperately wanted it to go much further. He suspected Luke felt the same way. He was right.

It was clear that Luke was somewhat shocked when Casey confessed that for money he danced naked for men, sometime blowing a load for an audience, and passing through an audience of men who often groped him. That was bad enough, but it was hardest to confess that he also went into small rooms where he let strangers blow him—and sometimes more—for money, and prostituted himself outside the theatre. "Now that I know you, I wish I hadn't done any of that stuff. I wish I wasn't a whore, because you deserve someone so much better than that."

Luke said, "I won't judge you, Casey. I've done a lot of things that I probably should be ashamed of—but I'm not. And I've had fun in all sorts of ways I wouldn't want my mother to have known about—like yesterday, with you." He took Casey's hand and gazed seriously into his eyes. "I don't know how you feel about yesterday, but I think … well … promise me you won't laugh when I say this, but I think I fell in love with you yesterday. I know it's way too soon, and we were strangers, and we got awfully wrapped up in fucking and getting fucked with a sailor we didn't even know, but … I know I want us to spend a lot of time together—just you and me—doing what we did together yesterday. I knew when I woke up this morning that I was in love with Casey Lowe—the hottest fucker, the greatest cocksucker, the most handsome man I've ever seen, much less had sex with. I wish to God I lived here; I'd do anything I could to make you my boyfriend. I don't know how I'd feel about … about what you do at the theatre, but I'd learn to overlook it if I had to, if that's what it took to be with you."

"Jesus, Luke," Casey said. "I feel that way about you. I could give up all that stuff if you lived here—or if I could be with you somewhere else."

"You don't know what your plans are after graduation." Luke said "Why not come to South Carolina and go to school at Farrar University this fall? We could live together, and we could be …"

"Boyfriends?" Casey smiled.

"I was gonna say lovers," Luke said, smiling even more broadly.

"Well, I don't know what kind of college I'm going to be able to go to. Like I said, I had really shitty grades last semester. But I've worked hard since then. So far I'm doing great this semester. My Counselor says if I keep it up, and graduate this summer, I might be able to get into college. But probably, I'll have to go to a two-year school and then transfer. He says that shouldn't be too hard to arrange."

"Are you gonna keep … working?" Luke asked.

"Casey laughed, "You mean hustling, and shaking my ass for the customers?"

"Yeah. I mean, I don't really see anything wrong with that if you can work it in with your studies," Luke said, but it was clear he didn't much believe what he was saying.

"Look, I know that what I'm doing isn't a career. I'm enjoying it, and I'm making a lot of money, but sooner or later I'll have to give it up." He laughed, "Eventually, I'll probably have to start giving it away!"

"You'll always be beautiful, and you'll always have … well," Luke stumbled.

"A ten-inch cock?" Luke grinned and nodded.

Casey continued. "Look, my dad has always told me, 'quit while you're ahead.' If something comes along to take the place of what I'm doing, I want to stop doing it while I'm still doing it well. Richard is one of the other dancers at the T 'n B, and he's thirty-eight—even if he hates to admit it. He's gorgeous, he looks ten or fifteen years younger than he is, and when it comes to sex, he does absolutely everything well—no, he does everything really, really well! But even he is gonna hafta stop some time, and then what will he do? He made some porn videos that were very popular—hell, they're still popular—and he admits he'll probably have to stay in the sex industry, because if he got into some other line of work someone would sooner or later recognize him from his videos, and he'd probably get fired. So, while I'm doing well, I know I've got to plan for something else. And that means graduating from high school and getting a college degree.

"I guess you've figured out by now, I'm horny as hell, and I think I really need sex. If I can go to college with someone I really care about, and who can satisfy me sexually, like keeping this ten-inch dick busy, and plugging my hungry ass when I need it, I can make it. I know I can. I just need to find that guy to go to college with."

"It's crazy, and it's too soon, and all that," Luke said, "but I think you found that guy yesterday."

"You mean that sailor, Gunther?" Casey asked. "I'll admit he was a great fuck, but …"

Luke stopped him in mid-sentence with a kiss. He said, "Very funny! Do you think I could be the one you need? Please say yes, and come to South Carolina in the fall, and live with me, and be my boyfriend."

Kneeling in front of Luke, Casey took his hand and held it. He looked up at him with great seriousness, and said, simply, "Yes."

They agreed that Casey would fly out to South Carolina during the week-long break between the end of the spring semester and the beginning of Summer School. If there seemed to be no hope of his getting into Farrar for the fall semester, he would prepare himself for acceptance by applying at the two-year tech school in nearby Seneca, where he was almost sure to be admitted.

It was nearing time for Casey to go to the theatre, and Luke pleaded to go along to see him perform. Even though Luke had watched him fucking with the sailor in the bushes the day before, to Casey, things were different now: Luke was more than just a cute guy he was sharing a sexual adventure with, and he wasn't sure he wanted Luke to watch him teasing strange men with his prick, strangers who would be drooling over it and trying to do more than just that. But he didn't want to hide anything from his new boyfriend, so he acceded to Luke's request. Moreover, there was a new guest porn star opening that day, and it was going to be a treat to see the one-named star "Lance" in person. Casey was scheduled to dance just before the guest star made his appearance but he would have time to get dressed quickly and join Luke in the audience, where they would be able to watch the beautiful and gloriously sexy Lance together.

They took a cable car up Powell Street to Market Street, its last stop. The T 'n B was only a short walk from there. They argued about who was going to buy Luke's ticket. Casey won. "Our first argument," he grinned.

Luke studied the lobby pictures of all the house dancers. He was impressed with the muscular bodies of Carl, Adam and Steve; predictably, Casey thought, he was most impressed by Richard. "Is this the Richard you were in love with?" Luke asked. Casey admitted he was, and Luke said, "I can see why."

"You'll probably meet Richard," Casey said. "He's scheduled to dance later on, but he always gets here early when a new porn star does his first show. He wants to get to know him better than anyone else does, so he stands a better chance of fucking with him more often than anyone else, and being asked to double with him." He had to explain about the guest porn star's traditional final show, where he would ask one of the house dancers to pair up with him, and they would have full-blown sex on stage.

Luke grinned, "Have you doubled with any of the guest stars? I'll bet they've all asked you."

"No," Casey smiled, "they haven't all asked me. Richard gets to double more than anyone else, probably because he sucks up to all the guest stars so much."

"Sucks up, or sucks off?" Luke laughed.

"Both," Casey said, "but I have to admit he is really hot. Sex with him is pretty damned intense. The general practice is that any guest fucks each of the house dancers if they want it—and they all do. Well, Adam used to claim to be straight, but he's finally admitting he likes a cock up his ass. Richard manages to be a better bottom than anyone else—and believe me, I know from experience, he's fantastic—so the star is probably gonna choose him to fuck in his last show. Still, to answer your question, I have doubled with a few of the stars."

"I don't think I want the details," Luke groaned in mock despair.

"Okay," Luke said, kissing him, "no details."

Eddie came out of the office, where he had just announced Carl's 'dance.' He spotted Casey. "I've been wondering where you were. You're gonna go on in a half-hour. Better get ready."

Casey introduced Luke as his boyfriend, which engendered congratulations from Eddie, and a huge grin from Luke. "Luke has a ticket for the day, but is it okay if he goes backstage with me?"

"Sure," Eddie said. "but don't get distracted by all the hot bods and cocks back there, kid." He told Luke. "You've got the hottest one around here—I envy you. Our new star, Lance, is already back there—go back and meet him. He's fuckin' gorgeous, but I think he might be a little nuts."

Casey and Luke went through the theatre while Carl was performing—at that point on stage and humping his ass so that his big erection flopped up and down while he massaged his magnificent tits. Luke was fascinated, and had to be led out. "Jesus, he's hot!" he exclaimed as Casey drew him into the backstage area, where they encountered—as expected—Richard, He was not scheduled to go on stage for more than an hour, but he was naked, and was sporting a very impressive hard-on, which he stroked as he chatted with a supernaturally beautiful, boyish-looking blond man who at first blush appeared to be sweet and even naïve. The young man was sitting in a chair, fully clothed, and his attention was clearly not on Richard's conversation, but on the monster cock Richard was stroking almost directly in front of his eyes.

Casey felt no compunction whatever about interrupting Richard's conversation or his casual masturbation. He knew Richard was merely working on seducing the blond—whom Casey recognized as the porn star Lance—and would continue until he wound up with Lance's cock in his ass. Judging by what he had seen in films, Casey thought Lance was probably not a bottom, but in his experience he had found that many porn stars who were strictly tops on-camera, loved to get fucked when they weren't being filmed doing so. Furthermore, he knew how persuasive Richard was, and how powerful his sexual allure. Lance was likely to discover at first hand how satisfying it was to be fucked by Richard. And if Lance was, as Eddie said, "a little nuts," he'd have to be completely insane to decline Richard's offer to take Lance's cock up his ass—an offer Richard would almost surely be making, very soon and probably very often.

Lance was fairly tall, rather light of build. Facially, he was innocent-looking, almost angelic in appearance, with a head of fairly long, virtually shining blond hair (his body hair, however, was dark). But perhaps his best feature was his cock. It was very long, probably at least nine inches when hard, and quite fat—a real lip-stretching treat. Moreover, Lance was definitely a show-er, not a grow-er. When his prick was soft it projected out slightly before drooping straight down, and almost as long when flaccid as when erect, suggesting to the uninitiated that he might have a twelve- or thirteen-inch cock when it was hard. The outstanding characteristic of his prick was not just its formidable size, but its sheer physical beauty—no other word would do. It was completely smooth and very light in color, showing no veins or blemishes of any kind along the shaft. The helmet of his prick was a light pink in color, and the perfect size for the shaft it surmounted. Anyone who had ever seen Lance in action, whether on film or in person, knew that his innocent outward appearance belied the raging stud within.

Casey introduced Luke to Richard. Richard, in turn, introduced both of them to Lance, who suggested they call him David—his actual name. He made this same suggestion to each of the staff at the T 'n B, but no one called him, or thought of him as anything but Lance — a sexy name for an incomparably sexy and beautiful man.

Shaking Casey's hand, Lance grinned and said, "I hear you've got the biggest dick around here. Is that true?"

"Guilty as charged," Casey smiled. "but Richard, here, is King Cock." He put an arm over Richard's shoulder. "Nobody can give it, or take it, the way he does," and he substituted his own hand for the one Richard had been stroking his prick with as he added, "and you can see he's got the equipment." Richard kissed Casey and grinned boyishly, obviously flattered — and eating it up. He did not modestly deny Casey's claim for his superiority, nor suggest that Casey was in any way his equal or superior.

About that time, Carl entered, having just finished his show. His naked muscular body was glistening with sweat, and his prick was fully hard, bobbing and swaying as he walked. Luke goggled at Carl's body and hard prick, but Lance said to him, "Good show." Actually, Lance had only watched the opening ten minutes of Carl's show from the wings before Richard lured him into the backstage room.

"Better get ready," Richard warned Casey. "You've only got about ten minutes before you go on."

Casey began stripping as he told Luke to go into the theatre and catch his show, promising to join him there so together they could watch Lance perform. Luke left, and Casey threw the clothes he was wearing into his locker, then took out his 'work clothes.' When Casey was completely naked, Lance's attention was diverted from Richard's cock and focused on Casey's equipment — not erect, but breathtaking nonetheless. Although he had little time, Casey was aware of how much his cock had impressed the new guest porn star, and couldn't resist stroking it until it grew hard. Lance was by then almost salivating over the sight, but Casey couldn't delay further by teasing the blond beauty any more. He donned the tiny g-string, which couldn't cover his monster cock when it was erect, as it was just then; the last couple inches of his massive shaft weren't concealed at all, but were held up against his belly by the waistband of the minuscule garment. He covered it all with his 'breakaway' pants. Stepping into his boots, he was ready to go on — just in time. Eddie announced his appearance and he went out to perform, trailed by Lance, who stood in the wings to watch his performance.

Richard was clearly displeased that Lance's attention had turned so obviously to Casey, and he went to stand next to Lance in the wings, still naked, and stroking his cock, which had lost some of its erection, but returned to full glory in a few strokes.

Lance shifted his attention from Casey on stage to Richard, and smiled as he reached over and substituted his own hand for Richard's, stroking his prick. He smiled at Richard while he stroked, looking sweet and almost saintly. With his other hand he pulled down the waistband of his warm-up pants, revealing the fact that: (a) he was wearing no underwear; (b) he had a perfectly formed, luscious cock; and (c) that glorious cock was rapidly getting hard—and enormous! The hand that was stroking Richard's hard-on shifted to the top of Richard's head, and pushed it down so that Richard knelt before him, his face only inches from Lance's cock. Richard had only to open his mouth to accept Lance's impressive offering. Both of Lance's hands held Richard's head as he began to fuck him in the mouth. Lance's offering was not only impressive, it was challenging, but Richard met the challenge bravely and eagerly, and was soon deep-throating every inch of the delicious mouth-stretcher. After several moments enjoying Richard's masterful blowjob, Lance murmured, "Gotta go get ready. I'll give you a load later on," and he turned to go back to the waiting room, causing his prick to pull from Richard's mouth with a distinct popping sound.

Out in the audience, Luke had been both fascinated and thrilled by his boyfriend's performance. During the part of his time in the audience while he wore his g-string, Casey had not lingered in front of Luke any more than he did with anyone, although he did lean down and kiss him, whispering, "Hey, lover!" as he did so. But during Casey's second circuit, performed nude except for his boots, with his dick hard and flopping, Luke was treated to a much longer and more intense experience than anyone else in the theatre. Casey pressed the tip of prick at Luke's lips, and pushed so that Luke had no choice but to take it inside his mouth—where he sucked it eagerly, Then Casey turned around and leaned over the seat in front of Luke. With one hand he reached down to place one of Luke's hands around his cock, and with the other he drew Luke's head forward so that his face was buried in Casey's buttocks, where he rimmed Casey's asshole while the blond stud wriggled his ass delightedly. Reluctantly, Casey moved on, and Luke was surprised to feel a hand grab the inside of his right leg.

He looked to his right to find a leering Richard, who had very quickly thrown on a warm-up jacket and pants and occupied the seat next to him. Casey had, apparently paid no attention to Richard sitting there when he interacted with Luke. Richard had pulled the waistband of his pants below his balls, exposing his prick, which was standing straight up as he played with it.

Richard moved his hand up Luke's leg, toward his crotch as he whispered, "He's fantastic, isn't he?" By that time, his hand had begun to grope Luke's crotch; Luke had developed a hard-on watching his boyfriend perform, which had become very serious when he was sucking him and eating his ass. Richard was massaging it through his pants, which was exciting, but Luke was not open to sex-play with anyone other then Casey at the moment.

Luke pulled Richard's hand away from his crotch. "Richard, stop. I'm Casey's lover."

"He only called you his boyfriend when he introduced you," Richard whispered. "No reason all three of us couldn't have some fun together. Casey can tell you, I'm a lot of fun in bed—and I know he's not opposed to threesomes. Are you?" Luke muttered a faint "No," and Richard continued. "I'll bet he told you what a great time he and I have had together. And we still do, too." His hand took Luke's right hand and brought it to his throbbing prick, which it grasped and stroked. Luke continued to fondle and stroke the considerable bulk of Richard's hard cock as Richard returned his own hand to Luke's lap, and he started to grope again, this time without Luke's protestations.

Casey had long since finished his show, and as Luke and Richard sat there, groping and masturbating each other, respectively, Casey appeared and sat down next to Luke's left side. He was irritated, but not at all surprised, to see that Richard had put the moves on his boyfriend. "Damn it, Richard, I told you he was my boyfriend."

Richard leered, "Yeah, but he's got a helluva hard-on that says he's enjoying it." Luke was too embarrassed to speak, and had stopped jacking Richard off when Casey appeared. "C'mon, Casey, don't be such a stick-in-the mud. Get your dick out and we'll all beat off while we watch Lance." Casey's performance had gone overtime, and the sound system announced Lance's appearance about that time.

"Okay with you, Luke?" Casey whispered.

"Sure," Luke said, but with some reluctance.

"What the hell, it'll be fun," Casey said as he pulled the waistband of his pants below his balls, and began to stroke his prick. For the next half hour Luke sat with two different men who were playing with his cock, while each of his hands was stroking and fondling two other extremely large and fiercely hard pricks. All three unconsciously paced their play so that no one would blow a load during that time.

Lance's performance was not very impressive. He seemed to be moving as if he were under water, but the sight of his angelic beauty and luscious prick more than made up for his apparent lack of interest in what he was doing to entertain the patrons. The sight of Casey, Luke and Richard, with their cocks bared and playing with each other, clearly piqued his interest when he visited them during his first circuit of the audience, while he was dressed only in a very skimpy, tight Speedo, which was well-stuffed, even though he didn't have an erection. Back on stage, he stripped off the Speedo and stroked his appetizing cock until it stood straight out, flopping and swaying, bobbing up and down with every movement he made. He jacked off enthusiastically while he was making his second circuit, and when he reached Casey and company, he stopped before them—directly in front of Luke. He ratcheted up his masturbation, and in a few minutes he gasped, "I'm gonna come! Who wants it?" Like just about everyone in the audience, the three were virtually hypnotized by Lance's languorous movements and the intense sensuousness of his performance, and all wanted it when Lance apparently offered his orgasm. As if they had rehearsed it, the three succumbed to the golden blond's invitation, craning their necks so their mouths would be at Lance's cock head when it gushed. Just as their mouths almost met, Lance's prick began to spew his hot white load, in five or six very generous spurts directed democratically on all three sets of lips and the tongues that eagerly extended and lapped to receive them. Many in the audience had by that time stood so they could better see what was happening—and many of those were well aware that two of the *Top 'n Bottom*'s hottest performers were involved Everyone who could see applauded the cum-facial delivered by the innocent-appearing, but gloriously sexy and sensual blond stud.

Casey, Luke and Richard unconsciously did their best to evenly divide what Lance had given them. Lance leaned over and pressed his mouth against theirs to share in the treasure he had given them. When Lance finally stood up and smiled seraphically into the glare of the spotlight, traces of his own discharge glistened on his cheeks, lips and chin, and even on his nose, while each of the three blessed ones on whom he had bestowed his largesse continued to lick the others' mouths clean.

Lance went back up on stage and simply stood there for a minute or two, seemingly oblivious to the wild applause he had earned. He stroked his still fiercely erect prick, and a string of cum oozed out to hang down from the tip, almost reaching the stage floor. He suddenly seemed to become aware of the audience, and he smiled the smile of an innocent child as he blew them kisses and walked off stage, the string of cum swaying pendulously as he did so.

Many in the audience rose and left the auditorium, but quite a few lingered to exchange blowjobs when they found a willing partner. The three upon whom Lance had bestowed his munificence still sat there, fondling each other's cocks, still thrilled by the rapturous experience they had just shared. Finally, Richard broke the silence: "Jesus, let's go somewhere and fuck," he panted. The three restored their cocks to their pants and headed backstage, where they found Lance dressing while he talked with Drake—one of two new dancers that Eddie had recently hired, and who was scheduled to dance next. Drake was naked, planning to don his show costume, and was doing most of the talking. Lance seemed to be only half-listening to him.

Drake was fairly tall—a bit over six feet—and was very thin. Skinny would be a more accurate term to describe his body. He was pleasant-looking, but not particularly handsome. He had one feature that set him apart, however, and which had already begun to endear him to audiences: his cock hung half-way to his knees when it was soft, and when it was erect it was even longer than Casey's—something like eleven inches. If his gargantuan prick wasn't as perfectly formed and aesthetically impressive as Lance's, its size made it glorious. It was clear Drake was impressed with Lance's beautiful equipment, however, since he apparently couldn't keep his eyes off it until Lance pulled up his sweat pants—but just as clearly, the memory of what he had been so hungrily eyeing was made manifest in the state of Drakes's mammoth cock, which projected out from his body, only half-erect, but arcing out at a forty-five degree angle, still a clearly formidable weapon.

When Casey, Luke and Richard entered, Lance grinned goofily at them and said, "You guys like my cum shower out there?" Drake looked annoyed at having been interrupted, but said nothing. The three recipients of Lance's generous bequest agreed it had been exciting — and delectable as well. "Y'all wanna come over to my hotel room and pay me back? You got some huge pricks," he said. His suggestion was a happy coincidence, since the three had been wondering, as they came backstage, where they could gather to fulfill Richard's suggestion, inspired by Lance's exciting attentions: *Let's go somewhere and fuck.*

Lance finished dressing, and the quartet went to the hotel room retained by the theatre, the site where Casey had taken part in such a wonderful threesome with Gundo Lopez and Joey Stone. Lance didn't say much, but in the elevator he groped all three of his prospective guests, paying particular attention to Casey; he wrapped his arms around Casey and began kissing him passionately while he fondled his ass even more ardently. Richard and Luke had to hold the elevator for a couple of minutes while Lance continued to devour Casey's mouth until Casey gently broke the embrace and led Lance into the hallway. Lance fumbled with the room key for a moment, but managed finally to get the door open, and the four entered, closing it behind them.

With no ceremony whatever, Lance stripped off all his clothes and threw them casually on the floor. He grinned at the others, saying. "I gotta take a shower. Y'all get naked and ready to feed me some dick." With that he went into the bathroom, and the shower could be heard as Casey, Luke and Richard prepared to honor Lance's request. Richard's clothes were on the floor before Casey and Luke were half undressed.

Casey enfolded Luke in his arms, saying. "This is gonna be fun." The two embraced and kissed for a few moments, and when they broke, they found that Richard was missing. They looked into the bathroom, and saw in the clear-glass shower stall that Richard was in there with Lance, who was on his knees, sucking Richard's cock. Casey chuckled, "Wouldn't you know? Richard never misses a trick. I'll bet he has Lance's big cock up his ass in no time." He smiled at Luke. "Wouldn't you like that, too?"

Luke smiled back, saying. "I don't care if he fucks Richard or not, but are you asking if I'd like his big cock up my ass? To be honest, yeah, I would, provided he gives you the same thing — and you give me the same thing, too." He said this last as he wrapped a hand around the fat shaft of Casey's cock.

"We'll hafta see how lucky we get, I guess." Casey replied.

They snooped casually around the room. Their cursory inspection yielded little information besides the presence of drug paraphernalia scattered about. They found no evidence of needles or pills, but to them it seemed obvious that Lance indulged in pot usage—which, they agreed, probably explained at least some of his detached, spaced-out actions, but only some. They may have been correct, but they never learned whether their deductions were founded in fact.

Soon, a naked Richard and Lance came out of the bathroom, toweling off, their hair wet and their cocks in a state of full arousal—Richard looking as smug as the proverbial cat that ate the canary, Lance smiling sweetly, not remotely hinting that actually he was the canary that had just eaten the cat. Casey's and Luke's dicks almost immediately grew to the same state of erection the other two sported. Both Lance and Richard were magnificently sexy, handsome men with big, hard pricks clearly willing to provide gratification, and—more importantly—capable of giving immense satisfaction. Under the circumstances, who would have been able to resist getting a hard-on?

Lance dropped his wet towel to the floor and brandished his erection. His smile appeared to be unfocused, and he looked innocent, even cherubic, in spite of the fact that he was stroking an immense hard cock. "Who wants this up his ass first?"

Luke had been sitting on the side of the double bed, and he stood and reversed his body so he was kneeling there, his toes hanging over the edge. He turned his head and grinned sheepishly, wriggling his bare ass, "Gotta start somewhere." Casey was somewhat surprised at Luke's forwardness, but he shrugged his shoulders and knelt next to his boyfriend on the bed.

Richard laughed and joined Casey and Luke, presenting Lance with a row of three hungry assholes waiting for service. He grinned at Lance, "Gang-bang the three of us, stud!"

"Nothin' I'd like better," Lance said. "but I wanna get you warmed up first." He knelt on the floor behind Casey and pulled his cheeks apart as he buried his face between them. Reaching around, he played with Casey's dick and pinched his tits as his tongue invaded the hungry asshole, flickering back and forth over it, darting in and out, and dancing around inside as Casey moaned his pleasure. "Sweet ass," he murmured as he moved on to service Luke the same way, and then on to Richard, who panted encouragement and wriggled his ass eagerly, stimulating Lance to greater heights of his practiced and joyous butt-munching. Standing, Lance dipped into a large, open jar of Vaseline on the nightstand and went down the line of eager receptacles again, preparing them this time for the onslaught of his dick. He took a bottle of poppers from the nightstand and began to unscrew the top.

Casey interrupted him. "Rubber, Lance?"

It was clear the blond stud had not even considered protection, but he giggled, "Oh, yeah, rubber." He put down the inhalant bottle and took a condom from the saucer on the nightstand. He rolled it on, then lubricated his sheathed cock as he opened the bottle of poppers. Taking a very large sniff in each nostril, he closed the bottle and palmed it as he seized Richard's waist and pressed the tip of his erection against his eager asshole. Pulling violently on Richard's body as he rammed his cock forward with equal intensity, he planted its entire prodigious length fully inside Richard, who yelled in combined surprise and pleasure. It was clear the poppers had done their work: Lance's plunging was insanely vigorous as he grunted and panted in what appeared to be fuck-frenzy. After five minutes of savage humping, he seized Richard's shoulders and pulled their bodies together as he gasped, "I'm coming! Take my load, stud!"

Lance continued to fuck Richard for a few minutes after his orgasm. He took another hit from the poppers bottle, and with almost no break in his rhythm, pulled his cock out of Richard and slammed it brutally inside Luke, not stopping to change the condom that now contained his first discharge. Luke cried out as he began to receive Lance's furious thrusts, and whimpered with joy while he reveled in the sweet-looking porn star's violent, protracted fuck. Casey was fully as appreciative as Luke when Lance turned his prodigious talents to him—still without changing the condom. Luke and Richard studied Lance's cute little, rounded ass as he fucked Casey for an extremely long, glorious time. As he had when he was fucking Luke, Lance took regular hits from the popper bottle.

After finally discharging his second orgasm, Lance fell heavily over Casey's back, pressing him flat to the bed, where the two lay in complete fulfillment. Richard began to caress Lance's ass and tease his asshole with a finger. "When do we get to fuck this little beauty?"

Lance turned his head and beamed his goofy grin back at Richard. "Sorry, man. I don't take it up the ass—even from a hot stud like you. But I'll suck all of you off as many times as you want. I like suckin' dick almost as much as I like fuckin' butt or eatin' ass." He demonstrated that he was a man of his word as he proceeded to blow all three — Richard, for the second time that day — as they sat on the bed and watched the beautiful blond head bobbing up and down and the cum glistening on his grinning lips after each orgasm he swallowed.

Bill Lowe had met many of Casey's school friends — most of them boys his son was having sex with, but he had to deduce that from the sounds he heard coming from his son's bedroom — and recently, he had even fucked with one of them. But so far, Casey had never brought someone home to introduce him as anything other than a friend — in actuality, usually a fuckbuddy. When he brought Luke home, however, he introduced him to his father without any clarification of Luke's status. Bill could tell by the glow in his son's eyes and the way he looked at Luke, this new boy meant more to Casey than the others he had brought home — more than just a friend, certainly. For a gay boy living with a single father, it was the equivalent of bringing a serious boyfriend home to Meet the Parents.

When Casey announced that he was planning on going to South Carolina in the fall, to start a college education — probably at Farrar University — Bill not only knew his son was in a serious relationship with an apparently nice young man, but he was also pleased that Casey now had a real incentive to graduate high school and go on with his education.

Casey had only known Luke for four days by then, but with each day he felt more sure that he was "the one." They spent the whole night together in Casey's bed, and it was the best sex they had shared, mainly because they had all the time in the world for gentle kissing and caressing as well as sucking and fucking. Furthermore, they were not being watched or sharing it with anyone else.

On Thursday, Casey begged off work, and spent the whole day with Luke, who was scheduled to fly back to South Carolina Friday morning. They wandered Lincoln Park together for hours, occasionally stopping to kiss and cuddle — only once having sex, when they went into the bushes to suck each other off. They went to the house where cousin Mike lived, when Casey met him for the first time.

And cousin Mike was something else! He was personable, even charming, and he was downright gorgeous: infectious smile; medium height and medium, but well-muscled build; straight coal-black hair, parted in the middle. He was also well-spoken, and seemed to be quite intelligent. He had a fairly large cock — probably eight inches — and an adorable, rounded ass. These last two features Casey was able to ascertain only by looking at the portfolio of photographs Mike's agent had prepared when he was working as a "Pete's Pal." The pictures showed that Mike was also sexually versatile and hot as hell—able to deep-throat an immense cock, and take it up the ass with obvious joy. And his cock might not always be as large as his partner's, but he could give as well as he got. This last was demonstrated when Mike showed Casey and Luke an advance copy of the video he had recently shot, which was being shopped around to several gay porn studios for distribution.

Casey liked Mike at once, and appreciated the fact that Mike did not try to get in the way of Casey and Luke sharing their last full day together, although he would have been more than happy to go to bed with Mike under any other circumstances.

The lovers took the dog Casey with them for a very long walk along the beach. Luke said he was really missing his three dogs back in South Carolina. It was the first time he had mentioned them. He told Casey that his lady friend Roxie—sort of a surrogate mother, who lived next door to him—was tending to the dogs in his absence. After their walk they went back to Mike's house for a late supper he had prepared. The distinguished older man who owned the house he shared conditionally with Mike, and who had long been one of Mike's most enthusiastic and generous admirers, joined them for the meal. Mike retired with the older man to his bedroom, while Casey and Luke retired to a spare guest room in Mike's part of the house, where Luke had been staying.

In the morning, Mike came in to wake the two lovers, Luke was awake, but still in bed. Just then, a naked Casey came out of the bathroom, his gargantuan prick fully hard, swaying and bobbing in spite of the workout it had received during the night.

Mike was as impressed with the size and beauty of Casey's cock as he had been with Casey's looks the day before. He was wearing a Japanese happi coat—an extremely short robe, made of light fabric and held closed by a sash, which barely covered the wearer's "private parts"—and his appreciation of Casey's most impressive private part was very obvious from the state of his own in spite of the workout his had received during the night. Seeing that, Luke offered to share the shower with his cousin as well as Casey, but Mike declined. "If this weren't your last day together, I'd be in there right away."

Luke grinned, "Dropping the soap?"

"Oh, yeah, and I bet it would take me a long time to pick it up — probably be bent over for quite a while," Mike grinned back.

Mike drove Luke and Casey to the airport. Casey promised to come out to South Carolina between the end of the school year and the beginning of summer school, so that he could check out Farrar University. In the meantime, he would be sending a conditional application to the school, and arranging for an interview with the Registrar when he got there. Luke's plane was, unfortunately, on time, so the lovers had little time to say goodbye.

As they drove back into The City, Mike apologized for having offered to join Casey and his cousin for sex in the shower that morning. "The offer still stands, even if Luke has left," he said, resting a hand on Casey's leg, "but only if you don't think that would be inappropriate."

"Look, Mike, I have sex with a lot of guys in my work at the theatre," he began — he had told Mike all about the *Top 'n Bottom*. "And even if — no, when Luke and I become full-fledged lovers, living together, I know we're going to be having sex with others guys from time to time." He laughed, "Shit, most of the time when we were fucking this week, there was at least one other guy involved."

"Does that mean I'm gonna get a crack at your big dick?" Mike asked.

"Sure, and you're gonna get a crack at my crack, too," Casey said, and moved Mike's hand up to his crotch. "In fact, I can hardly wait."

At Casey's suggestion, Mike lent him the tape of his porn movie, which Casey promised to show Eddie, with the hope that Eddie would hire Mike as a guest porn star. True he had only made one video, and it hadn't been distributed yet, but Casey felt sure that Mike was going to achieve great success in gay porn. Besides, there had been a few porn "stars" who had appeared at the T 'n B with equally slight credentials. (Pornography was similar to rock music, in that almost anyone who performed was called a "star." Porn stars who actually became stars were called "superstars.")

Casey took Mike's tape with him to the theatre when he went to work that afternoon. Eddie was impressed by "Mike Henson," and agreed to feature him for a week as soon as an opening came up on the schedule of guest performers. He preferred to hire only well-established porn stars with an established body of fans who would want to see them in person, but occasionally none who fit the bill were available, and he had to feature promising newcomers like Mike.

Casey had been somewhat negligent about studying during spring break, but he had really needed some relaxation of the intense concentration he had been affording his studies lately, and Luke had proven to be a very distracting diversion. But he had two papers due when he returned to school on Monday morning. He spent as little time at the theatre over the weekend as he possibly could, and managed to complete his assignments. He now had added inspiration for doing well in his studies: he wanted to enter Farrar University in the fall, and he wanted to be with his lover.

He did manage to squeeze in a little time to say goodbye to Lance on Sunday, however. Lance chose Richard to double with him for his final show on Sunday night—which surprised no one, considering how obviously Richard had been campaigning to be selected for the honor. However, after Lance's late afternoon performance, which immediately preceded Casey's final show for the week, he met the blond star as he left the stage. "You got time to come over to the apartment with me for a little while?" Lance asked. Casey agreed to accompany him, expecting Lance to say he wanted to fuck him again—something like "for old time's sake" he assumed, although "old time's sake" in this case had lasted less than a week.

Once in the apartment, Lance swore Casey to secrecy about anything that was about to occur. Casey agreed, and they both got naked and began caressing and kissing, rolling about on the bed in feverish passion. Then they swapped ends and began to suck cock in sixty-nine. Casey had blown his obligatory public load in the theatre earlier in the day, and he was in need of release; he hoped to achieve that release in Lance's throat, and he felt sure—hoped, actually—Lance would be achieving his release in his ass, as he had by then done several times during his tenure as guest dancer.

But Lance surprised him, before either of them blew a load. He stopped sucking and kissed Casey again, explaining why he wanted to keep their final meeting secret: "Everbody knows I'm strictly a top, but I've been drooling over that big ol' prick of yours all week, and I don't wanna leave without you shovin' it all the way up my butt and fillin' me with your hot cum." He did not mention it, but he had taken Drake's even-bigger cock in his ass the day before—and he had similarly sworn Drake to secrecy.

Needless to say, Casey was more than willing to oblige the strange, but beautiful and sexy stud who knelt on the bed, wriggling his small, round ass in anticipation. Casey took a condom from the dish on the nightstand, but before he tore it open, Lance told him he wanted to get fucked bareback. "I meant it when I said I want you fillin' up my ass with your cum — not some goddamned rubber." Casey knew it was inadvisable, but again, he was willing to accede to the request.

After lubricating his cock and Lance's eager ass, Casey seized the man's waist and positioned his cock-head at his asshole. Lance gasped, "Slam it in!" and Casey obliged with one savage thrust — eliciting a shout of "Yes!" Lance was tight, but it was clear he was no stranger to bottoming, and his cries of joy and encouragement inspired Casey to provide a truly masterful fuck. Casey's cry of triumph when he blew his load inside Lance was no sooner uttered than Lance begged him to keep fucking and give him another load — a request Casey was happy to honor; fortunately, he was able to do so as well, and it took a long time — adding to the enjoyment of both.

Casey told no one about his last encounter with Lance until much later, when Richard was reminiscing about Lance's beauty and sexual power. Figuring it really made no difference, he told Richard he had fucked the blond stud on Lance's last day at the theatre — twice, and bareback. Richard laughed, "He fucked me royally on stage that night, when we doubled. Then he took me over to the apartment, and I fucked him — bareback, and three times!" Casey had no idea if that were true, but knowing Richard's persuasiveness, and the magnificence of the fuck he normally administered, he believed it — even though it meant that the private meeting between Richard and Lance would have occurred on the evening of the day he, himself, had fucked the blond star twice.

11.

Tim's not Tiny, and

Chad's not Preppy

The second new dancer at the T 'n B was Justin. His frame was slight, and he only stood 5'5" tall. His clearly documented age was twenty years, but he appeared to be fourteen or fifteen. He was very cute, in a boyish way, and had a mop of straight, light brown hair that almost concealed his eyes. He had very little body hair, and only a very light thatch over his cock, adding to the illusion of immaturity. His prick was about seven inches long, but it appeared to be longer, given his stature. Eddie had not been interested in hiring him until Justin had pointed out that many of the theatre's patrons would probably be interested in fantasizing about sex with a young boy while watching a legal adult. Let Eddie give him a shot, and see how he was accepted.

Justin had been absolutely right about how he would be accepted. Although he didn't draw particularly large audiences, those who watched him reacted enthusiastically. In addition, he drew more patrons into the downstairs cubicles and out for more extended action than almost any of the standard house dancers. He was strictly a bottom, but that seemed to bother very few of his admirers. It certainly didn't bother Tim Kramer.

Tim Kramer was the next major star to be featured at the theatre. He was one of the most powerfully sexy men in gay porn at the time. He had a shock of straight, dirty-blond hair that draped across his forehead. He had something of a peasant's face—coarse features, large, rather thick lips and heavy eyebrows—usually featuring a petulant expression or a half-sneer. He seldom smiled. He had very long legs, and unusually wide shoulders. His chest tapered toward his waist only slightly, which made his upper body look almost rectangular. He was generally quite muscular, and he had a flat washboard stomach. His cock was big, but not more than nine inches, at best. Still, given the slightly threatening air his manner and his physical appearance suggested, his cock probably seemed larger and more menacing than it would if it had belonged to a more pleasant-seeming man. In any event, it was a serious assful — and an even more challenging mouthful.

He announced to all at the theatre that he was strictly a top, and his videos suggested he was not lying. He had bottomed only once for the cameras: his first porn work, a short 'loop,' where he was on a boat and was obviously uncomfortable the whole time he was being fucked. Like a great many of his generation's gay porn actors — perhaps even the majority of them — he was to succumb to an AIDS-related death in the mid 1990's, even though he allegedly never bottomed and the HIV virus was apparently transmitted through passive anal sex with an infected partner. He, himself, only wore a condom when he fucked if his partner insisted.

Tim fucked all the house dancers, as was the custom, and he seemed impervious to Richard's blatant wooing — much to the amusement of the others. He clearly admired Casey, who was one of only two house dancers he entertained alone in his assigned apartment. His compliments about Casey's masculine beauty and monster cock were couched in such macho terms they might easily have been the kind that straight athletes pay each other, without sexual overtones. His appreciation of Casey's talent as a bottom, however, elicited the kind of language only a gay man would use when making love. Furthermore, his eagerness in sucking Casey off and eating his ass — services he had performed for quite a few of the house dancers — bore testimony to his gay proclivities.

Shortly before Tim's brief tenure at the theatre, a scout from Eagle Productions, the San Francisco-based gay porn company, had offered to give Casey a screen test, saying he was sure the young blond could become a porn star of the first magnitude. Casey had promised the scout he would consider the offer, but he wondered how advisable it would be for him to appear in films, naked, having gay sex. He briefly chatted with Mike about it, but Mike had until then only made one porn video, which had not yet even been released, so he had no experience on which to draw in offering advice. He did, however, enthuse about his experience in making that one film: it had been great fun, and he had made love — his term — with a couple of the sexiest, most satisfying men he had ever encountered.

Casey decided to talk over the idea with Tim, an established porn star. Lying in bed with Tim in the theatre's apartment, after having just drained him of three loads—one down his throat and two up his ass—Casey asked for his advice.

"What do you wanna do with your life, kid? Tim had asked in reply.

"I don't really know. I'm hoping to go to college this fall. After that, who knows?"

"Well, if you think you might go into some profession, or work for a company of some kind, don't let 'em take pictures of you having sex. If you wanna spend your life selling your ass or posing for pictures of you while you're using your dick, that's fine, but otherwise, those pictures'll come back to haunt you somehow, and you'll lose your job. It's already happened to me."

Casey decided to heed Tim's advice, and advised the scout from Eagle that he wasn't interested in making videos.

The other house dancer Tim entertained in private was the new, young-appearing Justin. Tim fucked him, sucked him off and ate his ass several times in front of other dancers in the backstage area. He also took him to the apartment for private sex on three separate occasions—two of them 'all-nighters.' Whether or not Tim was a "chicken queen" (a gay man who likes underage boys for sex) who was enjoying sex with a legal boy who appeared to be "chicken" is not known. But his fascination with the boyish Justin seemed to suggest it was true. What was clear, however, was how much Justin enjoyed Tim's very powerful lovemaking.

In Tim's final show at the theatre, he doubled with Justin, fucking him so long and so ferociously that the young dancer blew a load across the stage without touching his cock while Tim continued to hammer his voracious ass until Justin blew yet another load in clear view of the audience, still without touching his cock. Justin's second orgasm erupted only a few seconds before Tim pulled his cock out of his ass, spun him around, and blasted his own huge orgasm all over the boy's face and body. Tim licked his own cum from Justin face and belly, and then locked his lips to Justin's in a long, passionate kiss that drew cheers from the audience.

As the school year drew to a close, Casey hewed diligently to the academic standards he had set for himself, and when semester grades were issued, he had made an "A" in all his subjects except one, and he got a "B+" in that. He lacked a Civics course and one in Trigonometry to graduate, and those he scheduled for Summer School.

Lately, he had been neglecting his fuckbuddies—at least that was what they told him—so he, Joey Stone, Rommel Chase, and two other boys he had fucked with fairly regularly during their high school years, planned an all-night orgy on the night of the Senior Prom. All went to the Prom stag, and then after the dance they went to a deluxe suite they had rented at the St. Francis Hotel—dressed in their tuxedos, and ready to say goodbye to their senior year in high style. All had taken long naps that afternoon, and were ready for a night of sex without sleep. They ordered room-service breakfast at 7:00 the next morning, and the boy who brought it up to the suite was clearly impressed with the five hot boys—all naked, and all apparently resting from a night of sex. They gave him a very good tip, but it seemed clear he would rather have joined in the fun, instead. No one was keeping tabs on the number of orgasms shared that night, but Casey knew he, himself, had delivered seven, and he doubted he had been the most fecund among them. After breakfast, they spent another three or four hours in total sexual abandon, and checked out at noon, again wearing their tuxedos.

Prior to that prom-night orgy, Rommel had become almost haunted by memory of the wild fucking he had once regularly celebrated with Casey. Lately, he had enjoyed it only on rare occasions, and his love for his younger, willowy lover had gradually dissipated in his growing hunger for a return to the ecstatic kind of sex he had known with Casey, Joey, and others. He had gradually, but gently 'turned over' his young lover to another boy at Serra High, one who had several times expressed his admiration for the young lover and his envy of Rommel's relationship with him. The young lover was hurt when he realized what was happening, but after having been fucked a couple times by the proposed replacement, who had a much bigger prick than Rommel's, and who used it with what he regarded as unbelievable skill, he accepted the situation with open arms—and legs.

One night, midway through his last semester in high school, Rommel was so eager to get fucked by Casey that on a sudden impulse he went to his house unannounced, hoping to find him home—and hoping to find satisfaction in his bed, as he had many, many times in the past. Since he had always before visited Casey's house during the day, it was not odd that he had never met Bill there.

Casey's father met Rommel at the door. Rommel said he was a friend of Casey's, and before he said anything further, he was invited inside. Bill had just taken a shower, and was wearing only a towel wrapped around his waist. Rommel was wearing small, tight walking shorts and a very tight sleeveless T-shirt. The utter magnificence of his body was obvious, and Bill was not one to overlook such beauty; there was no way he would not have invited such a mouth-watering sight inside.

Rommel was disappointed to learn that Casey was at work. He was going to leave when Bill asked him if he would like to stick around and chat for a minute or two. Rommel was fascinated: Bill looked like an older version of the gorgeous Casey — older, but no less attractive — fine body, the same golden crown of hair. He could not help but wonder if what was under the towel was as stunning as its counterpart in Casey. He accepted Bill's invitation, and sat as the older man went to get soft drinks.

Bill returned and stood in front of the seated boy as he made the kind of small talk one might expect. He couldn't help but drink in the glory of Rommel's body, and as he did so, his towel began to bulge. Rommel noticed the growing towel, and Bill noticed Rommel noticing. Bill almost never concealed an erection in a potentially sexual situation — the eye-popping glory of what he almost never concealed had led to a very pleasant resolution in so many of those situations. This was one of his son's classmates, of course, but he was regularly having no-guilt sex with another of Casey's friends. What the hell? In for a penny, in for a pound!

It was obvious to Rommel that the growing bulge in Bill's towel was caused by a marvelous ass-reamer like's Casey's. Nervously — but, surprisingly, not too nervously — Rommel looked Bill in the eye and said, "Casey sure does look a lot like you, Mr. Lowe." Then he slowly directed his gaze downward to the bulging towel as he added, "In every way, I think."

Seeing and hearing that, Bill knew exactly where things were headed. He reached out and rubbed a hand suggestively over Rommel's bare, muscular shoulder. "You might want to check and be sure." His hand moved down and inside Rommel's T-shirt to caress one of the boy's splendid, rounded breasts as he added, "It's strictly up to you."

Rommel reached for the knot in Bill's towel and pulled it free. The towel fell to the floor, and Bill's cock, which was by then mostly hard, rose to stand out in its full ten-inch glory as the boy's hand cupped Bill's balls and whistled in appreciation. "Oh yeah, Casey is like you in every way." He knelt on the floor and opened his mouth very wide as he welcomed all ten inches of throbbing cock deep inside his throat—no mean feat, but one he had honed to perfection on the lip-stretching challenge of the immense prick of Bill's own son. Bill ruffled Rommel's hair and murmured in satisfaction as he enjoyed the considerable cocksucking talent his son's fuckbuddy demonstrated. Rommel's hands fondled Bill's ass as it writhed and humped, driving the colossal meat into his throat.

"I'm gonna come if you don't stop," Bill gasped after a few minutes.

Rommel looked up admiringly at Bill, and stopped his sucking for a moment to say, "If I suck you off, you can fuck me that much longer. Okay?"

Taking Rommel's head in both hands, Bill smiled. "Sounds fine with me. Just be sure you're gonna be able to give me a load or two."

"You like to get fucked, Mr. Lowe?"

"Oh yeah, and I love to suck dick, too."

"Gee, Casey really is a lot like you."

"I know," Bill laughed. "Now get back to work." He pulled Rommel's head in toward him, and Rommel opened his mouth wide as Bill shoved his prick back inside and resumed his mouth-fuck.

Rommel was soon rewarded with a prodigious mouthful of hot cum. After he had savored and swallowed it, Bill pulled him to his feet, and began stripping off his clothes. "Let's get in bed."

Once the muscular boy was naked, Bill led him to the bedroom, where he had Rommel kneel on the bed on all fours, and he knelt behind him. Rommel used his hands to spread his cheeks, expecting Bill's huge prick, but he was surprised when the older man buried his face in his ass and ate him out thoroughly while his hands roved lovingly all over his magnificent body. Finally, Bill put on a condom, greased them both up, and sank his prick to the hilt in Rommel's hungry ass. He gasped, "Fuck me, Mr. Lowe."

"Under the circumstances, you might want to just call me Bill."

"Fuck me, Bill. You're fantastic!"

And Bill fucked him almost brutally, at great length, pushing the boy down onto his stomach, rolling him over, and raising his legs so that they rested on his shoulders. "I wanna see that gorgeous body while I fuck you," he panted, fucking even more hungrily as he stroked and fondled Rommel's shoulders, arms, and washboard stomach, cupped his breasts and sucked his nipples — not ignoring the boy's prick, but much more fascinated by his sumptuous body.

"Casey always fucks me this way, too, at least when he's coming. He says he loves to play with my tits while he's blowing his load."

"Casey's a smart boy," Bill laughed, and continued to fuck. He cried out loudly when he came a few minutes later, but his cries were muffled since he was sucking one of Rommel's nipples at the time. Rommel had always considered Casey the best fuck among the two-or-so dozen boys who had screwed him in the ass, but he had to admit to himself that for whatever reason — greater maturity, perhaps — Bill, who was almost a dead ringer for his son in so many ways, seemed to be even more exciting and satisfying.

When Rommel fucked Bill, he, too, also used the missionary position, so Bill could continue to admire his body visually and manually.

They spent the entire night in rapturous worship of Rommel's glorious body and Bill's stupendous prick. Later, they arranged ample opportunities for further lovemaking, working around Casey's and Joey's schedules. They had only the summer to make love with each other, since Rommel would be going off to college, but they made the best imaginable use of that time, and neither Casey nor Joey caught on to what they were doing.

If Bill felt any guilt over the fact that he was regularly having sex with two of his son's classmates, eighteen-year-old boys, he managed to stifle it and enjoy the rides.

Rommel had heard Casey talk about the Piedmont region of South Carolina, where he would, hopefully, be going to school in the fall. Maybe coincidentally, but more than likely not, Rommel had applied to, and been accepted at, Clemson University — only a half-hour down the road from where Casey would presumably be living. Rommel and Luke had not met when Luke was in San Francisco, but Casey felt sure his muscular classmate and his lover were going to impress each other, with predictable results.

For his part, Rommel was reluctant to abandon his very satisfying new relationship with Bill, but he knew Casey was sufficiently fond of him that even though they were going to be separated by several miles, the son would somehow find time to continue the body worship he always lavished on him — as he, himself, would continue the cock-worship he had been bestowing on father and son.

Joey Stone was going to stay in town and start classes at San Francisco State University. Neither he nor Bill Lowe had said anything about it, but it seemed obvious that Joey didn't want to be separated from Casey's dad. Casey knew that Joey and his father had become lovers, and in spite of the difference in their ages, he approved of the relationship wholeheartedly. He did, however, make it clear to both of them that he didn't want to know any of the details. He had no idea what Joey's parents thought about the arrangement, or even if they had any idea what was going on—nor did he have any idea that his father was regularly having sex with Rommel as well.

The other two graduating fuckbuddies were going off to school across the Bay, at the University of California at Berkeley, and were planning to room together. The attention they had paid each other at the St. Francis on prom night seemed to suggest they were going to have a very good time together as "roomies."

A week later, Casey flew to South Carolina, and was met at the Greenville-Spartanburg airport. The extended hug and kiss he and Luke shared there raised quite a few eyebrows among the other travelers in the airport—reactions that would probably not have occurred had they been in San Francisco. Casey had something over a week before he needed to start Summer School back in California, so he was able to spend six days with his lover. During that time he familiarized himself with the area around Oconee and met many of Luke's friends—chief among them his neighbor, a sixty-ish widow, 'second mother' and best friend, Roxie, and Luke's three dogs, Maggie, Jiggs and Sahara.

If the topography around Oconee was not as dramatic as that of the Bay Area, it was nonetheless beautiful. The people he met were mostly Luke's friends, many of whom were aware of Luke's sexual orientation. They had all heard of Casey, and they seemed to approve of him. Still, Luke made it quite clear to Casey that insofar as their public image was concerned, their status as lovers would have to be *sub rosa*. This was Bible-Belt country, after all.

Luke welcomed Casey with total enthusiasm; Maggie, Jiggs and Sahara also made it abundantly clear that Casey was completely welcome to their home, without reservation.

The house where Luke lived, at the edge of town, had only densely wooded property to one side and behind it, with a very large, fenced-in back yard. Roxie lived on the other side, and even her view of the back yard was screened by hedges. While Luke visited Roxie's house almost daily, without ever needing to give her advance warning (Roxie regarded him as one of the family), she only came to Luke's house when invited. She was well aware that Luke was gay, and had met many of the young men who 'visited' him at home — and all of the ones who did so with any regularity — but she didn't want to surprise or embarrass him by walking in on an 'intimate' moment. Luke had spoken about Casey in such glowing terms that she was worried she might not like him as much as Luke did. She had both boys over to her house for dinner the night Casey arrived, and before they left, she was convinced Luke had met a 'keeper' — the first time she had felt that way.

The three dogs did almost as much to make Casey feel at home as Luke did. Maggie — a six-year-old, twelve-pound, mostly white Shih Tzu — was the oldest. Jiggs, slightly larger and similarly colored was Maggie's male puppy, born about two years earlier. Sahara was a Yellow Lab that had been given to Luke when she was only about six weeks old, and that Maggie had adopted as her own, mothering her as she had Jiggs. Now, the full-grown Sahara was about six or seven times Maggie's size, but the latter still mothered her. In virtually everything the dogs did, it was clear that Maggie, the smallest, was in charge, and she apparently led without resorting to any kind of pressure on the other two. Like her two charges, she was sweet, good-natured and completely loveable. Casey succumbed to the dogs' charms as completely as they did to his.

Casey had not really decided what he wanted to do with his life post high school and the *Top 'n Bottom Theatre*. He had no idea at that point what he should major in when he went to college. The joy he experienced playing with Luke's dogs (not quite as much joy as he experienced in playing with Luke, of course) and observing Luke's obvious affinity for them, led him to consider a possible career in Veterinary Medicine. He and his dad had always had a cat or two around the house, but living in a big city without a yard, they had never been able to have a dog.

Luke thought the idea of Casey becoming a vet was a wonderful idea, and suggested he, himself, would be similarly inclined. "We could go into practice together," he said — a significant suggestion, as it was to happen.

On Monday morning Casey met with Farrar's Dean of Admissions. He had brought a transcript of his work at Serra High School through the semester just completed, and pointed out that he had made great strides in recovering from the disastrous grades he had received in the first semester of his senior year. In the spring semester he had a "B+" in Spanish, and an "A" in each of his other subjects. He had signed up to take the two courses he needed for graduation in summer school.

The Dean was impressed with the way Casey had recovered academically, and although he himself wasn't remotely gay, he was also impressed with Casey's looks and demeanor. He thought the boy would be an asset to the student body at Farrar University, but he agreed to admit him for the fall semester only on condition the that he do well in summer school at Serra High and receive his diploma.

Both Casey and Luke talked with a career counselor at the University concerning pursuing a course that could lead them to vet school. Farrar offered no formal "Pre-Vet" curriculum, as some schools did, but the counselor did a bit of research, and showed the boys how they could properly prepare for admission to a Veterinary program after graduation. Luke would have to abandon his Business Administration curriculum, but he would probably lose only a few credits in changing majors. Besides, he wasn't really interested in business and had only entered that program as one that could be potentially useful until he decided on a clear career ambition. The State of South Carolina had no Veterinary College, but the University of Georgia, in near-by Athens, had an excellent College of Veterinary Science, and had a quota for admission from students in South Carolina through an interstate agreement.

Casey pre-registered for the upcoming semester conditionally, and Luke made some adjustments in his registration for the fall to coordinate with his new goal of Vet School after graduation.

Scouting out the area by car, they wound up in Clemson one day, and looked up Rommel, who had already moved there to begin Summer School. Rommel's muscular body had never looked more fabulous, and Luke was quite impressed. His dormitory roommate had not yet shown up, and the three met in Rommel's room for an afternoon of three-way sex. Rommel said he had not especially missed San Francisco, but he had greatly missed Casey's monster cock, which he had not had access to for an unusually long time—unusually long in this case meaning about three weeks. He did not mention how he had been enjoying Casey's father's monster cock in the interim. Casey made up for Rommel's deprivation in a memorable way: he had him kneel on the end of his single bed while Casey filled his hungry ass with dick, which he drove in and out at a furious pace until he and Rommel both had orgasms, almost simultaneously. Luke had been lying on his back in sixty-nine with Rommel, so he ate Rommel's load while from a distance of only a few inches he was watching his lover continue to fuck the muscle stud. As soon as Casey withdrew, Luke extricated himself from his sixty-nine with Rommel and stood where Casey had been. He gave Rommel another memorable fuck, after which Rommel stood and had Luke bend over a chest of drawers while he returned the tall stud's fuck in expert style. Casey had not yet been fucked, so Luke and Rommel took turns making up for the omission.

As Luke and Casey were leaving Clemson, Rommel promised he would be visiting them often after school began for the fall.

On the way back to Oconee, the lovers talked about the fact that they had sex in threesomes so often. "I love you very much," Luke said, "but when the sailor was fucking me in the park that day we met, or when I was fucking him or we were sucking each other off, no matter how much I enjoyed it—and you could tell I enjoyed the hell out of it—I was thinking of you a lot of the time, and remembering how much I had enjoyed making love with you before that. I think I knew right away that I was gonna be in love with you. Then later, fucking and sucking with Richard and Lance, I enjoyed myself a lot, but it didn't make me stop thinking of you and our lovemaking. You know what I mean?"

"Yeah," Casey replied. "I enjoyed those times, too, but with Richard and Lance and the sailor … what his name…"

"Gunther," Luke supplied.

"Right, Gunther. I was having a great time, and enjoying them while I was enjoying sharing them with you. But with them, it was just sex. With you, I knew it was something more right away.

"I love sex with guys, but to me it doesn't mean I love you any less. If I can have sex with other guys and you at the same time, it's great—and I'm not jealous if other guys enjoy sex with you as much as I do. I know I should be, but honestly, I'm not."

"It's crazy, I guess," Luke responded, "but that's the way I feel, too. It was great sharing you with Rommel this afternoon, and I know there are gonna be other guys. But please, let me know right away if you feel jealous, and that will be the end of it."

"I know there'll be other guys," Casey said. "I've still got a couple of months to go before I leave San Francisco, and I'll be fucking as part of my job—and otherwise, too, I suppose—but it'll just be for fun."

Luke laughed, "Yeah, or for profit, maybe?"

"Yeah that too," Casey responded in kind. "And how about you? I haven't met any of the guys you've been fucking around with yet, but you're not gonna stop seeing them while I'm gone, are you? It seems obvious to me you need to fuck and suck as badly as I do—and maybe you need it as often as I do."

"I haven't been sure what to do about introducing you to the guys I've been having sex with," Luke said. "but I promise you, I've only been playing around with them. I'm not in love with any of them, and I don't think any of them are in love with me.

"I fell in love with a guy once, when I was in high school back in Irmo, and I thought he was in love with me—God knows he told me he was. He wasn't the first guy I ever had sex with—I'd sucked a lot of cocks before that—but he was the first guy who ever fucked me, and the first one I ever fucked. And I thought it was the most wonderful thing that had ever happened—not just to me, but to anybody! Benjie—that was his name, Benjie Eaton. He was a big-shot football player at Blessed Savior—the Catholic high school we went to. Handsome as hell, great body, and a big, fat 'dick of death.' I had a hell of a time taking all of it at first," he grinned, "but I learned fast. We spent our entire senior year fucking and sucking with each other, and quite a few of Benjie's teammates joined in the fun. I think I got fucked by most of the team, and I fucked most of them, too.

"Right before graduation Benjie told me it was all over between us, that he and his coach were in love with each other, and that he was going to go off to play football at a college in Tennessee where the coach had landed an assistant coaching job. That was when I found out that the coach had been the first guy to fuck Benjie, and Benjie'd really been in love with him ever since. Later, I found out that there were quite a few others on the team who had first been fucked by the coach, and several of those who were seniors moved to Tennessee to play on his team there, and to continue fucking with him. It all blew up in the coach's face halfway through his first season there, and he had to resign. Benjie called me, wanting to transfer to Farrar to be with me again, but I told him to get fucked—but I wasn't the one who was gonna provide that service for him any more. So anyway, you're not gonna meet Benjie.

"You can meet Chad Meredith while you're here, but Paul Ambler has gone with his family for the week, to a wedding in Florida. Chad and Paul They're the two main guys I have sex with regularly," Luke concluded.

"So, just two rivals for my affections?" Casey asked.

"Well," Luke began, sheepishly, "those are the two main guys. There are a few others I fuck around with once in a while, but nothing like regularly."

"Considering how much sex I've been having, with so many guys, I sure can't criticize," Casey said. "Maybe we'll both cut down on outside guys when we're living together as lovers, but let's try to share these other guys together when we do—and no jealousy or resentment, okay?"

"Okay," Luke replied. "It might get difficult or a little awkward from time to time, but if we stay honest with each other…"

"Communicate?" Casey interjected.

"Exactly," Luke affirmed. "We'll make it. Now let's go to my house and fuck each other's brains out. Oh, we're supposed to go to Roxie's for supper tonight first."

"It'll be hard to wait for dessert afterwards, at your house, but … "

Luke grinned, "Our house, okay? It's not just my house any more."

The next evening, Chad Meredith came over to Luke's house— invited not only to meet Casey, but to have sex with both him and Luke, about whom he had heard enough to make him more than eager for the meeting. The name "Chad Meredith," had conjured up in Casey's mind a sort of preppy, fraternity-boy type.

Chad turned out to be anything but what Casey had envisioned. He was short—only about 5'6"—and when he stood next to Luke, he looked especially diminutive compared to Luke's near-one-foot superiority in height. He was in his mid-thirties, and was ruggedly handsome, with deep-set dark eyes, sensuous lips, crinkling 'laugh lines' around his eyes, and an unusually strong chin. He was fairly burly, but well-built, with a generous butt and muscular legs that stretched his Levi's, seemingly almost to the bursting point. His hair was black and curly, which, combined with his swarthy complexion, made him look Mediterranean. His beard was so heavy it looked like he was in need of a shave, even though he had shaved that morning. Later, when he undressed, Casey learned he had a fairly heavy growth of chest hair, but otherwise his body hair was normal. Both Casey and Luke, in contrast, had very little body hair, aside from the normal armpit and pubic areas. Even fully dressed, Chad exuded a seething, powerful, almost electric sexuality.

Little time was spent in pleasantries. Chad told Casey how much he had heard about him, and how much he was eager to have sex with him—if that was agreeable with Casey. Casey assured him that it was at least just fine with him. All three went into Luke's bedroom and stripped for action.

Once Casey was naked, Chad laughed, "I've fuckin' died and gone to heaven: blond as an angel, gorgeous as a movie star, built like a brick shithouse and hung like a fuckin' mule."

"And ready to fuck your brains out," Casey laughed in return.

"Is all that gonna trump my dimples?" Luke asked.

A grinning Chad replied, fondling Casey's hard-on, "No reason I can't be enjoying the sight of those dimples while I'm enjoying this fuckin' huge dick"

At the same time Chad was stroking and praising Casey's cock, his own enormous prick reached full erection, and Casey fondled it admiringly. "Talk about a huge dick; I think I'm gonna be the one to do the enjoying!"

Given his relatively diminutive stature, Chad's cock appeared to be even bigger than Casey's glorious monster.

A physical comparison was inevitable, and a close evaluation of Chad's and Casey's respective cocks proved that Casey had a half-inch edge in length over Chad's ten inches, and Chad had an ever-so-slight edge in girth. Both admitted they had seldom had the opportunity to enjoy such magnificent equipment as each offered.

At Luke's request, Chad and Casey devoted their attention almost exclusively to each other during the four-hour fuckathon that ensued. Casey had been occupying most of his time for several days to making love with Luke, so he was willing to let his new lover be, more or less, a bystander while he and the magnificent stud with the gargantuan cock and the alleged sexual power of an inexhaustible satyr explored each other. Neither he nor Chad was disappointed, nor was Luke, who spent most of the next few hours in the role of fuckwatcher—but a fuckwatcher who still managed to fuck both of the studs he was watching, and get sucked off by each of them as well. Still, the four loads he produced were relatively few compared to those the two cum-machines gave each other.

The question of how Luke had so easily taken his cock in his mouth or his ass had briefly flitted across Casey's mind the first time they had made love. Many of Casey's conquests struggled to take all of his cock, especially those who were taking it the first few times, but it had not seemed to bother Luke in the bushes in Lincoln Park that day in the spring. Seeing Chad's equipment, it was clear why Luke was so well 'broken in.' Casey knew that this ultra-masculine, magnificently hung stud had been fucking his lover for over two years by then—since the day they met in a hardware store in town, only a few days after Luke arrived in Oconee following his high school graduation.

Chad had been born on a farm in upper Foothills County, not far from the town of Oconee. He had served as a Marine in Vietnam, and after his discharge, he had gone to work for Farrar University as a groundskeeper. He had gradually worked his way through various levels of responsibility in the University Physical Plant, and by the time Casey met him, he was its Personnel Supervisor, responsible for hiring and firing the University's workmen—electricians, carpenters, groundskeepers, etc. He had never married—had never, in fact, ever been interested in any female other than as a friend. He produced his first orgasm in the mouth of a teammate on his junior high school football team, and sucked cock for the first time about three minutes after that. Sex in his high school days had been limited to kissing and swapping blowjobs with a surprisingly large number of his classmates and several of his teachers who appreciated the glory of an expertly wielded, gargantuan prick. He enlisted in the Marine Corps within weeks of his high school graduation, and fucked butt for the first time in Boot Camp at Parris Island, only one night after he had bottomed for the first time—for a Drill Instructor who had spotted his enormous cock in the showers, and who had planned a rapid course of seduction that began with exchanged blowjobs in the Master Sergeant's room. Within a week he spread his legs to take the Sergeant's masterful and thoroughly enjoyable fuck—which he returned the next night and for almost every night after that until he graduated Boot Camp and left for Vietnam. By that time, several members of his Boot Camp company were fortunate enough to have shared in his sexual largesse, both as fuckers and fuck-ees.

In Vietnam, having sex was not as convenient as it had been at Parris Island, except for the occasional 72-hour pass that allowed him and a hot fellow Marine or two to check into a Saigon hotel for marathon sex. Other than those rare and keenly anticipated interludes, the combination of cramped quarters, miserable weather, short tempers, and almost constant danger made all but sharing surreptitious blowjobs difficult. Finding a place, a time, and a partner willing to fuck with was infinitely rarer, much less discovering opportunities to cuddle and kiss before and after fucking. Still, Chad managed to use his cock—fabled throughout his Company for its size and stamina—far more often than most of his fellow jarheads. He was further noted for using that same fabled cock very, very satisfactorily in service to the United States military—and not just Marines. He fucked a considerable number of Army "doggies" and an even greater number of Sailors— both enlisted and commissioned. For some reason, the Naval branch of his sexual partners fucked him back in greater percentage, and with greater expertise, than the doggies, jarheads, flyboys or civilians who fell prey to his ravening monster cock in "the Land of Peace and Quiet," as Vietnam had ironically been called, in spite of its tempestuous history.

For his activities in-country Vietnam, and even stateside, Chad should have been given a medal for his morale-building services to the U.S. Marine Corps. All he got from the Corps, however, was an honorable discharge, and a wealth of wonderful memories.

The day he met Luke in the hardware store, he encountered him in the section where nails, bolts, etc., were stocked, although Luke was actually looking around for a hasp, which he needed to repair a broken gate in the backyard fence. Chad accidentally nudged Luke as he passed him, and when he excused himself, Luke's smile as he mumbled "No problem" hit Chad like a ton of bricks—or, at any rate, like several hundred pounds of bricks: it was radiant, and totally charming.

Chad decided in an instant that he had to strike up a conversation with the very tall, very attractive young man. "Can I help you find something?"

"Do you work here?" Luke asked.

"No, but I know where almost everything is," Chad said, and looked around at the merchandise in that section of the store. "I'll be glad to help you." Then, a meaningful pause before he continued: "Are you looking for a screw?"

The double-entendre was not lost on Luke, who blushed as he hesitated very briefly before he said, "It seems like I'm always looking for a screw." He was thinking, This guy is older than anyone I've ever fucked with, but he is really hot! (He was misremembering, however: Father Tim, one of the teachers at Blessed Savior High school was older than Chad when he first fucked Luke, and Luke's scoutmaster, who fucked him only once at camp, was even older than Father Tim. But there was no question Chad was hot.)

Chad didn't blush or hesitate when he looked up very steadily into Luke's eyes as he said, "I'm always looking for a screw, too. I hope you just found what you were looking for. I'm pretty sure I did."

Luke laughed and said, "I need to buy a hasp, and then we can help each other find that screw we're both looking for." He raised an eyebrow inquisitively as he added, "Or those screws?"

"Definitely plural," Chad laughed.

Luke's house was closer to the hardware store than Chad's, so they went there. Luke's new dog, Maggie, was delighted to greet Chad, who was, in turn, delighted to meet her. When Chad peeled off his clothes, however, Luke got a look at his cock—which was by then fully engorged, bobbing and throbbing magnificently. If Maggie had greeted Chad warmly, Luke now greeted him joyfully. Luke had seen bigger cocks in porn movies and porn magazines, but never in the flesh—if something as hard as what he now wrapped his hand around could still be called flesh! Luke's own cock was equally hard and ready when Chad pulled his pants down and wrapped his lips around it.

Luke shucked off his shoes, pants and underwear, pulled his shirt over his head, and enclosed Chad in a close embrace as they kissed passionately. The considerable disparity in their respective heights made no difference as they fell to the bed, each frantically hungry for the other. They kissed for only a few minutes, their hands exploring and fondling each other's bodies, before Chad reversed his body and took Luke's cock all the way inside his mouth as he positioned his own cock at the boy's lips. Luke had to open his mouth very wide and work very hard to accept the combined length and girth he was offered. He had sucked cocks this long before, and ones that were as fat, but never one with the combination of dimensions that was both so challenging and so exciting.

Luke realized almost at once that this was a new experience. He had held many young men and boys in his arms, he had sucked many cocks, and he had fucked and been fucked almost as frequently. But Chad was clearly a fully-grown man—not a boy toying with his sexuality, as most of his former partners had been, no matter how joyous or eager their lovemaking had been. There was a seriousness and determination about the way Chad kissed and sucked cock, but it in no way detracted from the utter joy he evinced. Chad's fingers busily explored between Luke's buttocks, promising subsequent joys of even greater excitement. Soon Luke had three fingers fiercely fucking Chad's ass as he sucked, and although Chad's mouth was filled with cock, he managed, through his murmuring and squirming, to show how much he enjoyed what Luke was doing.

Luke relinquished the fat shaft for just a moment to ask, "If I suck you off, can you still fuck me?"

"Absolutely—if you can take it. A lotta guys can't," Chad replied, without seeming in any way to boast. It was a simple statement of fact.

Luke laughed, and promised he could take it, even though he knew he had never taken that much meat up his ass before; he would manage, come hell or high water. He returned with increased devotion to the expert blowjob he was administering, and soon Chad was warning of his impending orgasm, which inspired Luke to suck all the harder until his mouth began to fill with the huge, hot load Chad gave him while his cock plunged in and out savagely—actually fucking the younger man's mouth mercilessly. Luke appreciated Chad's mercilessness as he moaned his pleasure while he sucked every drop of cum from the mighty tool. Before he had finished, his own orgasm had loomed so suddenly and urgently that he filled Chad's mouth without warning—or without a promise to fuck his ass in spite of his having expended a load of cum at that point. Somehow, he knew Chad was going to want to be fucked—and he was as happy about that as he was about knowing he would be able to meet Chad's expectations in fine style.

After savoring the taste of the other's cum in his mouth, both swallowed and expressed their appreciation for what they had been given.

Chad again reversed his body, and they lay face-to-face. They resumed their passionate kissing for some time until Chad said, gruffly, "Get on your knees. I wanna eat that pretty ass out before I fuck it." Luke quickly knelt on the bed on all fours, and without any hesitation, Chad's face was pressed deep into his crack and his tongue began a thorough exploration. Whether Chad's tongue was unusually long, or whether he was simply an especially talented master of the art of rimming, Luke didn't know. What he did know was that no one had ever eaten his ass out more thoroughly or more excitingly.

Luke was in heaven, and was sorry when Chad withdrew his tongue, but he knew that the next step was Chad replacing his amazing tongue with the biggest, most exciting prick he had ever seen. There was—as always—a lubricant dispenser of the nightstand next to Luke's bed, and Chad used it to prepare Luke for the onslaught. He used three fingers to work the lube in, with deep strokes, revolving them and opening Luke up a little. Until one of his fuckbuddies grew used to the challenge of his prodigious prick, Chad always prepared him this way—unless it was a Marine. For some reason, Marines loved to have a huge cock shoved violently enough into them to cause pain—which they refused to acknowledge.

Chad had observed a strange phenomenon while he was fucking his way through his hitch in the Corps: most of the jarheads he encountered—certainly the ones who got a chance to see his hard-on— wanted to get fucked, roughly, and by the biggest cock imaginable (normally, at that moment, the biggest cock imaginable would be the one they were contemplating). If there was another Marine or two on hand to watch them bearing up bravely under the onslaught, so much the better. He'd had almost never met a Marine—or any other guy, for that matter—who wasn't impressed by the size of his cock when it was hard, and wanted to touch it. Most of them also wanted to stroke it, and most of those who did, wanted either to continue until he shot his wad or to take it in their mouths and suck it. Few who began sucking his cock stopped until he had blown a load in their mouths or on their faces. He had been sucked off by countless jarheads whom he thought were straight—even after they had blown him—and who cheerfully swallowed every drop of cum they sucked out of his magnificent dick. Their service to his cock was probably some sort of salute to his enviable manhood; Chad had never thought about that at the moment—he just enjoyed getting sucked off.

He had fucked hundreds of Marines in the ass—probably at least five or six hundred of them—and he felt sure that: (a) some of them were straight; (b) most of them thought they were straight; and (c) the few who confessed to themselves—as they often did to Chad—that they were queer, had probably enjoyed one of the more exciting experiences of their lives by the time he had finished with them. The distribution of repeat 'customers' was probably evenly divided among the three categories—including (a)!

He further thought that kissing was the real key to the sexual orientation of his fuckmates: (a) the truly straight ones wanted to kiss only while they were actually getting fucked; (b) the ones who only thought they were straight also loved the kissing that led up to the time when Chad shoved his behemoth up their butts, but they averted their lips once their assholes were filled with Chad's cum and they had blown their own loads; and (c) the truly queer ones also enjoyed lying with Chad, cuddling and kissing post-fuck. Those in the (c) category quickly learned that the pre-fuck/post-fuck cuddling and kissing usually led to another fuck, often within minutes, or even—best of all—a series of future fucks with the virile stud.

Chad loved sucking cock and getting fucked, but, for whatever obscure reason, he was far less often called upon to indulge those activities with Marines who blew him or got fucked by him than he was with other servicemen or civilians. In his fairly extensive experience with sailors, he found they were as likely to want to fuck him as to get fucked.

As Chad prepared to fuck Luke, he learned there were no condoms available for him to use. It should be noted, in Luke's defense that this was a time when it had not yet become widely understood that "safe sex" was advisable for such situations.

Given the preparation Chad had administered with his "three-finger lube job," Luke was physically ready to receive the administrator, although he had been mentally ready since Chad had first stepped out of his underwear.

If Luke had been a Marine, Chad would have entered his ass with one savage thrust, as he still did when he occasionally had a chance to fuck a jarhead or an ex-jarhead. Jarheads invariably wanted him to enter them roughly, even brutally, and fuck so savagely that he almost caused them pain. He did not think Marines were masochists, but that they liked to show the man fucking them—as well as other Marines they hoped might witness their toughness—that they could stand pain without whimpering or begging for mercy. But Luke was not a Marine, so Chad first teased the boy's asshole with his cock head, while Luke knelt on all fours before him on the bed. Then, gently, considerately, he began to insinuate the monstrous bulk and length of his weapon inside. Luke may not have been a Marine, but he was no stranger to getting fucked by a big dick—if not one quite as big as the one he was getting ready to accept. Furthermore, he was not used to being prepared quite so well to accept a big dick as Chad had done with his fingers. In all, he knew he was ready—and ravenously hungry—to get fucked by everything this stud could give him. He cried out, "Fuck me hard!" and violently shoved his ass backward to accept immediately everything Chad could provide. Chad complied with one counter-plunge, and both he and Luke cried out in pleasure. The most exciting fuck Luke had ever experienced got under way.

Chad clasped Luke's waist in his hands, and pulled his body inward each time he thrust his cock forward into the hungry ass that gripped it tightly while he fucked. The ferocity of Chad's fuck was unbelievable to Luke, but doubly enjoyable for that. Chad's huge prick hammered away with a speed that was almost as impressive as its intensity. Luke gasped and cried out in thrill, urging the ex-Marine to fuck faster and harder and deeper—pointless exhortations, as Chad's thrilling fuck seemed to Luke to be already attaining records in all those departments.

"Gonna fill this hot ass with so much fuckin' cum!" Chad panted.

Luke rose to his knees and moaned in rapture, "Blow that big load up my ass, you fuckin' stud!"

Chad's hands left Luke's waist and encircled the rapturous boy's body. He squeezed Luke's tits and pinched his nipples as he tongue-fucked his ear, whispering into it, "I love to fuck ass better'n anything in the world."

"And you never fucked an ass that wanted it more."

"You'll never believe how much it's gonna get fucked today," Chad replied, and his right hand went down to grasp Luke's prick, which Luke was busily jacking off. "Don't come for a while. I wanna keep you in the mood for a long time before you get your first load." He slammed Luke's upper body down and grasped his shoulders for purchase as his fuck seemed to go into overdrive and he screamed, "Take my cum, baby!" His busy ass froze in position and he virtually screamed in triumph as he discharged a massive load inside Luke's hungry chute.

Rather than falling over Luke's body in temporary exhaustion after such an explosion of fuck-lust, Chad surprised his sexual conquest by resuming his fuck, albeit in a more subdued manner—at least for the moment. He ran his hands lovingly over Luke's back, smiling and murmuring, "What a sweet ass!"

Luke was clearly masturbating himself as he asked, "Can I come now?"

"Shit, no," Chad laughed. "unless you can come at least three or four times. I've still got big plans for this hot butt of yours." With his cock planted deep inside Luke, and only missing three or four strokes, he manhandled the boy's body so that he lay on his back. Raising Luke's legs to his shoulders, Chad resumed his fuck—which was beginning to show signs of the savagery he had brought to his lovemaking before his orgasm.

Luke grinned up at Chad, "You gonna come again?"

"Jesus," Chad said, "just looking at those dimples almost makes me come, and I wanna keep fuckin' you forever. Yeah, I'm gonna come again—and we'll see how many more times; I think it might be a record number." He leaned down and they shared a long kiss—surprisingly tender, considering the fact that Chad continued to fuck profoundly, if not yet fiercely.

They continued to kiss, and as Chad's fuck grew more and more intense their kiss grew equally passionate. Luke moved his legs upward so that his knees straddled Chad's shoulders, and he used them as levers to pull his ass up to counter the ever more savage plunges of the magnificent cock hammering it. His heels pounded against Chad's back as both he and Chad grunted and gasped in increasing lust until Chad seized Luke's shoulders and again cried out in triumph as he discharged another massive load of cum.

Luke had been unable to resist the impulse to masturbate as Chad continued to fuck him so magnificently, in spite of Chad's repeated requests that he save his load. Just as Chad's cock erupted inside his ass, Luke's prick also exploded, plastering Chad's chest and his own stomach and chest with a prodigious amount of thick, white cum. Chad broke their kiss, and grinning hugely—and unbelievably, Luke thought—continued to fuck like a pile driver. The older man murmured his approval and delight as he used two fingers to scoop

Luke's cum from their bodies, which he sucked and savored as he fed himself the precious liquid, still driving his big prick in and out. With a mouth full of Luke's cum, Chad leaned down and shared it with the boy as they resumed their long kissing.

Although the speed and intensity of Chad's fucking lessened noticeably, he continued to pump Luke's ass. Luke murmured around Chad's invading tongue, "Jesus, are you gonna get another load?"

Chad broke their kiss and grinned into Luke's face, "Yes, dimples, I'm nowhere near finished fucking your pretty ass." He pulled out of Luke and rolled him to his left side. He then slammed his cock all the way back inside Luke with a merciless thrust and put his arms around him, holding him tightly as he resumed his seemingly tireless assault with renewed gusto.

"God, what a man—and what a fuck!" Luke exclaimed as he began driving his ass backward to counter each forward thrust of Chad's cock.

Luke had many times been fucked twice by the same man on the same occasion. Normally, in those cases, there had been a short break between fucks, but there had been a few times when fuck followed fuck without a break. He had only been fucked more than twice by the same man when an extended period of lovemaking was involved—usually an overnight session. But here was a magnificently hung stud who had blown two loads up his ass without stopping, and was clearly headed for a third. Who knew how many times Chad was going to fuck him? How much of this glorious and welcome abuse could his ass take before a rest was called for? Was Chad going to want to get fucked? Luke didn't care; whatever happened, he was enjoying himself as he never had before while he waited happily for those many questions to be answered.

Chad nibbled and kissed Luke's ears and shoulders while he fucked steadily and feverishly for another fifteen minutes, often gasping and panting his admiration and gratitude to the boy who was providing him with such pleasure. Finally, Chad wrapped his arms tightly around Luke's body, and as Luke was by then expecting, he blew yet another massive load of cum deep inside his rapturous partner, with his cries of joy almost matched by those of Luke.

When both had calmed down enough to speak rationally, by then facing each other and embracing, Luke looked into Chad's eyes and laughed, "Are you through?"

"Only for the moment," Chad said. "I've still got a lot of fucking for your sweet ass." Then he added, answering one of the questions Luke had mentally posed to himself, "And I hope you're gonna fuck me at least a couple of times." Luke promised to do his best.

The little dog Maggie, apparently sensed that a respite from the lovemaking was about to take place, since she jumped up on the bed and eagerly showed her love for Luke and lavished almost as much affection on her master's playmate. Although she always slept cuddled up against Luke's back when he slept alone, she went to her own padded pallet to watch the proceedings when Luke was sharing the bed with someone else.

"I need a drink," Chad said. "Got any bourbon?" Luke explained that he had only soft drinks or beer to offer. Chad accepted a beer, but said, "Lay in a supply of booze — Jack Daniels is good. I like a good stiff drink after I fuck, almost as much as I like a good stiff cock up my butt."

"Does that mean you're gonna come back again?" Luke asked.

"I sure hope you want me to," Chad said. "You are one hot piece of ass."

"Believe me, I want. Soon and often," Luke replied.

Among other things the two wanted to do next, Luke wanted to suck Chad off, and Chad wanted to eat Luke's ass, so they agreed a thorough shower was needed. It proved to be a lengthy proposition, since they embraced and kissed at great length under the hot spray, soaping each other down and rinsing each other off while they fondled and groped each other. The considerable disparity in their height was more noticeable while they made love standing up, but it in no way distracted from their enjoyment. Chad gave Luke another load, down his throat (*That's four*, Luke marveled as he drank the thick white offering) and he fucked Luke's ass with his tongue almost as passionately as he had fucked it with his prick. Luke also ate Chad's ass, and wanted to fuck him then and there, but the water was beginning to get cold, so they decided to wait until they could lie down again together.

By the time they left the shower and dried off, it was dark outside. Luke tossed the lubricant dispenser to Chad, grabbed a blanket and a couple of towels, and said, "Let's go in the back yard." Luke loved to make love *al fresco*, and frequently did so behind the house, weather permitting. The night was overcast, and enough ambient light from the town lighting reflected off the cloud cover that they could see what they were doing. The foliage surrounding the yard made it all but impossible that anyone else would be able to see. Luke spread the blanket in the middle of the yard. They lay down on it and began to kiss and fondle each other.

Maggie had gone out the door with them, a tennis ball in her mouth. She had a variety of tennis balls secreted all around the house and yard; they seemed to be her talismans. She romped on the blanket with Luke and Chad until their making out became passionate enough that she realized it was time for her to retire to the porch and assume her usual role as resident canine fuckwatcher.

At Chad's behest, Luke knelt, while Chad spread lube on his cock and on Luke's ass. No hesitancy was demonstrated this time as Chad rammed his huge prick inside again, and the brief respite had apparently recharged his sexual battery — if, indeed, the four loads he had blown, and the enormous energy expended in producing them had done anything to weaken the stud's glorious power and stamina. When Chad's load burst inside Luke after another twenty minutes of savage fucking, Luke's admiration and wonder increased. He thought, Five loads! No one has ever fucked me that many times without taking all night to do it! Had he known what still lay ahead, his wonder would have been boundless.

It was finally time for Chad to take a little of what he had been giving so prodigiously. Pulling his cock from Luke's ass, he twisted Luke's body so that he lay on his back. When it became clear Chad intended to mount his cock, Luke held it perpendicular to the ground and Chad sat on it, taking it all inside in one plunge. He rode up and down eagerly, fucking himself with obvious delight, moaning his pleasure while Luke groaned his own excitement. It took only a few minutes before Luke levered his body upward and froze in position as his load erupted inside Chad, Chad had been masturbating frantically during his ride, and after Luke filled his ass with cum, he rose to his knees, pulling Luke's cock out of his ass as he positioned his own dick over Luke's head and shouted, "Eat my load!" just before he splashed his sixth load of the night over Luke's face and open mouth.

Chad fell over Luke's body and licked his own discharge from the boy's face before they locked their lips in a passionate kiss that lasted for a long time as the two calmed down and their kiss turned tender. Maggie apparently sensed there was to be a lull; she left her tennis ball on the porch and trottted down to the blanket, snuggling up against her master's side while he continued to caress and kiss the seemingly tireless cum machine in his arms.

Considering how intense Chad's fucking was, it amazed Luke to find that he was very tender and gentle at making love when it involved kissing and snuggling. Although both still retained their erections, they lay together, saying almost nothing, but sharing very deep, unhurried kisses, and fondling each other lovingly and at length. After more than a half-hour of such sweet exchange, it was — surprisingly — Luke who broke the spell. He whispered, "Can I fuck you again?" into Chad's ear.

"As often and as hard as you want."

Luke rose, grabbed a towel and pulled Chad to his feet, leading him over to a picnic table and benches that were positioned in the center of the lawn. Throwing the towel on the table, he bent Chad's body over it and pressed down, so that Chad's chest lay against the tabletop. Chad had remembered to snag the lubricant when they left the blanket, but it wasn't much needed; Chad was still greased up from their earlier fuck, so Luke swiped only a small amount of lube on his cock and entered his ass easily.

In distinct contrast to the gentle and affectionate lovemaking they had just been experiencing, Luke's fuck was fierce, eliciting cries of joy and appreciation from its object. Luke was not the ever-ready fuck machine that Chad was, so he had to labor long and hard, but judging by Chad's litany of enthusiastic responses — "Yeah, fuck me hard, baby! Fill my ass with your hot cum!" and the like — he did not object. Luke pulled hard on Chad's shoulders, and Chad reached behind to pull Luke's ass in tightly to him when Luke cried loudly as he finally blew his load. The two froze in position for a long minute, savoring the thrill of Luke's orgasm and Chad's eager receipt of it.

As soon as it was clear that Luke had finished blowing his load, Chad rose to his feet and reversed their positions, bending Luke's body over the table and pressing his chest down onto it. Without ceremony, Chad sank his prick to the hilt in Luke's ass in one thrust. No lubrication was needed other than the residue of the five loads he had already blown inside the boy. In fact, as he began to fuck deeply and rabidly, some of his cum was forced out and splattered his pubes, also running down to drip from Luke's balls. He fucked for a long time, gasping his pleasure almost as enthusiastically as Luke was grunting his own. When the time came, Chad held Luke's waist in an almost painful grip as he hammered the last few inches of his cock in and out of the tight sheath holding it, in incredibly fierce and rapid strokes until he shouted out in delirious lust while he blew his seventh load of the evening deep inside the grateful boy.

Before Chad left for home, they showered together, and Luke sucked out an eighth load of cum from the incredible stud, who promised to return within a week, of Luke desired. Before leaving, he told the dazzled boy to whom he had that day given eight loads, "Like I told you a little while ago, you're a great piece of ass, and I'll be back for more of it. But don't go getting romantic about it. I've got a couple of other guys I fuck with regularly—and I don't let them start thinking we're in some sort of relationship either. We enjoy fucking, and so long as that's what you and I have, I'll fuck your brains out—regularly, if you want."

Luke kissed him and whispered, "I want." Chad was by then dressed and ready to leave, but Luke was still naked.

"Fine," Chad said as he undid his buckle and let his pants and shorts drop to the floor. "Bend over, and I'll seal the deal." With only a few strokes, his monster cock was again as monstrous as it had been all afternoon and evening, and as Luke bent over and braced himself against a table, Chad reached around and jacked off Luke's cock while he sank his own yet again into the ravenous, cum-filled ass still so hungry for it. He humped savagely for ten minutes until he provided a thrilling finale to their lovemaking with a ninth load of cum almost at the same time he coaxed out an explosive blast of Luke's cum, which splashed on the table as they both grunted and cried their excitement.

"Next time, I'll bring Paul," Chad said as he did up his pants, "and we can do a threesome. He's one of my three regulars—well, four now that I've met you. How's that sound? I think you two would really enjoy each other."

"Just bring that incredible prick of yours, and anything or anyone else you want," Luke smiled. "I can hardly wait."

Chad kissed Luke, and studied his face. "Smile for me." Luke complied. "God damn but you're cute! Greatest dimples ever!" They kissed again, and Chad was gone.

Luke had once been fucked five times in an all-night session with a high school fuckbuddy, and he had thought at the time that it was some kind of indescribably gratifying record, but he had just experienced a fuckfest he would not have imagined possible. And he had enjoyed it more than anything he had thus far experienced in his entire life. True, his asshole was a bit sore — much less than he would have thought, however, given how many times it had just been assailed — but it was not so much the number of times the incredible stud Chad had fucked him, but the prodigious size of the cock that he wielded — unmatched in his experience — and wielded so fiercely and gloriously. Gargantuan, mind-boggling, titanic, colossal, breathtaking, stupendous, immense — take your pick of adjectives for the prick that he was already longing to take up his ass again. the like of which he was not to encounter for a couple of years yet, in San Francisco's Lincoln Park.

As it happened, Luke didn't have to wait long. Only five days later, Chad called and asked if Luke was interested in getting together with him and Paul that night — at Chad's house this time. Luke was, of course, not only eager and hungry to meet with Chad again, but curious about Paul, as well. If Paul was hot enough to be one of Chad's regular sex partners, he had to be pretty special, Luke reasoned.

Chad opened the door to Luke when he arrived, naked, and with his monster cock standing straight out.

"Wow," Luke said. "good thing it's me." The sight of Chad's weapon started Luke's cock growing inside his pants.

Chad laughed. "All my friends and neighbors know to call before they come over — especially at night. A few complete strangers have gotten a shock, but a few of them have come in and enjoyed themselves. We got started without you, but just a few minutes ago. Neither of us has even blown a load yet." He started unbuttoning Luke's shirt. "C'mon in and get these clothes off."

Luke stripped, throwing his clothes onto a chair near the front door. He had no time to study Chad's house, since as soon as he had stripped, Chad kissed him, playing with his cock until it was fully hard, then, using it as a handle, led him into the bedroom. A tall, slim young man stood next to the bed, also nude, and also with a hard-on. "Luke, this is Paul. Paul, this is Luke."

Paul was tall, but still an inch or two shorter than Luke's 6'5". He was slim, but nicely muscled, with broad shoulders and very long legs. His cock was certainly above average in length, but very much above average in girth. It was what was later to be called a 'beer-can cock,' and was about eight inches in length. All in all, a formidable weapon, if not, in length, the ass reamer that Chad employed. He had a perfectly flat stomach and, as Luke discovered later, a perfectly rounded ass, somewhat more protuberant than normal for one with such a slim build. His hair was sandy brown in color, and was cut very short on his head. He had virtually no body hair except for the light thatch over his cock and under his arms. His skin was smooth and golden. Clearly, he sunbathed in the nude. His face was also thin, with a tall forehead, high cheekbones, v-shaped eyebrows—the points of which skewed outward—and a strong jaw. His nose was long and straight, his lips were slight, and his mouth seemed a bit small for his face. His most striking feature, however, was his eyes: intensely, impossibly, blue, and so arresting they almost seemed hypnotic; they crinkled when he smiled, and adorable laugh lines appeared at the corners. The overall impression he made on anyone who appreciated masculine beauty was that he was, in fact amazingly beautiful.

He extended his hand to Luke: "I'm Paul Ambler. Chad's told me about you, and I've been anxious to meet you." Luke shook his hand, and smiled the smile that was so universally appealing. It was met by one that was similarly winning.

Having introduced himself, Paul fell to his knees and took Luke's cock in his mouth while his hands went around to caress Luke's ass while it humped, instinctively driving his dick into Paul's mouth. The sensation was amazing to Luke. He had never felt anyone suck his dick with such skill. Regardless of his youth, Paul was clearly a virtuoso cocksucker.

Chad leered, "Ever feel anything like that? This kid sucks cock almost as well as a Marine buddy in the 'Nam, Gunnery Sergeant Rountree, who swore he could suck the chrome off a trailer hitch. He never proved that, but he sure as hell could suck the cum out of a dick better'n anyone I ever met."

Paul was obviously young. In fact, he was barely eighteen, and still a high-school student. Farrar University's Physical Plant hired a crew of temporary student workers every summer to carry out projects that were difficult to accomplish when the entire student body was in residence. Paul had signed on as such for the summer of his sophomore year. Chad had spotted his beauty immediately when he interviewed him for the job, and hired him on the spot. He then set about seducing the gorgeous youngster, regardless of his age; he had, after all, fucked literally hundreds of Marines as young or younger. Within two weeks,

Paul visited his boss's home, and spent the duration of his visit in bed with him. He was no stranger to gay sex: he had sucked off or been fucked by half the student athletes at Foothills County High school, a few teachers and coaches, and an incredibly sexy young janitor as well. By the time he went to bed with Chad, he was sufficiently seasoned that he had little trouble taking Chad's enormous cock down his throat or up his butt. While he liked fucking butt or having his own plowed, his favorite activity with a boy or a man was sucking cock; he did that with astonishing skill, and had yet to spit out a load unswallowed unless it was to be used as a lubricant for further activity. He never gave a blowjob that failed to elicit praise from the recipient—often extremely high praise. He also enjoyed getting a blowjob, of course (who wouldn't?), especially if it were accomplished while he was administering one in sixty-nine.

And he probably inspired a lot of cocksucking that might not have happened with another boy. Most men and boys who saw his cock—especially when it was hard, as it was so much of the time—wanted to touch it, whether they were gay or straight. Most had never before seen one so fat. Touching it almost always led to stroking, and stroking led to kissing it, and kissing it led to sucking, and a good many straight guys, as well as virtually all the gay ones, found themselves happily servicing a cock so fat it was hard to get their lips around it. Only a few of the straight ones who sucked it quit before it discharged in their mouths and sprayed its treasure on their faces—often with mouths open to receive it—but most continued to suck and savor the massive load Paul provided them as a result of their efforts. Following that, the decision to spit or swallow was probably evenly divided. Practically every gay man or boy who fondled Paul's prick wound up sucking him off—and with them, swallowing outscored spitting by a huge magnitude.

Although an amazing, inordinate number of partners wanted to give Paul a blowjob—and had their desires gratified—a fuck from his fat prick was hungrily sought by many of his sex partners as well. In most cases he managed to satisfy their longing—he enjoyed fucking butt—but it was sucking cock that he most craved, with taking a dick up his ass a definite second choice. If he was going to get fucked, he liked first to suck off his suitor so he could eat the first, larger or largest load he was going to receive, and could then enjoy a much longer fuck as a result of having relieved his fucker's urgency to make love.

Almost as much as he appreciated the expertise of Paul's blowjob, Luke was enjoying the sight of Paul's stunning eyes looking up at him in apparent adoration as he looked down at them, and the lips seemingly stretched to the maximum while they traveled up and down the cock in his mouth. Reluctantly, he removed his cock from the intense, hot vacuum, and raised the boy to his feet. He kissed him and said, "Let's get on the bed so we can sixty-nine." Paul returned his kiss with almost as much passion as he had brought to sucking his dick, and let Luke lead him to the king-sized bed that almost filled Chad's bedroom. Luke lay supine on the bed and held his arms out to Paul, who knelt over him in sixty-nine and returned to sucking ravenously as his partner opened his mouth extra wide to take Paul's challengingly fat cock inside.

Luke had almost forgotten Chad was in the room until, as he looked up at Paul's ass, humping busily as it drove his prick down into Luke's mouth, he saw Chad begin to eat Paul's ass. Luke was in heaven, as he looked up to watch Chad busily eating out Paul's asshole, only inches from his eyes, feeling Paul's balls sliding against his forehead as he sucked the unbelievable bulk of the boy's prick, and reveling in the stupendous blowjob he was receiving.

After about ten minutes, Chad replaced his tongue with the head of his monster cock, gleaming with lubricant as it pressed against the boy's asshole. Chad's cock began to enter Paul, who gasped around Luke's cock, "Give me that big dick, lover!" and Chad began to hammer away. Shortly after Chad began to fuck in earnest, Paul gasped again, and Luke felt his mouth filling with a load so copious and so forcefully blown that he was barely able to contain it without gagging or losing some of it around the mouth-stretching challenge of Paul's massive shaft. Paul's orgasm triggered Luke's own explosion of cum, eliciting murmurs of appreciation from Paul, who continued to suck with continuing eagerness as he swallowed the hot offering. Luke swallowed Paul's load as he watched Chad's huge cock fucking ever more rapidly and forcefully until, with a cry, Chad froze in place, with his monster organ completely buried inside Paul's ass as he filled it with his cum.

Chad had given Luke nine loads the first time they met—an unprecedented number for Luke, and a tie for the seemingly inexhaustible Chad—and on his second meeting with Luke, he again demonstrated his amazing ability to produce multiple orgasms, but only five of them on that occasion. Before the evening was over, Paul had sucked Chad off twice, Chad had fucked Paul once and Luke, twice. Luke had enjoyed Paul's amazing blowjob twice, and he had fucked each of his partners once. Paul had only produced three orgasms; he had been sucked off by each of his partners—who managed to get their lips around his beer-can prick only with well-rewarded difficulty—and had blown a load in Luke's ass. In all, it had been a very satisfactory encounter for Luke, but it was the only time he had a threesome with Chad and Paul. It was also one of the few times he went to Chad's house for sex—but Chad came to Luke's house with great regularity after that.

Oddly, the most vivid memory that Luke took with him of that night he met Paul was the sight of Paul sucking Chad's cock. The boy's beautiful, arresting eyes were looking upward at Chad as he sucked, and the massive girth of Chad's enormous prick appeared to be stretching Paul's lips to an impossible degree. Luke wondered, as he watched in fascination, how Paul had been able to get his rather delicate mouth around Chad's prick at all. But not only did Paul's lips manage to encompass the gargantuan shaft, they traveled back and forth its entire length, his throat somehow accommodating the entire length of the behemoth Chad was driving into it as Paul's lips disappeared into the thatch of hair above it. Just as he had could not remember ever having been given a more perfect blowjob than Paul's, Luke could not remember ever having seen one administered with greater skill or accomplishment than the two the high school boy gave Chad that night. The boy was a virtuoso. Even the many classmates who scorned him as a cocksucker invariably returned again and again to enjoy Paul's expertise, as did those who were more openly accepting of his unique talent.

Chad never invited Luke to share one of his 'regulars' again. He explained to Luke that he had wanted him and Paul to meet so that Paul would have an additional regular outlet. "The boy gives the best blowjob there is, but he wants to be sucking me off almost every day, and I've got to spread the wealth with my others. I'm getting with him about every fifth or sixth day, and that's fine, but he says he really needs more sex than that, And I think he really does—actually needs it. Anyway, I've got him fixed up with my preacher—he's one of my other regulars—and he's started going to bed regularly with one of the electricians at the University. Then he still sucks off a lot of his school buddies. He should be getting enough if you'll let him come over here quite a bit. I've been sucked off by hundred and hundreds of guys, but this kid gives as good a blowjob as I've ever got."

By the time Luke went to visit his cousin Mike in San Francisco, both Paul and Chad were regular visitors to his house and he was fairly well satisfied sexually by their enormous talents. His encounters with Chad were largely concerned with buttfucking of the most exciting order, those with Paul mostly with cocksucking of equal excellence. It was an extremely satisfying balance.

12.

Go East, Young Man

The required two months of summer school passed quickly for Casey. He studied hard for the two courses he needed to complete for graduation, and the work went easily, leaving him ample time for his more enjoyable labor at the *Top 'n Bottom*. He felt sure he was actually in love with the sweet, tall, dimpled Luke—not the kind of passing "love" he had felt for Richard, the hung, gorgeous, insatiably opportunistic satyr, however exciting that had been at the time—and he was anxious for the summer to be over so he could go to Oconee and be with him.

If it seemed that he and Luke had done threesomes an inordinately large percentage of the limited time they had been together so far, it didn't bother him; he kept telling himself that— especially when the likelihood of threesomes involving the superhung superstud Chad Meredith or the vaunted Paul lay ahead when he got to South Carolina. He had not yet met Paul, but Luke's description of his magnetic eyes, his unusually fat cock, and his cocksucking virtuosity promised to be wonderfully satisfying. Additionally, if he knew that the man he loved often had sex with someone else when he, Casey, was not a part of the equation, it didn't necessarily lessen the depth or sincerity of his love for him. The latter situation bothered him more than the other, but since he, himself was also regularly having sex with other guys, it would be hypocritical to object. In all honesty, he felt sure neither of those situations would change radically when he and Luke became committed, living-together lovers in the fall. But he also felt they would manage to deal with those factors in such a way that they did not become insuperable problems.

Luke's cousin Mike, now the new porn stud Mike Henson, appeared as guest star at the *Top 'n Bottom*, and was well received— unusually so for one whose "porn star" credentials were not yet well established. Mike was lacking in the excessive vanity that seemed to plague many porn stars, even though his dazzling good looks and profound sexual ability would have justified it. Perhaps, when he became better established as a porn star of the first magnitude — and every indication was that he would, indeed, become such — he might become a typically vain sex demigod, but it was not likely, as it as obvious to all who knew him that he was basically a very nice person.

Honoring the tradition of the theatre, Mike fucked each of the house dancers at least once, and he endeared himself to them by making sure each of them was given the opportunity to fuck his ass at least once. None of the dancers declined the opportunity.

Casey had felt a kinship with Mike, since he was his new lover's cousin, but that special relationship did not stand in the way of their having sex with each other. In fact, Casey doubled with Mike for his final show, and the two studs fucked each other on stage after extended double-sucking and passionate kissing.

The last porn star with whom he had shared the stage at the T 'n B was one of the most exciting he had encountered there. Casey had not seen any of Matt Ramsey's video work before Eddie introduced them, immediately following one of Casey's appearances, naked and fully erect as he exited the stage. Matt shook hands and said the usual "good to meetcha" kind of things as though there was not an 'elephant in the room' in the form of ten-and-a-half inches of Casey's fat, hard cock bobbing and swaying between them. They exchanged a few pleasantries, and then Matt looked down at Casey's monster and smiled, "Helluva cock!" although Casey's hard-on had by then subsided somewhat — but not entirely, since Matt Ramsay was clearly a walking wet dream: fucking gorgeous, his tight white T-shirt making it clear he had massive chest and great tits, and the equally tight, supple, faded jeans proclaiming he also had a helluva cock.

Casey could not initially study the contours of Matt's ass, but when Matt revealed it as he stripped to prepare for his first show, Casey was stunned at its perfection. "If that's not the sexiest ass I've ever seen," Casey gasped, "I'll eat my hat."

"You can eat your hat if you want," Matt grinned, "but I'd much rather you'd eat my ass. Or maybe this," he added as he stroked his prick and brought it to erection."

"Jesus," Casey said. "Eating that ass or that dick — which is just as fuckin' gorgeous as your ass, by the way — wouldn't just be eating. That would be more like dining. Or maybe feasting would be more accurate."

Matt bent over and used his hands to spread his asscheeks, exposing his hairless, pink pucker. "Feast away, and get me in the mood to go on stage. We've got a little while." Young Justin was out on stage performing as they talked.

Casey knelt behind Matt and fondled the plump, golden globes of the stud's ass as he licked his asshole and penetrated him with his busy tongue. Judging by Matt's enthusiastic groaning, Casey was doing an excellent job. Reaching between Matt's legs and grasping his cock, the evidence of Matt's excitement was clear. His prick was throbbing in full erection. And it was, indeed, a very full erection Matt was stroking — quite long, probably a full nine inches, unbelievably hard, and so fat he could barely close his fingers around the shaft. Matt turned his body so that Casey's tongue was pulled out of him, and his hard prick slapped the side of Casey's head. He said, "You better suck me off or I'll never be able to get this thing inside those little shorts I'm gonna wear to start my show."

Casey needed no second invitation. He seized Matt's waist and deep-throated the prodigious prick without the slightest hesitation. Matt held Casey's head tightly as he fucked his mouth eagerly, with brutal thrusts that would have made a less experienced cocksucker gag and choke When his orgasm arrived, Matt grunted and gasped as his load shot violently, deep in Casey's throat. Casey almost gagged and choked; he could not remember ever having taken a larger load, or one that was so explosive. He had to back his lips a couple of inches off Matt's shaft to avoid losing some of the hot cum that continued to fill his mouth, erupting in seven or eight explosive blasts. He managed, however, to contain all the precious liquid and savored it as he bathed Matt's cock in it for several minutes before swallowing. Matt murmured his pleasure and tousled Casey's hair as the feasting Casey savored his load.

Raising Casey to his feet, Matt kissed him at length, enjoying the taste of his own cum. He whispered into Casey's ear so that Justin, who had just entered following his performance, could not hear, "Fantastic fuckin' blowjob. If I can get my lips around that huge thing of yours, I'll return the favor. And I hope you're as good at takin' it up the butt as you are at suckin; dick."

"I'm told I'm even better," Casey whispered back.

Matt released him and grinned, "We'll find out soon."

During the course of that week, Matt fucked all the house dancers with a kind of rabid intensity that was as rare as it was enjoyable. He was less generous in reciprocity, however. He let Casey fuck him, and the muscular, big-dicked Carl, as well as Drake, who alone among the dancers had a prick bigger than Casey's. It seemed likely that he had also given his ass to Eddie, who, since he was a sane man, had surely also given his ass to Matt. Richard had been unusually diligent—and persuasive—with Matt, and he alone fucked him twice, as far as was known among the dancers. Unknown to the dancers was the fact that Richard had also spent two nights during the week in the apartment with Matt, where they exchanged fucks that might best be described as epic. The astonishing volume of Matt's loads, and their mind-boggling force became evident to all when he demonstrated them during his obligatory daily on-stage orgasm: he could blow six or eights ropes of cum as far as the seventh row of the theatre! The patrons ate up his act, and those fortunate enough to be in the line of fire when he blew his load ate that up as well.

It was clear that Matt was, in addition to being a masterly and seemingly insatiable buttfucker, also a talented and hungry cocksucker who liked taking a cock up his ass, particularly if it were a big one. Still, he told everyone he was really straight. If his post-coital kissing had not been so prolonged and passionate, some might even have believed him. A few years later, Matt appeared in a video with Rick Donovan, whose prick was arguably the biggest in the gay porn business at that time. Several years later, when Matt was performing in straight porn under a different name and claiming he was, and had always been, straight, the unmistakable joy he showed while he was taking Rick Donovan's dick up his ass on camera, or blowing one of his huge loads while he was riding Rick's gargantuan pole, certainly seemed to belie his claim to heterosexuality—as did the scenes in many other videos where he clearly demonstrated his appetite and expertise in bottoming.

Not surprisingly, it was Richard who Matt chose to double with him for his final show; God knows he had campaigned hard enough for the honor. Casey was disappointed Matt had not chosen him—he thought Matt Ramsey one of the sexiest men he had ever encountered. But there was really no reason he should have chosen Casey for his final performance duo, and his disappointment evaporated when Matt asked him to come and spend the night with him at the apartment following his last show. When Matt showed up at the apartment that Sunday night, it was Richard who greeted him at the door. Again, he was not surprised. And he was not displeased: the prospect of a threesome with Richard and the fascinating Matt Ramsey was extremely pleasing.

Their lovemaking was ultimately passionate—and all three seemed tireless. The most climactic among the many climaxes they all produced that night came early in the all-night-long, nearly non-stop fuckfest, when Matt and Casey double-fucked Richard.

Richard had been lying on top of Casey while they kissed. He rose to his knees and positioned the tip of Casey's cock at his asshole and began to sink down to ride it. Casey told Richard he was not wearing a rubber, but Richard continued to lower himself on his cock; no lubrication was needed—both Matt and Casey had already fucked him since they began their threesome. "Get in here, Matt, I want both of you," Richard moaned, smiling and licking his lips as he savored the massive bulk of Casey's cock filling him while the blond stud thrust it in and out.

Matt has been watching closely, so he knew Richard wanted him bareback, like Casey. He lubricated his cock generously—he knew this was going to be a very tight fit, in spite of Richard's invitation. He had no way of knowing how many times Richard had been double-fucked, but he suspected—rightly—it was a large number. Still, he was careful as he pressed against Richard's back to bend him over, then positioned the tip of his dick at Richard's asshole and began to enter it slowly. His fat shaft pressed hard against Casey's enormous cock, sliding against it easily as it continued to fuck Richard, who was beginning to eagerly pant encouragement to his two masterful assailants. Once Matt's cock was planted completely inside and began to thrust in and out alongside Casey's, Richard fairly screamed his thrill and urged them to hammer his ass as hard as they could.

They fucked Richard's ass savagely, and for an inordinately long time, since each had blown several loads in the previous couple of hours. The load Richard spewed out onto Casey's chest while he was receiving the glorious double assault didn't lessen his enjoyment in any way; he continued to wallow in unabated fuck-lust as Matt and Casey shared his excitement.

Both Matt and Casey had often been participants in a double fuck, if only rarely as recipients, and each was able quickly to pick up his partner's rhythm. As they knew from experience, both fuckers thrusting together in synchronization was especially exciting to the fuckee, but when the two wielding the cocks combined their thrusts and withdrawals, one pulling out as the other plunged, it was more gratifying to them—feeling one's cock sliding against another, with the speed and force doubled since one prick was going one way while the second went the other. The two fucking Richard switched between sync and alternation to grant maximum pleasure to all.

After a lengthy assault, Matt cried, "I'm gonna come!" He and Casey froze in position. Matt's cock bulged suddenly, there was a gush of very hot liquid, and Casey felt his own prick awash in the prodigious volume of cum that typically marked Matt's load. The two resumed fucking, but Casey became so excited by the sudden viscosity of the tight chute he and Matt were enjoying that he, too, proclaimed his imminent orgasm. He erupted inside Richard's ass, which was suddenly so full of semen that the thick fluid began to leak out around the base of the two fat dicks fucking it. All three studs remained motionless for several minutes, savoring the gratifying excitement of the moment, before they separated and collapsed on the bed, rolling around and sharing tender and appreciative kisses.

By the time morning came, Casey was convinced that Matt Ramsey was one of the sexiest men who had ever been born—and that Richard, with all his shortcomings, was equally irresistible. He mused, however, that "shortcoming" was not a word that should be applied to Richard: he had never come up short when it came to coming! But in spite of his admiration for the beauty and sexual power of the two men he had just spent such a gloriously exciting night with, he was in love with the tall, dimpled boy back in South Carolina—and he could hardly wait to join him there.

Near the first of August, Casey aced both of his courses at Serra High School, and was awarded his diploma. His father and his best friend—and former fuckbuddy—Joey Stone, now his father's lover, were on hand to congratulate him. Joey gave him a big kiss and Bill gave him the keys to his graduation present—a new car! With Bill's full approval, Joey also gave Casey a present: an all-night fuck session like those they had shared so many times in the past.

Casey had learned to drive in high school, where he had taken Driver's Education, even though there is little use for private automobiles on a day-to-day basis in San Francisco; the terrain is not particularly well suited to it, and the city's public transportation system is excellent and easy to use. Still, Casey had gained sufficient experience driving Bill' s car that he was in complete control when, on the morning after his graduation, he drove Bill and Joey down to Half-Moon Bay for a trial spin in his new 1983 Chrysler LeBaron convertible. The fact that his new car was a convertible was especially gratifying to Casey. The production of American convertibles had been on hiatus from the 1970s until the year before, when they had been reintroduced into the market. Joey sat in the middle and Casey drove, with Bill 'riding shotgun.' Casey was fondling Joey's left leg, remembering the hundreds of times they had shared sex so happily, while his father was fondling Joey's right leg, enjoying the knowledge that Joey was now his lover. Neither father, son, nor object of affection was embarrassed by the unusual situation.

His final performance at the *Top 'n Bottom* also occasioned a present for Casey. He had only worked there for fifteen months, but he was one of the most popular among the house dancers with audiences and the other dancers as well—probably rivaled only by Richard. It wasn't just their good looks, huge pricks, and apparent sexual insatiability that endeared them to their admirers, although those were probably the principal factors—especially insofar as the theatre patrons were concerned. Richard worked hard to be well-liked, but somehow it usually seemed he was doing so with some ulterior motive—normally scoring the biggest cock or the sexiest or cutest man or boy. Casey's popularity came naturally, arising, as it did, from his basic sweet nature and consideration for others. Everyone agreed he would be missed.

Casey was scheduled to dance last on the Sunday night of his last week. The guest porn star had a plane to catch, and had left for the airport before the theatre closed, but almost all the house dancers watched Casey's last show from the audience. They sat as a group in the front row, and as a literal climax to his last T 'n B show, he stepped off the stage and stood directly in front of the group of dancers, where he blew his obligatory public load of the day, aiming it generally at them, wagging his dick from side to side as his cum erupted, splattering most of them with at least some of it. They all went backstage while the last patrons left the theatre.

On-stage and still naked, Casey was receiving hugs, kisses, and best wishes from his fellow workers, all of whom were fondling his ass, in which each of them had found refuge a number of times, and stroking the huge prick that had filled them and thrilled all of them even more frequently. They were all here: the incomparable fuckmaster Richard, who had shared sex with Casey far more frequently than any one on stage; Steve, the muscle boy; Carl, also muscular, and wonderfully hung into the bargain; Mikey, of the huge body; Adam, who had by then abandoned all pretense at being straight; Drake, whose cock was even more enormous than Casey's; and one of the relative newcomers, Justin, who, in spite of the fact that he still looked to be about fourteen, was, at that point, getting fucked and sucked off more frequently by paying customers than anyone else on stage (the other newcomer, Drake, was just then fucking more paying customers than anyone else).

Eddie appeared on stage as soon as he locked the outer doors, bringing a case of chilled champagne. The arrival of the champagne was, apparently, the signal for all the house dancers to strip. In a moment, everyone on stage was naked—including Eddie, who seldom appeared before a group of his employees naked—even though he had serviced all of them individually at least once while he was naked behind them! The dancers watched in admiration as Eddie stroked his gargantuan prick to erection. All murmured in appreciation of its impressive dimensions—even Richard, who had been savoring and thrilling to those extraordinarily rewarding dimensions for nearly two decades.

Champagne was distributed in non-breakable flutes. Then Eddie called everyone to attention and a toast to Casey's future was drunk. Casey thanked everyone, and Eddie directed them to park their champagne glasses somewhere for the moment. With a wicked grin, he told Casey to lie on his back on a low bench that had been placed in the middle of the room and covered with a blanket. Assuming that whatever was planned was going to be fun, Casey did as he was told, lying on the end of the bench, with his feet planted on the floor.

"Now," Eddie said, "we all want to toast you again, Casey, but in the way we figure you'll like much better. And we won't be using champagne for this one."

Everyone moved in and stood around the bench in a rough circle, most of them grinning. All were holding their cocks, most of which were clearly erect. Looking at the beautiful, sexy Casey Lowe lying naked before them made that inevitable. They began stroking their cocks, and soon every one was throbbing in full erection—including Casey's. After all, lying in front of eight hot naked men who are jacking off will do that to a guy—any except the most unimaginative, irretrievably straight one.

The first blast of cum shot from Drake's huge cock, splattering Casey's own cock, balls and belly—and it was a very big load, delivered in seven or eight copious spurts. That apparently 'primed the pump' for some: Adam blasted a healthy load on Casey's belly just a moment before Mikey's jizz was added. Casey was, by this time, beating off as well, and Steve's cum was aimed at his hand as it stroked his monster cock. Steve's aim was very accurate, and ran off the back of Casey's busy hand and down his shaft, to coat his balls. Then two huge pricks erupted at the same time: Richard's and Carl's. By the time Eddie's enormous load was added to the mix, Casey's chest, belly, cock, and upper legs were virtually covered in glistening, thick white cum. His navel was completely filed with it. When Justin began to come, he threw his head back, closed his eyes, and waggled his cock around as he shot, moaning, "Jesus, Casey, you're so fuckin' hot!" As a result, Justin's load—the last one delivered—was the only one to hit Casey's face, a target that all had been instructed to avoid, fearing they would get cum in his eyes—which is very painful for a few minutes.

Casey opened his mouth to receive as much of Justin's load as he could, but his neck and chin were still thickly coated with it. For a young, diminutive guy, Justin shot a helluva big load. Casey sat up and said, "You're mighty fuckin' hot yourself, Justin. Get over here." As Justin approached, Casey stood, which made cum begin to ooze down his body and legs. He used a hand to swipe Justin's cum from his chin and neck, rubbed it over his throbbing cock, coating it thoroughly. He swiped his hand over his stomach, picking up a great deal of cum. "Turn around," he commanded, and he ran his hand between the cheeks of the boys ass, covering it and the boy's asshole with the hot natural lubricant. Then he turned Justin's body around and pressed on his back, which caused the boy to lean over the bench. Casey stood behind him and rammed his prick unceremoniously into his ass with one massive thrust. Justin cried out in pain and thrill as Casey began fucking him savagely, using long strokes only one with a dick as big as his could provide, and the boy's cries turned into gasps of sheer ecstasy.

Everyone watched closely as Casey hammered young Justin so
gloriously—stroking their cocks, all of which were hard in spite of the
fact they had all come so recently. "Eddie," Casey said, "my chest is
still covered with cum. Get some of it and fuck Richard," he added,
winking at the beautiful older stud. Richard grinned and bent over the
bench, Eddie coated a hand with cum from Casey's chest and covered
his cock and Richard's asshole. Richard cried out in sheer joy as Eddie
thrust his formidable weapon all the way inside with no hesitation, and
he continued to groan in pleasure as he savored the kind of fuck that
had made him first fall in love with Eddie so many years earlier.

Eddie and Casey fucked side-by-side for some minutes, until
Casey pulled his prick out of Justin and told Eddie, "Trade off." Eddie
pulled out of Richard, and the two studs effected the swap.

While Casey continued to fuck Richard, and Eddie maintained the
brutal fuck he was giving Justin, Adam bent over the bench while
Drake began to fuck his ass. For one who had long claimed he was
straight, and who was now being fucked by the biggest cock on the
premises, Adam seemed to be enjoying himself immensely. Mikey,
Steve and Carl simply watched, masturbating eagerly. Eddie and
Casey swapped fuck targets again.

Casey was the first to come, but after he announced his intention
to do so, and filled Justin with his cum, he announced his intention to
continue fucking the boy's hot little ass: "This sweet little tight ass is
too hot to stop now." The plan met with Justin's eager approval. Eddie
emulated Casey's example, and Richard was equally enthusiastic about
receiving two non-stop fucks from his former lover. Drake didn't give
Adam two fucks, but the one he gave him was very long and very
intense. The three self-service watchers apparently reached their goals
by the time the three fuckers and three fuckees had completed their
objectives.

Champagne glasses were retrieved and refilled. Eddie was toasted
for his efforts in arranging the send-off party for Casey, and the group
began to disperse, with hugs, kisses, and even a few tears as his fellow
dancers said goodbye to Casey. Justin overheard Eddie asking Casey
and Richard to go with him to the theatre's hotel apartment to spend
the night. He begged Eddie to let him go along, too, then turned to
Casey: "Please, Casey?" Richard seemed especially pleased at the
prospect of the very young-looking boy joining them for an 'all
nighter'—he and Justin had exchanged fucks quite a number of times

by then, to considerable mutual satisfaction. Eddie and Casey agreed to a foursome.

Everyone fucked everyone in the apartment that night, and ample oral stimulation and satisfaction was also a major part of the festivities. Most of the time was spent, however, with Richard and Eddie cuddling and kissing while Justin and Casey did the same. They had breakfast brought in from a nearby diner in the morning, and they satisfied their hunger for food as surely as they had apparently satisfied their hunger for sex—for the moment: only Justin wanted to get fucked "just one more time," but his three companions declared themselves "too pooped to pop."

Two days later, Casey loaded his car for the trip to South Carolina, helped by Joey. Bill had said goodbye earlier in the day, since he had to go to work. He told his son and his lover to say goodbye to each other "any way you see fit" as he winked at them and left for his office. Taking Bill at his word, the two spent the rest of the morning in bed, naked, saying goodbye—with Joey hymning the joys of father-and-son fucking partners.

As Casey began his trip to be with his lover, driving across the Bay Bridge, he could see his hometown in the rear-view mirror, receding in the distance. He would miss it, of course, but he was driving east into his future. He considered what was waiting there for him: a beautiful, dimpled, sexually exciting boyfriend whom he felt sure loved him as much as he was loved; the prospect of working side-by-side with that boyfriend as they trained for what he felt sure was going to be a rewarding career in veterinary medicine; one friend of his boyfriend who was a raging fuckmaster capable of delivering nine orgasms in a single encounter, using a cock of glorious dimensions; and another friend of his boyfriend who—although he had not yet met him—was reported to be not only gorgeous, but capable of, and anxious to, deliver blowjobs of incomparable quality. Also, three adorable dogs!

Perhaps as important as any of those considerations, he knew his boyfriend was more than willing to allow him access to said big-dicked fuckmaster or virtuoso cocksucker, either by himself or in concert with him.

He knew the countryside where he was going to live was beautiful, if not as exciting as San Francisco, and if the kind of hot boys and men he had found with such ease in 'The City' were not as easily found and conquered there, there were sure to be just as many in the South Carolina Upstate region — and together with Luke, he was going to find them.

The End

About the Author

John Butler retired after a thirty-six year career in music teaching and administration, ranging from elementary and secondary school music, to Dean of Liberal Arts at a major American university, where he also served as Professor and Department Head for twenty-seven years.

He has published widely in his primary career field, but his first publication in the field of interest that has occupied his mind since he started fooling around with the little boy next door at the age of nine or ten came with the publication of the erotic novel *model/escort* in 1998. Since then he has also published the novels, *WanderLUST: Ships that Pass in the Night*, *Boys HARD at Work (and playing with Fire)*, *This Gay Utopia*, *Teacher Is the Best Experience*, *Heels Over Head in Love*, and *Boys Will Be Toys*, as well as novels and short stories in the anthologies *Any Boy Can*, *Taboo!*, *Fever!*, *Virgins No More*, *Seduced II*, *Wild and Willing*, and *Fantasies Made Flesh*.

Following the death of STARbooks founder, John Patrick, He completed editing the anthologies *Seduced II* and *Wild and Willing*. He also edited an anthology of John Patrick's best writings, *Living Vicariously*.

All these are available from the publisher, STARbooks Press.

The author welcomes comments or questions through the e-mail address NotRhett@yahoo.com.

CPSIA information can be obtained at www.ICGtesting.com
Printed in the USA
BVOW05s1819160316

440597BV00024B/180/P